THE
ELEMENTAL
PROJECT

A Novel

CASSIE CORBIN

North Carolina

Published in the United States by BQB Publishing
(an imprint of Boutique of Quality Books Publishing, Inc.)
www.bqbpublishing.com

979-8-88633-024-3 (p)
979-8-88633-025-0 (e)

Library of Congress Control Number: 2024933815

Book design by Robin Krauss, www.bookformatters.com
Cover design by Rebecca Lown, www.rebeccalowndesign.com

First editor: Andrea Vande Vorde
Second editor: Allison Itterly

To the cleverest and prettiest engineer that I know.
Hey, NASA, if you're hiring, I know a girl.
Her name is Hailey.

Prologue

Mason pushed his legs faster than he ever had to, holding the small bundle close to his chest. His two fellow elementals, David and Robert, ran next to him, tucked low, using every amount of their training to their advantage. Their wives were waiting next to getaway cars outside the gates of the compound. The men only needed to reach them and they would be safe. It was a warm summer night without even moonlight to accompany the runaways. The air was thick and sticky with humidity. Thankfully, David had disabled most of the streetlamps earlier to provide some cover for their escape.

Mason's daughter, Vita, was sleeping snugly in her blankets, just like Robert's son and David's daughter in their respective fathers' arms. The sleeping serum the doctor had slipped them would only hold up for another few minutes. Mason prayed they would escape in time.

The threat of Tasers snapped behind them as they neared the back gate.

"Down!" he hissed, sliding on his knees behind the closest tree. David and Robert both tucked behind a tree as well. Mason's brown eyes transformed to a brilliant emerald green while he mentally commanded the trees to surround them and grant them cover. The ground quivered as shrubbery grew from the earth. Rich green leaves intertwined like fingers, forming thick foliage to hide the men's huddled frames.

Mason looked down at Vita with a heated desperation. *I'm gonna get you out of here, angel. Daddy's gonna take care of you.*

"Don't let them leave!" a familiar voice boomed out, followed by the rumbling of boots. Mason's best friend was hunting him down, and the man was a hell of a fighter. If Chief Jack Sawyer caught the runaways, their likelihood of escape decreased significantly.

Mason held Vita's little head closer, teeth gritting as he prepared himself for what would undoubtedly be the most important fight of his life.

I'm sorry, old friend, Mason thought. *I won't let you hurt my little girl.*

Jack's angular face slid into view, visible only through the tiny gaps between the shrub leaves. Sweat slid around his dark eyebrows and, though he was only in his twenties, the stress of his current hunt seemed to have aged him by ten years. The two friends locked eyes.

Jack and Mason used to tease each other about their differences—Mason's expressive demeanor versus Jack's stoicism. But tonight, Jack's clenched jaw and creased eyebrows only revealed his heartbreak.

Vita released a soft gurgle before cuddling closer to Mason's chest. Jack glanced down at the infant, then back up at his friend. Mason hoped he wouldn't have to use his abilities against him, not on his oldest friend. He hadn't told Jack—the newly appointed chief of guardians—that he was escaping because he knew his friend couldn't allow it. Jack *must* have known the danger they were in if they stayed. He *must* have known their children's generation wouldn't be protected and cherished like theirs. Like the twenty-two generations before them. Their children had been born with targets on their backs. What else were they supposed to do?

Jack squeezed his eyes shut and took a deep breath. When he opened his eyes, they were filled with a pained acceptance. "Go.

I'll buy you some time." Then he stood and yelled to his fellow guardians, "They're not here! Check the west gate!"

Without a second glance, Jack whipped around and sprinted in the opposite direction of where the fathers were going. He'd not only just lied to the entire guardian force he was leading, but he'd just allowed Elondoh's most sacred assets to escape. His life, and that of his wife and newborn son, would be at stake for it. And he'd done it anyway.

Thank you.

Mason nodded at David and Robert, then they continued their run to their rendezvous point. They ducked and wove around the underbrush in the woods that surrounded the compound, all while holding their babies with absolute care.

They'd made it. Robert's wife, Tabitha, and Mason's wife, June, were waiting by three cars, almost invisible down the off-beaten path where they'd chosen to hide. Tabitha paced and nervously wrung her hands. June, ever so defiant, had a baseball bat in her hands and stood tall, as if she could take down an entire guardian force on her own. It wasn't until all three fathers had approached that June released a breath and dropped her bat.

"They're here," June said as she grabbed Vita from Mason's arms.

"Oh, thank the angels!" Tabitha cried softly, taking baby Adrian from Robert's hands.

David's wife had left him this morning. She'd wanted nothing to do with the elementals or the danger that came with them. He seemed to be handling the breakup as well as he could, perhaps for his daughter's sake. He fumbled with Anila's car seat in the third escape car and muttered a curse under his breath.

"Oh, David, come with us!" Tabitha begged him, helping him

with the seatbelt. "The outside world is so big. We'll have to create entirely new lives while figuring out how to raise these kids. You shouldn't have to go through all of this on your own. We can help each other."

David shook his head. "Thanks, but . . . I can't. It's safer if we separate. I looked up the stats. There are thousands of single dads in the outside world, and they seem to be doing okay. I'll figure it out. Besides . . ." He rested a hand on the car seat and looked at his little girl. They both shared platinum-blonde hair and those crystalline-blue eyes that Air elementals were known for. "I won't be alone. I'll have Annie, and she'll have me."

"Annie." Mason repeated. Until now, Anila had gone by her full name. "It's cute."

Robert clapped David's shoulder with that gentle nature he always carried. "You can do this, David."

"The angels will guide you," Tabitha said with a reassuring smile.

All the parents stood together and faced each other with the same mournful gaze. If their escape plan worked out, then this would be the last time they would ever see each other. Mason tried committing their features to his memory: the way Robert's mossy-green eyes contrasted with his dark skin, how Tabitha always smiled with a softness like clouds, and David's signature easy-going grin.

Tabitha wept silently while June firmly squeezed her hand and wore a thin frown as she bit back tears.

"Their lives will never be easy," Robert pointed out, looking to the car seat where his son slept. "But at least they'll be free. Three of the four baby elementals, that is. I wish Winifred had come with us. To get a fresh start with her son."

David scoffed. "And leave precious Dr. Guyer? She'd never

dream of such a thing. I feel bad for the kid. We tried taking him, but Winifred found us and set off the alarm. We had to leave him."

"Winifred is no longer the girl we grew up with," June said. "This place destroyed her, and it would have ruined our kids, too, if we had stayed. We did the right thing, even if it meant leaving her."

Winifred Novak was the Fire elemental, and Mason had always viewed her as a sister. He knew her betrayal would sting for many years to come. Still, he wished he could help her and her son.

Mason looked into the grassy horizon where, some miles away, lay the secret region from which they'd just escaped. The place in which they had grown up.

Elondoh.

Now the entire community was going wild as they tried to find the runaway elementals and their ill-fated children.

"I'm not going to tell Annie about this place," David said. "No need for her to know about the things they do here."

"We won't tell Adrian either," Tabitha said. "But yes, I wish our children could grow up together. A part of me almost hopes they'll meet again someday. Perhaps the angels will bring us back together."

June laughed, but there were tears glimmering in her eyes. "And they'd all be the best of friends, right? Like we are."

"That would be nice, wouldn't it?" Robert said in a tight voice.

"Until then, good luck." Mason nodded at them for the last time. "And goodbye."

June started their drive under the cover of night toward the flashing city lights that waited ahead in the outside world. The promise of freedom and hope. Fresh rain slid down the windshield, washing away the threat of the condemned life they were all running from.

Mason tended to the waking baby in the back seat. Vita's eyes glowed green when she woke up, fading to brown as she yawned and whimpered. It was astounding to think that one day she'd be able to do all the things that he could now. These little fingers that barely wrapped around his thumb would one day bend the hardest earth to her will. It was hard to imagine now when she was so fragile and innocent.

"You're gonna live a good life, BellaVita," Mason promised, preparing a bottle for her. "Mommy and Daddy are gonna make sure of it."

Vita watched him with the most trusting eyes he'd ever seen, and he was reminded of one simple truth.

The guardians of Elondoh would stop at nothing to find them. They would scour the earth, use every dirty tactic imaginable, and spare no expense to find their elementals. But Mason would be ready for it. He would protect his daughter, be with her every single day, and teach her how to see the earth through the lens of a dreamer and not a weapon.

Mason smiled at his little girl, then at his wife. "Time for our new adventure."

CHAPTER 1

Generation 23

GUARDIAN

BellaVita Eastwood was completely unaware that someone was watching her through the hacked security footage of her plant nursery. She waved goodbye to her last customer and hummed along to the radio while she drifted around the rows of ferns. She wore a green dress and white flowers were braided into her curly brown hair. Her deeply tanned skin and splattering of freckles revealed her love of the sun. As beautiful as she looked, her earth abilities made her lethal.

"Hello, Agatha. Oh, you don't look too good. Here, let's fix you up," she said, a gentle hand cradling the bottom of a dying fern's fragile leaves. Her elemental mark blemished the inside of her right wrist like a dark burn, no bigger than a dollar coin.

All four of the elementals had these marks since birth, and hers was the alchemical symbol for Earth: an inverted triangle with a horizontal line striking through the bottom tip. To anyone else, it looked like a unique birthmark. But Guardian Lucas Sawyer knew better. It was a mark from the angels.

She tilted her head, and her hickory-brown eyes started to glow into a brilliant emerald green.

Lucas sat in his car in the parking lot of the nursery, watching her on a tablet. He had studied her relentlessly, read everything about her and her abilities, but he'd never seen her in person. A shiver of anticipation crawled under his skin as he watched the plant bloom from a crumbling brown to a refreshed and vibrant green.

"There, bet that's better, huh?" The girl smiled at the plant.

Incredible. He was frozen with reverence and ran through his mental inventory of her stats for the sixth time. *BellaVita Eastwood, goes by Vita O'Connell. Age: Eighteen. Element: Earth. Elemental Number: Four.*

Her angelic gifts made her dangerous. Her beauty could tempt even a blind man. Something that Lucas and the other guardians of Elondoh had trained to resist throughout his entire life.

His graduation from trainee to guardian was only a month ago. His first assignment was to find the lost Earth elemental and bring her back to Elondoh. This mission had been assigned to him by his father, Guardian Chief Sawyer. Being a chief's son meant one thing: Lucas would one day take his father's place as chief of guardians. The other guardians didn't think Lucas was up to the task, so this was more than an ordinary assignment. This was his first step in proving himself to his community and his father.

He had to do this. His people and all of humanity, not to mention his own future, depended on his success.

He stepped out of his truck and slid on a ballcap. In order for this to work, he needed to look the part of a friendly gardener. The guardians had even given him dirty boots, worn jeans, and a muddy T-shirt to complete his facade. What he didn't account for was how stifling the afternoon Georgia sun would feel compared to the air-conditioning in his car. *Angels, how did anyone live in this heat?*

He walked into the plant nursery and rang the bell at the counter.

"Hi, friend, welcome in!" Four's singsong voice greeted from the doorway of the greenhouse. She spoke with a strong twangy accent. "I'm Vita. How can I help you?"

"I need help selecting a new addition to my garden. Do you have any blueberry bushes?" he asked, repeating the line he'd rehearsed.

"You came to the right place," She said, motioning around her. She gave him a quick once-over and a smile that made his face flush. "Right this way."

He followed her out to the greenhouse, wondering if she was sizing him up for an attack. She was surrounded by potential weapons with all these plants, and he was one guy with a tranquilizer in his pocket. But he had a plan, and that plan would work as long as he stayed focused. Her smile was admittedly distracting, but that was an effect of her abilities. He carefully pulled the needle out of his pocket, concealing it in his palm.

As Four walked, she talked to him as if they'd always been friends, making him more uncomfortable. He'd never been good at conversations with strangers, much less with women.

"You must be new around here," she said. "Just moved in?"

"Yes."

"Have you explored much of the area? I know it looks like a no-name town in the middle of nowhere, but she's got a lot to offer."

"I haven't."

"Well, the first place you should try is Lucy's café just down the block, and be sure to get a helping of that berry cobbler. So good it'll make you slap your momma." Four flashed another smile, forcing him to hide the needle behind his back. "I could take you sometime if you'd like. I'm friends with the owner."

Oh. Did she just ask a complete stranger on a date? Angels, these outside-world women really were bold. She was staring at him, and he had to say something.

"Sure." He offered a smile that he hoped wasn't too awkward.

"Cool." She flicked some hair over her shoulder and turned her back to him again.

This was his chance. Ready the needle, knock her out, and bring her to the rendezvous point where a few other guardians would finish the escort. But as he flicked the cap off the needle, he hesitated. It felt dishonorable to do something like this to someone so kind. But he knew what she really was. She wasn't the pretty and friendly face she put on. She was part of the most violent generation of her elemental line. If Lucas didn't do this, humanity would suffer for it, and nobody would trust a chief who had the chance to capture an elemental but chose to let her go.

Just beneath his breath, he whispered, "I'm sorry about this." Then he lunged forward and sunk the needle into her neck.

AIR

Annie Scott sprayed the finishing touches to her graffiti on the blades of the wind turbine before blowing out a powerful gust of wind to spin the blades faster. Her blue irises glowed white as she floated to the ground using her air abilities. The birthmark on her right wrist—a triangle with a line striking through the top—peeked out of her jacket sleeve as she gained her balance. Once both feet were planted on the ground, she slicked her fingers through her platinum hair and smiled proudly at her small act of rebellion.

Her dad was going to be so pissed when he found this. He was a wind turbine tech, and last night he'd given Annie the scolding of a lifetime when he found out she'd been partying underage again. She was eighteen, and a little fun wasn't going to hurt her. He didn't like that explanation and took away her car keys. He used the whole "My house, my rules" argument.

Naturally, as way of revenge, she decided to sneak out and spray-paint "Anarchy" all over the wind turbines he'd worked on.

Hell, it was better than the time when she'd spray-painted a rather *unladylike* image on one of them. At least now the faster speed of the turbines would produce more energy than it did before. So, in a way, this was humanitarian work.

You're welcome, SoCal.

Annie proudly stuck her hands into the pockets of her jacket and marched out of the field. All she needed to do now was hop the fence and get home before her dad woke up and realized she had snuck out.

Again.

As Annie neared the ten-foot barbwire fence, she took a running start and kicked off the ground. Her eyes glowed white as her body lifted into the air, a smile spreading on her lips as she glided upward. There was something so deliciously freeing about coursing through the sky with nothing to hold her down.

But just as she was halfway up, a heavy chain whipped around her waist and yanked her down.

Cursing, Annie hit the grass back-first. She whipped around to see four men dressed in gray uniforms, one of them holding the chains that bound her. They didn't look like the average security guys she snuck around, not with the weird insignia—a test tube between a pair of angel wings—on their shirts.

What the hell?

"Let me go!" she screamed, trying to wiggle out of the chains.

"We come in peace, Anila," the guy holding the chain announced. "We're from Elondoh. We're here to help."

"Screw you, you've got the wrong girl," she hissed, squeezing her eyes shut. A gust of wind encircled her, then pushed out, releasing her from the chains and gusting the men away from her.

Just as she got to her feet and started running, a sharp sensation pierced her back and sent her to the ground. The fight was over before it even began.

WATER

Adrian Capers started the long walk off the practice football field, helmet in one hand and a sweaty jersey in the other. One of the volunteer girls, Jessie, held out a basket for the dirty jerseys so that it could be taken to the school dry cleaner. Everyone knew she needed the volunteer hours for her sorority, and all the other volunteer opportunities had been taken. Three of the newer players joked around with each other, absentmindedly tossing their jerseys at her feet instead of in the basket.

"Hey!" Adrian barked loudly enough to make the trio stop and look over their shoulders at him. "She's not your maid. Pick it up and do it right."

They rolled their eyes and muttered to each other but did as they were told. Even though he was only a freshman in college, he was a good enough player that his teammates listened to him.

Jessie offered Adrian a grateful smile. "Thanks."

He shrugged, then dropped his jersey into the basket. "Thanks for taking these. You know, my girlfriend was just telling me a volunteer slot opened up at the library. You should check with her and get the hell out of here. I can ask her to drop in a good word for you, if you want."

Jessie lit up, her face already red from the sun. "You're an angel, Adrian. Thank you."

He waved a friendly goodbye to her and continued his trek to the locker rooms. The walls of the hallway were decorated with sports banners and a tattered poster of this year's game schedule. Hopefully enough time had passed so Adrian would have the showers to himself.

Rule number one for hiding the fact that you're a freak is to not let anyone see you in water.

Unfortunately, football practice under the South Carolina

sun meant he *had* to shower today. Thankfully, the showers were empty and quiet. Before he got into the stall, he took a few long, deep breaths and tried calming his anxiety. *It's just water, right?*

He quickly lathered up, his mossy-green eyes glowing a brilliant aquatic blue as soon as he touched the hot water. Adrian tried, as he always did, to suppress his weird water abilities. Most of the time, it worked. But sometimes, when he was really exhausted from practice, it was harder. His mind just naturally started interacting with water, without Adrian giving it permission or thought. The water sputtered from the showerhead, threatening to blow.

"No, cut it out," Adrian muttered angrily. The water burst out in a higher pressure, emitting a high-pitched whine as if arguing with him.

"Stop. *Stop!*" he shouted, turning off the faucet.

Sighing, he stepped out of the shower and dried off the remaining soap bubbles from his body.

Damn freak, he cursed at himself. His head throbbed like it always did after he tried to stop the water. He didn't understand why he had to be this way. His dad had water abilities too, but rarely used them. He always told Adrian how important it was that nobody ever found out about their abilities. If only Adrian could make it go away. He *hated* this constant fight with water.

"Capers!" a booming voice barked through the locker room.

"Yes, Coach?" Adrian answered as he stepped into his jeans.

"Someone in a suit is here to talk to you. Said he's from your dad's work."

There was only one reason the fire department would be here right now, but he hoped that wouldn't be it. He quickly finished getting dressed, shoving on his shirt and shoes before picking up his bag and walking out to the coach's office.

A man stood in a gray uniform with an insignia on his right breast pocket that Adrian didn't recognize. He didn't look like the usual firefighters his dad worked with. He couldn't have been much older than Adrian, with brown skin and a tall, lean stature.

"Can I help you?" Adrian asked.

The man kept his hands clasped in front of him and didn't bother with a smile. "Adrian, my name is Jason Boyd. It's a pleasure to meet you."

That indifferent face says otherwise.

He had a weird accent, like a real proper guy. British, maybe? "Is my dad okay?"

"Coach, could we have the office please?" Jason asked.

Coach glanced at Adrian, who nodded in approval.

"I'll be right outside, son," Coach said, closing the door behind him.

"Your father is fine," Jason said. "I'm not here with the fire department. Our parents used to work together in Elondoh. Have you heard of us before?"

"No. Does he know you're here?"

"He is being informed, but I'm here for you. I'm sure you've noticed some peculiar abilities about yourself. Things you can do that no one else can." His eyes flicked down to Adrian's weird birthmark on his right wrist—an inverted triangle, the same as his father's.

"What makes you think that?" Adrian asked, subconsciously hiding his wrist.

"You see, in Elondoh, we specialize in helping people like you. We can teach you to control your abilities, use it for good, rather than needing to avoid showers."

Oh, that definitely didn't make Adrian feel any better about this. Most guys wanted to be like the superheroes in *X-Men*. Adrian wanted to be like Tom Brady, and as far as he knew, Tom Brady did not have weird water abilities.

"All right." Adrian nodded. "You say my parents know you? Let me call them and ask."

"Of course. Tell them my father said hello," Jason said, his stiff tone betraying his friendly words.

Adrian pulled out his phone and turned away while he called his mother's cell.

"Hey, honey," his mom answered.

"Ma, there's this guy here who said he—"

A sharp sensation pierced into his neck and cut him off. He dropped his phone. The world went sideways as he lost all feeling in his body and toppled to the floor. The last thing he saw was Jason, his face twisted with a cruel smile, as he put the phone to his ear.

"Hello, Tabitha. This is the son of Guardian Isaac Boyd. Dr. Guyer believes it's time for a reunion. We'll see you in Elondoh."

CHAPTER 2

GUARDIAN

T wo guardians sat in the front seats of the SUV, remaining quiet during the long drive. Occasionally, their eyes flicked to the rearview mirror to get a glimpse of the back seat, where Lucas sat next to the unconscious Four. She remained asleep while they drove through the mountains, well into the night. Whenever she did wake up, the silver impulse bracelet on her wrist would shock her if she tried to use her abilities. These bracelets were one of the guardians' most effective tools, and Lucas was glad she was wearing one now because it meant she couldn't hurt anyone.

Finally, they turned onto the long dirt road that led to Elondoh's hidden community. The community itself was tucked away deep in a valley of mountains in Virginia. The road was impossible to spot if one didn't know what to look for. That was one of the reasons why they'd been able to remain hidden from the outside world for centuries.

The car jostled on the bumpy road and caused Four to stir.

She groaned, her eyebrows creased as she blinked open heavy eyelids. At first it seemed like she didn't know she was in a car, but then she blinked again and stared out the window with confusion. Lucas jolted when she suddenly straightened up and looked around, wide eyes landing on him.

He held up his hands in a placating gesture. "Please remain calm."

She screamed, her eyes flickering from brown to green only to subject herself to a shock from the bracelet. Four grunted in pain and frantically tugged at the bracelet, but nothing was going to detach it except for a guardian's key. The bracelet shocked her again as she continued to try.

"You're hurting yourself," Lucas said. "That bracelet will continue to shock you if you do not stop."

Tears welled up in her eyes as she scooted as far away from him as she could. "Who are you? What do you want from me?"

"My name is Lucas Sawyer. I'm a guardian. This will all be explained to you soon, but we need you to remain—what are you doing?"

Four pulled at the door handle and tried unlocking it, but the back doors only unlocked from the outside. When that didn't work, she banged on the window with her fists. What was her plan? Jump out of a moving car in an unfamiliar territory?

"Get her under control, Sawyer," one of the guardians up front grunted.

"You're making this worse for yourself. Will you please just—" Lucas reached out to pull her back from the window, but she shoved him away.

"Don't touch me! Let me out, I don't have whatever you want."

"We are trying to help you!" Lucas huffed. Yes, this was probably a bit much for her, but how many times did he have to ask her to calm down? He exhaled from his nose and tried again in a softer voice. "Nobody is going to hurt you."

"You stabbed me with a needle and kidnapped me. How is that not hurting me?"

He winced. That was a fair point, but it was necessary to his mission. "As I said, you'll get a full explanation soon. Look, we're here. This is Elondoh, the hometown of your parents."

The car finally approached the iron gates of Elondoh. Two

guards stood at the front outposts, rifles in their hands. One of the guards approached as the driver rolled down the window and flashed a badge. The guard inspected it and peeked in to look at Four. She stuck her chin up and glared at him. He nodded at the driver and let the car go through.

The land itself was about the size of the small town where Four had grown up, with no more than a few hundred occupants. They drove past rows of structured white buildings fronted with gold lettering labeling the bank, tailor, school, and many other businesses that a regular town would have. The buildings lacked the frivolous decor that the outside world was so fond of. At this late hour, most businesses were closed, and everyone was home from work or school.

They drove past signs pointing to an orchard, where late-night workers carrying baskets of fruit stared in awe at the car. The community itself was so small that cars weren't necessary except for their missions to the outside world. To see a car meant the guardians, Elondoh's private military, had returned from a mission.

Another sign led to the small festival grounds and Elemental Avenue, the street of townhomes where the elementals were to live.

The car stopped in front of a building marked LAB: Laboratory for Alchemy and Biology. More guardians waited outside, escorting a blonde girl who thrashed about and cursed loudly enough to wake the community. That must have been Elemental Three, the Air elemental: Anila Holiday. She went by Annie Scott in the outside world. The guardians managed to drag her into the building before Lucas got out of the car and walked around to open the door for Four.

She glared at him and ignored his offered hand, pushing past him as she stepped out of the vehicle. Lucas and the other two guardians escorted her into the laboratory. Thankfully, she didn't resist, but there was hesitance in her every step.

The lobby was similar to a hospital waiting room. Plain white walls, pristine tiled floors, and a small sitting area that led to a series of hallways. A receptionist at the front table watched the guardians enter with a pale expression of fright. Other guardians lining the walls stood tense, watching Four as she walked past them.

Lucas led her down the middle hall to the conference room, where the other two elementals waited. The conference room had glass walls so anyone could see inside.

Down the hall, someone watched them from a distance with glowing red irises. Two, the Fire elemental. He was the only elemental who had grown up here in Elondoh. Lucas had always found him unsettling. How did he manage to not show a single spark of passion in those dark eyes? Now they were glowing red, a stark contrast to his golden skin and black hair. He was probably reading the emotions of the other elementals.

Lucas scanned his badge and opened the door for Four, then walked in behind her and closed the door.

The other two elementals sat quietly at the table. Sitting tall and nervously picking at his sleeve was Elemental One—the water elemental. Adrian. Last name Jackson, undercover name Adrian Capers. He had an athletic build, dark skin, and mossy-green eyes. Apparently, he played a sport in the outside world and did quite well for himself there. Elondoh didn't have games such as football, and the little that Lucas did know of it came only from studying Adrian's file.

Four timidly walked up to them. Lucas took his post next to his fellow guardians and nodded at them, knowing they were just as nervous as he was. But he was their leader; he couldn't look afraid.

Timothy Hogan, with dirty-blond hair and a round face, was

in the same graduating class as Lucas and had been part of the extraction team that had picked up Three.

Next to Hogan was Guardian Jason Boyd, who was overseeing One. Boyd was tall and lean like a light post. He had dark hair and brown skin. He had graduated a year ago and mostly worked security at the front gates. This was his most important assignment so far, and he couldn't be taking it more seriously. His father had worked closely with Dr. Guyer for many years, so this was Boyd's opportunity to earn Guyer's favor as well. Lucas was never fond of Boyd. He had a tendency for cruelty, but it didn't matter. Future chiefs could work with anyone at any time so long as the mission was accomplished.

"Welcome to the party!" Three cheered sarcastically. "Let me guess, the invite wasn't optional for you either?"

Four shook her head and held out her hand. "I'm Vita."

"Adrian," One responded, shaking her hand.

"Annie," Three said.

"Do you know why we're here?" One asked, He nervously glanced at the guardians before lowering his voice to the other two elementals. "Can either of you . . . do things?"

Three cocked a pierced eyebrow. "If by 'things' you mean make the air do what I want? Yeah."

"Air?" One echoed. "My problem is water. I didn't know there were other people like me."

"I'm Earth," Four said, looking around the room. "If there's one for each element, we're missing Fire."

"That would be Two, the Fire elemental. You'll meet him soon," Lucas added from his post.

"She didn't ask you, GI Joe," Three snapped.

"Did he say 'two,' as in the number?" One asked quietly.

"I'm sure they number all their token freaks," Three said, sneering at the guardians.

"What's his actual name?" asked Four.

"Just Two," Lucas answered.

She cocked an eyebrow at him. "You're honestly telling me you people decided to number a person instead of giving him a name? Doesn't that seem wrong to you?"

The door opened, interrupting the conversation, as two of the most influential people of Elondoh entered the room: Chief Jack Sawyer and Dr. Joseph Guyer, the head alchemist and leader of Elondoh.

CHAPTER 3

EARTH

The young guardians straightened to attention when the two other men walked in. The man wearing a uniform looked to be in his forties. He had a buzz cut of black hair and blue eyes that widened slightly when they landed on Vita, as if he were surprised to see her there. His name tag read Chief Sawyer.

The other man was older, hobbling on an elaborate wooden cane. His white doctor's coat hung loosely, as if it had fit him once upon a time but was now too big. His wispy white hair was combed back and matched his thin white beard. Veins bulged from beneath his pale skin, and as frail as he looked, his blue eyes remained sharp. He nodded at everyone and sat at the head of the table, casting a quick glance at Lucas before focusing on Vita, Adrian, and Annie.

"You must have so many questions," he said in a raspy version of the watered-down British accent everyone here had. "My name is Dr. Joseph Guyer. I am the head alchemist of Elondoh. I knew your parents, and believe it or not, I actually remember the days you were all born. It's wonderful to see you all grown as you are."

"Let's just get to the point," Annie said. "Why are we here? Who are you freaks? What do you want from us?"

Vita winced at how brash Annie was talking to an elder like that, but the same question was running through her own mind.

But she kept her mouth shut. She didn't ask questions. She didn't interrupt. She listened and hated every word she was hearing.

Dr. Guyer smiled, making his appearance softer and almost welcoming. Like Santa Claus without the red suit. "You are what we call 'elementals.' You come from a long line of element-wielding beings who have been blessed with angelic blood. You'll get a more in-depth explanation on that later. My community of alchemists has trained and studied your kind for centuries since your creation in the Elizabethan era. Our efforts are funded by the government. As a matter of fact, previous generations of elementals have served the United States government on many occasions. Your ancestors have stopped potential wars, curved dangerous weather patterns, even saved dying soldiers during battles. You're all very special."

The three elementals exchanged strange looks.

"What does that have to do with us?" Adrian asked. "I'm not trying to be a soldier or whatever."

"Oh no, you children are in Generation 23, what we call the 'Stone Generation,' meaning, you will be the generation to create the philosopher's stone."

"Isn't that the *Harry Potter* book?" Annie asked.

"The philosopher's stone is a substance in alchemy that is said to grant immortality and immunity from all disease," Dr. Guyer explained. "Our mission as a community is to create enough of the substance to be evenly distributed throughout the country to eliminate all diseases without granting immortality. This is the magnum opus of our work, and you're all predicted to be the generation to create it."

"Predicted by who?" Vita asked.

"Dr. John Dee. He was an alchemist and adviser for Queen Elizabeth I. He is known for his works in angel summoning, and he summoned the very angel that created you. He wrote predictions for each generation, and you're the generation that will finally create the stone. It is a wonderful opportunity to save humanity!"

"And if we don't agree to it?" Annie challenged.

"Well, you technically belong to Elondoh. According to the US government, you are our property. What we are doing is by direct order from the highest-ranking office. In other words, you have no choice. You may try to run, but you won't get far. We'll find you again, and we'll find you as many times as we need to in order to create that stone," Dr. Guyer said, his tone remaining nonchalant despite the threat he'd just made. "But please understand, we do not want to go through all that trouble. We will treat you well here. You will want for nothing, and when that stone is created, we will let you go."

"Just like that?" Vita asked.

Dr. Guyer nodded. "As simple as that. We'll provide whatever is needed, training included. So, either you delay the process and constantly live your life looking over your shoulder, or you agree to help humanity and live your life as you want to. Do we have a deal?"

"Not much of a choice," Adrian muttered, glaring at the table. "I was in school on a football scholarship. They'll revoke it if I stop showing up. I have a girlfriend back home, and friends."

"We'll smooth things over with your school. As for any former lovers, well . . . you won't be able to speak to them for a long while. Perhaps as long as a year."

"A *year*?" Adrian repeated, aghast. "No communication at all? That's ridiculous."

"We cannot risk you telling anyone about us. Hopefully you will create the stone quick enough to minimize damage to your relationships. The process will take as long as you allow it to. Your parents have been informed of your return to Elondoh and we'd like to have them back. We wouldn't want them to lose their senses and run to any media about you." He chuckled, like it was all a funny joke.

"For now, your guardians will take you to your new homes. I have prepared a file for each of you, detailing information about the elemental line you come from. Your parents needed to change their names and appearances in order to blend in with the outside world, so I imagine your knowledge of your heritage is quite skewed."

Chief Sawyer stood and offered each of them a file with their names on it. "I'm Chief Jack Sawyer. I lead the guardian force of Elondoh and will oversee your security. My son, Guardian Lucas Sawyer, will lead your protection detail. Your guardians will escort you throughout your day and help you acclimate to Elondohnian culture. Whatever you need, they'll retrieve it for you. Please be aware that you are being monitored, and breaking any Elondoh laws will result in punishment appropriate to that infraction. Guardian Sawyer, you may take them, and you may remove their bracelets for now. I am allowing this as a show of good faith that the elementals will not hurt anyone using their elements."

"Yes, sir." Lucas turned to the elementals and pulled out a key from one of his many pockets. "Let's go, then."

———————————

Every house on the community streets looked like the same cookie-cutter design, with the windows all in the same location, the grass perfectly kept, and not a single car in sight. The only difference was the colorful flags with animal designs flying over each front door.

The elementals had their own street, away from the rest of the neighborhood. Lucas had called it Elemental Avenue, as if the name added some grandiosity to it. It didn't. There were only two buildings on the street, each made up of four townhomes.

Lucas explained that the spare building was meant for when the elementals were old enough to start their own families and move out of their parents' home. Lucas led Vita to the last townhome on the street and led her inside.

Vita scanned the room. It was minimalist. Everything was white, even the furniture. But there was a full kitchen, two bedrooms, and two bathrooms. No TV or entertainment of any kind.

"Your room is this way, Four." Lucas motioned up the stairs.

Vita stopped with a huff and glared at him. "My name is Vita. I'm a person, not a number."

His eyebrows raised in surprise. Vita didn't give him a chance to answer. She breezed past him and up the indicated steps.

The bedroom was bigger than the one she had at home, with large balcony doors. Beyond the balcony was a wonderful view of an orchard that stretched farther than Vita could see in the night.

The only color in her room was the green scrubs in the closet. Even the underwear and socks they'd given her were a basic white. Vita shivered and swallowed the reminder creeping down her spine that she was an "elemental" and not just Vita anymore.

Oh yeah, I should probably ask about the whole "angelic blood" thing too.

How was it possible that her parents had lied to her about her origins for her entire life? She'd never heard of Elondoh, or elementals, or anything like this. Her father had told her the two of them had received their gifts from the earth and that she could never tell anyone about it. When Vita had been small and her eyes began to glow in public, her mother diverted other people's attention. Then she decided to steer Vita away from plants or animals altogether until she was old enough to control the impulse. When she was old enough, Vita was known to have a green thumb, but now she wore contacts to hide her glowing eyes. She knew she and her father were different, but she'd never dreamed they were . . . *angelic.*

"If you're trying to plan an escape, it won't work," Lucas said, bringing her out of her thoughts. "This place is surrounded by cameras and guardians. You won't make it far."

"Yeah, your boss already said that." Vita sighed, cracking open the balcony doors. She breathed in the sweet air from the apple trees and slowly exhaled. "He never explained the whole angelic thing though. Is this like a biblical thing?"

"No, we don't necessarily believe in one God. We pray to many angels, but the main one is King Carmara. He's the angel who created you with the help of Dr. John Dee. Your parents really never explained that?"

"Obviously not. We went to the same old Catholic church that everyone else in our town did. I've never heard of any of this." She flipped through the file in her hand, staring at the photo of her father. He was missing his bearded smile in this picture. Her mother had blonde hair and green eyes in her picture, but Vita had always known her with brown hair and brown eyes. Vita apparently didn't even know their real names. She always knew them as Mary and Jared O'Connell, but they were actually June and Mason Eastwood. She wished her dad were still alive so she could ask him about this, maybe get a little angry and demand answers.

A tree branch extended out toward Vita, and a leaf gently caressed her cheek and swiped away a tear that slipped out of her eyes.

"It has been years since another soul has called to us before," the tree said in a wispy voice inside her mind. "You are Mason's daughter, aren't you? I remember you as a babe. Is Mason here?"

"No, I'm sorry. He died three years ago. I'm Vita." She blinked away her tears and held back the rest. Her father had always said trees were the most innocent souls on the planet. They wanted for nothing and had no need for violence. Vita could trust the trees, and even though this entire situation was horrific, she felt a little relief at knowing there were still trees to protect her.

"Do not cry, dear Vita. Sorrows never do the soul any good. My name is Sera. My sisters and I will take care of you. Please accept this gift and know that you are not alone here." The tree produced a beautiful, crisp apple and dropped it into her hands. "Welcome to Elondoh."

"Thank you," Vita mustered a smile for Sera as the branches drifted back to their original state. She turned and noticed Lucas had a hand on the bracelet on his belt, his jaw clenched tight. He seriously had the nerve to be afraid of her after what he did?

"I'm tired," she said in a tight voice. "It's been a long day."

"Right. If you need anything, there's a landline in the kitchen. It's only wired for calls within Elondoh, and the lines are monitored, so I don't recommend trying to call anyone from the outside world. It won't work. My number is written in that folder if you need something."

"A landline? That's so old school."

"We don't allow ourselves to be distracted by unnecessary technology, so a landline is all you'll have. Only those in leadership positions have cell phones. I'll be back in the morning to collect you."

Vita rolled her eyes and shrugged. "Fine, whatever."

Lucas nodded once and turned on his heel to leave. She waited until she heard the front door close, then she slumped against the balcony railing and let herself cry. Today really had been too long of a day.

CHAPTER 4

FIRE

The echo of black combat boots followed Two's steps as he marched alone to Dr. Guyer's office to make his report. Dr. Guyer's office was in the laboratory. At this hour, it was the only light in the dark and empty halls of the lab. Two had watched the other elementals, noting their emotional frequencies and patterns.

For the most part, they were afraid.

He was just as afraid as they were, but he didn't dare to express it. Now that the other elementals had arrived, the prophecy of Dr. John Dee, famed alchemist from the sixteenth century, would start to come true.

Beware the children of this day, for they carry a power that shall change humanity forever. They will mirror Generation 6 and wield powers of the mind.

There was some damage to the written prophecy, so there was another line somewhere in the prediction, but nobody knew what it said. Of course, there was a plethora of rumors and fantastical stories about a hidden prophecy, but none of it had been proven. It didn't matter anyway because the message was clear: the twenty-third generation of elementals was dangerous and not to be trusted. Generation 6 had been one of the deadliest generations in the history of elementals, and Two's generation was prophesied to mirror it.

Previous generations of elementals were praised. His generation was feared.

Now, fear was an emotion he knew well. It glowed in small lime-green spikes around the shoulders of both the captured elementals and their guardians. Its acidic smell was strong enough to make Two's eyes water. His additional gift of perceiving emotions allowed him to observe the otherwise hidden display of emotions from those around him. While some might find it to be a blessing, for Two it meant that he could see everyone's fear grow when he walked into a crowded room. Everyone except for two people: Dr. Guyer and Dr. Novak.

He stopped in front of Dr. Guyer's office and knocked twice.

"Enter," Dr. Guyer weakly called.

Two stepped inside and closed the door behind him, keeping his eyes low as he had been taught. "I am here to make my report, sir."

"Ah, yes." Dr. Guyer opened his notepad with a shaking hand, every vein bulging beneath his graying skin. He had been sick for all of Two's life, but recently, the disease had seemed to take a drastic turn for the worse. "Let us start with One. What did you notice?"

"Fear, the same as it was for Three and Four. Though, Three carried more anger than the others."

Dr. Guyer made notes, flipping to a different page dedicated to each element. At the top of each page bore the corresponding alchemical symbols. For Air, a triangle with a line striking through the top point. For Water, an inverted triangle. And for Earth, an inverted triangle with a line striking through the bottom point. Two's symbol for Fire was a standard triangle, but Dr. Guyer didn't make any notes beneath it. The alchemists at Elondoh already knew everything they needed to know.

"Did any of them show any sign of dangerous intentions?" Dr. Guyer asked, finishing his notes for Earth.

"Not that I observed. They simply do not know whether they are safe here."

Dr. Guyer flipped to another page featuring a different symbol, one that Two had never seen before. Two triangles—one standard, one inverted—pressed together, pierced by two parallel lines. It looked as if the four basic symbols were merged into one.

Two did not dare show his confusion, as the scientific leaders did not appreciate any sign of his emotions, but he was unnerved by the sight of the symbol. He had studied alchemy his entire life. He had memorized every sign and symbol that existed. Why did he not recognize this one?

"And what of the guardians?" Dr. Guyer asked, readying his pen over the page with that odd symbol.

Two tore his eyes away. "They were nervous as well."

"Yes, but was there any sign of . . . something unexpected? Perhaps a feeling of confidence or solemnity?"

"Nothing notable."

Dr. Guyer frowned, one side of his mouth curling in as he made a note. The notes were written in a series of Roman letters that did not form words in any language Two knew. They seemed to have no pattern or organization.

"Sir . . ." Two started carefully. "What is that symbol? I do not recognize it from the alchemical tables."

Dr. Guyer gave a start and closed his notebook. "Nothing to worry yourself with for now. You may report to Dr. Novak for the night and be ready to meet the other elementals in the morning. Remember that you are to keep them calm should they react poorly around Elondohnians."

"Yes, sir."

Two quietly made his way out of the office, wondering how his first meeting with the elementals would go. They were not the only ones who were afraid. But unlike them, Two was not allowed to act on his fear.

Dr. Novak would not take his weakness kindly. His mother was never one for compassion. So, he must appear as apathetic as possible around the elementals, even if he was truly terrified.

CHAPTER 5

GUARDIAN

Lucas entered his home and closed the door behind him. Today had been a long day, the first of many to come now that he was a qualified guardian and on the path of proving himself as a future chief. He'd turned in a report to Chief Sawyer but hadn't received a review yet, and waiting for one was daunting. Had he performed well? Had he made mistakes? Hopefully, Chief would have an answer for him at dinner.

His mother bustled around the kitchen, preparing dinner. She upheld one tradition from growing up in the outside world: Every night, the family must enjoy their meal together rather than in the dining hall with the rest of the community.

"Lucas, is that you?" Mom called from the dining room.

"Yes, ma'am," he answered, taking off his boots.

She stepped out of the kitchen and visibly sagged in relief when she saw that he was injury free. His mission to the outside world was dangerous, and she worried about him. "How did everything go?"

"It went as expected. Though, I suppose we'll have to hear Chief's notes before I can truly determine that."

Lucas went about setting the table as he did every night. Plates first, then napkins, followed by cutlery and glasses. Systems had a fond place in his heart. As he set down the last glass, Chief walked in.

Lucas watched his father walk into the dining room and held

his breath. Chief kissed his wife in greeting, poured a glass of wine for her, then got a drink for himself before acknowledging Lucas.

Finally, when they all sat down to dinner, Chief looked up at Lucas. "You did well, son."

Lucas exhaled and smiled. "Thank you, sir. You read the full report?"

"I did. The accompanying guardians reported to me as well, and they said that, with a few exceptions, it was almost perfect."

"Almost? Was there something that I missed?"

Chief shrugged. "They believe your retrieval could have been quicker, but you dedicated more time to earning her trust. That's not necessarily a bad thing, but more time spent during a mission leaves more time for potential error. As I said, all things considered, you did well."

"But not perfect."

"Well enough," Chief grunted.

Mom shot Chief a sharp look before changing the subject. "Did the elementals seem all right when they arrived? No injuries?"

"No," Lucas answered. "Four had been shocked a few times from her bracelet, but I'm sure she'll be fine."

"Poor thing, those bracelets can be awful. Her father used to constantly complain about them when he lived here."

"She looks just like him, Natalie," Chief added quietly. "Down to the freckles, it's incredible."

Was Lucas imagining the glint of grief in his father's eyes? As quickly as it appeared, Chief blinked it away and continued eating.

"She's quite peculiar," Lucas said. "I didn't expect her to be so ... friendly."

"As long as you're careful around her. Earth has been known to have strong emotional reactions. As you know, the elementals' abilities respond to emotion, which can be dangerous, especially after going so long untrained," Chief advised.

"Yes, sir. I think we'll need to dedicate a little extra time to their education. She doesn't even know about King Carmara or her heritage. She's never heard of Dr. John Dee. Seems a little irresponsible that their parents didn't tell her anything."

"Do not criticize what you do not understand. They had their reasons to keep certain information a secret, and it is not our place to question them."

"But to not know anything at all?"

"Well, that's what you're for," Mom said. "You can share the knowledge you have."

"I suppose so," Lucas said, watching Chief with curiosity. Chief had quickly turned defensive the moment the elemental parents were brought up. Yes, they used to be friends, but the elementals of Generation 22 had run away and betrayed him. Why did he care what anyone said about them?

"I'll bring her one of my books," Lucas said more to himself. "Perhaps that'll help her."

"On to other things, I heard you got an introduction this morning." Chief now smiled proudly. "From none other than Miss Callie Dawson. Her father told me about it over lunch today."

"Really?" Mom's eyebrows raised. "Angels, she's pretty."

Oh, right. This morning, Lucas had eaten a quick breakfast in the dining hall before the mission, and one of the kitchen workers had approached him to offer her introduction. Callie Dawson came from a decent enough family, House of the Gopher. Her father served as one of the school security guards. This was his first introduction, and of course, it just had to happen in front of an audience.

Lucas blushed and shrugged one shoulder. "It wasn't that big of a deal."

"Just remember what I told you," Mom said in a warning tone. "Girls will do anything to be a chief's wife. The pay you'll receive, the additional perks, the social status, and promised security? Any girl would want that. But just because they look the part doesn't mean they'll act the part of a chief's wife. Now that you're eighteen and starting to receive introductions, you can expect to be flooded with them. You must be mindful about who you choose to pursue. When you ask someone on a date, you must ask yourself if this is really someone you want a serious courtship with. Be sure they care about *you* and not just the financial gain they'll have by marrying you."

"Yes, of course," Lucas answered. It wasn't enough to just be a good chief, which apparently was something he still needed to prove, but he had to be the example of Elondoh culture and standards. Whoever he chose to marry needed to be able to fit that role. Mom was a great example of that as the head doctor of Elondoh. She contributed a lot, but she faced some scrutiny because she was originally from the outside world.

"He knows all this," Chief said, waving a hand. "Let's discuss how he'll attract more introductions. We'll enter your name into the swordsman tournament for the upcoming Clarice Day Festival. Once you win, you'll have the entire community's attention."

Mom pursed her lips. "Lucas will attract plenty of girls on his own without all that brutish nonsense. Honestly, he has such a winning personality, he won't need silly tournaments."

Lucas grimaced a little. A mother saying her son had a "winning personality" didn't exactly boost his self-esteem.

"Well, it worked on you, didn't it?" Chief smiled at his wife with the kind of lightness that only she could bring out of him. "It's time that our son learns how his father earned the affection of the world's smartest woman. See if it doesn't help you too, Lucas. I still remember the first day your mother joined us. I fell in love the moment I saw her. I just knew I was going to marry her. I'm telling you, son, I was the smoothest talker she'd ever seen. I walked right up to her and offered to give her a tour of the grounds. The rest is history."

Mom raised an eyebrow. "Really? Is that how you remember it? I seem to remember you tripping over your shoelaces and tumbling into the pond. Then blaming it on the laces being longer than regulation requirements."

Chief's smile grew. "All part of the plan."

CHAPTER 6

GUARDIAN

The next morning, Lucas knocked twice on the front door of Four's townhome, holding a small book in his hands. Boyd and Hogan waited in front of their respective elemental's door to collect One and Three for breakfast. Two didn't need a guardian. He simply left his home and walked to the dining hall by himself.

Lucas remembered that Four wouldn't respond if she was referred by her elemental number. Maybe he should call her by her outside-world name.

Vita.

It was strange to use this name. Ever since the moment he'd received her file, he'd always referred to her as "Four." But her cooperation was vital to his mission, so if he had to call her a different name, then so be it.

Vita opened the door, her curls tangled around her fingers. "Sorry, I'm almost done tying my hair. Come on in."

Lucas surveyed the room to ensure it was safe, then stepped inside and closed the door, resting his hand on the tranquilizer gun on his belt. Since last night, Vita had acquired more fruits of different varieties and a cluster of wildflowers from the gardens. The fruits were piled neatly on her countertop and the flowers sat in a vase of water by the kitchen window. All were brighter and bigger than he'd ever seen before. Likely from the trees in the orchard, like that apple tree last night.

It had been strange to see a tree move of its own accord and caress Vita's cheek. He'd noticed she was trying to hide her tears, but he didn't think it was appropriate to say anything. He always assumed Generation 23 would be apathetic and cold. But something as simple as her crying reminded him that she had a human side as well. For some reason, that reminder was even more disturbing than her simply being a monster.

"Did you pick those flowers?" Lucas asked.

She nodded, tying her hair back into a braid. "Yeah. They're pretty, aren't they? Wildflowers are my favorite."

"Doesn't it hurt them to be plucked like that?"

"No. Flowers to plants are like eyelashes to us. They don't hurt. But it could hurt them if you pull at their roots and aren't careful. Plus, these are so sweet and keep complimenting me, I just *had* to take them home. I only went out to the backyard this morning, so don't worry. I wasn't rampaging around your precious community."

Lucas knew that, historically, Earth elementals had always bonded easily with various plants and animals and could literally speak with them the way they did with humans.

Speaking of history, Lucas held up the small book in his hand. "This is for you. It's the history of your ancestors."

Vita took it and raised an eyebrow at him. "This is a picture book."

"It was mine when I was a child. I thought it would be helpful to have the portraits in there so you could put a face to the names, and the textbooks don't have portraits. The history is still accurate. Here, I'll show you."

He opened the book to the first page. This had been one of his favorite stories: the fantastic legend of angels and knights. Who wouldn't be excited about that?

When he was a little boy, Lucas would run around with toy

swords and pretend he was one of the great knights, anointed with heavenly power, a hero to all of humanity. His mother claimed that he'd refused to go to bed until his parents referred to him as "Sir Lucas." She retold that story to anyone who would listen. It haunted him to this day.

"It's a great legend. You see, Dr. John Dee—that's this man with the pointed beard here—was an alchemist and adviser to Queen Elizabeth I. He was known for his ability to supposedly summon angels with the help of his scryer, Edward Kelley. That's this man—he's missing an ear beneath that hat. The story goes that one day, Dee heard news of a great attack on Her Majesty's kingdom and summoned an angel to ask for protection. That's Queen Elizabeth I here. You've heard of her, right?"

Vita smirked in amusement. "*Everyone* has heard of Queen Elizabeth."

"Just wanted to be sure. Strange that you would know about her but not John Dee or the angels." Lucas shook his head and got back on track.

"Anyway, the angel that appeared was King Carmara. He appeared several more times for John Dee, but this was the first and only time he granted Dee a favor. He told Dee to bring forth four of his best knights at midnight before the attack. He requested knights who were known for strong chivalry and battle-worthiness. Carmara personally tested each knight's character by searching the depths of their mind. Apparently, this test was most challenging—the Fire elemental nearly didn't make it. That's the painting of your ancestor, Sir Michael Schafer, the Earth elemental. He was raised on a cattle farm before his journey into knighthood."

"Looks just like me, beard and all." Vita pulled her hair beneath her chin to make a fake beard.

Lucas was surprised to find himself smiling at her. "He's only missing the freckles. When the knights finally passed the test, the angel blessed each of them with the ability to manipulate one of the four elements. He did this by giving the knights some of his own blood to consume. The story says wine, but we learned the truth when we were older. I suppose blood is a bit too gory for children. Anyway, the blood gave these knights angelic genetics.

"The angel then marked them with the alchemical symbol on their right wrist to designate each of their elements. That's why you have that birthmark on your wrist. Those knights were able to defeat the enemy and went on to have one child each, passing down their angelic genes. Because the genes are so strong, they can't wash out throughout the ages. Thus, the creation of the elementals. Each elemental is said to have the beauty of angels and the worthiness of knights. You are part of Generation 23."

Lucas shyly caught his voice growing louder with enthusiasm and cleared his throat. "Or that's what legend says. There are all kinds of stories about the individual elementals we grew up with. Supposedly, Sir Schafer could move mountains."

"Can I move *mountains*?" Vita asked with an excited wonder in her eyes.

"You could if you wanted to."

Vita studied the symbol on her wrist. "So, we're descended from knights and angels, huh?"

"According to one legend. Other texts describe an elixir created by alchemists and given to each knight before their great battle. Some believe that's actually where the abilities come from and that the mark was branded. It depends on whether you believe in science or angels."

"What do *you* believe, Lucas Sawyer?"

"I've always wondered why both couldn't be true."

Vita smiled and flipped through the picture book. "My daddy used to call me 'angel,' so I believe it."

She had a wistfulness about her when she spoke about her father, a distant spark twinkling in her soft brown eyes. The legends were clearly true; she really did have the beauty of an angel. It was eerie how naturally perfect all four elementals were, but there was a distinct warmth in Vita's beauty.

Remember who she is, he reminded himself. Blades could be beautiful, too, before they gutted someone. These elementals were predicted to be bloodthirsty and violent. Just because they hadn't displayed this yet didn't mean it wasn't to come. John Dee had never been wrong before, and he wouldn't be now.

"In our elemental lore, each element represents something that humans need in order to thrive," Lucas continued. "The root of everything, if you will. Earth is life itself, Fire is passion, Water is creativity, and Air is energy. There are countless stories about all that as well. Sometimes it's hard to keep up with it all."

Vita flipped through the pages of the book. As she did, Lucas caught sight of a fresh burn on her wrist.

"What happened to your wrist?" Lucas asked.

She held it up and quirked an eyebrow at him. "It's from that bracelet you made me wear yesterday. It left a couple of welts when it shocked me."

"I didn't know it would do long-term damage. I'm sorry, that must hurt." Then he remembered the legends. "I saw you heal that one fern in your plant nursery. You can heal yourself using plant life, right? We can make a stop to a tree on the way to the dining hall."

Vita shook her head. "I don't like to. Healing myself means taking their life preservation; it takes longer for them to restore. If I take too much, they might not restore at all. I don't want to kill a tree just for me."

"They're just trees."

Vita tilted her head and frowned "And we're just humans. We

cause destruction, chaos, and death. I've never once read about trees starting wars, but I know plenty started by men. Even though we kill their kind every day, they still take care of us. Pretty unfair, don't you think?"

A hot shame burned Lucas's face. "I hadn't thought of it that way."

"Most people don't until it's too late. Then they start wondering what happened to all the rainforests and why so many animals went extinct. Humans like claiming power over things that can't fight back. It's their way of feeling strong in such a big world. Anyway, are we ready?"

"Um, yes. Let's go." Lucas swallowed his shame and led her out.

Of course she is going to care more about the trees than I would. I'm just a human.

But she was right, wasn't she? Lucas was so quick to dismiss the death of trees, but she could actually befriend and speak to them. He'd witnessed it himself. He supposed that if he could hear and feel what Vita could, perhaps he'd feel the same way.

But for her to be so empathetic and gentle, it contradicted the natural violence and cruelty that Lucas had been taught about the elements. This didn't make sense to him, but for now, he dismissed it. Just because she was kind to trees didn't mean she would be kind to him.

Boyd and Hogan and their assigned elementals were up ahead. Annie glanced over her shoulder and brightened up at the sight of Vita. "Hey!"

"Good morning, Annie," Vita greeted, joining her side. She noticed the burn on Annie's wrist and rested a hand on her shoulder. "Oh, you got stung by that bracelet too. Here, I can help."

Vita's eyes glowed green, and Annie's burn simply faded away as if someone had wiped it off.

Annie cursed and inspected her wrist. "How the hell did you do that?"

"Can't you . . . oh." Vita stumbled a step and pressed a hand to her forehead. "Sorry. Got a little dizzy for a second."

"You good?" Annie asked, raising an eyebrow at her.

"Yeah. Just hungry is all. Been a while since I ate." Vita offered her a friendly smile and carried on as if nothing was wrong. "Anyway, can't you do something like that too?"

"Um, no?"

Lucas remembered from history: Healing herself took energy from plant life. Healing others took energy from herself.

She's willing to give part of herself to heal others, but unwilling to use plant life to help herself, Lucas realized. It was surprisingly selfless.

"You all have different connection abilities," Lucas explained. "I'm sure Dr. Guyer will further explain this to you."

Annie rolled her eyes. "Great. Another thing I don't know about myself."

"Good morning, Adrian," Vita called out, catching up to his side.

"Hey." Adrian nodded, slowing down to walk with them. Boyd and Hogan hung back while Lucas took the lead.

As they walked, Elondohnians parted ways for them to pass, mouths agape and eyes wide. Their whispers were like a ripple in the wind that passed by the elemental group. A cluster of girls smiled appreciatively at Lucas and gave him a quick bow of their heads. He nodded back out of courtesy but remained focused on his path.

Vita smiled and waved at the crowd, but no one responded. Rather, they all shrank back and averted their eyes.

In the dining hall, the elementals had their own table

separated from the rest of the community. For years, Two had been the only one to occupy this table during every meal.

Vita leaned toward Lucas and lowered her voice. "Who's that?"

"That's Two, the Fire elemental."

"He's hot. No pun intended," Annie added.

Hot? Lucas thought. He should have been at a regular temperature. Two had a constant fever due to his abilities, but he received an injection every morning to regulate it.

Vita nodded. "He reminds me of cacti. Prickly on the outside but maybe nice on the inside. I've always wanted to befriend a cactus. They're really sweet."

"It looks like the man has never smiled in his life," Adrian muttered.

"We can change that," Vita offered.

Lucas couldn't help but admire her ability to see the best in any situation. He wondered how she was able to do it so effortlessly, as if by reflex rather than a conscious decision. But again, that kind of behavior didn't align with the prophecy. Perhaps the violence would come with time? If that was the case, he would need to keep an eye out for potential triggers.

The food trays were already waiting for the elementals. They weren't yet permitted to go through the buffet line unaccompanied. Two ate quietly, keeping his eyes focused on his tray rather than his new company.

"We'll gather you before your morning training. You have thirty minutes to eat," Lucas instructed. "Enjoy your breakfast."

He and the other two guardians went to the buffet line, and all simultaneously breathed a sigh of relief. So far, the morning was going smoothly. Now they just needed to get through the rest of the day without any incidents.

CHAPTER 7

FIRE

"Is your name really Two?" One asked. His accent was Southern, like Four's, but not as strong. One grew up in South Carolina, while Four was raised in Georgia.

"I have no name in the traditional sense. It is the order in which we were born," Two answered.

"But . . . why?"

"Names provide attachment, which can be triggers for unnecessary violence. My element is historically the most temperamental of the four. In order to prevent danger to human life, they have prevented me from having attachments."

"Two is lame," Three sighed, picking at her nails.

She was the one who intrigued Two the most. Her platinum-blonde hair fell in a perfectly straight sheet to her shoulders, and she had crystalline-blue eyes. She had a nose piercing and several more on each earlobe. When she was carried in, she'd worn a leather jacket and black makeup smudged around her eyes. Now she wore the issued scrubs that the officials had given her and no longer had the makeup around her eyes. She tried to make herself appear intimidating and bored, but Two could see right through that.

Two's irises glowed a ruby red as he read each elemental's emotions.

Four was staring at her tray with yellow starbursts of annoyance dancing above her head, the sharp scent of lemons drifting with the emotion. She offered One her plate, as he had already finished his.

"What's wrong with it?" One asked, inspecting her food.

"I can hardly eat any of it. I'm a vegetarian," Four said, taking the small fruit cup from the tray and sliding the rest his way. "I don't mind other people eating meat, but I just can't do it."

A vegetarian? Two had heard of such a thing, but everyone here ate meat.

One accepted and began eating the food, a strange emotion shimmering behind him in a blurry haze. It had no color or scent yet.

Strange. An emotion that Two did not recognize. What was it?

"I have read of vegetarians," Two said. "Some eat eggs. Do you?"

"Yeah, but the bacon was all over mine and now it's got grease all over it." Vita shivered. "Poor pigs."

"You can have mine. The eggs have not touched the meat on my plate." Two slid his tray toward her, keeping his eyes low. His face heated up and embarrassment tightened in his core. He'd never offered to share any of his things before. Most people took from him without permission, but he couldn't allow Four to react in an anger caused by hunger. Would she think he was inappropriate for offering his food?

She smiled and picked up her fork. "That's really sweet, thanks—uh . . . sorry. It's weird calling someone by a number."

"Yeah, I'm not calling you Two," Three stated, eyeing him. "You're gonna have to pick a name. And by the way, I'm Annie. Not Three."

"I'm Adrian," One cut in, talking through a mouthful of bacon.

"And Two is lame." Three—*Annie*—repeated.

Two looked at his hands. "My limbs have full function."

Four—Vita—giggled. "Bless your heart. We haven't used 'lame' in that way since like, I don't know, the seventies?"

"Then I do not know the new meaning of it."

"It's like... hmm." Vita tapped her chin. "Like, boring or not so favorable. If you don't like something, you just call it lame."

"It means exactly what it sounds like." Annie sighed. "And the name 'Two' is lame. Until you can pick a name, I'll call you Dos. At least it's got some flavor."

"The Spanish word for 'two?'"

"Yeah, you take languages around here?"

"Yes. As elementals, we are to honor the traditions of our medieval forefathers, one of which is the appreciation of languages. I know Spanish, French, Italian, and Latin."

"A bit over the top, but whatever." Annie studied him, her eyes flicking quickly up and down his body, before she looked back at her nails.

Yet again, another strange emotion that he did not recognize. This one swished around Annie's chest like a ribbon blowing in the wind, but he could not see the color. It only appeared as a dark gray.

"So, what were y'all doing before you came here?" Vita asked, poking at the eggs with her fork. "I worked at my daddy's plant nursery."

"I just started college for sports medicine, and I was a quarterback on my University's football team," Adrian answered.

"Football?" Two repeated. He knew very little of games from the outside world, but he had heard of football. It seemed a strange pastime for an element who represented peace. "Is that not a violent game?"

"Nah," Adrian chuckled. "Sure, it looks rough from the outside. A bunch of big dudes running after a leather ball? Anyone would run the other way, but I see it differently. It's all about teamwork and being creative enough to know which plays will work at the drop of a hat. That's when I'm in the zone."

"I see," Two said, though he still didn't quite understand. Perhaps he needed to witness a game to fully comprehend it.

"What about you, Annie?" Vita asked. "What were you up to?"

"I worked at a café, and I just got accepted into my dream art school," Annie said, and sadness dripped around her in navy droplets along with the scent of rain, but she did not display it. She looked bored. "I was supposed to start in the fall."

"Starting school in the fall upsets you?" Two asked, his eyes glowing red from observing her emotions.

She quirked an eyebrow at him. "No. Being in this hellhole instead of going to school upsets me. It was going to be the time of my freaking life, and now I'm here wearing these ugly scrubs and surrounded by possibly the most boring people I've ever met in my life. No offense."

"Why would I take offense to that?" Two asked.

She rolled her eyes and nodded to the other two elementals. "You guys leave anyone important behind?"

Adrian nodded, the ruddy brown of regret zigzagging above his head with the smell of rust. "Besides my friends? I had a girlfriend. We've been together since we were kids and talked about getting married after college. She's probably losing her damn mind about me disappearing."

"Maybe she'll file a missing person's report and we'll get sprung out of here."

"That will not work," Two cut in. "Dr. Guyer works closely with the American government. Anything having to do with us will disappear, so if a report is filed about you, it will be dismissed."

Annoyance danced around Annie. "Great. What about you, Vita? I'm sure you had plenty of guys back home."

Vita shook her head. "Just my mother, my friends, Otis, and Lula. Otis is our guard dog. Poor thing must be so worried about me. Lula, she's my cat. She's probably worried too, but she's a little calmer than Oty. I hope when my mom gets here, she brings them with her. I miss talking to them."

"You *talk* to them?"

Vita nodded, looking between Annie and Adrian as if they were the strange ones. "Well, it would be rude to ignore them."

Annie and Adrian exchanged an amused look and carried on a conversation about their lives from the outside world. Topics such as musicians, foods, and sports—all things Two had never heard of.

He would need to study these elementals closely if he were to understand them. They were more mysterious than he'd anticipated.

And . . . it was strange that they did not wear fear around him. Perhaps they had not been in Elondoh long enough to know better.

CHAPTER 8

AIR

God, could this place feel any more like prison? For once, Annie didn't break a single law, but here she was, wearing scrubs and being escorted around. All she needed was handcuffs, not that she couldn't pick her way out of those.

Once the thirty minutes for breakfast were up, the three guardians came back to their table.

"We need to go to your first session," Guardian Sawyer announced.

Annie cocked an eyebrow and jerked a thumb at Two. "Why do *we* need babysitters but Dos doesn't?"

"Dos?" Guardian Sawyer asked.

"Yeah, it's what we're calling Fire Boy."

"Two was raised here and has been trained to properly control his reactions. He doesn't need a guardian," said Hogan.

"What the hell is that supposed to mean?" Annie demanded. All the questioning looks and glares they received in passing were bad enough. Now they were being contained like a disease.

"You are unpredictable," Two explained. "No one knows how you will react or what you will do. You might try to hurt someone or lose control. You are a liability."

Annie gave him a bitter glare. "Cult freak."

"I do not understand that."

Vita stood, breaking the tension. "What should we expect for our first session?"

"You'll be doing a series of physical tests. They'll take your blood and ask questions. You'll also be asked to demonstrate your abilities," Sawyer explained as he led them out.

Their little entourage walked to the laboratory. Two followed at a quiet distance behind, keeping his eyes low. Annie found him annoying. What was his problem? Did he think himself too good to talk to them? Why wouldn't he even look them in the eyes? It was as if he were pretending no one around him existed. *What a tool.*

"Hey, Hoagie," Annie started, nodding at her guardian. "How long do we have to be here?"

"It's Hogan," he corrected in a mutter. "You'll spend weekdays in the laboratory, and the scientists will release you before dinner."

"So, what kind of jobs do you have around here? Like obviously there are guardians and scientists, but what else?"

"We have a multitude of job opportunities. Various medical staff, teachers, daycare workers, business owners, scientists, and other opportunities to contribute to Elondoh. Someone needs to ensure our electricity and plumbing works properly. There are landscapers, farmers. I can't imagine it is so different from the outside world. As a matter of fact, the outside-world government often employs our guardians as reserves if there is a matter that requires more stealth. We've assisted countless missions while remaining undercover about who we are. We work a lot with your CIA, I believe."

"So, everyday stuff, right?" Annie said sarcastically, watching Sawyer and Vita take the lead of their entourage. Those two seemed to get along well enough. Adrian and his guardian, Boyd, acted as if the other didn't exist. "What's school like here?"

"We undergo a general education in our adolescence. Once we turn fifteen, we start studying strictly for our assigned duties."

"So, at fifteen you're expected to know what you're going to do for the rest of your life? Little Hoagie just knew at fifteen that he wanted to escort a couple of outsiders around? Must feel like you're really changing the world."

Hogan blushed and averted his eyes from her. "Most boys follow their father's footsteps in the path of guardians. It's not the only choice, but it is a fulfilling one."

"Oh, I get it. So, you're telling me the guys get to have all the fun, but the girls have to cook and take care of kids?"

"We have female guardians," Hogan insisted. "My mother was a guardian before becoming an instructor. She prepares the trainees by teaching our tactical strategies. My father is a tailor and spends his days helping his community feel confident through his work with fabrics. It isn't extravagant, but I'm proud of the work they do."

"Oh." Guilt immediately bubbled within her, making her wince at her own attitude. She had a habit of finding people's buttons and pushing them. Hogan looked embarrassed. Sure, he was like a skittish cat around her, but he wasn't a jerk. He hadn't given her a reason yet for her to be such an asshole.

"That's awesome . . . that your parents do that," she said earnestly.

Hogan flicked his big eyes to her and offered her a nod. "Thank you."

Once they arrived at the LAB building, Sawyer scanned his badge and the doors slid open with a soft hiss.

The group entered the spacious lobby of the laboratory, where a desk sat in the center and people flurried about in white uniforms. Last night, it had been late enough that there weren't many people around, but now it was prime working hours and there were dozens of people. They all stopped what they were doing to watch the new lab rats walk into the building.

Guardians were stationed all around the inside of the building in front of every possible exit. Annie wondered if they were there for the elementals' safety or for everyone else's. The elementals' guardians exchanged respectful nods to their colleagues before leading their charges to the center of the lobby.

"Guardian Sawyer," a middle-aged woman greeted him with a bright smile. Her graying black hair was tied in a bun, and her brown eyes hid behind a pair of glasses. "Good morning."

"Good morning, Dr. Sawyer," Sawyer greeted with a similar smile. He faced the small group and motioned to the woman. "This is Dr. Natalie Sawyer. She's one of the best doctors Elondoh has to offer and will be in charge of your physical well-being. She's also Chief Sawyer's wife."

What is this, a family affair?

"Good morning," Vita smiled first. "I'm Vita."

Dr. Sawyer nodded. "BellaVita Eastwood, Earth elemental and a gifted piano player. I was friends with your parents when we were children. Angels, you look just like Mason. You have no injuries to date. But it was noted that your connection ability is to heal. Am I correct in assuming you have trouble maintaining energy?"

Vita raised her eyebrows. "Yes, ma'am. It takes a lot out of me."

"An exchange of energy. You can either give from yourself to heal others or take from plant life to heal yourself. Many of your ancestors could heal as well, and all had the same issue. We'll be working with you to help that." The doctor then turned to Adrian. "You must be Adrian Jackson, our Water elemental. I heard you played ball. An accomplished quarterback, correct?"

Adrian lit up like a match. "Yes, ma'am."

She then turned to Annie. "Anila Holiday. Air elemental, and I hear you can also paint quite nicely too. You have your father's eyes."

"Impressive," Annie commented, eyeing the woman. She

seemed nice enough, except Annie detested being called anything but Annie Scott. The stupid file she'd received last night said her father's actual surname was "Holiday." But that wasn't Annie.

"Dr. Sawyer, they're here for their first session," Guardian Sawyer interjected. "We were told to bring them to you."

"Yes, sir. Guardians, you may stay here and wait for your charges. Adrian, you'll be in room one. Anila, room three. BellaVita, room four with me. Two, your shot is ready for you in room two, as always," Dr. Sawyer instructed.

"Thank you, Doctor." Two nodded, heading to room two.

"We call him Dos now," Annie said. "And I go by Annie Scott, by the way. She's Vita. And he's just Adrian."

Dr. Sawyer smiled warmly. "Dos, Annie, Vita, and just Adrian. I like it. Come along."

CHAPTER 9

EARTH

Vita didn't always have the ability to heal. It was a gift that had shown up when she was fifteen after her father died. She'd desperately wished that she'd never feel that heartbroken again, and then the earth answered her prayers.

When she first got a handle on her healing abilities, Vita was too generous with them. She would sneak out and visit hospitals as an act of charity. Whenever she left a hospital room, she would hear the cries of a miracle, shouts of praise to whichever deity they believed in, or even claims of seeing an angel. Suddenly, dying children were no longer sick. Cancer patients were now survivors. Accident victims could walk again.

It was incredible. There wasn't a single ailment she couldn't heal. As long as the patient was alive, she could heal them.

Even though the images of tubes and needles haunted her, Vita had continued her charity. It was like a calling to her. An itch she couldn't satisfy.

There were times where it felt like she had no control over it. It felt like someone had possessed her body and forced her aside as she watched in awe.

But it took so much out of her. At the time, she hadn't yet known the capacity or cost of healing until the day she healed a child who was on his deathbed. Inky black clouds of sickness were bundled in that kid's body, and Vita could see that it was a battle he'd lose if she didn't do something.

Vita had healed him completely, took every last sickness out of his body. Then she'd passed out.

She awoke two days later in a hospital bed. Her poor mother was hysterical, not knowing what had suddenly made Vita so weak. Vita finally confessed to her actions, confessed that she was the reason all these patients had miraculously healed, and then she cried for an hour.

If only she had known of her healing abilities when her daddy was dying in the dirty street. If only she'd been able to catch him in time after he had been shot. She could have healed him. He would still be with her now. She saw her inability to heal him as her greatest failure, and not a day passed that she didn't think about it.

As repentance, she made sure no one else felt such a magnitude of loss, but she didn't know that it would cost a bit of herself.

Even still, she desperately wanted to continue. It was her mother who had forbidden it and offered a solution that she work at the plant nursery. Healing sick and dying plants was much easier on Vita, as they typically required a lot less energy from her. It satisfied her craving enough that she wouldn't lose control, but there was always that desire to do more.

"How are you with needles, dear?" Dr. Sawyer asked, bringing Vita out of her thoughts.

"I'm fine if I don't watch," Vita said, staring at the plain white wall to her right. She felt the prick of the needle, the slide of it settling into her vein, and a gloved finger pressing down a piece of cotton and tape to hold the needle in place. Vita was glad for the cotton. She never liked seeing the needle in her skin.

Vita looked back at the doctor. She had the same concentrated crease in her brow as Lucas, and the same dark hair and eyes. But the rest of Lucas's features—his narrow nose and observant gaze—came from his father.

"You said you knew my daddy?" Vita asked.

Dr. Sawyer smiled ruefully. "My husband grew up together with the elementals. I grew up in the outside world and had no friends when I moved here, so they welcomed me into their little group. Mason was quite the character. So lighthearted and funny, always told stories with such energy."

"Even then?"

"Yes. And the way he adored your mother, too, like she was the finest jewel he'd ever seen. I've never known anyone to be more in love, and when they had you, my goodness." She chuckled and shook her head. "You had him wrapped around your tiny finger from the moment you were born."

"Did you know when he passed?"

Dr. Sawyer put away the last vial of blood and started the process of removing the needle. Vita looked away while she talked. "All this time, we assumed he was alive, but . . . we got the news a few weeks ago when they found your whereabouts. It broke our hearts to hear it. Jack read the report, but he didn't tell me the details. He couldn't get through it. Mason was always like a brother to him. To hear that he's been dead for years was a bit of a shock."

Vita looked down at her shoes. "We were picking up a plant from a client in the city. He said he had a phone call to make and told me to wait inside the client's store. I heard the shots, and when I ran outside, he was already gone. The police said it was gang related or whatever. I was fifteen."

"I'm so sorry, sweetheart." Dr. Sawyer laid a gentle hand on Vita's. "He raised a beautiful young lady. I know you must be scared being here, but I promise you, our family *will* keep you safe. We owe it to Mason."

Vita studied the doctor and saw the eyes of a mother. The same endearing and protective eyes that Momma had. But there was a firmness in the way she spoke, as if she never questioned herself. Dr. Sawyer may be the first person Vita had met here whom she just *knew* she could trust.

Vita smiled warmly at her. "Thank you for being their friend when they needed it."

"I'll be monitoring your abilities to see what I can prescribe for your healing. Come, I'll bring you back out to your guardian."

Vita followed her out to the main lobby, where Lucas was currently deep in conversation with another girl. Vita took this opportunity to ask another question.

"You said you moved here from the outside world. Were you about my age?"

Dr. Sawyer shook her head, eyeing the girl that her son was talking to. "No. My father was a high-ranking member of the Army. The guardians recruited him here to train them, and they offered to let me study to be a doctor here. It was either move here or pay for medical school. I had just turned sixteen."

"Have any advice for an outsider?"

"Things are pretty old school here. They value tradition and etiquette, but don't let that scare you from speaking your mind. It's been far too long since anyone around here has been properly challenged."

Lucas finally finished his conversation and joined Vita and Dr. Sawyer. "Ready? We're nearly two minutes behind schedule, so we need to hurry. This way."

Vita followed his quick pace down the hall. She wondered if he'd ever been "properly challenged" before.

CHAPTER 10

WATER

B oyd spoke quietly to Dr. Guyer while everyone else filed in to the designated training room and sat at one of the many tables in the center of the room. To Adrian, it reminded him of a high school classroom except the floors and walls were a spotless white and the fluorescent lights beamed brightly above them. Dr. Guyer sat at a desk, reading over a messy stack of papers. No windows and the only door was protected by Sawyer. Dr. Guyer whispered something to Boyd before sending him back to his position at the back of the room.

Adrian didn't like Boyd. There was something shady about him and the glare he always wore. What was the guy's problem? Last night, Boyd could've won an award for the world's worst introduction, starting the brief speech with, "My name is Guardian Jason Boyd, and our relationship will be strictly professional. I suggest that you do not try to escape, or I will be forced to subdue you."

What a nice guy.

Adrian had dealt with guys like that before, the kind who were too big for their britches. He'd always been able to turn those kinds of guys into friends, so he tried his usual tactics. Guys like that talked most about one thing: themselves. So, Adrian asked Boyd about himself and tried to keep a friendly tone. It was better to make peace early on with this type of person. But Boyd wasn't having it. He ignored Adrian unless he was telling him that it would be inappropriate to share such personal information to a dangerous elemental. Adrian guessed they wouldn't be braiding each other's hair anytime soon.

At Guyer's side was Dr. Wilson, who reminded Adrian of a weasel. The ruddy-brown hair didn't help his pinched-in features and lanky height. Wilson was obviously Guyer's assistant and did most of the talking for both of them.

"You will all demonstrate your abilities now. Three, why don't you start." Wilson held up a small pinwheel and waited expectantly.

Annie looked at her nails as if she didn't hear him, a bored expression on her face.

"Elemental Three?" Wilson repeated. "You may now demonstrate your ability."

"Her name is Annie," Adrian explained.

Wilson cleared his throat. "Miss . . . Annie, you may demonstrate your ability."

Annie's irises glowed white, then the pinwheel spun so fast it became a blur of red paper.

"Happy?" Annie asked before completely stopping the wind altogether.

"Yes." Wilson carefully set down the pinwheel as if it were made of poison. He made a quick note on his clipboard. Then he picked up a potted plant that looked nearly dead.

"Element—"

"Vita. My name is Vita," she corrected politely.

"We'll see yours now."

Vita walked up to the plant and gently touched it with her finger. Her eyes glowed green, and the once wilted plant now seemed to dance as its rich green leaves grew and sprouted white flowers. She released the plant and smiled. "His name is Eli. He prefers low light and warm water. Oh, and he likes jazz music."

"Vita," Dr. Sawyer interrupted. "Come over here so I can read your vitals."

Vita walked over and let Dr. Sawyer do so.

"Excellent." Wilson scribbled something down before he held up a glass of water, looked at Adrian, and paused.

"Adrian, it is your turn," he said.

Adrian stared at the glass of water and scratched the back of his head. "I . . . don't really know how. It usually just happens by accident."

Wilson frowned. "You have no control over your abilities?"

"I can usually stop it if it starts. But I get migraines."

"Well then, we will mark this as attempt number one."

"I don't know *how*. I've never been able to on command."

"It usually helps if I visualize it," Vita offered. "When I'm healing, I imagine the illness leaving the body or the wound disappearing. Maybe try imagining the water moving."

Adrian tried to imagine the water in motion within the glass, moving the way a snake would out of the glass and rising up into the air. The fluid rippled, but it didn't move the way he wanted. But his eyes were glowing.

"Okay, we have a glow." Wilson notated that on his clipboard. "Keep trying."

Adrian nodded and took a deep breath. He thought about it again, and again. The water rippled a little harder, even splashed a bit, but refused to move the way he wanted it to.

Frustrated, Adrian tore his eyes away and rubbed his temples. His head throbbed so hard it shook his vision. "I can't."

"You can do it, Adrian. You're on the right path," Vita encouraged. "Maybe take a break and come back to it."

"We have no time for breaks. I need to see that your abilities haven't been affected by years of dormancy." Wilson scrutinized Adrian. "Move the water out of the glass."

"I just *told you—*"

"You must do it! We cannot afford for your abilities to fail because of your parents' irresponsibility."

"That's not fair," Vita stood up. "He's trying. Give him some time."

"We do not have time," Wilson snapped at her. He set the glass on the table and waved a dismissive hand at her. "Stop talking. I have not invited you to speak yet."

"Would you lay the hell off?" Adrian growled. The water trembled as if it didn't like the tension in the air. The glass frosted over, and the top layer of the water froze into a thin sheet of ice.

"I didn't even want to be here, I've never used these stupid abilities, I don't know anything about them," Adrian ranted. "But now you expect me to be an expert? It doesn't work that way."

Again, the water vibrated, cracking the ice and splashing a few drops onto the table. A quick succession of zaps sounded in the room, followed by a sharp sting at Adrian's back.

He yelped and jerked forward. His eyes instantly glowed blue as the water gushed out of the glass and whipped behind him. It blasted Annie in the face, sending her sprawling backward. A Taser was in her hand, sending the guardians in a frenzy as they tried to figure out how she'd gotten her hands on one of their Tasers.

"What the hell?" Adrian gasped, rubbing the tender spot on his shoulder, his eyes returning to their mossy green.

Annie sat up, drenched with water, and smirked at him. "You're welcome."

"Put down the Taser!" Boyd demanded, reaching for his tranquilizer gun.

"Oh, *honestly*." Dr. Sawyer huffed in irritation. She walked over to Annie and held out her hand. Annie dropped the Taser into her hand with a sheepish smile. The doctor gave it back to Boyd. "If she wanted to use it on you, she would have. Don't threaten my patients again."

Annie winked at Boyd as Adrian helped her up. Adrian shook his head. "I'd say sorry for splashing you, but . . . you tased me."

"What you *should* be saying is 'I owe you, Annie.' To which I'd agree." Annie called up a brisk wind to dry off the water from her hair as if using a blow dryer.

"Let's try that again," Wilson suggested, refilling the glass with more water.

Adrian rubbed his temples again. His head pounded tremendously now. He'd had hangovers, but they paled in comparison to this.

"May I?" Vita offered, approaching him with a studious look.

"May you what?" Adrian asked.

Vita placed her fingertips on his temples as her eyes started to glow. Her Mona Lisa smile changed to a concentrated purse of her lips.

"Oh . . . you've got a lot going on here. Hm." Her eyebrows furrowed as she looked at Adrian—not into his eyes but through them.

"What's happening?" Adrian asked tentatively, stopping himself from inching back.

"I think I found your block, Adrian. This is complicated. Because you've suppressed it for so long, I think it just got stuck. I can sense your pain from just using that small amount. It's kind of like a knot in your brain. Let's see if I can loosen it up a bit." She took a deep breath and closed her eyes.

Then Adrian felt it. A breathtaking flush of warmth from his head all the way down to his toes. He closed his eyes as the pain in his head was almost instantly replaced with astounding relief.

Old injuries from football disappeared as if they never existed. Like moving a dam from a river, allowing the body of water to rush through at an incredible speed.

Vita opened her eyes at the same time he did. He released an amazed laugh. "How are you doing this?"

She didn't answer in her usual chirpy tone. Her skin became pale and clammy, almost gray compared to her sun-kissed pallor.

"Vita?" Adrian asked.

She puffed out a ragged breath before her eyes fluttered close, and she collapsed.

CHAPTER 11

GUARDIAN

Lucas predicted what would happen a second before it did. He surged forward when Vita collapsed and barely caught her in time. Now he laid her down and held an ice pack to her forehead while his mother pulled various tools out of her case and muttered to herself. Lucas knew Vita grew weak from healing, but this was quite different from what he'd expected. Then again, she hadn't eaten much of the breakfast earlier, and she didn't eat last night either. He just assumed the stress had averted her from food, but maybe there was something else?

Dr. Sawyer pressed her stethoscope to Vita's chest. "Okay, sounds good . . ."

Lucas was used to seeing his mother in doctor mode. Guardian-related injuries happened all the time, some worse than others. She was the head doctor for a good reason. Chief had always said there was never a wound that Dr. Sawyer couldn't fix.

Vita stirred, opened her eyes, and moaned.

"How are you feeling?" Dr. Sawyer asked, brushing hair from Vita's cheek.

"Hungry," Vita muttered, pushing herself to sit up and rubbing her head. "I blacked out again."

"Yes, I know." The doctor smiled. "Guardian Sawyer, take her to the orchard and get her some fresh fruit."

Lucas quickly got to his feet and helped Vita stand. She was dizzy, but she could walk on her own. Lucas kept a hand on the small of her back just in case. He wouldn't let another elemental get hurt on his watch ever again.

He led her on the short walk to the orchards and brought her to the nearest tree. Vita sat in a patch of sunlight, leaned against its trunk, and held out her hand. A branch extended down to her and dropped a pair of bright red apples onto her lap.

"Thank you, dear friend." Vita gave the branch a tired smile as it slinked back to its original state. She looked up at Lucas. "Why don't you take a seat? Want one? You look awkward just standing there."

Lucas rubbed his fingers together in discomfort, wondering if such a thing would be inappropriate. He looked around to ensure the workers wouldn't see them and think something scandalous, then sat next to her by the tree and accepted the spare apple.

It was the juiciest fruit he'd ever tasted.

"Angels," he blurted. "Our fruit have never been so sweet."

"Plants usually save their best fruits for people who take good care of them," Vita said. Perhaps it was a benefit that his charge could produce such delicious fruit.

"You'll have to thank the trees for me. This apple is delicious."

"It's Honey Crisp, actually." She smiled at him and his immediate desire to return it was instinctual. He withheld the smile, however. Like a good chief would.

"So, was that your girlfriend earlier?" Vita asked as he ate. "The girl in the lab?"

"No, of course not. She offered me her introduction today."

"What do you mean?"

"Well, after Elondohnians graduate from school, we're allowed to court. However, the girl needs to formally introduce herself to the boy first. It's a sort of invitation to pursue them. Don't they have something like that in the outside world?"

"No. If a boy or a girl wants to date someone, there's this whole song-and-dance thing of awkward flirtation until one of them fesses up and they start dating. It's not so . . . stiff. So, you really can't ask them out till they introduce themselves to you?"

He nodded. "We have a system to follow. After a girl offers her introduction, the couple may go on a few casual dates. At that point, it isn't exclusive, just an opportunity to see if they like each other. Assuming they do, the boy will ask for courtship, which is when they start discussing serious matters such as marriage. Usually, a courtship will last about a year before they wed. Truthfully, I'm terrible at receiving introductions. It's embarrassing and awkward, especially in front of other people. I never really know what to do."

Why in the angel's name did he confess such a vulnerable thing to her, a veritable stranger? It had just slipped out. He'd have to pay more attention to what he said around her. He didn't want her to think he was incompetent.

"Strange," Vita muttered. "Nobody does things like that anymore."

"Well, you're from the outside world. A lot of things *you* do are strange."

"The outside world. What a weird way to label the people just outside your fancy gates," she mused, chuckling to herself. "So, what does a formal introduction sound like, anyway?"

"Well, typically, the girl will announce her name and the house she represents. I think if the boy wants to accept, he'll say the same. For example, I am Guardian Lucas Sawyer, House of the Lion."

"The lion, huh? I've always wanted to befriend a lion. I think they'd be real sweet. Does everyone have a different animal?"

"Every family, except for the elementals. The family is to embody the qualities of that animal."

"And what's the lion?"

"Oh, it's a lengthy list. Courage, justice, military might. The Sawyers have always been the chief of guardians, so we have a lot to uphold."

"Sounds like a lot of pressure." Vita's eyes dropped to the lion emblem on his lapel.

Lucas shrugged. "It is our duty."

"But if it were up to you, would you choose it?"

"Well, what else is there to do? Become a gardener in some no-name town?"

"If that's what makes you happy, why not? I tell you what, we no-name-town folks smile a heck of a lot more than the people around here do."

"Must be the berry cobbler," Lucas muttered sarcastically.

Vita scoffed. "Yeah, must be. It's a shame you'll never get to try Lucy's café. Might actually get you to smile for once."

"If I may, that was bold of you to ask a complete stranger on a date like that when we first met. We don't do things like that here. It's considered improper."

She blushed and crossed her arms. "First of all, it wasn't a date. I was trying to be nice to a newbie in town who obviously didn't have any friends. Second of all, I think it's pretty funny that the guy who kidnapped me is telling me about proper behavior. And you don't have to worry about me wasting my boldness on you anyway. I'm not interested in the stiff, schedule-keeping kind of guy. I find it to be boring."

A hot sting heated up his face. He wasn't boring, he was efficient. "Good. I'm glad we could agree on that. Speaking of schedules, we should be heading back now. Are you feeling better?"

"Oh yeah. I guess we gotta go back to that chicken coop of a lab, huh?"

"You talk oddly, do you know that?" Lucas asked, holding out a hand to help her up.

She scoffed and accepted his help. "So do you. But that's a bridge we'll cross another time."

CHAPTER 12

GUARDIAN

T he afternoon training consisted mostly of ability demonstrations under the careful instruction of Dr. Guyer and Dr. Wilson. The three guardians stood at their posts and kept a careful eye on their elemental. Lucas watched with curiosity as things floated around him with a flick of Annie's hand, water splashed from one bucket to another by Adrian's will, and plants moved as Vita made them dance.

Two joined them this time, quietly observing in the background. His training was more complex than this, but it was encouraged that he spend time with the other elementals so that they may be influenced by his naturally calm behavior.

The other two guardians kept their distance, a disturbed grimace creasing their faces. Lucas could understand why they were frightened, but he was more intrigued. These seemingly normal beings could do incredible things, yet they weren't naturally violent as he'd been taught his entire life.

Annie and Adrian worked together to make a small snow flurry, the icy breeze carrying snowflakes and rogue flower petals from Vita's plants. Vita was standing in front of Lucas, holding up her palms and catching the snowflakes, giggling as they landed on her cheeks.

"I've never seen snow before," she said. She looked at Lucas. "Is this what it's like?"

"It's colder," he answered.

She giggled again when a snowflake landed on the tip of his nose. Lucas blushed and hurriedly wiped it off, unable to withhold his shy smile.

Vita tilted her head at him. "Huh. So, all it takes to make you smile is a little snowflake. Good to know."

She turned away and joined Annie and Adrian for the next part of their training.

"Ready, Adrian? Here goes." Vita threw water from a glass his way.

Adrian's eyes glowed blue as he threw out his hands in front of him. The water stopped in a clear wall, as if it had hit a window. He held it there for several seconds before it became unsteady, wavering as if trying to break loose from Adrian's hold.

"No, no. Come on . . ." Adrian hissed through gritted teeth, focusing his eyes harder.

Thin streams dripped down like melting ice. Just as it did before, the water vibrated, becoming too unsteady for him to hold, and splashed down on the floor, joining the puddles from his last attempts.

He wiped his forehead. "Damn, this is harder than I thought it'd be."

"You're getting the hang of it though!" Vita encouraged with her bright smile. "I'll bet by this time tomorrow, you'll have it down lickety-split."

Annie was lounging in midair as if she were sitting on an invisible chair. By now, Lucas had grown used to seeing her randomly float.

Annie offered a cocky smile and nodded at Two. "This isn't a free show. When are you gonna show us what *you* can do, hot-head?"

Two brought his dark eyes on her before casting them down again. "I was not invited to demonstrate my abilities."

"I'm inviting you now. Go on, light something on fire," Annie encouraged. Her encouragement was much different from Vita's. More like pushing rather than an excited guidance.

"Go ahead, Two." Dr. Guyer smiled with approval.

"His name is Dos now," Annie informed stiffly.

Two shot her a look of warning before his eyes fell.

"Dos," Dr. Guyer repeated, as if sounding it out. "I like it. Go on, Dos."

Two motioned to the potted shrub Vita had been using for her ability demonstration. "May I take a leaf from your plant?"

She approached the shrub. "I'll need to borrow a leaf, is that okay?" A green leaf detached itself from the tiny branch and drifted into her hand. "Thank you, dear friend." She handed him the leaf and stepped back.

"Thank you." Two stood in the middle of the room and took a deep breath. His eyes glowed a brilliant red as the leaf began to smoke. The edges burned a bright orange before the entire leaf completely caught fire and turned into a ball of flame in the palm of his hand.

Annie scoffed. "That's all? You spent your whole life training just for a little flame? A lighter could do that."

His expression unwavering, Two turned his hand down and dropped the ball of fire. Instinctively, everyone but Annie jumped back. She hung safely in the air, or so Lucas thought.

The ball of flame spread into a long body of a snake, slithering in zigzag motions as it stretched its way across the floor and rose to face Annie. The serpent of fire stared Annie right in the eyes, calculating and composed, and opened its mouth to expose its fiery fangs. Heat burned Lucas's face as the flames rippled and lapped each other. He took another step back.

Annie smirked and raised her chin at the serpent. "Now that's what I'm talking about. What else can you do?"

Just as quickly as it appeared, the serpent shrank back into a ball in Two's hand and disappeared altogether, leaving the unharmed green leaf in its place. Two held out the leaf to Vita, who accepted it with a bright smile.

"Wow, Dos, that was amazing!" She giggled, cupping the leaf in two hands. "I can't believe you could do all that without hurting this leaf. You'd be a hit at magic shows."

Vita used her abilities to reattach the leaf to her plant, smiling proudly.

Two creased his eyebrows, studying her excited expression for a few seconds. "What is that emotion you are experiencing?"

"What do you mean?"

"I can read and deliver emotions. I can see them. I can smell them. But I cannot read yours. It is new to me. If I have not experienced it myself, I cannot understand it nor can I deliver it."

Lucas had heard rumor of this ability, but he'd never seen it in person. He wondered if Two had ever made Lucas feel a certain emotion without his knowing. That idea sent chills down his spine.

"Oh," Vita's smile faded. "Well, it's happiness."

"Now you feel sad," Two pointed out without any question. "Some sort of pity."

"Well, yeah."

"Why?"

"I feel bad that you don't know happiness but you know sadness. Hasn't anyone or anything ever made you smile?"

"No," Two answered simply.

"Bless your heart." Vita rested a hand on her chest and deflated.

Now that Lucas thought about it, he'd never seen Two smile or laugh, and he'd known Two his entire life. A ball of pity formed in Lucas's stomach, and perhaps a little guilt. He supposed that he could've done more to make Two smile at least once in his life. He'd just never thought about it.

"I'll have to study it," Two noted with a shrug.

To everyone's surprise, Vita opened her arms and wrapped them around Two—a move that was highly inappropriate for people who were not family or in a serious courtship.

Two jerked back slightly, eyes widening, seemingly at a loss for how to react. He stiffened and did not touch her as she rested her chin on his shoulder, whispering something that only he could hear. His eyebrows creased as if he couldn't understand.

"What is she doing?" Hogan grimaced. "Is this allowed?"

"Control your elemental!" Boyd hissed to Lucas.

Lucas shook his head. "There's a reason she's doing this."

Dr. Wilson nearly dropped his clipboard, along with his jaw, as he watched them in frozen horror. Annie and Adrian simply exchanged a nonchalant look and a shrug. Dr. Guyer smiled to himself and glanced at Lucas.

When Vita pulled away, she rested her hands on Two's shoulders and smiled at him. "Okay?"

Two still looked confused, the most emotion that Lucas had ever seen on him. He nodded stiffly.

Vita smiled even brighter and patted his shoulder before returning to Annie's side.

Dr. Sawyer walked in before anyone could even process what to do next. "It's time for dinner. No more training for the day." She stopped and looked around the room, seeing the expressions of shock. "Is everyone well?"

"Hell yeah, except I'm starving. What's for dinner?" Annie asked.

Dr. Sawyer smiled and led the elementals out, except for Two, who stayed behind and stared at the floor with a furrowed brow.

Lucas hesitated at the door. "Dos, are you coming?"

Two looked up with a confused frown. "You are calling me Dos?"

"Isn't that your name now? That's what the others call you," Lucas answered. "Would you prefer something different?"

Two lowered his eyes again, the corners of his lips twitching up just slightly. "No. Dos is my name now. Thank you, Guardian Sawyer."

"Sure." Lucas shrugged. "Will you be joining them for dinner?"

"Not tonight. I have work to do."

"Okay, then. Goodnight."

"Goodnight."

CHAPTER 13

FIRE

os ... Dos ... Dos ...
That was his name now.
He had a name.
Dos.

He liked his name. Even though he had not thought of it himself, it was his. It was something that no one could take away from him or punish him for. It was him.

Dos.

He said his name aloud in the privacy of his home, that strange emotion glowing as he spoke it. He stood in front of the mirror and repeated, "My name is Dos."

All around him, the gray emotion flourished into a golden burst, encasing his entire body like a cloud. It felt warm. Lightweight. Similar to the heat from sunrays in spring. Not overbearing and uncomfortable, but enticing and soothing. Happiness carried with it a certain hum in his chest, like a steady note played on his cello. It smelled as sweet as freshly cut pineapples.

He had never sensed such a thing from anyone in Elondoh before. At least, anyone in his presence. But Vita carried it so effortlessly, almost all the time. To hold such an emotion for so long should be tiring, but she seemed energized by it. Adrian experienced it every time he ate.

Was happiness different from the other emotions Dos had learned? Emotions like anger, depression, and anxiety were draining. Like a leaking faucet, constantly dripping energy from the person's mind and body.

He'd felt positive emotions too, like peace. He'd learned that emotion from Dr. Sawyer and had often felt it while playing his cello. It was his favorite emotion to transfer. He'd transferred peace a few times to Annie since her arrival. She hadn't seemed to notice yet, but they never did. Most people believed they were wise enough to calm themselves, but if that were the case, then Dos would not be needed.

Annie was quite the proud character too. She always looked bored, but he could sense her fear inside. Much like himself, she hid it well. But when he produced that fire, he did not sense fear. He sensed that strange, unknown emotion again—the one that showed as a ribbon encircling her body. It reminded him of hunger.

Dos liked studying emotions when they were undisturbed. That was when they were the most effective. He'd only asked Vita about her emotion because she had been wearing happiness all day, and it frustrated him that he could not understand it.

But Annie wore an emotion that made him think of one word: *rebellion*. It felt hot in his core, like a used piece of coal resting in his lower gut. He liked that emotion too. He'd only felt it for a few seconds, and he was addicted.

Dr. Novak was not home yet, and she wouldn't be for some time. This gave Dos the privacy he needed to study the emotions, using a book that Guyer had given him for reference.

Dos took out his notebook and clicked his pen. It was the same notebook he used for all his emotion studies ever since his connection ability had activated the day he turned twelve. The notebook contained his notes on the different emotions he understood, what they looked like, what they felt like, and where he felt them.

He quickly wrote down his analysis of happiness.

Happiness.

A positive emotion that humans feel when something favorable has occurred. A warm sensation in the chest and face. Smiling and sometimes laughter occurs to the recipient of happiness. A notable lack of negative emotions during this particular experience. The color is gold and appears as an afterglow. The smell is similar to pineapples.

Happiness can be given and received.

Dos thought about the words that Vita had whispered into his ear: *Everyone deserves to be happy, including you.*

No one had ever told Dos that he deserved anything. Fundamentally speaking, it did not make sense to deem someone worthy of an emotion because the brain naturally produced them. But to hear that he deserved to feel the golden rush, as she did so freely, made him experience it just a little bit himself.

Then when Guardian Sawyer called him Dos, that made him happy as well. But why?

Because it made my name official, he realized.

Guardian Sawyer was an important member of the community. He held a great influence over the other guardians, even those senior to him. If Sawyer started to acknowledge him by an official name, that made it real. It made *Dos* real.

Guardian Sawyer had always been more kind to him than the rest of the boys in school. He never went out of his way to befriend Dos, but he was never cruel either. He was simple, civilized, and polite. He treated Dos like another person, and he'd stopped the other boys when they took turns beating Dos during guardian training.

Dos wrote down examples of when he'd experienced happiness today. He even wrote that he almost smiled when Guardian Sawyer used his new name.

But the smile quickly diminished as his mind traveled down the path of the guardians. In addition to developing his ability, Dos had been forced to attend guardian training with the other boys. He learned strategy and fighting alongside them. He'd taken every class they did. And he'd excelled.

But the other boys were cruel, open in their discomfort toward him. They would steal his things: books, uniform articles, and shoes. They would break in to his locker and no one would reprimand them for it. During sparring matches, the others would throw hits that were not allowed, and the instructors would say nothing. They openly discussed what they would do if he lost control around them. What they were *trained* to do.

The prophecy was taught in school, and the other students would look at Dos as if he were a monster. The guardian trainees relished in the idea of simply hazing the evil out of Dos. Chivalry applied to everyone except for him.

Of course, this would cause his element to react, to defend the body. But Dr. Guyer forced Dos to wear impulse bracelets that shocked him whenever he used his abilities without permission. Rather than defend himself, he would get shocked as he was taunted and beaten. The bracelets were vicious things, too, sending shockwaves of electricity through every nerve in his body, and only growing sharper with every attempt he made to use his ability. He still bore the marks on his wrists from those damn bracelets even though he hadn't worn them in years.

Dos had always been taught that his element was dangerous, and as a result, he was dangerous too.

Historically, the Fire element had always been the most violent of them all, and therefore was viewed as a thing that needed to be controlled. Despite the bruises and bloodstained shirts, Dr. Novak warned him to never react and to never complain about it. One small sign of rebellion from Dos would lead to his punishment.

The punishment he had faced for simply existing was enough to stave off his need for revenge.

Dos had to be incredibly careful with his words and actions because he could not defend himself, and there was no one else who would. *When in doubt, say nothing. Look at no one. Attract no attention.*

He had to live his life as if he did not exist. That was the only way to be safe. Eventually, the boys became bored and would ignore him. He preferred it that way.

The part that frustrated him the most was that he was just as qualified to be a guardian as the others were. He had even taken the same oath that the guardians did when they graduated. He had descended from the best of knights, with angelic blood in his veins, and yet he was reduced to a liability. His ancestors were worshipped, treated as highly as gods. Dos was treated as a worthless rat because of two sentences written centuries ago. If he were an ordinary Elondohnian like the rest of them, he could live a simple life. If it were not for his fire abilities, he would be a guardian. He would be respected.

One would think that being the only living Fire elemental would grant him that, but alas.

Unlike the other elemental parents, Dr. Winifred Novak had lost her abilities. No one knew why. There was only one instance in history when an elemental lost their ability completely, and that was Generation 6. The angels deemed those elementals unworthy and stripped them of their abilities before they were killed for their violence. Dos wondered if the angels thought the same about Dr. Novak and had punished her for it. What had she done that angered the angels in such a way?

She frequently wore the emotion of bitterness when Dos needed to use his abilities around her. He had never noted that she smiled or wore happiness around him.

He scribbled down a quick note:

Happiness is available to all, but few choose to accept it.

Dos felt the wave of disdain before he heard the door open. Dr. Novak was home now. She walked through the door without acknowledging him, per usual. He kept his eyes on his book.

"Oh. You are home," Dr. Novak greeted, placing her briefcase on the countertop.

"Yes. I skipped dinner," Dos answered without raising his eyes. He knew better. Dr. Novak did not like to be looked in the eyes. It angered her. She had never said it out loud, but he could sense it.

"You are studying the emotions again. Have you learned something new?"

"Happiness."

He could sense the slight shock from her end, followed by a spike of anger.

"Give me your notes," she requested, holding out her hand.

Dr. Novak frequently looked through his notes. There was nothing private for him, save for his own body. Even then, he'd been experimented on over and over again, so that was not necessarily true either. Dr. Guyer frequently used beatings, electrocutions, or drug-induced hallucinations in an attempt to artificially advance Dos's abilities, and Dr. Novak would just watch. She wasn't a mother so much as a jailer.

He handed over the notes.

Dr. Novak read with a slight frown that she always wore when she was focused. "You learned happiness from Elemental Four?"

"Yes," he answered without bothering to correct her on Vita's name. She wouldn't use it anyway. "The elementals carry strange emotions that I have never experienced before."

"Mm," Dr. Novak grunted, reading further. "Guardian Sawyer called you 'Dos,' and that has given you happiness?"

"It is what the other elementals call me. They did not think a number was an appropriate name."

"'*Dos*' is still a number."

"Yes, but they say it is a name as well."

"I would advise against letting those from the outside world give you names. They can be vulgar and pointless. '*Dos*' is just Spanish for 'two.' It makes no sense to change one translation of a number to another. You do not even have Hispanic heritage. Ours is of Asian descent."

Dos kept his eyes low. "Yes, Doctor."

She slapped the notebook down. "And I would recommend caution around the elementals. Earth is known to show heightened emotions. If you are learning emotions from Elemental Four, be aware that it likely will not be practical."

"She is kind," Dos defended meekly. "They all are."

Dr. Novak scoffed. "They *appear* that way. Such is their camouflage."

He wondered if "they" meant just the other elementals or him as well.

She left before giving him a chance to answer. Dos did not like the way she spoke about the other elementals with such disdain. They were welcoming to him. They openly conversed with him, did not wear a negative emotion around him.

Adrian was kind to him. Dos almost wanted to impress him, as he'd never had a male friend before. Or any friend, for that matter.

Vita did not seem like she could withstand the mountain of hate from Dr. Novak. It made him protective of her. She was gentle, and the scientists here did not treat gentle things properly. They used, manipulated, and took whatever they wanted from whoever they wanted, all in the name of science. He didn't want to see her perpetual happiness broken because of their greed.

Then there was Annie. She may have been brash, but she

was unique. He liked the way she spoke her mind, and the way she smiled as if there was no challenge she could not face. It was different from the false politeness the other women wore. There was just something about her that intrigued him. A curiosity that made him smile to himself.

This emotion, he did *not* write down.

CHAPTER 14

GUARDIAN

Vita hummed to herself as they walked home from dinner. Again, Elondohnians stopped and stared, making Lucas terribly uncomfortable. He never liked extra attention. Vita, however, seemed to enjoy it.

She waved and smiled at the spectators. "Hi there. Hello. Oh, you're just as pretty as a peach!"

They merely cast their eyes down, afraid to disrespect or offend her. Vita didn't seem to notice, however, and continued peppering the community with compliments and friendly greetings. It wasn't until they got closer to her townhouse and away from the crowd that she said anything about it.

"Why is everyone here so afraid of me?" she asked. "Weren't y'all raised knowing about us and what we can do? Why do they all look away from me?"

Lucas wasn't exactly sure how to answer that without lying or sounding rude. "Um, they just aren't used to you yet."

"That's not the whole truth, is it? You look like you're hiding something."

"Guardians are forbidden to lie."

"You lied to me when you came to my plant nursery."

"That was for a mission. It was crucial, so an exception was made, but I don't make a habit of telling lies."

They reached her front door, where she stopped and raised an eyebrow at him. "What's the big deal? Why is everyone being so skittish around me?"

He sighed and relented. "Do you remember how I told you about Dr. John Dee?" She nodded so he continued. "He wrote prophecies for each elemental generation. King Carmara supposedly told him which generations would have the connection abilities and the great things they would do. He's never been wrong—every prophecy he made came true. For the sixth generation, he predicted they would be overcome with great evil."

"And he was right?"

"Yes. They were responsible for the deaths of thousands of people. Not just Elondohnians but civilians too. They burned down villages, flooded towns, caused terrible storms, and created earthquakes so devastating that it still marks the earth. The guardians had to kill them. Thankfully, they already had children, so the line could live on, but . . . it was a dark time in our history."

"What does that have to do with us?"

"John Dee believed your generation would mirror that one. We're all taught about the prophecy so that we can be prepared for when it comes to pass."

"And what's gonna happen if it does? You'll kill me like your people killed mine?"

He hesitated, seeing the fear in her eyes. He didn't *want* to kill any of them, but in guardian training, he was taught that, if there was an out-of-control reaction, he *must* kill them. Generation 23 could not be a repeat of Generation 6.

At his silence, Vita looked down and hugged her elbows. "So, not only was my entire life thrown to hell, but now I have to live the rest of it, however short it may be, with people who hate me for whatever my ancestors did. Wow, that sucks. I've never even met my ancestors."

"It's just a precaution, Vita."

Vita glared up at him with a look sharp enough to dry his tongue. "Can't you see how unfair that is? Do I look like a killer to you? Have I acted violent at all? I'm the one who's being nice to everyone here, you included, and all of you are just counting the days until you can shoot me down. You think I haven't noticed how you're always holding on to your holster? You haven't even given me a chance to prove you wrong. Need I remind you that I'm not even here by choice? I had a life and friends and a home, but all of that is gone just so your people can take what you want from me and kill me."

"That's not fair," he argued, face flushing. "We're not treating you as a prisoner. You have nice lodging, you have whatever you want for free, you have protection—"

"But it's not my choice!" she hissed, tears welling in her eyes. "You don't even care enough to provide food that I can eat. It's not fair for you to take everything away from me, treat me like I'm a loose cannon, and then toss me away when you're done with me. I'm human, just like you."

"You can't eat the food? Is that why you've been so irritable?"

She scoffed and opened her door. "You're clueless, you know that? Goodnight."

She slammed the door behind her and turned off the porch light, leaving him alone in the dark.

Lucas sat at the dinner table, absentmindedly picking at his food while drowning out his parents' conversation. Vita, again, was upset when he'd left her, and he was starting to understand why. Maybe he'd always known, but avoiding the topic made his job easier. It was easy to focus on the task at hand when the task didn't carry emotional baggage. But that wasn't a fair expectation for a girl who had a life stolen from her and now knew that one step out of line could result in her punishment.

It was a pressure that Lucas knew well. One mistake and those in charge would start to question his every move.

At the end of the day, they were simply trying to figure out how to prove themselves. Lucas was trying to prove that he could be a good leader, and Vita was trying to prove that she was innocent. That didn't seem fair. Neither of them asked for this, but it was tossed in their laps, and they had to do the best with what they were given.

Granted, it didn't help that she'd called him clueless.

"Do Earth elementals traditionally have dietary restrictions?" Lucas asked, interrupting the current conversation.

Chief considered. "Mason never ate meat if it came from an animal that he'd met. He liked chicken until one day he talked to a chicken, and he wouldn't eat it after that. I think fish was still on the menu, but where around here would he meet a fish? Why do you ask?"

Lucas rubbed his forehead. "That's why Vita passed out so easily earlier. She's barely had enough to eat. I didn't think to ask, and I didn't see any notes about it from previous Earth elementals, so I didn't do anything about it. The kitchen staff needs to be notified immediately. Angels, she must be surviving on fruit and maybe eggs? Eggs aren't meat, right?"

"Mason ate eggs. I think it's just meat that they avoid. I'll have a note sent to the kitchen first thing in the morning."

"Oh, that reminds me," Mom said, setting down her wine glass. "I picked up some caramels for Vita. Have her eat one after she heals. The sugar will hold her until she can get in a decent meal. Is your concern for her the reason you've been so quiet tonight?"

He shook his head. "Did John Dee predict that the previous

generation would run? Did he predict that Dr. Winifred Novak would lose her abilities or that Mason Eastwood would die the way he did?"

Chief creased his eyebrows. "No. Otherwise, we would have done something to prevent all of that. He predicted that Generation 22 would stop the deaths of thousands of people, and they did through their various missions in the outside world."

"But he missed incredibly crucial parts, so that must mean that he can be wrong," Lucas said.

"Well, it's not as if he saw every detail of their lives."

"No, but if he failed to predict that, then why do we believe we understand the whole truth about his prediction for Generation 23? Maybe there's something that we're missing."

Mom and Chief exchanged a quick glance before Mom turned to Lucas with a stern look. "Why are you saying this? Did you learn something new?"

"The prophecy says Generation 23 would carry a power that shall change humanity forever. Why did we decide that was a bad thing?"

"It also says they mirror Generation 6," Chief said.

"There are *many* similarities," Lucas argued, frustrated. "In the portraits, the Water elemental looks just like Adrian. The Earth elemental held a cat in his painting and Vita has a cat—or *had* until she was brought here."

"I spoke with her mother, by the way. She'll be here tomorrow, as will the other parents." Chief looked tiredly at his wife. "June hasn't changed a bit. Bold as ever."

"My point is," Lucas continued, "I think we're endangering ourselves by making this generation believe they're destined to be murderers. If we don't present that option to them, if our people stop treating them like monsters, then maybe the elementals will actually *want* to do good for us. Maybe we can earn their loyalty and we won't *need* to fear them. They can be revered as their ancestors once were."

"And what do you propose we do?" Chief challenged. "Dr. Guyer believed caution to be an important part of your education. It is ingrained into everyone's core belief system here. You can't change that overnight."

"No, but I can make a start, and that's better than nothing, isn't it? Isn't it my responsibility as their lead guardian to provide an environment where they will feel comfortable? I think I know how I can start too."

"Oh, really?" Chief scoffed.

"Jack," Mom snapped. "Let him speak."

Lucas swallowed his frustration and nodded firmly. "The elementals were always made to honor the traditions of the original knights. That includes an appreciation for the arts, which is why Dos learned how to play the cello. Perhaps they can present something at the upcoming Clarice Day Festival. Elondohnians will love it, and it shows they are still civilized and honorable, despite being from the outside world. I would like to propose the idea to Dr. Guyer in the morning."

Chief actually looked impressed with a simple head nod. "That's . . . a good idea."

"I think it's kind of you, darling," Mom said, smiling at Lucas. "Another idea? Perhaps you should try befriending Vita. It would help to have an ally among them, and from what I've seen, she's the most welcoming."

"She called me clueless."

"Happens to the best of us," Mom said, shrugging. "I'll bet you two will be the best of friends soon."

Not likely.

CHAPTER 15

FIRE

It was a little after 4:00 a.m. when Dos woke up from a strange dream.

He was sitting across from Annie in the dining hall. They were alone, and she was eating. Dos freely watched her, unafraid of her catching his eyes. Then she looked up at him and raised an eyebrow.

"What are you looking at, hothead?"

Then he woke up.

That was it. A simple, meaningless dream, and yet, he wished he could stay there longer. Why did he dream about her? Why was she on his mind? Probably because she was so . . . intriguing. Yes, that was the most logical reason.

Dos rolled out of his bed to crack open the balcony doors and take in some air. Another cool August night, with a light breeze to carry in the earthy scent of the orchard. Dos took a deep breath and was about to head back to bed when he heard Dr. Novak's voice from below the balcony.

"Not a single reaction since the arrival. It's been forty-eight hours. There should have been signs by now," she whispered, pacing back and forth on the concrete patio.

Dos knelt down and hid behind the balcony wall, listening carefully. She was on the phone with someone, likely Dr. Guyer. This early? What could be so important?

"No," Dr. Novak continued. "Two has not reported any signs.

Are we sure we got it right? We should have made another batch
. . . Yes, I understand, but clearly something is off about our
hypothesis."

Signs of what?

"Sir, I am concerned. If V is not active, we will be unsuccessful
in creating the stone."

V? Dos sorted through his mental library of alchemical
substances. V was not something he could remember. It must be a
code or perhaps an abbreviation? Alchemy was full of hidden codes
and mysteries, created in fear of the wrong people discovering the
wrong thing.

"Yes, you are right. We still need to fully develop the others.
One and Three have not unlocked their connection abilities, and
we still need to build strength in One's water abilities. Two? His
abilities are fully developed, we need not worry about him."

Dr. Novak listened for a second. "Yes, he is still discovering new
emotions, but . . . is that really necessary? He is ready. Understood,
I will allow him more time with the others. Yes, sir. Goodnight."

Dr. Novak hung up but didn't go inside right away. Dos peeked
his head over the edge of the balcony and watched her. She chewed
her nails in thought. A lemon-yellow starburst of annoyance
danced above her head, following her as she paced.

Why is she so upset?

She suddenly looked up in Dos's direction, narrowly missing
him as he ducked down and held his breath.

He heard the back door open and click closed. Dos hurried to
his bed, slid beneath the covers, and rolled over so that his back
faced the bedroom door.

Just as he settled in, his door opened.

Dos kept his eyes closed and forced himself to breathe deeply,
in and out. Then his door closed. He counted to one hundred just

to be safe, then barely peeked through his cracked lids. She was gone.

Dos released the tension from his shoulders and stared at his ceiling in thought.

V . . . what does that have to do with the elementals?

———————————

The next morning, Dos stopped at the hospital before breakfast to receive his injection to keep his fever at bay. The connection abilities brought their own set of side effects for the elementals. There was only so much their human genetics could withstand. Vita was depleted of energy, and Dos had a constant fever. Sometimes the effects could worsen when the connection abilities were used too often. Dos had been reading and delivering a lot more emotions than he was used to, so the medicine was needed.

He waited in his assigned room with the door open for a nurse to come in. As he waited, he heard voices. One of them was Dr. Guyer.

"I need you to study him, Jason. Be sure to note every behavioral or physical change. Every detail matters, understand?"

Guardian Boyd answered, "Yes, sir. And we are still under the agreement that if I perform well, I will be considered for chiefhood?"

"If you perform well, then yes. I will consider your application."

Dos stood and made his way to the door. The elementals had slightly heightened senses, which meant they could hear and see very well due to the purity of their angelic blood. However, they couldn't hear through walls, so Dos needed to move closer to eavesdrop. He wasn't quite sure he heard the conversation correctly.

Boyd for chief? Lucas Sawyer was meant to be chief. According to Elondoh history, the Sawyers had always been chiefs, as it passed down through the family line. Why would Dr. Guyer ever consider anyone else? And who was Boyd meant to study? Perhaps Adrian?

Just as Dos made it to the doorway, Guardian Boyd stepped out of another room across the hall, where Dr. Guyer sat in the background with some kind of IV needle in his arm. Dos and Boyd both froze once they saw each other.

"Good morning, Guardian Boyd," Dos said, looking down. "I was just coming in for my morning injection, I did not expect to see you here. Is Adrian all right?"

"I am here for personal matters, not elemental."

"Then I hope the angels bless you with quick healing."

"Thank you, Two."

"Actually, my name is Dos now. I no longer answer to Two."

Boyd scoffed and smiled in cruel amusement, the way he did when they were children as he'd watched Dos get pushed around by the others. "You answer to what Elondoh says you do. As far as I know, there is no official report that your name is different. I'll see you for training, Two."

Dos let him walk off, anger rising within him like a kindling fire. He ignored it and nodded in greeting to the young nurse who approached him.

"Good morning, Dos," she greeted politely. "I have on file that you'd like to be referred to by that name from now on?"

"It does not matter," he muttered. He rolled up his sleeve for the injection and followed her into the room. "It is only a name."

CHAPTER 16

GUARDIAN

Lucas knocked on Vita's door with a bundle of delicate blue flowers in his hand.

As he waited, Boyd and Hogan raised their eyebrows from their respective doors. Boyd gave Lucas a bitter look of judgment. Hogan simply looked confused, as if wondering whether he was supposed to bring flowers to his elemental.

Vita opened the door with a polite but tight smile. "Good morning."

"Good morning. May I speak to you for a moment before we go?"

Vita shrugged and stepped aside to let him in, then closed the door behind him. "Don't worry, I don't have any hidden traps around here to hurt you."

"I wasn't going to accuse you of—" He stopped and realized he probably wasn't going to earn her trust with a tone of annoyance. He tried again. "I wanted to discuss our conversation last night. I understand you probably feel frustrated and afraid. I would be, too, in your place. After some consideration, I think we should start over. I propose a pact between you and me. A friendship, if you will. The pros of this agreement will include a high-ranking ally who can pull most strings for you within reason, an appropriate amount of comfort when required, and a solution to gain more sympathy from the community for the elementals. In return, I ask that you refrain from ever using your element to hurt anyone, adhere to Elondohnian guidelines, and above all else, you must create the philosopher's stone. I believe that to be a fair start to our friendship. Do we have an agreement?"

Vita blinked and snorted. "Wait, was that you asking me to be your friend? Is that how you approached all the other kids at recess when you were growing up?"

His face heated up. He'd rehearsed that proposal at least five times in the mirror this morning. There wasn't a flaw in it. It was concise and well thought out. What could she possibly have to laugh at?

"I didn't spend much time in recess as a student. I started guardian training earlier than the others, so I spent that time at my father's side, learning from him."

Vita still had a spark of amusement in her eyes. "So, I'm your first . . . friend proposal, I guess?"

"I would call it a proposition, not a proposal. But . . . yes. Do we have a deal or not?"

"Yeah, all right. I accept. We're friends, you and me."

"Good." He held up the blue flowers. "These are for you. A peace offering."

Vita's smile dropped when she saw the flowers in his hand. "Oh gosh, where did you get that? That's leadwort!"

"Is that bad?"

Vita's eyes glowed green, and she wagged a finger at the flowers. "That's not nice. We are not mean to people just because they look a bit different from us. His nose looks just fine to me."

"S-sorry?" Lucas stammered, self-consciously touching his nose. What was wrong with it?

"Oh no, don't touch your face! Sorry, leadwort's poisonous, and they have such bad manners. We'd better hurry or you'll get a nasty rash. Here, dump it so I can heal you." Vita led him to the kitchen where he begrudgingly tossed out the flowers and sat on a stool. Of all the flowers to pick, he chose the poisonous one with bad manners.

Outstanding, you idiot.

Vita stood in front of him and held both of his hands in hers, eyes glowing green. A rush of euphoric warmth shimmered throughout his body, starting at his hands and spreading through his muscles. His previous annoyance at his failure dissipated as he took in the sensation of her healing. He'd never felt something so vibrantly beautiful before. According to history, people had gotten addicted to the high of Earth's healing and would purposely hurt themselves just to experience it. Now Lucas understood why.

It was over all too soon. Vita's eyes faded back to brown as the euphoric high reduced to a soft buzz in his chest.

"Incredible . . . why does it feel like that?" Lucas asked in awe. "It's like . . . wow."

"I feel it too. My momma says it's kind of like my spirit hugging you. To heal, I have to share my life with you. So, for a moment, we're kind of connected."

"Well, you feel good." Lucas sucked in a breath and hastily corrected himself, his face growing hot. "Your healing, I mean. Er, your spirit? Whatever you call it."

Heavens take me now.

Vita smiled warmly. "It was sweet of you, but maybe leave the flower picking to me, okay?"

His hands still rested in hers. All those years of training and fighting had given him rough skin, sturdy and scarred compared to her delicate fingers.

Lucas felt a shy smile spread on his lips. "I hope this isn't an indicator of how the rest of our friendship will play out. I do intend on being a good friend to you. Oh, here. My mother suggested you eat one of these after you heal."

He fished a caramel out of his pocket and handed it to her. She smiled and popped it into her mouth. "Well, look at that, you're doing better already!"

"Wait until you hear my new idea. Everyone will love it."

"You've got to be out of your damn mind," Annie hissed. "I am *not* gonna let you parade me around these cultish freaks. No way in hell."

The elementals were not receptive of Lucas's solution. He heavily relied on Vita's help with this, though she didn't seem very enthused either.

"Why are we doing this?" Adrian asked, watching him with wary eyes.

"To change Elondoh's opinion of you," Lucas explained.

"Like I give a rat's ass what they think about me!" Annie snapped. "You're just trying to embarrass us, make us submit to your precious little ways. I see right through you."

"Now, Annie, I don't think that's fair," Vita defended. "Maybe this could be good. A festival sounds like fun. Plus, it's not like they're asking us to do some impossible thing. Dos and I will play some music, you'll paint something beautiful, and Adrian will . . . do something great, I'm sure."

"Is fun even allowed here?" Adrian asked, looking at Boyd and Hogan. Boyd scowled, and Hogan watched the interaction with wide eyes like a tennis match.

"Festivals are a big part of our culture," Lucas answered. "This one in particular is to celebrate Dr. Guyer's late wife, Clarice. She was an enthusiast of the Middle Ages, so that's the theme of the celebration. You'll have costumes made, there will be tournaments, food, and all varieties of entertainment, including a dance at the end of the night. All I'm asking is for your participation."

Dos brought his eyes to Lucas. "Our performances and artistic talents do not change the prophecy."

"I know. But the point is to prove that you are more than a prophecy made hundreds of years ago. This is how we will show them that you are more like the good generations than you are the bad one. Everyone bonds over art, right?"

Dos grunted and looked away, a downward twitch on his lips.

Vita was the first to speak up. "Are you sure this'll work?"

He wasn't, and according to the guardian code, he wasn't allowed to lie. "I'm hopeful."

Vita exchanged a look with the other elementals. Dos nodded once in approval.

Adrian shrugged. "At this point, as long there's free food, I don't really care."

Annie huffed and glared at Lucas. "Just so we're clear, I think this is a dumb idea, but I don't have a choice, so fine. I'll grace this boring hellhole with my art."

"Well, Lucas Sawyer," Vita said with a half-cocked smile. "Looks like we're trying it your way. Hope it works."

He returned her smile, finding it surprisingly easy to do so. "Yes, me too. Let's go, we have a full schedule for today, and if we hurry, we'll get there five minutes early."

CHAPTER 17

GUARDIAN

"Two, please demonstrate your connection ability," Dr. Wilson instructed.

Dr. Guyer sat at the desk, looking slightly worse than before. Dr. Sawyer sat by his side, not only to watch the elementals but also to monitor Dr. Guyer's health.

"So, is anyone actually going to explain what a connection ability is, or am I supposed to take a wild guess?" Annie asked, lounging in one chair with her feet kicked up in the air. Vita and Adrian sat on either side of her.

"Your abilities offer you a connection to the human side of you as well. For example, Two can use fire, but he can also read and deliver emotions so long as he understands and experiences them first," Dr. Wilson explained, pushing up his glasses.

"His name is Dos," Annie grumbled beneath her breath.

Dos stood in the center of the room and nodded at Dr. Wilson. "Who would you like me to read?"

"Miss Vita is fine."

Vita brightened up in her chair and smiled at Dos.

Dos's eyes glowed red as he visually studied her. "You are experiencing happiness and a form of irritation at the same time. It is a specific form . . . hunger?"

"Oh my gosh, yes! I'm starving. I didn't know hunger was an emotion."

"It isn't, but the shade of irritation can vary based on physical factors. Hunger is a brighter shade."

Dr. Wilson spoke up. "Now distribute an emotion to her."

"Which one?" Dos asked cautiously.

Dr. Wilson scribbled on his clipboard and held it up for only Dos to see.

"Is there not a better option?" Dos asked. "Perhaps peace or—"

"This is the one you will distribute."

Dos proceeded with what might be a ghost of a frown. He never showed much emotion, but there were twitches that came out every now and then. He locked his glowing eyes on Vita. Then something shifted. Her eyebrows pressed inward. Her lips slowly fell, turning into a distraught pout. Her eyes glossed over and turned pink at the rims.

"Oh," Vita muttered, blinking rapidly.

Was she about to . . . ?

Vita sucked in a shaking breath, then tears spilled from her eyes down her cheeks. Her hands flew to her face to try and hide them.

"Hey, what the hell? Stop it!" Annie demanded, jumping to her feet.

"Oh no." Adrian gently patted Vita's back and wore an empathetic frown. "Hey, it's okay. You're fine."

In the corner of his eye, Lucas caught sight of Boyd smiling cruelly, as if he were watching something funny. Lucas shot him a furious look.

"Do not laugh at her," Lucas demanded.

"It's funny," Boyd said dismissively. "Why do you care that I laugh at her?"

"It's cruel. The guardian code demands empathy and kindness to others. I suggest you start practicing that."

"Right, I'm sure the code is what you're concerned about."

Dr. Guyer watched with distant interest, rubbing his chin and observing Vita and Lucas. He wrote something down. Lucas left Boyd alone for now, but he would definitely make a note about this in his report to the Chief.

Dos blinked himself out of his hold, a look of horror cracking the usually blank facade. "Oh!" he blurted, stumbling back. "Vita, I am sorry. It is not normally so strong. I can fix it." His eyes began to glow again, but Vita only cried harder. Dos's eyebrows furrowed. "Angels, I have never seen emotions so strong before. I will deliver you a different emotion."

Annie stood between him and Vita and gave him a harsh shove. "Don't you screw with her again!"

"I—I am not. I can calm her down," Dos stuttered, holding up his hands.

"Like you calmed her down just now? I don't think so."

"Annie, stop," Dr. Sawyer insisted. "Step aside."

Annie looked like she wanted to do anything except that. Dos's chin flexed the slightest bit while he refused to meet Annie's eye. She leaned forward and poked his chest. "You make it worse, and I'll make *you* worse."

Adrian pulled Annie aside and held her back.

Dos focused his eyes on the crying Vita and said in a quiet voice, "It is okay, Vita. You are feeling peaceful now, right?"

Vita's sobs died down, her cheeks red and splotchy. She opened her eyes and blinked away the last of her tears.

"Oh, Dos, I'm so sorry." Vita wiped her cheeks and stood from her seat. "I feel so silly now. I didn't expect it to be so much."

Dos's eyes dropped to the floor. "Excuse me."

Without a further word, he stepped out of the room.

Vita started to follow him, but Dr. Sawyer stopped her. "No, no. Let him be."

"But . . . I overreacted. It's my fault, not his."

"That's actually accurate," Dr. Wilson added, writing notes, completely unaffected by the events in front of him. "The Earth element is known to feel their emotions intensely, which is why I had him work on her so that I could see it in action. I asked Dos to give her a sense of low spirits, but clearly, she amplified it into despair. You all have your vices. Air is disobedient, Fire is violent, Earth is emotional, and Water is passive. I need to observe how this affects you."

"You're a dick," Annie spat.

Now the guardians tensed, all three of them watching Annie's eyes for a reaction. Dr. Guyer smiled slightly and leaned forward with interest.

"How could you turn us against each other like that? You *knew* that was how she'd react, and you still had him do that? What the hell's the matter with you?" Annie demanded.

Vita's face was prickling red. "That's an awful thing to do, Dr. Wilson. You should be ashamed."

Dr. Wilson was apathetic in his response. "This is about science, not feelings. She needs to control her emotions or she could be a hazard. You all do. Let's proceed."

"Proceed?" Annie scoffed. "I'll proceed myself out. Come on, Vita. Adrian, are you coming?"

"Yeah, this is screwed up." Adrian draped an arm over Vita's shoulder and guided her toward the door.

"Go? You can't go anywhere. We're in the middle of—excuse you!"

Annie held up her middle finger at Dr. Wilson and pushed open the door.

"Hold on!" Boyd shouted, stepping forward. "You're not going anywhere."

"Are you going to stop me?" Annie challenged. "I'd like to see you try."

Boyd unholstered his tranquilizer gun and aimed it at her. Vita immediately locked eyes with Lucas, her cheeks still glistening from her tears, as she seemed to silently say, *Now is the time to prove yourself.*

Lucas held up a hand. "Stand down, Boyd. Let them go."

Boyd scoffed and nodded at Annie. "Get back here at once and I won't shoot. That's an order."

"I just gave you an order," Lucas said incredulously. "You're going to disregard it for what?"

"Because it's weak."

Annie fully faced him, her eyes glowing white. "Does it look like I'm scared of you? Go on then. Shoot."

Boyd's finger moved to the trigger, but before Lucas could stop him, the tranquilizer discharged. Lucas ran forward to protect Annie but was thrown back by a gust of wind. He landed on his back in time to see the tranquilizer dart flip around and sink into Boyd's shoulder.

Angels above . . .

It had only taken a mere flick of Annie's hand before Boyd fell unconscious in an ungraceful heap, and the elementals dashed out of the room.

If she could do that with a simple movement, what else were they capable of?

CHAPTER 18

EARTH

Vita was shaking. Not out of cold or fear, but anger. Vicious, harmful anger. This stupid town was filled with too much hatred. She didn't ask for this; none of the elementals asked for this. Least of all Dos. What did he have to endure while growing up here? Vita couldn't imagine a lifetime of this nonsense.

Annie led them back to her place, ranting the whole time about the injustice of this "cultish nightmare."

Vita stopped just before entering the townhome and looked around.

"Vita?" Adrian asked.

"We need to find Dos," Vita insisted.

"Um, did you forget that he was the one who made you cry?" Annie rested a hand on her hip.

"That was just as much against him as it was us," Vita said. "He was only doing what he was told, and it's not fair for us to act ugly because of it. I'm going to find him."

She spotted an apple tree next to the house and approached it. She rested her hand against the bark, her eyes glowing.

"Hello, dear Vita!" Sera greeted happily.

"Hi, Sera. I need to find a friend. Can you help me?"

"Any friend of Vita's is a friend of ours. Let's see . . ."

Vita was shown a vision of what the tree had seen in the past hour. This was a trick she'd learned when Otis was a puppy and kept getting lost. The images were fuzzy and usually in grayscale, but it worked. The vision appeared like a memory in her mind's eye as if she'd lived through what the tree had seen.

Finally, she saw Dos walking toward the orchards with a sullen look on his face.

"Thank you," Vita quickly whispered. "I'll meet y'all in a minute!" she shouted as she raced off to find him.

Vita raced through rows of fruit trees and vegetable patches. She ran until she saw a figure sitting by a man-made pond, then paused to make sure it was Dos. A puff of fire shot out from the figure's hands and sizzled onto the pond's surface.

Gotcha.

She rushed over and plopped down beside him, then threw her arms around him. He was just as stiff and afraid as he was the first time she'd hugged him, but she didn't care.

"It ain't your fault," Vita promised breathlessly. "You're not a bad person."

"Vita . . . stop," Dos warned.

"No. Not until you hug me back and admit it to yourself."

"I cannot."

"Yes, you can. You're a good person, Dos. You're worthy of happiness and joy. Regardless of what anyone says, thinks, or feels."

Dos shook his head.

"Hug me, Dos. It's okay."

His arms tentatively wrapped around her in return. Hugs around here were so timid and stiff, but this was progress, and sometimes progress was messy.

"I am sorry, Vita," Dos whispered thickly. "I did not mean to—"

"No, don't. Don't you dare take responsibility for the things those people do. Dr. Wilson said he knew I feel emotions stronger than the others, and he knew your ability would be stronger on me. That's why he had you do that. You're not the monster."

"But I hurt you. You are kind, and yet I hurt you."

"No, you showed me your abilities."

He scoffed bitterly. "My abilities . . . they are destructive and vile. You and the others have life-giving abilities. You come from honorable lines. I come from an extensive line of violent elementals, and I am just like them. I hurt people and burn things down. I share all the dreadful things I know."

"But you can do good things too. You can give people warmth when they're cold. You can light the way for others when it's dark. You can share good emotions too, like joy. You can spread all of that love and light just as strongly as you can with sadness. It's such a beautiful gift."

"I do not understand those emotions."

Vita's heart broke as righteous anger coursed through her.

"You are angry with me," Dos noted.

"No." Vita hugged him tighter. "Not at you. I'm angry with the cowards who raised you. Elondoh failed you, so Annie, Adrian, and I will teach you the good things in life. We'll show you all the wonderful emotions you should know. You're not alone anymore. You have friends now."

"I do not know how to be a friend."

"That's okay, you'll learn. I'll see to it myself."

"Why?"

"Because that's what friends do. But first, you need to tell yourself that you're not a bad person."

"I . . . I am not a bad person," he whispered.

"Do you believe it?" Vita asked.

"Not yet."

Vita pulled away and smiled. "Yet. But you will. Okay?"

Dos's weighted expression lightened just a bit, as if, for once, he understood what hope felt like. "Okay."

Vita felt a tremor in the ground, and she straightened. Soft warmth and a familiar scent of fur traveled to her. She gasped. "They're here!"

"Who is?"

She didn't need to answer. A blur of black and white fur came hopping over to her.

"Otis!" Vita squealed as her American Staffordshire Terrier tackled her to the ground and covered her face in dog kisses.

"Vita, Vita, Vita!" Otis exclaimed, tail wagging faster than lightning.

Vita pushed herself up, giggles exploding out of her as she scratched Otis behind his ears. "I missed you so much, you good boy!"

"I thought you would never come back, but then Momma gave me a treat and I fell asleep, and here you are!"

"Are Momma and Lula here?" Lula was Vita's black cat and Otis's best friend. Though, Lula would never admit that out loud. Vita had caught them snuggling too many times to believe Lula's claims that she was too good for a mutt like Otis.

"Yeah, they're at our new home. Momma gave me a new ball too! It squeaks!"

"That's wonderful!" Vita exclaimed.

Dos was smiling wide, and his eyes were glowing. Vita caught on to what was happening: he was studying her joy. And he laughed. It was a short, breathy laugh, but it was a laugh, nonetheless. His hand flew to his mouth, eyes widening in surprise. Was that his first laugh?

Vita giggled. "Otis, I have a friend for you to meet. His name is Dos."

"Dos! I like Dos," Otis answered.

"Go say hi."

Otis turned his affection to Dos, who jerked back at the dog's wagging tail and wet nose.

"It's okay, he's friendly. You can pet him," Vita promised.

"How?" Dos asked, flinching at Otis's excited whimpers.

"Like this." Vita demonstrated by scratching Otis, who was happy to partake. It occurred to Vita that Elondohnians may not know what a dog was like. She hadn't seen any domesticated animals since her arrival. This would be a first for Otis, who thought the universe was his friend. But now the Elondohnians would get to know him well because she would be taking him with her everywhere. He made her feel safe.

Dos tentatively reached out his hand and carefully stroked the dog's head. Otis happily responded, tail wagging back and forth.

"Dogs can create happiness." Dos laughed again when Otis licked his cheek.

"Petting them actually produces more serotonin. Some people have dogs that are specially trained to help them. They're called service dogs," Vita explained.

"Those dogs have responsibilities?"

"They do, big ones. And they do it well."

"Do *I* do a good job, Vita?" Otis asked, tongue dangling from his mouth.

"You do the *best* job, Oty," Vita cooed, scratching his back and turning to Dos. "My daddy had him trained as a guard dog by a guy from the Army. He can get really scary if he wants to, but he doesn't fool me. Otis is seventy pounds of pure love."

"Ah, there she is," a voice announced from a few feet away. It was Lucas, walking toward the pond with Vita's mother at his side. They were alone, so Annie and Adrian must have been greeting their own parents.

"Vita!" her mom shouted.

Vita stilled. Her mom hurried up to her, then stopped when she saw Vita's guarded expression. They both watched each other, as if frozen in time, while a million questions silently flurried between them. In that single look, they both knew that a wedge had been formed between them. Vita's parents had lied to her, and as a result, she had been drowned in a whirlwind of life-changing revelations. It felt like she didn't really know who her parents were, and as a result, who *she* was.

After all, her daddy had died without Vita even knowing his real name. What other secrets did he take to his grave, and was her mother intending to do the same thing? Had they ever planned to tell her?

There were so many things Vita wanted to say, but for now, she stood up and ran into her mother's arms for a much-needed hug. At the very least, her mother still felt as strong and loving as she had before.

"I'm so sorry," her mother started in a thick voice, squeezing Vita tightly. "Are you all right?"

Vita pulled away and nodded, casting a quick glance to Lucas, who inched away from Otis's curious sniffing. "I'm okay. We've got a lot to talk about."

"Yes, we do, and we will, I promise." Momma pushed aside Vita's curls and offered her a sad smile. She looked over Vita's shoulders, her eyes widening. "You must be Winifred's boy. You look just like her."

Dos kept his eyes down, almost shrinking into himself. "Yes, ma'am. I am Two."

"Two?" Vita asked. "Is that still what you want us to call you?"

He flicked up his gaze at her and shook his head, a shy smile just barely making an appearance. "No. I am Dos."

Momma smiled and walked up to him, holding out her hand.

"You don't remember this, but there was a time I helped your mom take care of you. I'm Mar—June. I'm June Eastwood."

Confusion creased above his brow as he took her hand and shook it.

Lucas shouted in surprise, jumping back as Otis excitedly tried to lick him. Vita laughed and hurried over to yank Otis off. "We've got to be gentle with these friends, Otis. They ain't used to seeing dogs like you."

"Do you think he likes to play fetch?" Otis asked.

"Probably not."

Lucas brushed dirt from his shirtfront and grimaced at a new stain before looking to the others. "Dr. Guyer has scheduled meetings with you all. Dos, he's requested to see you this afternoon. Mrs. Eastwood, there are workers who will help you move in while Vita finishes her training for the day. But first, Dr. Guyer would like to meet with you and the rest of Generation 22."

Momma scowled at him before turning to Vita and whispering, "Is he treating you properly? If not, just say the word and I'll handle him. These guardians can be brutish. I don't trust them."

Vita rolled her eyes. "Yes, he's fine, and if not, I can handle it myself."

"I want you to be careful around them, especially Dr. Guyer. Don't be alone with him, and definitely do not trust him. Do you understand?"

"Yeah, okay. I'll talk to you after training." Vita had always thought her mother was overprotective.

Momma glared at Lucas as she left Vita's side. Dos joined her and offered to walk her to Dr. Guyer's office. Once Lucas and Vita were alone, Lucas's shoulders relaxed just a bit.

"Your mother really does not like me," he said. "On the way

here, she told me that if she found a single bruise on you, she'd make me pay for it."

"Don't take it personally. She once made the pastor's son cry at church because he cheated on me. I just about died from embarrassment."

Lucas raised his eyebrows. "I didn't realize you had suitors in the outside world."

Vita shrugged one shoulder. "There are a lot of things you don't know, and I ain't telling you. What do we have next? Dr. Wilson's not gonna make us turn on each other like that again, is he?"

"No. We have a new guardian joining us while Boyd is in the infirmary, so we'll do introductions, and you'll start studying the different methods Dr. Guyer has for the stone. Even though we don't have everything in place yet, it will be important to learn the process early."

"Right. The sooner we get this done, the sooner I can go back home and get out of your hair." She reached over and plucked an apple from a tree branch. "I'll need one of these."

Lucas offered her a polite smile and motioned down the path. "After you."

CHAPTER 19

FIRE

D os walked June Eastwood to the conference room of the laboratory, where the other parents sat, including his own mother. Dr. Novak glared impassively at Dos as he walked in.

The other parents greeted June like an old friend, exchanging hugs and apologies when they received the news of Mason Eastwood's death.

"Our crazy little plan almost worked," David Holiday sighed.

"Almost," Tabitha Jackson agreed. "What are we going to do now?"

Robert Jackson flicked a glare at Dr. Novak. "Nothing we can discuss yet."

Dr. Novak evenly met his gaze and did not speak. Curious, Dos waited outside of the room and remained silent. The door was cracked open and the single glass wall allowed him to observe as he had with Generation 23's arrival. He was curious about their parents' generation. Why did they run? What would they do now that they were back?

Dr. Guyer walked into the room, and all the parents froze, glaring at him. According to their shared emotions, they were afraid.

Strange. Dos thought the parents would be angry, but to wear fear instead? Why? Dos had his reasons, but what were theirs?

Dr. Guyer smiled. "Oh, how glad I am to see you are all well."

"Let's not play games, Dr. Guyer," June shot back. "You're only as happy to see us as we are to see you."

Vita must have gotten her gentle temperament from her father, Dos thought in amusement.

Dr. Guyer's smile dropped. He hobbled to the head of the conference table and motioned to the seats. "Let us discuss this as calmly as we can, yes? After all, we have shared interests."

"None of us are interested in being here," David pointed out as the parents sat.

"You are interested in keeping your children alive, are you not? Quite frankly, I'm impressed you were able to avoid a reaction in the outside world, so full of sin that it is. What if Vita were to witness animal abuse? Or if someone were to disturb Adrian's peace? Or if Annie's freedom were to be taken? What would you have done?"

The parents didn't say anything. Rather, they all exchanged uncomfortable looks. Dos realized this really had been a worry for them.

Dr. Guyer spoke directly to June. "I am deeply sorry for the loss of your husband. It must have been quite difficult."

"I'm not here to discuss Mason," June said calmly. "Let the kids go. We all know what you'll really do with them."

"They are of no use to me dead, June. I understand you all had some . . . predetermined misconceptions about my intentions with Generation 23, but I can assure you, I wish only for the stone. You had no reason to run back then, and you have no reason to run now."

"You held that damn prophecy like a weapon against us," Robert barked. "You promised the entire Elondohnian community you would protect them against the 'children of darkness,' as you called them. But they were our *children*. At the time, they couldn't even hold their heads up on their own."

"Not to mention," June added, "Your wild accusations that *we* were the reason Clarice passed when she'd been battling her illness for years."

"You left us with no choice," Tabitha said in a soft-spoken voice. "We could either run from you or willingly give up our children. What else did you expect a parent to do?"

"Winifred stayed, and her son still lives," Dr. Guyer pointed out.

Being alive does not equate to living, Dos thought bitterly.

"Winifred is a shell of who she used to be," David argued.

If Dr. Novak was offended, she didn't show it. Who had she been before? Dos couldn't imagine her any other way than she was now.

Dr. Guyer sighed heavily and sank back in to his chair. "Yes, I will admit I have said a few things I shouldn't have. I was lost in the grief of losing my dear Clarice. I regret the pain I have caused you, but I can assure you that I do not wish harm upon your children. Once the stone is created, they may leave. You will never need to return to Elondoh again. But now I will be frank with all of you: none of you can leave until that stone is created. You are too great a risk. I am not a fool. I know you could run to media outlets, local governing officials, law enforcement. That is a lot of damage you do not wish to inflict upon yourselves, so I will make every effort for you to live comfortably in Elondoh."

The parents weren't as shocked as their children had been when they'd received the same treatment. They seemed to be familiar with the customs.

June scoffed. "Do you expect us to forgive you after all these years? How do we know you won't turn against our children the next time you miss your wife again?"

Dr. Guyer's eyes darkened. "How do I know you won't train your children to harm me or my people? I suppose we are all relying on faith. I will have guardians escort you to your old townhomes on Elemental Avenue. Your children have already moved in. Don't worry, their guardians will keep them safe. I'm sure you all remember Chief Jack Sawyer. His son is an excellent guardian."

June remained silent. She was worried. They all were. The guardians escorted them out and left Dos alone with Dr. Novak. Dr. Guyer left for his lab, coughing into a handkerchief.

Dr. Novak stood and walked out the door, pausing in front of Dos. "Your frivolous absence from training today was unacceptable. You will meet Dr. Guyer in his lab for due punishment."

"Yes, Doctor," he muttered. She walked away, and Dos forced himself to report to Dr. Guyer's lab.

Show no emotion. Do not grant them the satisfaction of your fear.

He chanted this in his head, like he had since he was a child.

Dr. Guyer was alone in his lab, wearing gloves and safety goggles, as he watched a black chemical burn over a small flame. Dos recognized this procedure. Dr. Guyer was creating an elixir for his ailment. Modern medicines didn't work for him, but these strange concoctions seemed to stave off the disease enough to buy him more time. The flames needed to be hotter to burn the impurities away from the minerals he used.

Dos rolled his shoulders back and took a deep breath. There was nothing they could do to him that he had not already endured by their hands. The pain, the fear, and the anger were all gifts from them. He could endure anything they gave him so long as he remembered one thing.

Show. No. Emotion.

Dos knocked twice on the frame of the open door and cast his eyes low. "You called for me, sir?"

"Ah, yes! Come in, son." Dr. Guyer waved him in.

Dos looked up for a mere second, wondering if Dr. Guyer realized that he was speaking to Dos and not one of the other guardians. He had never called Dos "son" before.

Nonetheless, Dos stepped in and waited, his hands clasped behind his back.

"You know, I think 'Dos' is a wonderful name for you," Dr. Guyer started with a smile. "I'm envious that I hadn't thought of it first."

Dos said nothing. This was a test, it must be. Guyer wanted to gauge Dos's loyalty to Elondoh. To ensure their years of arduous work had not dissipated because of the other elementals.

"I know Dr. Wilson was a bit brash. I understand your disdain for him," Guyer continued, sprinkling a powdery substance into the beaker. "Truthfully, I agree that he can lack bedside manners. But what he lacks in decorum he makes up for with intelligence. We must show some grace his way. I sincerely apologize to you on his behalf."

No one had ever apologized to Dos before. Why was Guyer doing so now? What did he want from Dos that he could not take by force?

Dr. Guyer limped his way over to Dos, resting a frail hand on his shoulder. His hunched stature made him shorter than Dos, but if he stood at his full height, they'd be eye to eye.

"Dos, you've served our purpose your whole life with a splendid sense of loyalty. I couldn't be any prouder of you. But now, I wish to make it up to you. I would like you to get close to the other elementals, to learn what it's like to make friends and build relationships. I would like you to be happy."

"Why, sir?" Dos dared to ask.

Dr. Guyer patted his shoulder. "Because you deserve it. Don't you agree?"

He would have given anything to discreetly sense Dr. Guyer's emotions. If only his eyes were not a beacon to his abilities.

"After all, the other elementals can teach you emotions that we cannot. It is time we expanded your emotional range. You need to be at full capacity to develop the stone," Dr. Guyer added.

Ah, there it was. This was not about Dos's welfare. This was about the stone. It was *always* about that damn stone.

Dr. Guyer limped back to his chair in front of the beaker and sighed. "Could you help me with this, son? I can't get the burner to heat. Fickle thing."

Dos nodded, his eyes glowing. The flames burned blue as they heated up. The chemical now boiled into a clear yellow substance.

Dos lowered his eyes, catching a glimpse of that mysterious symbol that was drawn in one of Guyer's notebooks.

Dr. Guyer caught Dos's eyes before Dos could tear them away. He smiled. "You know, there are some things I wish I could tell you. Some things that I have sworn my secrecy over. These things must remain hidden. But just because we cannot speak of them does not mean we cannot *seek* them." His eyes glanced fondly at the baby grand piano at the side of the lab and then back at Dos.

Dos's brows flicked inward for just a second before he could prevent his confusion from showing. He simply nodded once more and stepped out of the office.

Did Guyer just tell me to seek the symbol? Why?

————————————

Dos was walking into the training room when Annie approached him. The other elementals were waiting for their new guardian to join now that Boyd had been disposed. Dos was glad about that.

Boyd was always the most annoying of the three guardians. Even Hogan, who carried less grace than a pigeon, was more bearable than Boyd.

"Hey." Annie nodded at Dos. "Can we talk?"

"Are we not talking now?"

Annie motioned him to follow her out into the hall where they would be alone. Dos followed, not allowing himself to sense her emotions yet. He liked the mystery she wore.

Annie leaned against the wall and crossed her arms. "So, listen. I was thinking about the whole emotion-slash-Vita thing, and . . ." She sighed and looked him in the eyes. "I'm sorry I was a dick to you about it. I don't know how you grew up or what you were taught, but you were only doing what you were told. We're friends now, and I should've given you the benefit of the doubt."

Dos's eyebrows raised. "You are apologizing to me?"

Annie shrugged. "Yeah."

Two apologies in one day. Were the angels suddenly taking pity on him?

"Um, thank you," Dos muttered shyly. He lacked practice accepting apologies and was unsure of the appropriate response.

"I think it's cool that you can do all that stuff with emotions. I never even knew we had . . . whatever it's called."

"A connection ability. Has yours not unlocked yet?"

"No. But at least Adrian's hasn't either, so I'm not alone."

"You are not alone," Dos repeated firmly. "Vita has declared we are friends now, and therefore, none of us are alone."

Annie smirked. "Right. It'd be cool to do something like you and Vita, though. Healing and emotions . . . that's awesome. I don't even know what mine would be, if I receive one at all."

"You will."

Annie's eyebrows creased together as if she were confused. "Are you actually encouraging me?"

"Oh, I am not encouraging you. It is a scientific fact. Dr. John Dee predicted it, so that means it will come true. Sometimes it takes certain stimuli to unlock it and the ability itself can differ for each generation that has it, but it will come when the angels feel you are ready for it."

"Angels, huh?" Annie chuckled. "Yeah, I don't know about all that."

"Do you know of our heritage? About how or why we were created?"

"I know Guyer mentioned a few things, but I don't know anything in depth. I always figured we just . . . soaked up radiation or something."

Dos allowed himself a small smile. "Allow me to tell you about the history of the elementals. At one point, even the greatest kings bowed to us."

CHAPTER 20

GUARDIAN

Guardian Ethan James had been more of a friend to Lucas than the other guardians while they were in school. He was the closest ranking to Lucas and practically oozed chivalry. If there was a poster child for the guardian code, it would be Ethan James.

After, of course, Lucas.

He came from a prominent family too. His father worked as a liaison between the guardians and the Navy in the outside world. Having an individual liaison for each military branch helped that specific person become an expert in their given tactics and finding the best ways that the guardians could assist. It was a good job to have. They answered directly to Chief and often doubled as advisers. No doubt, Ethan James would follow in his father's footsteps. The only group that Chief directly handled without a liaison was the CIA. They tended to be picky with their communications.

The only reason Ethan hadn't been on the elemental team initially was because the Boyd family was close with Dr. Guyer. Favor pulled a lot of weight in Elondoh.

Ethan was half a foot taller than Lucas, with light-brown hair and blue eyes. Rumor had it that he'd been quite successful in receiving introductions but hadn't acted on any of them yet.

"Guardian Sawyer!" Ethan said with a friendly smile as he walked into the training room. His eyes swept the room and widened when they landed on Vita, visually sweeping from her shoes up to her face.

"Welcome, Guardian James," Lucas said, pulling Ethan's attention back to him. "I'm glad you could join us on such short notice. I'll introduce you to the elementals, and then they need to get back to training."

Lucas introduced each elemental. Ethan shook Annie and Adrian's hands until he got to Vita. For her, he offered her a charming smile and planted a kiss on the back of her hand.

"Ethan James, ma'am," he said in a smooth, almost rehearsed voice. "House of the Black Bear. It's a pleasure to meet you."

Vita blushed brilliantly and returned the smile. "Well, aren't you the sweetest."

Hogan shot an impressed look at Lucas and whispered, "Angels, *I* almost swooned."

Lucas didn't realize he was frowning until he noticed Dos watching him with glowing red irises. He cleared his throat. "They have work to do. Guardian James, you'll take up the rear exit."

Ethan nodded and took up Boyd's former spot, while Hogan took the west side of the room and Lucas stood at the front door. Dr. Guyer and Dr. Wilson were busy preparing a station at the front of the room with various tools laid out on a table.

Vita placed an apple in front of Dr. Wilson. "I forgive you for being rude with my emotions earlier."

Dr. Wilson blinked at it, then creased his brows at her.

"You know what's worse than finding a worm in your apple?" Vita asked. "Finding half a worm."

Lucas snorted, failing at holding his chuckle in. Then he blushed when Vita raised an amused eyebrow at him. "That was clever," he said.

Vita grinned. "Y'all don't have dad jokes around here? If you liked that one, wait until you hear the one about the fish wearing a bow tie. He's real so-*fish*-ticated."

Lucas bit back his grin and looked away from her. The outside world had clever humor, but it wouldn't look good for a future chief to giggle during training.

Hogan leaned toward Adrian and whispered, "Are there a lot of fish in the outside world that wear bow ties?"

"Yes. Yes, there are," Adrian said confidently, clapping Hogan's shoulder.

Annie rolled her eyes.

"Let's get back to work," Dr. Wilson announced, moving the apple out of his way.

A porcelain crucible sat above a small stack of wood. Dr. Wilson placed a yellow crystal and a chunk of copper in the bowl, then poured a pitcher of water into it. Once done, he slid on a pair of protective glasses, picked up a clipboard, and turned to the elementals.

"Are we ready?"

"Ready for what?" Annie asked. "You still haven't told us what we're supposed to be doing."

"We want to test different methods to create the stone. We can't really create the tincture itself, as two of the four elementals still do not have their connection abilities, but we can perfect the method until then." Dr. Wilson tapped his pen on the crucible. "According to Mary the Jewess's methods, creating the stone is the same process as turning a lesser metal into a more precious one, such as gold or silver. Otherwise known as transmutation. You will use your elements to purify this copper and sulfur into gold. We'll start with fire."

"He literally didn't answer my question," Annie muttered.

Dos stepped forward. "I will slowly heat the water to a soft boil.

Adrian will collect the steam and process it back into the bath so that it does not run dry. Annie will assist me with the flames by using her air to shape it in one direct spot. And Vita will fuse the copper and sulfur, as they are natural earth elements."

He raised his hand toward the stack of wood and flicked his index finger at it. A spark danced on the stack of wood before erupting into a small flame. "Adrian, I cannot see the water like you can. You must tell me if the heat is too strong. This process must be slow for it to work."

Adrian nodded, his eyes glowing blue. "Could be a little hotter."

Dos's flames turned blue with the added intensity. "Annie, be sure to maintain the focus of the flames."

"Got it." Annie's eyes glowed white, moving her hands in a cupping motion like a potter would when shaping a bowl. The flames whooshed up and encased the bottom of the bowl. She sniffed the air and scrunched her nose at the scent of rotting eggs. "Damn, it stinks."

"Yes, that is the sulfur," explained Dos, who seemed unbothered by the scent. "Vita, the materials will begin to melt soon. You must ensure they mold together evenly."

Vita's glowing green eyes focused on the crucible. "Wow. I can actually see the materials moving around each other. I didn't know I could move minerals like this."

"If it comes from the earth, then it is yours to manipulate," Dos said. "Adrian, the water?"

"If you want it to boil, you need more heat. Or maybe sprinkle some salt in there. You know, like how they do with pasta?"

Dr. Wilson looked positively repulsed by the mere suggestion and physically recoiled behind his clipboard. "We certainly will *not* be doing that!"

"I'm just joking." Adrian focused his blue eyes. "We're boiling now."

"The materials are melting," Vita said. "I'm kind of sewing them together."

Hogan sniffed the air and grimaced. "It smells awful."

"Should we have done this outside?" Ethan asked, covering his nose.

"Silence, it is working!" Dr. Wilson shouted, peeking into the crucible and grinning with excitement. "The material is turning red. We are entering the *rubedo* stage! This is the final stage of the process. Shouldn't be much longer until it is complete."

A wave of nausea passed through Lucas, as if slamming him into a brick wall. He grunted and stumbled back into the wall for support. Dizziness blurred his vision. His stomach twisted in knots, as if his insides were trying to run off without him. He'd never felt so sick before.

Dr. Guyer suddenly straightened up, his eyes lasering in on Lucas. "Are you all right, Guardian Sawyer? Do you feel something odd?"

"Just nauseous and dizzy. Perhaps the smell is getting to me."

"Oh!" Dr. Wilson exclaimed. "They've done it! We have gold."

He used a pair of tongs to carefully pick up the crucible, then poured out the glittering gold substance into some sort of circular mold. Dos stopped his flames, allowing Adrian to relinquish control of the water and Vita to take her focus from the materials. Annie reached out and pulled at the air around her, as if catching fireflies, and bundled the sulfuric smell into a yellowish ball of air. Hogan escorted her outside to release it. As soon as the smell was gone, Lucas's sickness went away.

Vita hurried over to him and rested a hand on his shoulder, her eyes glowing again. "I know you said you feel sick, but I don't see anything wrong with you. If you were about to throw up, I'd at least see some clouds by your stomach."

He was a little embarrassed by his reaction. "It's gone. Stopped once Annie took the smell away."

Dr. Guyer was scribbling furiously in his notepad and smiling as if he'd just solved a puzzle. "This is wonderful! We will practice this more often. I need more data. You are all dismissed for now. I want you all well-rested and ready to begin again early in the morning."

Vita patted Lucas's shoulder and offered him a conspiratorial smile. She whispered low enough that only he could hear. "If you pretended to be sick to end training early, then you're officially awesome."

He was going to say that he really had felt sick, but he stopped himself. He was once again distracted by her smile and the warmth of her hand resting on his shoulder. He smiled back. "Thank you."

CHAPTER 21

GUARDIAN

I t had been about two weeks since the arrival of the elementals. In that time span, they'd practiced their transmutation at least four times, and every time, Lucas had felt sick. It didn't matter what he tried. Holding his breath, taking medicine, chewing on mint—none of it worked.

But it wasn't all bad. The elementals were acclimating well to Elondoh, and Lucas and Vita had mostly gotten along nicely. He had to admit that she was . . . fun to be around. Perhaps his mother was right when she predicted they'd be friends.

This morning, Lucas hurried down the stairs and found Dr. Guyer sitting at the kitchen table with a bright smile on his face. Mom served him and Chief coffee, and smiled at Lucas.

"Good morning," his mother greeted. "Coffee?"

"No, thank you. I'm already running a little late," Lucas answered, stepping into his boots. "Good morning, Dr. Guyer."

It wasn't unusual for Dr. Guyer to visit the Sawyer home. He frequently met with Chief or sometimes just liked to check in on Lucas.

"Ah, just the man I came to see!" Dr. Guyer greeted happily in a croaking voice. "Come sit. I'm sure Vita won't mind you being a few minutes late."

Lucas obeyed and sat across from Dr. Guyer and next to Chief.

"Tell me, son." Dr. Guyer patted his hand. "How is it being around the elementals?"

"All right, I suppose." Lucas shrugged. "They're actually not as intimidating as I thought they'd be. Well, Annie is, but I think that's just her personality. She's nice when she wants to be."

"Hmm." Dr. Guyer rubbed his chin. "And you haven't noticed anything out of the ordinary with them?"

"No, sir. Should I?"

Dr. Guyer tilted his head slightly and observed Lucas. "Nothing to be concerned with for now. If you notice anything strange, report it to me right away. Yes? We want to make sure everything is going according to plan."

"Yes, sir." Lucas glanced at his mother. She smiled and refilled Chief's coffee.

"You are aware of the dangers of the elementals, I'm sure," Dr. Guyer continued in a serious tone. "Their minds are not like ours. Yes, biologically, they are humans like us, but their spirit is that of the angels. If their elements are threatened, their angelic side will take over to destroy the threat and anything near it in the most unholy ways. Even though their human side knows us, they won't recognize us."

Mom's smile faded and was replaced with a scowl.

Lucas nodded. "So we're taught in training."

"Yes, but I'm afraid your training may not have been severe enough." Dr. Guyer leaned forward with a fervent gleam in his eyes. "It isn't just their uncontrolled power that is a threat to us. It's their comfort in violence. There are key principles that are sacred to them. If threatened, they *will* kill for it. For example, let's discuss your own charge, the Earth elemental. Do you know what is sacred to her?"

"Well . . . the earth, right?"

"Think deeper, son. *Why* is the earth sacred to Vita?"

Lucas thought back to his conversation with Vita about the

trees healing her. There was a moment when she seemed nearly detached, as if someone had deeply hurt her.

Humans like claiming power over things that can't fight back.

"Because it is innocent," he answered. "Those who cannot fight back, their lives are sacred to her. She bears the responsibility as their protector."

"Exactly," Dr. Guyer confirmed. "She is the *defender* of innocence. Such as Air defends freedom, Water defends peace, and Fire defends virtue. It's in their DNA, and they cannot help it. We kill animals to eat, we cut trees to provide shelter, and we fight monstrous beasts to survive and assert dominance. But Vita doesn't understand that the way we do. She sees death and destruction where we see survival and adaptation. For example, if the Earth elemental were to see the construction workers cutting down trees, do you think she'd see innocent men earning a paycheck for their families?"

Lucas's stomach turned cold as he shook his head.

Dr. Guyer nodded. "She will see a threat, and therefore, her angelic mind will take over her body in an effort to save them— even at the cost of human life. She will viciously kill any man in her path to do it, even you. *This* is why you must be vigilant around the elementals. Yes, they do appear human and even act that way, but deep down inside, they can be . . . vicious. You, Lucas, must react properly if something goes awry."

"I think that's enough," Mom said firmly.

"You speak of the angels as if they are cruel," Lucas pointed out in a small voice.

"They are beings far beyond our understanding," Dr. Guyer continued. "Their creations are no different. No matter how beautiful they look, you must never forget that the elementals have slaughtered men before and can do it again." Dr. Guyer tapped his chest and flashed Lucas a grave, knowing look. "They are unforgiving creatures. I know the truth about them. I know it quite personally."

"I said that's enough!" Mom snapped, slamming the coffee pot on the counter. "Lucas, you're late. Go."

"Natalie," Chief warned, though his face was just as pale as hers was red. Lucas couldn't believe his mother would snap at Dr. Guyer like that. It wasn't like her at all.

"Oh, that's all right." Dr. Guyer smiled now and patted Lucas's hand. "Forgive me, I'm just an old man of science letting magic plague his mind. I will see you soon, son."

"Yes, sir." Lucas stood. He glanced at his parents one more time, but they refused to meet his eyes.

As he left the kitchen, he heard his mother hiss, "You promised you wouldn't meddle."

"Sacrifices must be made," Dr. Guyer answered gently as Lucas closed the door behind him.

Lucas went off to collect Vita, trying not to focus on that conversation with Dr. Guyer. Perhaps the elementals in the past were violent, but this generation couldn't be. They were too free to be that way. After all, Vita could turn anyone into her friend. Dr. Guyer said it didn't matter if they were beautiful, but no one could look like Vita and be as cruel as he described.

Not that Lucas cared much about her beauty. It was just a passing thought. But even as he walked to her home, he found himself looking forward to seeing her.

He knocked on her front door and she opened it, stepping out in a similar outfit that she'd worn when they first met, except this dress was in a shade of cream and her curls were braided with purple flowers. Now that the elementals' parents had returned and brought their things, they were wearing their clothing from the outside world. It was a stark difference to the plain gray uniforms the Elondohnians wore.

"That's a nice dress," Lucas said.

She smiled. "Thanks. I'll let you borrow it sometime if you want."

"A kind offer but one I'll have to refuse."

Otis joined Vita's side, along with a lanky black cat that cocked her head at Lucas. Vita had introduced Lucas to both of her pets a few days ago, and he quickly determined that Lula was his favorite. No offense to Otis, but the purring cat that slipped around noiselessly fit Lucas's personality best.

Lula rubbed herself around Lucas's ankles and sauntered out the front door. She mostly hunted mice all day in the orchards but occasionally would track down Vita during training, particularly during lunch time. Vita picked up her bag from the counter and followed Lucas out on their path.

Small yellow butterflies flitted around Vita. A few landed on the flowers in her hair before taking off again. A ladybug landed on Vita's index finger, and she whispered something close to it, then lightly blew so the ladybug flew away.

She opened her bag and pulled out two blueberry muffins, handing one to Lucas as she did every morning. The elementals had requested to enjoy breakfast and dinner with their parents, so the only time they ate at the dining hall was for lunch. Vita packed her own lunch since the dining hall didn't offer much in terms of vegetarian options. "There's only so much lettuce a girl can eat," Vita had claimed.

Lucas gratefully accepted the muffin. "Thank you. I didn't know you could speak to insects."

"Oh, I can't. They don't understand our language. But if a ladybug lands on you, they'll grant you a wish. You just gotta whisper to it and help it fly again," Vita explained as if it were the most obvious thing in the world.

"What grants them the ability to do so?"

"How would I know? I don't go around asking that stuff. It's rude."

"Oh. Well, what did you wish for?"

"That I'd get to meet a new friend soon, preferably a new plant. I think that ladybug was lucky too; it had four white spots. Four's my new lucky number."

She believes in the strangest things.

Lucas again wondered how anyone could believe her to be a weapon or dangerous at all. Simply being in her presence had a calming effect on him. He took a bite of the muffin and a blueberry burst onto his tongue, surprising him with how deliciously sweet the fruit was.

"I didn't think baked goods would come with our friendship. I'm glad, because these are wonderful," he said, going in for a second bite.

"We should probably add muffins to our contract, huh? Don't worry, I'll have my people call your people." She playfully winked at him and tossed Otis the last bite of her muffin without noticing the warm blush that spread on Lucas's face.

She was awfully pretty.

No. Do not go down that path, Guardian Sawyer. Don't even entertain the thought.

He tore his eyes away from her and focused on his muffin.

CHAPTER 22

AIR

D r. Wilson pushed up his glasses and avoided meeting Annie's eyes. She glared at him, ready to challenge him if the opportunity came up. She hoped that it would.

The elementals had all gathered outside by the pond for training today. They weren't going to try to create the philosopher's stone again until the afternoon because Dr. Guyer wanted to meet with each elemental individually today. Adrian was just called in to meet with him first, Annie would be next, and then Vita.

Dr. Wilson stood in the center of a white spray-painted circle in the grass, big enough to comfortably fit about ten people in it. The elementals sat on a bench outside of the circle with their guardians standing guard behind them.

"Good morning, everyone. It is our theory that in order to create the stone, we must fully develop your abilities. You must be able to activate your connection ability, use your element for combat, and have full use of your main ability or else this project may not work. The purpose is for you to have the same skill level that the original knights did when King Carmara created the elementals. The closer you are to the unity with your angelic side, the easier the process will be to create the stone."

Vita shifted uncomfortably. "Combat? I don't think I can do that. I can't ask the earth to be violent for me, and I don't want to hurt anyone."

"We won't ask you to physically go into danger, of course.

Combat was the original purpose of your elements and requires a different level of skill. We'll train you in a safe and humane way."

Annie was excited that she'd finally get to do something better than make things float. It was about time things livened up around here.

"I'll have Dos demonstrate it first. Then we'll pair you up for sparring. Your goal will be to knock the other out of the circle." Dr. Wilson motioned for Dos to step into the center.

Dos stepped up and removed his jacket, his muscles peeking from his T-shirt sleeves. This was so unfair. Weren't super-hot guys supposed to know they were hot? Guys with muscles were loud, constantly bragging, and drawing attention to themselves. Why did Dos strut around like he was just another guy?

He stood in the middle, took a deep breath, and closed his eyes.

"The key," he said, breathing out with his palms together, "is allowing your element to move your body for you. Its purpose is to protect you, and it will show you what to do. Listen to it."

His eyes opened, a brilliant ruby red taking over his black irises. Then he moved his arms apart, and a string of fire connected his palms. The fire grew so powerful that the heat took Annie's breath away. A protective barrier built around Dos, bending and twisting with his every move.

Everyone took a step back, gasps of surprise leaving their mouths. Except for Annie, who'd never felt such a surge of powerful awe. She stayed rooted in her spot, her eyes locked with Dos, who for once didn't dare to look away.

His hands moved side to side in slow movements, like water. The band of fire swished outward toward Annie. It surrounded her like it did with Dos, trapping her in a barrier of flame. The heat kissed her back, heart racing as she took a daring step forward. The circle of fire enclosed her ever so slightly, still careful not to touch her.

Was she an idiot for wanting to touch the flames? To reach out her hand and grab it for herself, hold it close, and dare it to burn her?

Yes, she definitely was an idiot, but that didn't change a damn thing.

Dos's eyebrows creased and sweat droplets slid down his temple as he moved the band of fire with care, as if testing his limits with Annie but without allowing his control to slip.

Annie had no such qualms about that. She almost wanted to see what would happen if he did slip just a bit. The adrenaline coursed through her veins, pushing her one step farther with a breathless smile that put her hunger in full display.

Annie prowled, step by step, closer to him, like a hunter stalking its prey. The flames swayed around her, as if inviting her to an intimate dance. Dos's eyes followed her, head tilting as he watched her irises glow a pure white.

With a shiver, she could feel the air telling her bones what to do, how to move. As if she were born with this instinct in her. Wearing a half-cocked grin, she tilted her head and pressed her palms together. "Like this, Dos?"

In a wide-arching push, Annie pressed cold air outward from her, forcing the circle of flames to dissipate.

In the moments that Dos used to recover, she brought up her hands and pushed toward him. The force of her wind shoved him backward, causing him stumble to the edge of the spray-painted boundary.

His eyes flashed with the acceptance of a challenge, body moving with the grace only defined by years of training. His band of fire tightened to a rope, lashing out at her feet.

She ran a couple of steps toward him, deftly jumping up and using the air to push herself upward for a second. As she landed, her hands sliced sideways, ripping the flames apart to create a pathway. Dos was right; her body moved of its own accord, and she was in for the joyride of her life.

Dos's eyes widened, watching Annie race toward him with that hungry smile.

Be still her beating heart, he smiled back and kicked it up a notch.

Dos made quick flicks of his hands, and sparks the size of golf balls bounced by Annie's feet. She leaped and skirted around, still moving forward. Something about his half smile and head tilt spread goosebumps down her back, but she kept moving, demanding herself to focus.

Cute boys were *not* enough to distract her.

Right?

With a push, a gust of wind knocked him back a couple of steps. His recovery was quick enough that Annie barely had time to plan for it. He was strong—that push was supposed to knock him down. Instead, he leaped forward, a small arc of fire flourishing toward her.

Annie swiftly dropped to her knees and watched the bottom of the flames glide mere inches from her body. By the time she jumped to her feet, Dos was close and reaching toward her.

Annie tried ducking out of his way, but he was nimble enough to close the distance between them. Dos wrapped his fingers around her wrist, then with a firm but gentle flick, he whipped Annie around and pushed her forward. He managed to push her just slightly out of the circle while keeping himself inside, her wrist pinned behind her back. He was careful enough to never hurt her, but she had a feeling that he could do some serious damage if he wanted to.

"Fine," she huffed. "You win this round, hothead."

His breath tickled her ear as he spoke. "You were close. But I have had years of training, and you are still new at this. You need time, and maybe one day you will beat me. Maybe."

"You held back on me, didn't you?"

"Yes. Playing with fire is dangerous." He released her wrist, his eyes still red as he studied her. An amused smile cracked that serious mask he usually wore. Still, he looked away.

Annie tossed a lopsided smile at him. "Don't hold back next time. I want to see what you can *really* do."

His eyes followed her as she walked back to join the crowd of shocked spectators. The skin on her wrists still tingled with heat when she flipped her hair over her shoulders and did a damn good job of looking bored.

God, he's so hot.

CHAPTER 23

WATER

Adrian waited nervously as Guardian Ethan James knocked on the door to Dr. Guyer's office and opened it once given permission. Adrian walked in first and took in his new surroundings. Dr. Guyer was seated at a table, setting up a small station with beakers and tools.

The room was cluttered with books and yellowing papers. One large table sat at the center, adorned with tools and jars of weird ingredients.

Was that a snake head in one of those jars?

To the left was a wall of floor-to-ceiling shelves stocked with vials of more unknown substances. Several cabinets lined the other walls, leaving hardly any wall space except for the single window that had a potted plant sitting on the sill. To the right was a white baby grand piano that remained the only surface completely clean and clear, save for the photo of a woman with long blonde hair and a peaceful smile.

"Ah, welcome in," Dr. Guyer greeted with a raspy voice. "I am glad you came to see me. I wanted to meet with you as soon as possible, but sometimes that does not happen with our busy schedules. Come, Adrian. Sit with me."

Adrian did so, sitting across the table from Dr. Guyer with his back facing the door.

"Have you ever studied alchemy before?" Guyer asked.

"No, sir. Isn't that like chemistry?"

"Very good. It is the predecessor. According to your transcripts, you weren't fond of chemistry in school, were you?"

Adrian smiled meekly. "No, sir."

Guyer chuckled. "I do not blame you. I admit, I was not the best at it either. It took great studying to understand what I do now. You were studying exercise science in school, correct?"

"Yes, sir. Apparently, football isn't a real major, so I had to pick something. My girlfriend is really good at science and math, so I figured she would help me with it."

"Smart man! I am only where I am because of my dear Clarice. She was the most intelligent woman I've ever met."

"I always say the same about Naomi. She can solve anything you put in front of her. I bet she'd know all about this alchemy stuff."

"Perhaps she will make a positive addition to our mission. I met my Clarice through my studies as well. She was my mentor's daughter and the first girl to offer me her introduction. The only one I cared about too. We were married thirty wonderful years before cancer took her."

"I'm sorry to hear that. Must've been hard to lose her."

Dr. Guyer offered him a small smile and patted his hand. "It was and still is. But as always, she is still teaching me. I have learned to serve my people selflessly, and I have an example of grace through fire because of my dear Clarice. When I see her again, I hope to hear that she is proud. Now tell me again, what is your sweetheart's name?"

"Naomi Brooks. She's studying biology, wants to work on diseases and stuff. Probably wondering where my ass disappeared to. Oh . . . sorry, excuse my language, sir."

Guyer placed an empty beaker in the holder over a burner and smiled at Adrian. "A beautiful name. I admit, being unable to hear my Clarice's voice has been . . . heartbreaking to say the least."

Adrian picked up on the possible opening. "I understand. It really sucks to be away from Naomi. I hate to think she's worried about me and distracted from her studies. If I could only call her and let her know—"

"Unfortunately, we cannot risk it. If you tell her the wrong thing, if she asks the wrong questions—"

"But—"

"The answer is no." Dr. Guyer lightly patted Adrian's shoulder like he was consoling a child who didn't get what they wanted for Christmas. "I am sorry, Adrian. But the sooner you help me create the stone, the sooner you will go back home to her. View this as motivation. After all, they say distance makes the heart fonder. Your return home will be a joyous one, I'm sure."

Adrian deflated. He could imagine his girlfriend at home with books scattered across her bed, wearing his old sweatshirt with a forgotten pencil tucked behind her ear. The image made his heart ache. All he wanted was to go home to her. But he'd settle for just one chance to tell her he was okay.

Instead, he nodded. "I'll do my best to get you that stone."

Adrian followed Guardian James outside. Vita and Guardians Sawyer and Hogan were all standing aside, watching Annie and Dos finish their elemental sparring, a puff of smoke drifting between them. Annie grinned to herself, despite obviously losing, and walked over to join Vita on the bench.

God, he's so hot.

The voice echoed in Adrian's head, nearly blaring in his eardrums.

Adrian flinched and pressed a hand over his ear, scowling at Annie as he approached her. "Damn, lower your voice."

"Huh?" Annie said. "I didn't say anything."

"I heard you. I'm sure heaven and hell heard you too."

"You've lost your damn mind, Water Boy."

"Adrian, I was looking at her and she didn't say anything," Vita offered, petting the sleepy Otis.

"Look, I clearly heard you." Adrian pointed at Annie. "You said 'God, he's so—' "

"Shut up!" Annie snapped, eyes widening. "How did you hear that?"

"Who were you even talking—" Adrian then looked at the curious Dos and noticed the way Annie kept nervously glancing at him. It clicked. Adrian tilted his head back and laughed. "Oh, you're *kidding*."

"Say anything and I'll rip off your jewels and feed it to the dog," Annie hissed, taking a threatening step forward.

Otis raised his head, tail wagging. Vita gasped and covered his ears, casting a dirty look at Annie. "No, Oty, it's *not* a treat."

"It is according to my girlfriend!" Adrian boasted proudly, holding up his hand to Guardian Sawyer for a high five. "Ain't that right, big dog?"

"Um." Guardian Sawyer gave Adrian a confused grimace.

"Just high-five me and say yes."

"My goodness, why haven't I thought of that before?" Dr. Wilson muttered to himself, flipping through his papers.

And somehow, without moving his lips, Dr. Wilson continued speaking. *Adrian's great-great grandfather was said to know the thoughts of those around him. I'm a genius.*

"Humble, aren't you?" Adrian teased.

Dr. Wilson nearly shrieked. "Eureka! Adrian, we found your connection ability. You can read minds."

"I can?"

"He can?" Annie repeated in horror.

"We need to find a way to control it," Dr. Wilson said, picking up his clipboard. "Is this the first time it's happened?"

Adrian thought for a second and shook his head. "I don't know. I was always good at guessing the opposing coach's play when the game got heated."

"Interesting. It must have developed when Vita healed you. Let's play around with it. Vita, come here."

Dr. Wilson wrote something on his clipboard and showed it to her. "All right, I gave Vita a word. See if you can read it."

"How?" Adrian asked.

"Try eye contact to aid you."

"Okay." Adrian looked into Vita's eyes. His eyes glowed aquatic blue as he took a deep breath and felt his mind slip into hers. Like tuning to the right radio station, Vita's voice rang clear in his head.

Wow, I'm so jealous. He has such pretty blue eyes! Wait. Focus. What was the word? Oh, 'hydrogen'!

Adrian grinned. "Hydrogen."

"Good job!" Vita giggled.

"Try delivering a thought back," Dr. Wilson said.

Adrian focused on Vita again, and this time thought of a word to deliver.

Tacos. Tacos. Tacos.

Vita grinned. "Tacos!"

"Yeah," Adrian answered, laughing.

"Excellent!" Dr. Wilson exclaimed. "Let's continue."

Imagine all the funny stuff I could pull with this dandy trick. First person I'll go after is Hogan. He'll start thinking he's haunted.

Vita giggled again, trying to cover her mouth.

Oh damn. I didn't mean to tell her that.

"Oh, it's okay," Vita assured.

"I can't turn it off." Adrian rubbed his knuckles into his temples.

God, what if they all hear the embarrassing stuff?

"It's okay, Adrian," Vita repeated calmly.

"Adrian, take a deep breath and pull out of her mind," Dr. Wilson instructed.

Adrian breathed in, but the thoughts seemed to flurry about his mind in rapid-fire succession. All the embarrassing moments he wanted to hide, all the thoughts he didn't want anyone to know, they *screamed* at him, getting more desperate by the moment.

Vita winced, hands on her head. "Ow, Adrian, please stop. It's too loud."

"I can't!"

Stop, stop, stop!

Guardian Sawyer knelt next to Vita and placed a protective hand on her back. "Vita? Are you okay? Adrian, turn it off."

"I'm trying," Adrian snapped.

They'll know about every time I snuck off with my girlfriend, or the stupid stuff I did at parties, or that one time when I—

Adrian felt his shoulders relax and his mind slow. His racing heart slowed to a steady beat.

His thoughts didn't sound as loud now. They were quieter, less insulting. He could feel himself slip out of her mind and back into his own, like reeling in a fishing line.

Vita released a breath and rubbed her forehead.

Dos's eyes faded from the red glow.

"Did you do that?" Adrian asked, wiping the sweat from his forehead.

"I just delivered some peace. It is harder to control our abilities when our emotions are heightened," Dos answered quietly. "My apologies, I should not have done it without your permission."

Adrian shook his head and clapped Dos on the back. "Nah man, you saved my back. You can calm me down whenever you want. Thanks."

As Adrian stared into Dos's eyes, he was hit with a dozen flashes of Dos's memories like a slideshow. Images of a young Dos trapped in an iced-over room, wearing those thin scrubs and chained to a corner. Dos shivered violently, limbs going numb, and tears burning the rims of his eyes as his mother and Dr. Guyer observed him from the sole window in the room. Dos chanted to himself to not react, because if he did, the bracelets would shock him and he would need to stay in the room even longer. He couldn't have been any older than ten years old.

We must strengthen your discipline, Two, Dr. Guyer said before throwing him in the room. *You are far too emotional, and that is dangerous. If you behaved properly, we would not have this problem. Instead, I am receiving reports that you burned a boy. I expect better from you.*

Please, sir, Dos begged. *He hit me first . . . he held me down and hit me. I did not mean to burn him, I only wanted it to stop. I'm sorry. Dr. Novak . . . Mother . . . please, do not let him put me back in there."*

Dr. Novak looked away from him, clutching the clipboard to her chest with an impassive expression on her face.

Dos cried. He prayed to the angels. His wrist was bleeding from the shocks—

Adrian snapped out of Dos's mind and back into his own. He reached over and gently squeezed Dos's shoulder. "Hey, man, you're a good guy, you know that? I'm glad we're friends."

Dos blinked, his eyebrows twitching from his confusion. He stiffly nodded. "Likewise."

Adrian let him go and barely spotted the dark scars on Dos's wrists. He didn't say anything about it, and he didn't know if he ever should. He watched the others in the room around him—the guardians, the other elementals, Dr. Wilson—and he wondered if they had dark pasts that haunted them. How many of them were hurting or broken in irreparable ways but carried on like nothing was wrong?

He wondered if there was a way to help them at all or if his help would even be enough.

CHAPTER 24

AIR

Guardian Hogan walked Annie to Dr. Guyer's lab, keeping quiet as usual. Annie didn't want to meet privately with Dr. Guyer. This morning, her dad had been adamant that Guyer was not a man to trust. She was still pissed at her dad for not telling her about this place. She thought about all the times she'd been grounded for lying about stupid stuff when he was lying about the *biggest* part of their lives. It seemed a little unfair.

Either way, there was something about Dr. Guyer that made her father nervous, and that put her on edge. Her dad wasn't normally a skittish guy. He was confident, but Dr. Guyer brought out something that made him anxious. What did Dr. Guyer do that made her father run away all those years ago, and why wouldn't anyone just talk about it?

"Are you ill?" Hogan finally asked.

"Do I look sick to you?" Annie snapped.

"You're uncharacteristically quiet. You haven't cursed once since we left the pond."

Annie rolled her eyes. "A girl can't think every now and then?"

"That's not what I meant."

"You don't happen to have a cigarette, do you?"

"Smoking is bad for your lungs," Hogan pointed out in confusion. "Shouldn't you be against smoking since it pollutes the air?"

"Whatever." She blew a strand of hair out of her face. "Hey, is this Guyer dude creepy or something? What's his deal?"

"His deal?"

"Yeah, why are people so afraid of him?"

"I don't think anyone is really afraid of him. Dr. Guyer is a good man."

"I asked my dad about it, and he said to be careful."

Hogan shrugged and knocked on the door.

"Come in!" Dr. Guyer called out.

Hogan opened the door and followed Annie inside, stationing himself at the door.

"Ah, Anila, come in." Dr. Guyer waved her in with a smile.

Annie rolled her shoulders back and strutted toward him, hands in her jacket pockets. "It's Annie."

"Annie, how nice. How have you been adjusting, dear?" Dr. Guyer asked, setting down his tools.

Annie shrugged one shoulder. "Fine, I guess."

"Are you comfortable in your given conditions?"

"I prefer the air in California, but I don't have a choice, do I?"

Dr. Guyer smiled that infuriatingly kind smile and moved on. "I understand you have not developed your connection ability yet. Are you concerned?"

"Should I be?"

"No, not at all. It has been shown in history that sometimes the connection simply takes longer to develop. These are fickle things, so I wouldn't worry if I were you. If we really need to, we have humane methods of guiding it along. However, we won't need to think of that quite yet."

"Hm," Annie grunted, eyeing him. All the other elementals had a connection ability. It was embarrassing, like being a late bloomer with puberty. Was there something wrong with her?

Dr. Guyer observed her for a moment. "You look so much like

your father. Except for your hair. Your mother's hair was perfectly straight, like yours."

"Good for her." Annie didn't know anything about her mother. Dad had no pictures, didn't talk about her, didn't even mention her name. All Annie knew was that her mom had walked out when she was a baby, and last night, Dad finally confessed that when given the choice to run with her husband and daughter, Annie's mother had decided to split up the family and go her own way. Apparently, her daughter wasn't worth the trouble.

"I can imagine how hard this must be for you," Dr. Guyer said, pouring some white powder into a beaker filled with a red fluid. "To walk the paths that she once walked and meet the people who knew her. It is a terrible shame that you had to grow up without a mother. It is a confusing kind of pain."

"I'm sure you know all about that."

"I never met my mother. She died in childbirth. They say my father was a kind man, but I never met that version of him. My mother's death haunted him, turned him cold and cruel to the world and everyone in it. I was always told that I looked just like my mother, and it is my belief that was the reason he never liked me much." Dr. Guyer swirled around the contents, watching as the red fluid turned a darker red with each swirl until it was black. "Our parents mold us like clay. However, we are like *wet* clay. We never dry, and so we have the opportunity to reshape ourselves from their mistakes. We can either remain the grim mess they created, or we can become something better. Something we can be proud of."

He studied the liquid, then looked at Annie. "I can see you have already decided to reject the weight she has given you. That, my dear, is true wisdom."

Confusion finally cracked Annie's hardened expression. Was this guy actually trying to be nice to her? Why did he care? Even more important, why did his words make Annie feel just a little better about this whole situation?

"Thanks," she muttered.

Dr. Guyer patted her hand. "Thank you for taking the time to meet with me. I am looking forward to your connection unlocking. Air has always been my favorite of the elementals, the most diverse of the four. However, I am not supposed to pick favorites, so let's keep that a secret. I have a little gift for you, just something that might make your time here a bit easier."

He slid a small blue book across the table and offered her a knowing smile. "Air values freedom, which often means you hate rules. But for the time being, I thought it best that you have this rule book on hand just to be sure you don't find yourself in any dangerous situations."

Annie stifled her eyeroll and picked it up. It probably wouldn't hurt to know a few of these. Dr. Guyer stood and leaned on his cane. "I'll be joining the next part of training before lunch. There are a few things I'd like to see. Don't wait for me, I'll only slow you down."

Annie shrugged and walked off, Hogan joining her side.

"Well, that meeting had a positive ending, didn't it?" Hogan said as they walked outside.

"Yeah, I guess." Annie flipped through the book, stopping on a single highlighted line.

Elementals are—under no circumstances—to mix romantically. The result of breaking such a rule shall be the immediate punishment and solitary confinement for the elementals in question.

Annie stopped walking and snapped her eyes over her shoulder. Dr. Guyer was hobbling toward them, appearing every bit weak and frail. Like he'd fall over if someone so much as sneezed on him. But the sharp gleam in his icy-blue eyes, the righteous smile

. . . he was not to be toyed with. He was not to be trusted. He was not to be underestimated.

How did he know? She didn't even think much of Dos until this morning, and Guyer hadn't even been with them.

How?

"Annie?" Hogan said, noticing her frozen stature.

Her heart raced as she realized that Guyer had just threatened her with her worst fear. *Confinement.* He didn't even say a word, but he could do it. Snap his fingers, have the entire guardian force throw her in some prison, toss away the key, and forget about it. All because she liked a guy who could walk through fire.

Dr. Guyer finally caught up to their side and offered her a sympathetic expression. "Are you all right, dear? Is there something you need to tell me?"

She shook her head, pressing her lips together to avoid blurting out whatever empty threat she could make up. Dr. Guyer nodded, and to anyone else it would have looked like understanding, but Annie already knew it was his satisfaction. And it made her *sick.* He continued on his walk, not showing any signs of the silent confrontation between them.

Annie swallowed the fear lumping in her throat, raised her chin, and continued down her path. To be extra sure that nobody would suspect anything, she shoved her trembling hands into her jacket pockets.

CHAPTER 25

FIRE

D r. Guyer sat at the nearest bench outside and watched Guardian Sawyer with a studious gaze, despite the elementals actively practicing their abilities in front of him. He'd been doing that a lot lately. Perhaps Dr. Guyer wanted to observe how the future chief would react if one of the elementals stepped out of line.

"Instead of element versus element, we will do element versus man. Guardian Sawyer and Dos, you'll handle this."

Dos restrained his annoyance and stepped forward, holding out his right wrist just as he had always done. He wasn't looking forward to wearing the bracelet again, but Dr. Guyer wasn't someone to argue with.

Dr. Guyer shook his head. "No. For today, I want you to use your abilities."

Guardian Sawyer whipped around. "You do?"

"You wish for me to use fire against Guardian Sawyer?" Dos asked. During his training with the guardians, the instructors had always made him wear the impulse bracelet so his abilities wouldn't give him an unfair advantage. Even still, it was forbidden to use his element against a human.

"Yes," Dr. Guyer said.

"Why, sir?"

Dr. Guyer's eyebrows twitched, a look that told Dos he should be silent. "Your goal, Guardian Sawyer, is to latch the impulse bracelet onto Dos's wrist before he can knock you out of the circle. Do what you must. You may choose one practice weapon to use."

Dr. Wilson laid out several practice weapons, such as swords, staves, and shields.

Guardian Sawyer hesitantly picked up a shield.

If Dos were in his shoes, he'd be furious. All the practice weapons were made of wood and would only kindle the fire. In all actuality, Sawyer had no weapon.

His strategy, then, would be to use brute force. This meant Dos would need to move fast and keep distance between them.

This should be easy enough.

Sawyer carried his shield over to the pond and soaked it in water until it dripped at his feet.

Smart. The water would buy him a few seconds. However useful those precious seconds may be.

Dos and Sawyer stood across from each other and waited for the go-ahead. Sawyer held the open bracelet in his right hand and the wet shield in his left. Dos had sparred with him a few times in training but always with the bracelets on. This would be a first for both of them. Why was Dr. Guyer doing this? How did this help with the stone's creation?

"Begin." Dr. Guyer waved a hand.

Dos immediately created a rope of fire and lashed it forward.

Sawyer dodged out of the way, keeping his shield away from the flame as he ran toward his opponent.

Dos pushed a wave of flame toward Sawyer, leaving enough room for him to hit the ground.

Sawyer slid on his side, holding the shield over his body as the flames just barely sizzled over it. Sawyer was back on his feet and heading toward him in the time that Dos managed to lash out another rope of flame.

Sawyer stumbled back, nearly reaching the edge of the white-painted circle.

Another lash from Dos prompted Sawyer to dig his heel into the ground and push back with the shield.

Dos gritted his teeth, upping the intensity of his fire just enough to make his opponent sweat. Water sizzled against the shield, and the smell of burning wood permeated the air.

Sawyer dropped to his knees and tucked forward, just beneath the flames.

Dos released his flames and focused on Sawyer's movements. Sawyer charged, but if Dos was quick enough, he still had enough distance to push him back over the line. Just as he raised his hands to conjure flames, Dos barely saw a purple flash before the shield collided with his face.

Dos stumbled back, his vision blurring as Sawyer gripped Dos's wrist and pulled him down.

Out of instinct, Dos grabbed Sawyer's forearm with a heated hand, his hot touch instantly burning his opponent.

Sawyer sucked in a sharp breath and latched the bracelet on to Dos's wrist, thus stopping the heat all together. Then he jolted back, grimacing in pain over the new burn on his arm.

Dos was familiar with these bracelets from his lifelong training. It felt like his veins had filled with lead. When he tried to use them, his abilities wouldn't respond, and the bracelets would shock him.

"My apologies," Dos huffed out, and sat up to rub his throbbing cheek. "You caught me by surprise."

"Ah." Sawyer clicked his tongue. "I think that was the point."

Vita rushed over to Sawyer and placed her hands on his burn. "Hold still."

Dos dared to shoot a quick glance at Annie. Did she see him fumble? She quickly looked away, hands in her pockets and cheeks turning red. Damn these bracelets for blocking his ability to see her emotions.

Sawyer walked over and unlocked the bracelet. The elemental's abilities would be stunted until the bracelet was removed and only a guardian's key would remove it. Luckily, all the keys for the bracelets were universal, so if one of the guardians lost theirs, they could use another's.

The rush of Dos's abilities flowed back through his body, as if his nerves had awakened again.

Dr. Guyer sighed heavily. "Bring me Vita after lunch." He limped off with a disappointed grimace.

What had upset him? That Dos had lost a sparring match? Dos had spent years learning how Dr. Guyer worked, and yet there were still things he didn't understand about the mad alchemist. He wondered if he ever would.

CHAPTER 26

GUARDIAN

A fter lunch, Vita and Otis followed Lucas to Dr. Guyer's office. "What does Dr. Guyer want me to do?" Vita asked.

"He just wants to meet you. It should be quick."

"My momma warned me to stay away from him. She said he was dangerous."

"I trust Dr. Guyer. He's a brilliant, selfless man. I'm unaware of the history between him and your parents, but I've known him to be nothing but a hero."

Once they arrived, Lucas knocked on the door and waited for permission. At Guyer's welcome, he opened the door and followed Vita inside. Dr. Guyer was leaning on his cane and carrying a beaker filled with a clear liquid. Then he stumbled, and the beaker slipped from his hands and shattered on the floor. His cane slipped on the water, and he lost his balance.

Lucas barely reached him in time and caught the old man before he hit the floor. Vita rushed to their side and helped Lucas straighten up the doctor.

"Sir, are you okay? Vita, call my mother," Lucas instructed.

"Oh no, don't worry yourself over an old man's poor balance. Just get my cane, please." Dr. Guyer coughed, leaning on Lucas.

"I could heal you," Vita offered, handing him the cane.

Dr. Guyer settled into his chair. "I couldn't ask you to do that. I'm not even sure that you can."

"At least let me try," Vita insisted, taking his hand in hers.

Lucas badly wanted Dr. Guyer to say yes. If anyone could help him, it would be Vita.

"Perhaps one day, but not today. No, today, I'd like to talk more about you. Guardian Sawyer, can you sweep that glass away? I fear that someone will step on it. There is a broom in the closet across the hall."

"Of course, sir." Lucas hurried out of the room to the broom closet. When he came back with a broom in hand, Vita and Dr. Guyer were already deep in conversation. He knelt down and carefully swept up the glass.

"I am so sorry about the fate that befell your father," Guyer said, patting Vita's hand. "I sent our best guardians to find Mason's killers, but we were unable to find them. It will forever be considered my greatest failure."

"I didn't even know you tried. Thank you, anyway," Vita answered softly.

Lucas didn't know about that mission either, which was strange because he knew most of the outside-world missions the guardians were sent on. True, some were confidential, so he wouldn't be able to see those files until he was a chief, but his father shared everything else with Lucas and used them as training opportunities. Even so, he couldn't understand why the hunt for Mason Eastwood's killers would be confidential.

"Well, what do you say, dear?" Dr. Guyer asked Vita, motioning to the piano in the corner of the room. "Do you like it?"

"Oh, it's beautiful!"

"Clarice would play the sweetest music in here while I worked. It was our way of bonding during the long hours. Even after her death, I keep it tuned for her. As if I can somehow still honor her. But those keys have not been touched in years, and I feel it is an awful shame. I wonder if, perhaps, *you* could change that?"

Vita gasped. "You'd let me play it? Are you sure?"

"I heard you were a gifted pianist. It would do this old heart such good to hear it."

"It would be an honor, sir. Do you have any requests?"

"Play me something that makes your heart swell in delight."

Vita eagerly took her seat at the piano. Lucas couldn't help but watch the gentle way her fingers rested on the keys and how her back straightened in pride.

The moment she started playing, Lucas's breath caught, and he stopped cleaning the glass just so he could watch her. She played such a delicate tune, the melody as soft as clouds. She had the most peaceful smile, like the world around her no longer existed and it was just her and that song.

Dr. Guyer smiled at Lucas, then at Vita before silently going back to his work.

Vita looked up, still playing, and caught Lucas's eyes. He didn't dare look away, he couldn't. It was impossible to see or hear anything but her and that song.

He was totally and effortlessly absorbed in her gaze.

Angels above . . . I have feelings for her.

It was like a million stars suddenly flickered to life within his core and shimmered all the way to his fingertips. Somewhere in the back of his head, reason was screaming at him for falling for someone who didn't fit the mold of a chief's wife in any way. But reason was quickly drowned out by the sound of her music.

Vita smiled at him, and for a moment, Lucas felt dizzy from the sudden rush of emotions he felt for her. This was awful and wonderful all at the same time. He rested his hand down on the floor and caught a shard of forgotten glass in his palm.

Lucas jerked back, blood sprouting from his palm in a bright-red line. The music stopped and Vita was at his side in seconds.

"Oh no, that looks painful." She grabbed his hand, plucked out the bloody shard of glass, and began to heal him. Again, that rush of euphoria shivered throughout his body. His blood sucked back into his skin, and the wound sewed itself closed as if it were never there.

"Is that better?" Vita asked.

He blushed and nodded stiffly. "Yes. Thank you. You may let go of my hand now."

She blinked in surprise and released him. Not a moment too soon, his palms were sweating, and the last thing he wanted was for her to see that. Lucas stood and dumped the glass into the trash.

"Vita, dear," Dr. Guyer started, "I've heard a little rumor that Guardian James has asked you to join him for dinner tonight at the Guardian Club. Is this correct?"

Lucas went rigid and looked to Vita. "When did that happen?"

Vita pushed a curl behind her ear. "During lunch, when you went to turn in your report."

"And you said yes?"

"I did."

Dr. Guyer smiled brightly. "Well, in that case, I wouldn't want to hold you any longer. You have a date to get ready for, my lady! And he is a wonderful young man. I am sure he will show you a great time."

"Thank you for letting me play, and for our talk."

"Oh, it was my pleasure. I hope it's all right if I request your music from time to time?"

"I would love that."

Dr. Guyer nodded. "Thank you, dear. Enjoy your night."

"Good night, sir." Vita turned and walked out, an annoyed Lucas and excited Otis in tow.

As soon as the door closed and they were alone in the hall, Lucas blurted, "You're honestly pursuing Guardian James?"

Vita rolled her eyes. "It's just one dinner. Why do you care?"

Oh, he did *not* like that sting of jealousy that coursed through him. It was suffocating and made his entire body feverishly hot. How could anyone think clearly like this? "Of all people, why him?"

"Why not? He doesn't seem so offended by my boldness, and he's cute. Are you seriously worried about us dirty outside girls mixing with your precious guardians?"

"It's not that at all. You just met him! How can you possibly want to date a person you barely know?"

"That's the whole point of the date, genius. To get to know each other. If you've got such a problem with it, why aren't you talking to Ethan?"

He leaned forward, an annoyed twitch in his brow. "Should I really have to swat away all the men who desire you? I have better things to do. Can't you handle that yourself?"

Vita poked his chest. "You wanna know something, Lucas Sawyer? You're a mean old prick with the temper of a copperhead. I would knock the sense clear from your head if it weren't for the fact that you ain't got none! You don't know the first thing about girls, do you? Maybe you should ask Ethan for advice and take some notes. He's got twice the charm you ever will. Otis, come!"

She whipped around and stormed away, Otis scampering after her.

Lucas grunted. "Where are you going? I am meant to walk you home."

Vita scoffed over her shoulder at him. "Don't worry, I'll ask Ethan."

She slammed the door behind her and left him there in the training hall more frustrated and confused than he'd ever been.

I can't believe I thought I had feelings for her.

Clearly, those feelings were nothing but fleeting hormones. It was a trick of her angelic beauty. He trained and prepared, and yet he had still slipped up and almost fallen prey to her appearances. These elementals were tricky beings. It was a good thing he got this little confusion out of the way early on so he could focus on more pressing matters.

Creating the philosopher's stone and earning his place as chief held much more importance than whatever silly crush he thought he had. That was for children, and he was a guardian. He was better than this, for the angel's sake.

CHAPTER 27

FIRE

D os spent a lot of time out on the balcony these days. He never used to sit out here, but now it was his favorite spot in all of Elondoh.

Why?

Because *she* lived next door and liked sitting on her own balcony railing to enjoy the night's cool breeze. Her blonde hair flicked in the wind, and her ivory skin illuminated by the moonlight. At night, she wore a long T-shirt that went down to her thighs.

She frequently showed off some part of her skin during the day, be it her legs or stomach or arms. Most women around here dressed modestly, but not her. She had piercings in her ears and eyebrow, wore dark makeup around her eyes, and her clothing— shorts and strange T-shirts—were always in black. Whenever she walked past him, he caught a slight whiff of her jasmine perfume, like a curse pulling him under her spell.

Tonight, Dos caught sight of a black tattoo on her hip. He only saw the corner of it, not the whole thing, but he wanted to. What was so special about the design that she had it inked on her body?

She was just so different from anyone he'd ever seen before. He had questions about her, wanted to understand her more, but he didn't know where to start, or if he should. Restraint was one of the skills he'd perfected over years of practice. Still, she was his greatest challenge yet.

"Annie!" her father, David, called from inside their home.

Annie sighed and rolled her head back. "Yeah?"

"Come in here, I need to talk to you."

Annie groaned and scooped her long legs over the railing. The balcony doors shut behind her, leaving Dos alone in the darkness yet again. Back to the bleak silence of his plain white room.

He made a quick stop to his kitchen for water before bed. Dr. Sawyer was always telling him that he needed to drink twice as much as other people since his body burned it off more quickly.

Dr. Novak was sitting at the counter with her notebook in front of her and a pen in her hand. She glanced up at Dos and then back down at her notes.

"How have the elementals been in training?" she asked.

"They are adjusting well," he reported, grabbing a glass.

"Any discovery on Three's connection ability?"

"Not yet."

"We might need to start stimuli training."

Dos fumbled with his glass, barely catching it. His heart raced as memories flooded his mind of the shock treatments and unbearable experiments they called "stimuli training." Memories of him begging for them to stop, and yet they kept going. When he was young, they had unlocked his connection abilities by force rather than letting them develop naturally. He would *not* allow them to do that to Annie.

"I do not believe that will be necessary. It should unlock soon with training." Dos's tongue was dry.

"I will suggest it to Dr. Guyer in the morning. We have no time to waste."

Her phone rang, Dr. Guyer's name lighting up the screen. She picked it up and stepped outside. "Novak. Yes, I am reading it now."

Dos watched her step away, and he quickly peered over her

notes. A bundle of letters arranged in strange fragments lined the page. Not a language that Dos knew.

But he did recognize the strange symbol drawn on the top right corner. The same one that Dr. Guyer had written in his notepad.

Dr. Novak opened the door and stepped back in. Dos skirted back to the sink, filling his glass and trying not to give away his actions.

Novak took one look at him, then at the notebook, and rounded on him. "Did you read my notes?"

"No."

Dr. Novak lashed out, slapping him hard enough to make him drop his cup. Glass and water shattered onto the floor, the acidic scent of his fear building bile in his throat. Dos recoiled and held his hand over his throbbing cheek.

"Do *not* lie to me," she warned through gritted teeth. "Did you read them?"

Dos kept his eyes and stature low. "I could not understand them. I only saw the symbol and recognized it from Dr. Guyer's lab."

"Do you know what the symbol is for?"

"No, Doctor."

She threateningly raised her hand again.

Dos flinched. "I swear it, I do not know, and I will tell no one of what I saw."

She studied him, but he kept himself low and small.

"Clean up this mess." Dr. Novak snatched up her work and stormed out of the room.

Dos squeezed his eyes shut and took a few deep breaths until the wretched fear left him. Until he could pretend that he was not as weak as he felt.

One day, she will get what she deserves. They all will.

He gritted his teeth and set about cleaning up the broken glass.

As he dropped the shards into the trash, a piece nicked his thumb. He sucked in a sharp breath and angrily bandaged the cut. The sulfuric scent of anger quickly replaced fear.

Someday.

Dos walked into the training room early the next morning to prepare the crucible for their next attempt at the stone. He liked being sure that the wood was stacked properly, the bowl of the crucible was fixed straight in its holder, and that other, smaller details were taken care of. Dr. Wilson often missed small details that Dos would rather fix ahead of time. He needed to collect a sample of lead from Dr. Guyer's office, and then he could go off to breakfast.

Dr. Guyer's door was cracked open, leaving just enough space for Dos to hear Dr. Guyer's yelling.

"You lost your temper, and that cost you valuable time to do as I asked!"

"Please, sir," a man begged. It sounded like Boyd. "I can make up for it. Give me another chance to prove myself. Put me back on the guardian detail for the elementals and I will complete the task as required."

"You expect me to give you another chance after that terrible performance you gave? Absolutely not!"

"There must be another way. There must be something I can do. I am meant to be chief—I can do a better job than Sawyer can."

"I cannot add you back to the guardian detail. Guardian James is already in, and he's doing an excellent job. If I replace him with a guardian who lost his patience, there will be questions. However, you will act as my personal guardian. This way, you can still keep an eye on the elementals, but it shouldn't raise too much suspicion. Many believe I should have a personal guardian due to my health anyway, so it will work. You are to notify me the moment a reaction happens in our favor. You know the severity of our task and the consequences if you fail. You will be seen, not heard, until I say otherwise. Is that understood?"

"Yes, sir. Thank you for this—"

"Enough. You may go."

The door opened before Dos could scramble away. Boyd sneered and pushed past him, not bothering with a polite greeting. That left Dos in the doorway, visible to Dr. Guyer.

"Dos," he greeted, shuffling papers on his desk. "When did you get there?"

"Just a moment ago, sir. I need a lesser metal for the crucible."

Dr. Guyer waved a hand and focused on his papers. "There is lead in my stores that you may take."

Dos nodded, walking to Dr. Guyer's wall of ingredients, and picked out the jar of lead shavings. On his way to the wall, he peeked over to Dr. Guyer's notebook and noticed a strange mixture of letters beneath that unknown symbol. This time he made sure to keep his eyes down before Dr. Guyer could catch him. With the jar in hand, Dos headed to the door of the office but stopped when Dr. Guyer spoke up again.

"Dos, remind me again about the second rule of the elemental guidelines. I seem to have forgotten it."

Dos kept his expression devoid of any emotion, but inside, protective anger prickled beneath his skin like a thousand biting ants. "Elementals are not to mix under any circumstances."

"No one knows what would happen if two elementals had a child together. It would be an abomination against the angels. We would have no choice but to punish those who disregard this. You don't think the others would break that rule, do you?"

"To do so would be foolish."

Dr. Guyer smiled, but his voice remained cold. "Yes, it would be. Thank you. You may go."

Dos turned and walked out, sparks flickering around his fists. Of course, Dr. Guyer knew about Dos's feelings for Annie. He knew everything.

And now he had another set of eyes watching over them.

CHAPTER 28

GUARDIAN

Lucas Sawyer was a man of discipline. He exceeded expectations, maintained his schedules, and certainly never went against Elondohnian culture. So, when he woke up thinking about Vita Eastwood, he was a little . . . annoyed. It didn't help that he felt sorry about their argument last night. They'd made a pact to be friends, yet he was letting his emotions get in the way and making foolish decisions.

So, two things happened in the lazy minutes he spent lying in bed. First, he decided immediately that he wouldn't acknowledge his feelings for Vita. If he ignored them, they'd simply go away. He even made a mental list as to why it would be a bad idea to pursue her.

1. She is from the outside world. Many people complained about an outsider becoming a chief's wife. They said my mother wasn't as deserving as an Elondohnian girl. They will complain about Vita too.

2. She is an elemental in a dangerous generation. She could snap at any moment, and I would have to be the one to stop her. That would likely cause a lot of tension between us, and she has a short enough fuse as it is.

3. She might not feel the same way.

But angels, she was magnetic. There was a wildness about her that was somehow both terrifying and addictive. Her laughter alone was proof that angels existed.

Lucas sat up in bed and forced himself to get ready for the day. The second thing was to make amends for their argument. Feelings aside, they had an alliance that he needed to maintain.

———————————

Lucas knocked on Vita's door, holding a little blue teacup in his hands. In the teacup was a tiny succulent that he'd clipped from his mother's garden. He couldn't find a pot small enough to hold the plant, so the teacup was his next best option. Hogan and Ethan talked to each other as they waited for their elementals. Ethan looked over to Lucas, his smile starting to waver.

"What is that, Sawyer?"

"Oh," Lucas held it up. "It's just a gift for Vita. We had a disagreement last night, so I'm hoping to make amends."

"She seemed in good spirits at dinner last night," Ethan said. "I'm sure she wasn't thinking of your argument."

"Well, just in case, the plant will help."

"Huh," Hogan grunted. "I wonder if I should be bringing Annie gifts. She can get awfully sour with me. Maybe I somehow offended her? Yesterday, she said I looked like Humpty Dumpty."

He looked around and plucked a flower from a nearby bush. Annie just opened the door with a yawn and raised an eyebrow at Hogan's flower.

"I'm not interested," Annie grunted, breezing past him.

Hogan blushed a scarlet red and dropped the flower before hurrying up to her. "Oh no, that wasn't my intention!"

Poor Hogan. That man had such terrible luck with women.

Vita's door opened and she stopped with a gasp, her eyes glowing green when they landed on the teacup. She broke out into a bright grin. "Well, hello! Aren't you just the cutest little thing?"

Lucas held it out to her. "I know you said you wanted a cactus, but I don't think we have any of those. This is in the same family, right?"

Vita brought her eyes up to him. "Is he for me?"

He nodded, suddenly blushing. "I'm sorry about our argument yesterday. I acted out of line and disregarded our pact. Can we still be friends, you and me?"

"Yes, you and me. I love him, thank you!" She giggled and threw her arms around him in a hug.

Lucas froze, his cheeks growing even hotter. In the corner of his eye, he saw Ethan watching with an offended gasp and Adrian tugging him away while explaining how comfortable the outside world was with touching. Lucas knew that, but it didn't make this any less shocking. He awkwardly patted her back.

Vita pulled back and took the teacup, still smiling at it. "Hi Bo, welcome to your new home. I'll be right back, Lucas. I'm just gonna put him on my desk."

She hurried into her home, leaving him there standing like a stunned idiot. He was glad Adrian had pulled Ethan away or this would have been even more awkward. Vita came back out with Otis at her side and her bag over her shoulder.

"Ready?" she asked.

"Yes." He held out his hand. "Um, I could carry your bag for you, if it's heavy."

She brightened up and handed her bag to him. "So, he *can* be a gentleman. Thanks. Care for a strawberry muffin?"

"The strawberries are my favorite. Thank you."

Lucas was overcome with nausea yet again as the elementals rehearsed their transmutation process. It had gotten so bad this time that he excused himself from the room and hurried outside for some fresh air. The smell of that burning sulfur was awful, and it was annoying that no one else was as affected by it as he was.

"I brought you some water."

Lucas looked over his shoulder. Dos had followed him out and held out a glass of water.

"That's not the same water from the crucible, is it?" Lucas asked, grimacing.

"No, it is from the tap. If I am being honest, that is not really why I came out here. Vita offered to check on you, but I needed to speak with you."

"Oh. Thank you," Lucas said, a little disappointed. He accepted the water and watched as Dos looked around to make sure they were alone.

"Dr. Guyer is planning something dangerous with the elementals."

Lucas blinked. "I'm sorry?"

"Dr. Guyer has been writing to Dr. Novak in a strange code, using a hidden symbol that I do not know."

"Okay. Is that a bad thing?"

Dos sighed. "It is obviously a bad thing. Dr. Guyer has always secretly hated the elementals, and I believe this symbol might represent some sort of weapon to use against us."

"Dos, come now. Dr. Guyer would never choose to hurt the elementals. He cares too much about all of you. Perhaps you misinterpreted something."

"I did not. I overheard him and Dr. Novak discussing something called V. I think we need to find their notebook and figure out what it is they are plotting."

"You want us to dig around Dr. Guyer's notes? That would get us in a whirlwind of trouble. Why don't we just ask him?"

Dos scoffed. "I do not trust Dr. Guyer or Novak. They are hiding something from us, and I think you should know that Boyd is after chiefhood. He has made a deal with Dr. Guyer to have his application reviewed if he can keep an eye on the elementals."

Lucas's lip curled down at that. "Plenty of people have tried to change who gets the role of chief, and they have all failed. What could Boyd possibly have to offer that would change tradition?"

"I am not sure. Tonight, I am going to the archives room."

"The archives room? That's just another silly myth. It doesn't actually exist."

"I have seen it. It is a floor down from Dr. Guyer's office, and I have been there several times. It is sealed off from the public, but I found the entrance some years ago. I will invite the others, and I believe you should come with us. I need answers, Guardian Sawyer, and you do too."

Lucas's jaw dropped. "Do you hear yourself? That would be trespassing into a restricted area, breaking and entering into the archives room without a key, endangering the well-being of prized elementals, and, oh right—breaking curfew."

"Yes," Dos answered bluntly. "Can you manage it without inducing a panic attack? It would also mean spending a few extra minutes alone with Vita, if that helps."

Lucas's heart skipped a beat. "I'm sure I don't know what you mean."

"Guardian Sawyer, I know what attraction looks like. I see the emotion flaring within you at the mere mention of her name. You have feelings for her."

"How do you know what attraction looks like? Who taught you that emotion?"

"Do not turn this back on me. We are discussing you."

"I believe we are discussing breaking several community laws." Lucas sighed and rubbed his forehead. "Fine. If we do this, we will do it right. Let's all meet at the orchard at midnight. It's late enough that no one should be working or commuting. Be sure to stay away from the streetlamps. I'll tell the others. Just so we're clear, I'm doing this to prove that Dr. Guyer has honorable intentions. I don't believe he wishes to hurt the elementals."

"I do not care why you do it. I only care that you do it," Dos said. "We have been out here for too long. We should go."

Lucas followed Dos inside and pressed his lips thin. Dos, although usually level-headed, must be mistaken. Dr. Guyer was honorable and kind. He was a man of science, not cruelty, and he obviously liked the idea of Lucas as chief; otherwise, he wouldn't have dedicated so much time to Lucas throughout guardian training.

This was all one big misunderstanding, and Lucas would find a way to prove it.

CHAPTER 29

FIRE

Dos had just slipped out of the back door of his townhome when Annie drifted off her balcony and planted both feet on the ground in a soft thump. The darkness of night was pierced by her glowing white eyes, like stars. Adrian and Vita joined them, along with Vita's cat.

Vita was wearing an all-black outfit and pulled a black beanie over her head. "What do y'all think? Fits the mood, right?"

Annie raised an amused eyebrow at her. "You've never snuck out before, have you?"

"No, why? Should I change?"

Annie ignored the question. "Are we sure Dr. Guyer's asleep and not pulling an all-nighter in his office?"

"I suppose there is no way to be sure," Dos said.

"I could swing by his house and read his thoughts," Adrian suggested.

"That's a good idea," Annie said. "You do that, and if you can't find his mind there, pop into one of our heads and let us know. Meanwhile, Dos and I should get a head start at the lab. It's stupid for us all to go in a big group. We'll get caught."

"Guardian Sawyer suggested we stay together, and he is well trained in guardian tactics," Dos countered.

"I'm going to take a wild guess and assume that tonight is Sawyer's first time sneaking out like the spy princess over here." Annie jerked her thumb at Vita, who pursed her lips in response.

"Groups are louder and easier to spot. We'll go in pairs. Vita, you should probably meet up with Sawyer so he knows what's going on."

"Yeah, okay. Come on, Lula-bean." Vita hurried off to the orchards with Lula in tow. Adrian took off for Dr. Guyer's house, which left Dos and Annie alone.

"I am impressed," Dos said, starting their walk toward the lab.

Annie shrugged. "You learn a thing or two in the outside world."

"May I ask you something about the outside world?"

"I guess."

"That tattoo on your side, what is it? Elondoh does not allow tattoos here, but I have read about them. The art is significant, is it not?"

Annie smirked. "Yeah. It's something I designed myself. Maybe I'll show it to you one day."

He didn't know how to respond to that, so he remained silent and averted his eyes from her. His cheeks warmed and an excited flurry twisted in his gut. These symptoms were similar to happiness and nervousness, but he did not recognize this emotion. That strange ribbon appeared around her, but he still hadn't been able to find the name for it. It couldn't be attraction, because attraction was an icy-blue cloud and smelled of honey. He would have to research it later.

They continued noiselessly toward the lab building and waited by the doors for a confirmation from Adrian. A few minutes later, his words popped into Dos's mind.

Dr. Guyer's asleep. We are a go.

"Adrian cleared us," Dos said, pulling open the door to the lab building and following Annie inside.

"So, where exactly did you plan on finding this information on Dr. Guyer?" Annie asked as they hurried through the halls.

"There is an archives room beneath us," Dos whispered as he led Annie toward Dr. Guyer's office. "There is a secret door in Dr. Guyer's office. That is where they keep all the documents from every study done on elementals. No one throws anything away for fear that it may be a clue to something, as was most things in alchemical history. Many Elondohnians think the library holds all our records, but they only see what Dr. Guyer wants them to see. Can you pick this lock?"

Annie scoffed. "Can I pick this lock? This is nothing." She plucked a pin from her hair and bent it until it was one flat piece. Dos stood guard while she fiddled with the lock.

"Break into a lot of places, did you?"

Annie smirked up at him. "Wouldn't you like to know?"

The lock clicked and Annie pushed the door open. "All right, hothead, we're in."

They walked through the lab and stopped at the piano. Just under the lid was a small red button that no one would notice if they hadn't been looking for it. Dos pressed it. One of the closet doors propped open, revealing a dark staircase that led down into the shadowy depths.

"Holy hell," Annie breathed. "How did you find out about this?"

"Sometimes as punishment, they had me clean Dr. Guyer's office. They trusted that I would not snoop through his documents unlike the janitors. I never knew what they would check, so I took care to clean every space. One day, I accidentally bumped against this button and found the archives."

"That sucks. That they punished you, I mean."

Dos shrugged. "I always preferred that method of punishment compared to the others."

"What others?"

Dos formed a ball of fire in his hands for light. He shouldn't have said anything. The freezer room they'd locked him in for hours. The bracelets that shocked him if he used his ability just to stay warm. The beatings. The ice baths. The scars on his wrists that would never go away. Novak and Guyer had said it was all for training, but he never believed it.

No, he did not want Annie to know any of that.

He ignored the question. "We should hurry. The others will be here soon."

Once they reached the bottom of the stairs, Dos touched his fireball against an oil lamp. The row of lamps on the walls ignited, one by one, until the expansive room was entirely lit. The room itself resembled a cave with stone walls and hard-packed stone floors. Spider webs were in the corners, and there was a messy wooden desk that looked older than Dr. Guyer. The left side of the room was spacious enough for a desk and several file cabinets. The rest of the room housed long rows of carefully organized book shelves. Most of the shelves covered in dust or cobwebs.

It was twice as cold down here than it was upstairs, as proven by the cloudy puffs of Annie's breath and the way she hugged her elbows. Dos made sure to radiate a bit of heat when he stood next to her.

Annie looked around. "This is insane. There are hundreds of shelves here. Where do we even start?"

Dos nodded to the desk that was littered with yellowing rolls of parchment and various leather-bound books. "I'll search there.

You should start with section A. Look for any mention of an elemental weapon."

Annie hurried off toward the shelves, leaving Dos to look through the desk. He took care to remember how everything was placed before he touched it so that he could leave it exactly as it was.

He carefully unraveled several rolls of parchment and discovered ancient records of family trees. One record was of the elemental line dating back to the original knights, and another was of other original families from the Elondoh records.

Dos knelt on the ground and studied the elemental line. These records were listed in the library for the public to see, but something about this particular illustration looked different. Something in his family line was tangled like a knot in a string. He traced his finger from the top of his line down to where the confusion rested at Generation 6, born in 1660 and died in 1683. Then he blinked and inspected it closer, because surely, he wasn't seeing the chart properly.

Katherine Ambrose, the Fire elemental of that time, was a name that Dos knew well. They shared the same connection ability, and she was reported to be the first elemental to ever have an angelic reaction. Her reaction had sparked a domino effect with the others and got the rest of them killed.

Connected to her spot on the tree was the Earth elemental, Peter Cole. Peter was the second elemental of that generation to have reacted. They had children together. Twins. One Earth, one Fire, both boys. These elementals had mixed.

They will mirror Generation 6 . . .

Dos looked across the room to Annie, who stood at a shelf, flipping through a book.

He had never heard of this before. According to the charts in the library, Peter and Katherine had married humans. If that was correct, then they'd been unfaithful to their spouses to be with each other. But that made no sense.

No elementals had ever mixed before, or at least that was what Dos had always been taught. But if these elementals had fallen in love, had children together, and even went as far as died together, why couldn't Dos do the same? If Dr. John Dee, with the help of the great King Carmara, predicted that Generation 23 would succumb to the same fate, why try to prevent it? Did that mean Dos and Annie were fated only to be condemned?

He closed his eyes and could hear Dr. Guyer's voice in his head. *It would be a sin against the angels.*

Nobody knew why Generation 6 had reacted, but Dos had a feeling that the alchemists of that time believed it was because the elementals had mixed. They sinned against the great angels and were punished for it. That would explain why that rule was put in place and why Dr. Guyer was suspicious about it. If Generation 23 was to mirror Generation 6, then it would make sense to be wary of every individual indicator.

Annie snapped her book closed and raised a pierced eyebrow at Dos. "You look like you're thinking really hard over there."

Dos glanced down at the parchment. "I am coming to terms with the fact that emotions can be potentially fatal."

"Why do you say that?"

He tapped the family tree. "Vita and I are very distant cousins. Our ancestors had children together."

"Really?" Annie put her book back on the shelf and walked over. She leaned against his shoulder as she read through the chart. Her arm was cool against his, the scent of her jasmine perfume swirling around him and dragging him into her clutches. Goosebumps shivered down his spine when she tilted her head and let her silky platinum hair drape against his shoulder. He'd never been so physically close with someone he was attracted to, but angels, the mere presence of her was heady.

"I wonder how they got away with their little affair," Annie said. "They were probably together a while before their reaction."

She turned to him, and her face was within an inch of his. He could see the dancing firelight flicker in her eyes and the long shadows that her lashes cast against her cheeks. Her eyes dropped down to his lips and back up into his eyes. Again, that ribbon-shaped emotion flourished and wrapped around her chest, blowing in the imaginary storm that was her desire.

"If they were smart, then they would have developed a code of some sort to speak to each other without anyone knowing," Dos said. "They would have had to sneak around in the dark, keeping their private moments a secret. Dr. Guyer would certainly not approve."

"Who cares about what Guyer has to say? He's just one man."

"A very powerful man."

Annie shrugged a shoulder. "I'm stronger than he is."

Her irises glowed white, and a gust of air swept up, causing the flames from the lamps to grow until the light was nearly blinding. The flames slowly fell back to their normal state as Annie's eyes faded back to blue.

"See?" Annie said with a teasing smile. "I'm not scared of a little fire."

"You should be," Dos said. His muddled thoughts were interrupted by shuffling and whispered arguments from upstairs. Vita's accent, Adrian's loud footsteps, and Guardian Sawyer's annoyed sighing. "The others are here."

Dos stood and offered Annie a hand to help her up. She grabbed his hand, her eyes locking on his while she rose. With a cocky smirk, she released his hand and walked back to the bookshelf.

CHAPTER 30

GUARDIAN

Lucas waited for the others deep in the orchards beneath an apple tree. He fidgeted, tapping his finger against his thigh as the minutes ticked by. There was a new moon tonight, which was perfect to ensure they wouldn't be seen by any cameras.

The grass barely rustled when Lucas clicked on his flashlight and caught Lula peering up at him with a cocked head and reflective yellow eyes. Then Vita stepped into the light, wearing all black, complete with a black beanie over her curly hair.

"What are you wearing?" he asked, lowering his flashlight.

"You said to be sneaky," she whispered, motioning to her outfit. "So, I dressed the part."

"I'm surprised you own so much black," he mused. "Are any of the others with you?"

"I caught up with them when I left. Annie and Dos went ahead to the lab, and Adrian is gonna make a quick stop to Guyer's place to make sure he's still sleeping. It's just us for now."

"That's not part of the plan. We're all supposed to go together."

"What does it matter? It's already in motion."

He sighed through his nose. "We have plans for a reason. We cannot just frivolously break them because we feel like it. You weren't even supposed to bring your pets with you."

She pointed a finger at him and gave him a cold glare. "Don't *ever* call them pets again. They are my friends. They're free to leave or stay, and I treat them with the same respect that I would to any human. Besides, Lula's silent as a ninja, she won't be any trouble. You're starting the night off by acting real petty."

"I'm petty for trying to stick to a plan?"

"You're petty for acting ugly just because we had a better idea than you did. Now, are we gonna sit here all night and argue, or are we gonna go?"

He huffed and clicked off his light, then led Vita and Lula toward the laboratory.

Adrian joined Lucas and Vita as they entered the building.

"Guyer's definitely asleep," Adrian reported. "He's also dreaming about his wife. It was a little weird."

"Poor thing," Vita said. "They must've been so in love."

"They were," Lucas said, pushing open the door to Guyer's office. "She was Elondoh's favorite citizen, but her illness took her too soon. Some Elondohnians believe she became an angel after her death because a white rose was found by her side when she passed. Adrian, you can see dreams?"

"Yeah," Adrian said. "It's all happening in your mind. Cool, right?"

"You've never done that to me, have you?"

Adrian quirked an eyebrow at him. "Not yet, but thanks for the idea."

"Holy Moses. It's *actually* a secret door." Vita's jaw dropped as she spotted the door to the archives room. "This is like *National Treasure*."

"Love that movie," Adrian said mostly to himself as he peeked through the hidden door.

Lucas stood next to them in stunned silence. He'd been to Guyer's office hundreds of times but never once had he seen this hidden room. He'd heard rumors of the archives room, but he never believed them to be true. Lucas turned on his flashlight, and descended the stairs with Vita and Adrian in tow. Lula elected to sit at the top of the stairwell and stay in the office. Smart girl.

They followed the faint glow of firelight as they reached the bottom of the stairs.

"Oh, it's freezing down here," Vita said, hugging her elbows. "I hate the cold."

"Here." Lucas shrugged off his jacket and held it out for her. She smiled warmly at him and accepted. Adrian wiggled his eyebrows at Lucas and wore a proud smile. Lucas ignored him.

"I've seen this in a horror movie before," Vita whispered.

"I was just thinking that. Some creepy demon is gonna pop out and eat us or something." Adrian added. "Sorry in advance, but I'll probably use one of you as a sacrifice so I can get away. No hard feelings."

"That's okay. I'll just haunt you in the afterlife."

The room was cavernous and damp. The frigid air laced with the musty smell of old books and the stone walls jutted out with uneven textures. If not for the rows of lit torches, it would be pitch-black and admittedly terrifying. Lucas did his best to ignore the massive black spider sewing its web in the corner. It wouldn't do well for a future chief to be squeamish.

Annie and Dos were standing on the opposite sides of the wide cellar, Dos at an antique desk and Annie at a book shelf. Dos nodded in greeting at them. He was holding a leather-bound book in one hand and a pen in the other.

"Good, you made it," Dos said. "I believe I found Dr. Novak and Dr. Guyer's latest notes. It appears as if they wrote messages to each other using the Caesar cipher. Guardian Sawyer, you know that method, correct?"

Lucas nodded as he turned off his flashlight. "It's a basic

method. If they were trying to truly hide their notes, they should've chosen a more difficult code."

Dos shrugged. "I assume this was quick enough for Dr. Guyer's ailing mind. I am trying to find their chosen number now. Sawyer, you can help me decipher these codes while the others assist Annie with her search? If you can find anything regarding some sort of elemental weapon, that would be most helpful."

Vita and Adrian joined Annie while Lucas walked over to the desk where Dos stood. He noticed the unrolled parchments and pointed at one of them. "That's the Sawyer line."

Dos looked up from his work. "So it is. Does it mean anything to you? I found several others, but this one appears to be the most worn, which means it has been read more than the others."

Lucas shrugged, tracing his lineage with a finger. There was a long line of Sawyer men before him, all of them highly respected chiefs. He hoped to make them proud. "The Sawyers are one of the oldest families in Elondohnian history. Did you find anything yet?"

"No. Dr. Guyer wouldn't have just written it down. He would have made it invisible if he could." Dos's eyes glowed red as he held one hand over the pages and emitted heat waves from his palm over the notebook. He flipped through each page and scrutinized it with careful eyes. Then he smiled when a dime-sized number five appeared on the center of the last page. It was written in thermochromic ink. "Ah, there it is. That old man should not have taught me so well."

Dos hurried to a spare piece of paper and dug a pen from the desk's cluttered surface. He quickly wrote the alphabet and then wrote it again, five letters from the first row. The letter A was disguised as the letter F. This would explain the strange jumble of letters on these pages.

"Help me decipher this. This should be H, correct?"

Lucas checked the alphabet and nodded. "Yes. Next letter is I."

Together, they scribbled out messages using the cipher until half of the notebook was written out. As he deciphered the last message, Dos set down his pen. Though his expression was impassive, his skin was pale even in the dark firelight.

Lucas stared dumbly at the notes, and for a moment, wondered if he'd suddenly become illiterate. "Surely, this can't be correct."

"You are at liberty to check again," Dos said, pinching the bridge of his nose.

Lucas read it over again, making sure to check each letter for accuracy.

Code: CDYYZI KMJKCZXT DN FZT

Message: Hidden prophecy is key.

"There *can't* be a hidden prophecy," Lucas said.

"If there is a hidden archives room, why can there not be a hidden prophecy? I have heard rumors, but I never knew whether they've been confirmed. Perhaps Guyer has found it. If so, we will need to find it as well. Assuming it is real."

"But why wouldn't he say anything about it to the elementals?"

"Perhaps that is because of the next message. Look." Dos tapped the next series of letters.

Code: JWNZMQZ Z4

Message: Observe E4

"E4," Lucas said, looking over to the bookshelf where Vita was flipping through a book. "Elemental Four. She is somehow involved in the hidden prophecy."

"That worries me because of the last code we deciphered." Dos's eyebrows twitched in the smallest show of his concern.

Code: V. YVGZ HZOCJY

Message: A. Dale Method

"A. Dale?" Lucas read aloud, a crease forming above his brow. "Why does that sound familiar?"

"Dr. Alfred Dale of Generation 20. He was the lead alchemist at that time." Dos looked at the others. "Have any of you found anything from Dr. Alfred Dale?"

"Oh, yeah." Adrian plucked a red leather book from one of the top shelves. "Dude was nuts. I saw the theories he had about the philosopher's stone."

Dos nodded. "In order to create the stone, he believed the gift of life must be given by a willing sacrifice, specifically by the elementals. Because our blood holds angelic power, we are immune to diseases and experience prolonged life."

"We're immortal?" Annie asked, brightening up.

"No, not immortal. We just tend to live another hundred years or so longer than the average human. We can still be killed, and we have an expiration date. Dr. Dale believed that the blood of the elementals is what will create the stone. When he took pints of blood from the elementals and nothing happened, he waited until they all reproduced and then killed them so that he could take all of their blood. Clearly, that was still unsuccessful."

Vita brought a hand over her mouth. "Oh, that's awful. They died for nothing."

"Why does he matter right now?" Adrian asked.

"Because his theories were still entertained by his students. Some thought that it was not the literal blood they would need, rather the organs, or perhaps the souls trapped inside our bodies. That created the theory that our connection abilities are what fuel the actual stone: the bond between the human body and the angelic soul."

"Is that what y'all found over there?" Vita asked.

"Among other things," Dos said, looking over to the stairs at the sound of gentle thumping.

Lula finally worked up the courage to slink downstairs and prowled across the stone floor toward Lucas. She was probably searching for more food. He'd made the mistake of sharing a piece of his lunch with her once, and ever since, she liked to stay close by.

A booming thump sounded from a few aisles down, where Annie had accidentally dropped a large book. Lula leaped wildly into the air and sprinted upstairs, followed by more crashing sounds from Dr. Guyer's office.

Lucas held his breath and listened closely for any signs of voices. After a few seconds, he released a long sigh and gave Vita a knowing glare. "Silent as a ninja, right?"

She winced. "So, maybe Lula won't come with us next time."

CHAPTER 31

GUARDIAN

The next morning, the elementals were waiting in the training room to run another transmutation when Otis pawed at Lucas and stared up at him with expectant eyes. That was Lucas's cue to take Otis outside for a bathroom break. Vita always brought Otis to training with her, but she couldn't take him outside while she trained, so Lucas had volunteered to do it. It was just as well; he hated being in the room when the transmutation began. He seriously needed to find a way to curb his nausea—it was getting embarrassing.

Lucas walked Otis outside to the back of the laboratory. It had just started raining, so Lucas stayed in the doorway and waited for Otis to go about his business. When the dog was done, he trampled inside and shook the rain off, splattering water all over Lucas.

"Must you be so messy?" Lucas wiped his uniform front and grimaced.

Otis's ears tucked in, his big whale eyes centering on Lucas. Guilt immediately made Lucas's shoulders slump.

"That's not to say you're a bad dog! You're still a good boy, but that wasn't your best moment. Please forgive—" Lucas stopped and closed his eyes for a second when he realized what an idiot he must have looked like. "I'm pleading forgiveness from a dog. I've officially lost my mind. Come on, Otis."

Once back in the training room, Otis shook again and caught Vita's attention. She brightened up.

"Is it raining?"

"Yes, why?" Lucas asked.

Vita grinned. "We have to go outside right now!"

Dr. Wilson looked up from his clipboard with a disgruntled frown. "You haven't even begun the transmutation yet. We cannot start without you."

"I'll be right back, I promise." Vita ran out of the room, not waiting for anyone to convince her otherwise.

"Vita!" Lucas called as she breezed past him. He and Otis jogged after her. "What are you doing?"

"The Earth sings when it rains, and I want to hear it." She pushed open the back doors and ran out. The rain had picked up now and went from a drizzle to full showers of heavy raindrops.

"You'll get drenched!" Lucas groaned. He grabbed an umbrella from the holder by the door, popped it open, and ran after her. Elementals couldn't get sick, but she'd still be freezing, and Vita hated the cold. Otis had no problem. He seemed to love the rain and frolicked about with a wild burst of energy.

Lucas caught up with Vita at the entrance of the garden, where she stood with her head tilted back and a smile on her face. Thankfully, the garden wasn't a far walk from the lab building. He held the umbrella over her, resigned to getting soaked.

"Is it really so important that you had to run out right this moment? Couldn't you have sat by a window?" he griped.

She opened her glowing green eyes and shook her head. "I wanted to feel their music. It hadn't rained since I left home. This is my favorite aspect of my gift, listening to the earth sing to me."

His annoyance melted away as he listened to the awe in her voice. How could she make something as dismal as rain seem so magical? "What does it sound like?"

"They don't use words when they sing, just voices. Each plant sings a little differently, but they're unified, and they believe in every note they sing. It's like they *want* someone to hear their music. It surrounds me, and I swear they're singing just for me. I think this is what angels must sound like. I wish you could hear it." She suddenly realized that Lucas was standing in the rain. "Oh, I'm sorry. Come closer. We can share the umbrella. I just want a minute longer and then I promise we'll go inside."

She looped her arm through his and pressed herself against him so that they could both fit under the umbrella. He was going to argue that it was fine but stopped himself.

It might have been a cool, gloomy day, but she radiated such warmth that he could have sworn he was beneath the sun's light. The gentle weight of her head against his shoulder made him feel like the strongest man alive. This was one of those rare moments that felt like the angels themselves had designed it for him.

As if he was designed for her. He knew in his bones that he had far surpassed a vain crush. Lucas was in love with her, and though it was wrong, he mentally prayed to every angel above that this feeling of falling would stay with him forever.

"It's all right," Lucas said in a soft voice. "We can listen to the rain for as long as you like."

Days without schedules made Lucas anxious. He didn't like having nothing to do because it made him feel useless. Normally, he kept a list of productive activities to accomplish on the weekends. Shine his shoes, study the guardian manual, read through the guardian mission files. But all of these options bored him today. Today, he wanted to see Vita again.

But that was a bad idea. So, when his parents asked if he'd like to join them at the tearoom for brunch, he agreed. The distraction would be good for him.

Or so he thought.

Lucas was listening to Chief retell another story from his youth when he saw Vita and Guardian Ethan James walk in together. Vita was holding a small bundle of flowers that Ethan must have given her, and she laughed at whatever he'd said. They must have been on another date. A pretty waitress led them to a table for two. In Elondoh, a couple only went on a handful of dates before discussing courtship. How many dates had they been on so far?

The waitress took their order, and in that moment, Ethan glanced over to the Sawyer table. He grinned and said something to the waitress, who looked at Lucas, who quickly tore his eyes away. He discreetly peeked over and saw Vita turning red and hissing something at Ethan. The waitress walked over to his table.

"Oh no," Lucas muttered as she approached.

"Pardon me," the waitress said, pushing a lock of blonde hair behind her ears. "I'm sorry to interrupt your meal. I just wanted to offer my introduction to you, Guardian Sawyer. Guardian James mentioned you might have interest in me. I am Isla Peters, House of the Cheetah."

His mother and Chief watched with wide, interested eyes while Lucas just sat there like an idiot. Since his graduation, he'd received around ten introductions but never acted on any of them. Mostly because he didn't have time, but also because he felt too awkward. Now Lucas realized he didn't want their introductions in the first place. Not when his mind stayed on Vita.

Ethan had an almost giddy smile, and Vita watched him with lips pressed thin. It was in that moment that Lucas realized his feelings for her weren't returned. If they were, she wouldn't be with Ethan right now or would have let him send a woman to Lucas. He shouldn't be surprised. Why would someone like Vita, someone with the beauty of angels and the worthiness of knights, want to be with a man as awkward as Lucas?

Isla was still watching him. It was time to dismiss the silly idea of being with Vita and accept someone else. Even if he didn't really want to.

Lucas forced himself to smile at Isla and hold out his hand. "It's a pleasure to meet you, Miss Peters. I am Lucas Sawyer, House of the Lion."

He took her hand and dropped a kiss on the back of it, and her smile grew. He'd never done that before, but he wanted Vita to see that he wasn't a joke. He could be smooth and charming if he wanted to be. He could fit whatever damn role was required of him. He was tired of needing to prove himself in every aspect of his life.

"I hope to see more of you, Guardian Sawyer," Isla said. "I'll let you get back to your meal for now."

Isla left him to attend to another table. Lucas spared a quick glance at Vita's table. Ethan raised his glass in congratulations and grinned. Lucas raised his glass to Ethan and returned the smile. Vita didn't so much as look at him.

CHAPTER 32

GUARDIAN

Vita and Lucas didn't say a word to each other on Monday morning. He picked her up for training, escorted her to the training room, and pretended that he was completely unbothered by the tangible silence between them. He even knew she was angry by the occasional twitching of her nose and how she happily picked at a muffin in front of him without offering one to him like she usually did. He noted with some annoyance that it was strawberry. She knew that to be his favorite.

It's just a silly muffin. It means nothing.

Now, the elementals rehearsed the process for the stone. Dr. Guyer was absent today. Dr. Sawyer reported this morning that he wasn't feeling well and had to be hospitalized, but the elementals were under strict instructions to carry on under Dr. Wilson's supervision. Lucas watched as the materials in the crucible bubbled up and exploded out of the top, narrowly missing Dr. Wilson.

"What in the angels' name?" Dr. Wilson shrieked, slapping his clipboard to the table. "Which one of you lost control?"

The elementals remained silent, avoiding his eyes. Dr. Wilson sighed and raised his chin. "I will ask you one more time. Which one—"

"It was me," Vita snapped. "Sorry."

"Sorry?" Dr. Wilson repeated, aghast. He waved around at

the splattered remains of the sulfur and copper. "You could have seriously injured us because of your carelessness."

"I didn't mean to hurt anyone. I would've healed you."

"Is that after you've burned the flesh clear off my bones?"

"Dr. Wilson," Lucas said, stepping forward. "Perhaps they could break early for lunch. I'm sure she is just hungry."

Vita scowled at him. "You're assuming I lost control because I'm hungry? You don't know a damn thing about me."

Lucas blinked and felt heat rise to his cheeks. "I'm looking out for you."

"I didn't ask you to do that."

He restrained his annoyance and looked to Dos. "Perhaps you could help her?"

"Oh!" Vita huffed. "Now you're dragging Dos into this so you can control me? Guardian Lucas Sawyer just can't *stand* somebody arguing with him, huh?"

Dos held up his hands in surrender and took a step back. His eyes glowed red but he didn't do anything to treat Vita's outburst.

Lucas tried again in a stiffer tone. "You need to calm down."

She stepped up to him with wide, fiery eyes. "Make me."

He didn't know what to do. If she were using her element, he'd snap the bracelet on her. Defuse the situation, maintain safety, avoid casualties. That was what he was taught to do. But to regulate her heightened emotions? He was driving blind, and she knew it.

At his stifling silence, Vita scoffed and pushed past him. The door slammed behind her as she stormed out, and all anyone could do was stare at Lucas, watching for the next move.

Ethan had the nerve to offer a sympathetic smile. "I'll go handle her. Poor thing is probably so embarrassed by her mistake—"

"Are you her guardian?" Lucas snapped, his palms prickling as he balled his fists by his side.

Ethan dropped his smile. "No, sir."

"I didn't think so. You will stay by your elemental's side as you are meant to, and I will take care of Vita. By the way, she is not a problem to be *handled.*" Lucas exhaled through his nose before turning on his heel to follow Vita's path out.

He could almost feel Dos's emotional prodding at the back of his mind when calming emotions watered down his infuriated ones.

Oh, so he thought to treat my emotions but not Vita's? How is that fair?

Lucas stormed out of the laboratory and made his way to the pond. It wasn't a far walk from the lab, and there was plenty of plant life to talk to. He knew Vita would be there.

Sure enough, as he approached her pacing figure, he could hear snippets of her rant to the blue lilies that swayed above the pond's surface.

"I didn't want to feel this way, and yet, there he is! I can't *believe* what a . . . a *prick* he is!"

"It's rude to gossip, you know," Lucas said by way of announcement. When she whirled around and glared at him, he pointed to the flowers. "Even to those who cannot spread it."

She continued her pacing. "Get away from me."

"I can't do that. I need to know why you're so upset."

"Maybe because my guardian is a—"

"A prick? Yes, I gathered that. I think it's funny that you continue to call me names like that when you spent your Saturday morning teasing me in the tearoom."

"Teasing you?"

"Letting Ethan send Isla to me like that. I know how this game works, Vita. I'm not smooth or charming like the other guardians and they like watching me fumble. They have since we were in school. It's bad enough they don't think I can handle being chief, but now they do things like *this* and you just let it happen. I can handle all of them being crass, but you . . ."

You were better than that to me.

He stopped himself and took a deep breath. "I hope I didn't ruin your precious date by proving him wrong."

Vita stopped pacing and stared at him with wide eyes. "That's what this is about? So, you don't even like her? You just did that to prove a point?"

Lucas shrugged. "She is beautiful. She was born and raised in Elondoh. What's not to like?"

"That's what you look for? A proper Elondohnian girl with a good family? You're not even gonna ask what's important to her?"

"That's what dates are for, remember?"

"Oh!" Vita grunted. "I told Ethan up and down how rude it was to poke fun like that, but there you are acting like it's all just a game! Giving that girl false hope like that. She's probably waiting up all night thinking about you, and here you are pretending like she means nothing. Bet you feel real good about yourself now. It turns out you're just like every other idiot guy."

He blinked as guilt washed over him. He hadn't thought about how Isla might feel about the interaction and he certainly didn't expect that Vita had reprimanded Ethan for it. "Is that why you're upset?"

"A lot of things upset me about this stupid place, but you make it worse. You *always* make it worse."

"Oh, do I? I'm trying my best, but have you ever considered that maybe your unbearable wildness is making it impossible for me to do my job? You act so pleasantly with Guardians Hogan and James; would you rather have them instead?"

"Is that what you want? You want to get rid of me?" Vita

stepped up to him, tears pooling in her furious eyes. "We might as well tear up our stupid pact and forget all about you and me!"

"I would love nothing more!" he shouted back. "I would much rather spend my time with someone who isn't so argumentative. You know, I don't even pursue the introductions I've received because I am constantly wasting my time with you."

"Wasting?" Her tears slid out, and his heart broke at the sight of them. She quickly swiped them away and continued to glare at him. "You obviously hate me, so fix me up with Hogan or whatever. I don't care."

He didn't hate her. He could never hate her. But she looked at him with such an unforgiving light, and he couldn't take it anymore. The constant battle between his feelings for her and the importance of his duty. The arguing and then the desire to make her smile. The need to prove that he was strong, and then the gut-wrenching guilt that came with seeing her cry. It was too much. If there was a problem that kept getting worse, it was best to step back until the emotions could settle themselves and a clear solution came to mind. It was what a good chief would do.

So, he swallowed the lump in his throat and nodded. "Fine. I'll do the paperwork during lunch, and you'll have a new guardian in the morning. It'll be best for both of us."

Vita hugged her elbows and chewed on her lower lip, her lashes coated with tears. There was nothing to say or do now. He didn't like seeing her cry, and he hated even more that he was the cause.

Luckily, he kept tissues in his pocket for moments like this and handed one to her. She watched him with a confused glare as she accepted it and wordlessly dabbed at her eyes.

Hogan came jogging out to them. "Sawyer! Vita is needed in the hospital right away. Dr. Guyer is . . ." He stopped and gasped out the next words. "They say he is dying."

CHAPTER 33

GUARDIAN

Lucas quickly escorted Vita to the hospital, where they were immediately greeted by nurses who brought them to Dr. Guyer's room. His mother was operating some kind of heart monitor, her lips pressed thin as she worked. Dr. Novak sat in a corner of the room with a clipboard and pen. Dr. Guyer lay in bed and looked . . . like death itself.

It was terrifying to see such an esteemed man lying down, so sick like this. His skin had a yellow tint to it, dark half-moons beneath his eyes, and his veins practically bulged beneath his paper-thin skin. He was incoherent and barely opened his eyes when Vita and Lucas walked in.

Vita brought a hand over her heart, eyebrows creased upward. Dr. Guyer held up a shaking hand toward her and tried to say her name only to enter a coughing fit. Blood splattered on his lips as he took a rasping gulp of air. Vita ran forward and took his hand.

"It'll be over soon," Vita promised. "I'll fix it."

"Hold on," Dr. Sawyer said. "I'm going to give you a dose of your vitamin injection first. You'll have to give a lot. Have you had lunch yet?"

Lucas shook his head. "She hasn't eaten yet. Is Mrs. Eastwood aware of this?"

"Yes, and she was adamant that Vita shouldn't heal him." Dr. Sawyer placed a hand on Vita's arm. "It's up to you. You can decide to not heal him."

"I'll never leave someone in this much pain." Vita's eyes started to glow green. "Whatever happens, don't make me take from the trees. To take this much energy from them will kill them."

"You can't give that much," Lucas said. "I think you should wait."

"You're not my guardian anymore, remember?" she said, sparing him a quick glare. "I don't have to do what you say, and I can't leave him like this."

Dr. Sawyer hurried out of the room to get Vita's injection. Vita closed her eyes and let her healing begin.

Lucas watched in awe as Dr. Guyer's skin flushed with color. The veins in his skin diminished, the wrinkles and spots disappeared, and his posture straightened. Even his white hair filled in more. Dr. Guyer released a sigh of relief. He closed his eyes while he received his healing. No doubt, he was feeling that high of Vita's spirit.

Vita, however, looked progressively worse. Her eyelids drooped slightly in weariness, and her curls wilted like dying flower petals.

"Vita," Lucas said. "I think that's enough."

"Do not interrupt her, Guardian Sawyer," Dr. Novak snapped.

"She is exhausted, look at her!"

"I'm fine," Vita said through gritted teeth. "I've almost got it. It's . . . it's unlike anything I've ever seen before. I think it's alive."

A commotion of shouts broke out from the lobby and prevented Lucas from asking what Vita meant by 'alive'. He poked his head out and saw June arguing with a pair of guardians who were blocking the corridor.

"Don't touch me!" June shouted as the guardians grabbed her by the arms. "My daughter is in there!"

"Let her through!" Lucas demanded as he stepped into the hall.

"Under whose authority?" grunted one of the guardians.

Lucas straightened his posture and tapped his lion pin. "Under Guardian Lucas Sawyer's authority. If you've got an issue with it, take it to Chief Sawyer. Mrs. Eastwood, come in. I'll bring you to Vita."

June sneered once more at the guardians before shoving past them and following Lucas down the hall to Guyer's room. June immediately gasped at Vita's weak state.

"She's given too much," she said, hurrying toward Vita.

Dr. Novak stepped in the way, her tall figure glowering down at June. "Do not interrupt her. You will ruin everything."

"You move out of my way, Winifred, or I'll move you myself."

"Do you always have to be so emotional?" Dr. Novak hissed. "This is bigger than your silly feelings."

"You mean my feelings of being a mother? Maybe you should try it sometime."

Lucas had only a moment to admire June's tenacity, realizing where Vita got hers from, before he stepped between them. "Let's not lose ourselves here."

Dr. Sawyer ran in with a small case in her hand and observed the tense room with a deep sigh. Vita grunted, then released Dr. Guyer's hands and fell to her knees.

Lucas surged forward, catching Vita before her head could hit the tile floor. She lay completely limp in his arms, eyes closed, sweat glistening on her skin.

"Vita?" Lucas asked, heart racing as he lightly shook her. "Angels. Mom, she's not waking up."

June and Dr. Sawyer rushed to his side. Dr. Novak stood by Dr. Guyer's bedside and scrutinized Lucas. Dr. Sawyer pulled a syringe out of her case and, with trained hands, gave Vita a vitamin injection.

"We have to bring her to a tree," June said frantically. "Your vitamins won't be enough."

"We can't. Vita asked us not to. She didn't want to hurt the trees." Dr. Sawyer said. Then she checked on Dr. Guyer. "Sir, how do you feel?"

"It doesn't matter how he feels!" June roared, waving at hand at Vita. "Look at what he's done to her. As far as I'm concerned, Guyer can die in a ditch."

"June," Dr. Sawyer said in a warning tone. "Careful. Don't make this worse for her. I'm sorry, but I have to follow Vita's latest request."

"Did it work?" Dr. Guyer asked, clearly still reeling from Vita's high. "Was there a reaction?"

"No," Dr. Novak answered quickly. "Do not speak, sir. You are still recovering."

Reaction? But that didn't make any sense. What reaction could Dr. Guyer want to get from Vita? Perhaps an angelic one? But that would be catastrophic.

"We should get Vita home," Lucas Lucas suggested. "She'll need rest."

"Yes, that's a good idea," Dr. Sawyer sighed. "Take her home and stay by her side until she wakes."

June clearly didn't like the idea of Lucas staying, but she nodded anyway. Lucas carefully lifted Vita and followed June out.

Once they were outside and away from any prying ears, Lucas spoke up again. "Mrs. Eastwood? We can take her to a tree to heal. I won't tell anyone."

June stopped walking and faced him with a scrutinizing look. "That goes directly against your mother's orders. You would have to lie if they asked about it."

"I know."

"You could lose chiefhood for lying."

He nodded as he stared at Vita. She looked so serene when she slept, with her head leaning against his chest. What if she'd given too much of herself to heal Dr. Guyer, and the last thing she would remember Lucas saying to her was that she was a waste of his time? What if the last emotion that she felt was the anger that Lucas had given her? Angels, what was wrong with him?

"I know," Lucas repeated in a softer voice. "But if there's a chance at saving Vita, then it's worth it."

June's eyebrows creased upward the way Vita's always did when she tried not to cry. "Let's hurry, we have to find a strong enough tree."

Lucas checked over his shoulder once more to make sure no one was watching, and then he hurried after June.

CHAPTER 34

EARTH

Vita woke up to the sight of the paper flowers and fairy lights she'd pinned to her ceiling. Otis and Lula snuggled close to her, keeping her warm. Her throat was unbearably dry, and her body was weak. Groaning, she sat up and rubbed her eyes.

Lucas appeared at her side, wearing a worried grimace. "How are you feeling?"

"I . . ." She cleared her throat and blinked away the grogginess. "I feel like I just got hit by a truck."

A memory resurfaced of a pearlescent white cloud blocking Dr. Guyer's heart and lungs. It had been strange because most diseases appeared as inky black clouds, and Vita would always know the name of the disease just by looking at it. But she'd never seen anything like this before, and it had felt . . . violent. Alive and parasitic.

Vita had pulled on that white cloud until it was mostly gone. There was just one spot that clung to Dr. Guyer's lungs with everything it had, like an oil stain on fabric. Vita's last memory was that cloud slipping away before she passed out.

"I . . . didn't completely heal Dr. Guyer. I've got to get back to him." Vita tried to sit up.

"No, no. Stay down," Lucas insisted. "You healed him enough for now. No more. Are *you* okay?"

"I think so. I just feel weak."

"Your mother is making dinner now, so you can eat soon. We tried taking you to a tree, but for some reason it wouldn't heal you."

"What? Lucas, how could you? I told you that it's hard for them to restore!"

"What else was I to do?" Lucas demanded. "You weren't waking up. I was afraid."

Vita's anger died off on her tongue. "You were?"

"Yes," he answered. "I don't want you to do that again. I don't want you to sacrifice yourself. Not for anyone."

After all that fighting, did he still care? Oh, Vita couldn't stand how much it made her heart flutter. She thought he was handsome from the moment they'd met in that plant nursery, but ever since then, she told herself that she *wouldn't* like him. But then beneath the rain, she knew she'd fallen for him. It was the first time that touching someone felt so right.

In between the arguing, the stiffness, and the obsession with his schedule, he was kind, passionate, and selfless. She liked that he was more balanced than she was. She liked that he fought back a little, unlike all the other boys who agreed with whatever she said because she had a pretty smile.

But Vita knew that Lucas would never be with a girl like her, he practically said it himself. His duty and future demanded it of him.Either way, it didn't matter. Lucas would choose Elondoh before he chose her. But it still broke her heart that he didn't want to be her guardian anymore. Did he really hate her?

Vita almost worked up the courage to ask, but Otis nudged his head against her arm.

"What is it, Oty?"

Otis merely watched her and whined. Lula meowed and pawed gently at Vita's knee.

"What is it?" Vita repeated. "Why can't I hear y'all talk?"

"Your eyes aren't glowing," Lucas pointed out. "Usually, your eyes glow when you talk to them. Is there something wrong with your abilities?"

"What? Don't be silly, I can still feel them. Come on, y'all, speak. What's wrong?"

Both animals stared at her with dismay in their glassy eyes.

Vita shook her head. "No, no, no . . . what's happening?"

She kicked off the comforter and pushed past Lucas, stumbling into the succulent on her vanity.

"Vita, be careful," Lucas called, steadying her.

Vita ignored him and picked up the little teacup. Bo had a sweet, tiny voice, and she just noticed that he hadn't said a word since she woke up. "Bo? Can you hear me?"

Silence. The most aching, painful, violent silence that Vita had ever known.

"*Bo?*" she cried, the air becoming thin around her. "Bo, please say something!"

No answer.

"Just sit for a second," Lucas tried. When Vita dropped to her knees, he called out, "Mrs. Eastwood!"

Pain erupted from Vita's chest as she called the names of all her beloved friends. All the plants, the trees, Otis, and Lula. No one answered her. She was . . . alone.

No, not alone. It was as if her very spirit ceased to exist. As if life itself continued to move on without her. What was life if not the opportunity to dance with the animals and listen to the song of the flowers? How was someone meant to survive without doing the one thing that formed their very soul?

"Please . . . say something. Please don't leave me alone," Vita sobbed, shaking as if caught in the dead of winter without a coat.

Vita wasn't ready to face the silence of the world. She couldn't face the horrible secrets hidden in the burrows of loneliness. She lived her entire life hearing the earth sing to her, and now that was gone. She never even knew she was afraid of such a thing, but now the very thought of facing it all by herself squeezed the air from her lungs.

She felt . . . meaningless.

Lucas was at her side, arms around her as she sobbed into his shoulder. The crushing weight of desperation sank in faster than she could handle.

Vita fell apart. June slid in front and cradled her head in her arms. Vita couldn't even look her mother in the eyes. She simply shook her head and folded in to herself.

"Her abilities," Lucas started quietly. "They're gone."

CHAPTER 35

GUARDIAN

"She'll be okay." Dr. Sawyer stepped out of Vita's room and closed the door behind her. "We've seen rare cases like this before ... with her ancestors."

"You have?" Lucas asked, just as nervous as June, who had been pacing the hall until Dr. Sawyer returned.

"Yes. During war or plague times, which required a lot of healing. The strain on her abilities was simply too much. She says she can still feel them, but they aren't responding. Believe it or not, that's a good sign. It means she still has them. She'll need to rebuild herself and get plenty of rest. They should come back on their own."

"When?" June wrung her hands.

"There's no telling. History shows that sometimes it ranges from a few hours to a few months. The longest documented was a year, but that hasn't been since the Spanish Flu."

"Months?" June repeated in dismay. "Oh, my poor Vita. What am I going to do?"

Dr. Sawyer took June's hand and lowered her voice. "I just gave her a sedative to help with the hysteria, so she'll be asleep soon. You need to keep an eye on her. You remember what happened to Winifred. I don't recommend leaving her out of your sight for too long, understand?"

June's eyes watered. "You don't really think . . . she's such a happy girl . . ."

"I'm not saying she would go that far. There's still so much hope for her. She's healthy with grit like her father. She'll recover eventually, but with the heightened emotions of Earth elementals and the pain of losing an ability . . . we need to be careful. Lucas will help keep an eye on her."

June gave Lucas a sad yet grateful smile. "You really came through for my little Vita. Thank you, honey."

Lucas simply nodded. He wanted June to warm up to him but not at Vita's expense. He'd face a thousand years of cold glares if he could reverse what happened to her.

"Lucas?" Vita called from the other side of her door.

He slid past the two mothers before poking his head into Vita's room. She lay in bed, eyes blinking heavily from the sedative. She wasn't crying anymore, which was a good sign.

"Oh good," she mumbled. "You're still here."

"I'm here." He walked over and sat on the edge of her bed. "My mother says your abilities will come back with time."

"Yeah, she told me. Look, I know you said you wanted to spend your time somewhere else, but . . . do you think you could be my guardian until my abilities come back? I feel safer with you around."

He took her hand in both of his and nodded. "I will always be your guardian. I'm sorry about what I said earlier. I didn't mean any of it. I was just . . . well, it doesn't matter how I felt. What I said was wrong. I don't want to argue with you anymore."

She offered a tired smile. "Me neither. I don't want you to hate me."

"Don't be silly. I could never hate you."

"Do you think we can start over? You and me?"

"You and me."

Otis snuggled up to Vita's side, and Lula curled up next to her head on the pillow. Lucas waited until Vita fully fell asleep and her grip loosened on his hand. He gently laid her hand down and stood up to leave. His mother and June watched the entire interaction from outside the room and were exchanging surprised looks with each other. He ignored them and closed Vita's door behind him.

After June assured them that she wouldn't need anything else, Lucas and Dr. Sawyer walked out, a heavy weight on their shoulders.

"Mom," Lucas said, exhausted from the day's events. "After Dr. Novak lost her abilities, what did she do that makes you so afraid for Vita?"

His mother was silent for a moment before she sighed heavily. "She tried to kill herself."

The next day, Lucas entered the training hall alone. Vita's usual humming and chatter had become such an ordinary part of his day that its absence was unbearable. His world was so eerily still without her. He could only imagine how empty she felt.

Ethan straightened up per usual when Lucas walked in, then sagged a little when he didn't see Vita follow. Lucas ignored his curious look, took his usual post by the door, and looked straight ahead.

Hogan walked in with Annie by his side. He was usually so quiet that he could easily be forgotten. But today, he was animatedly talking with her

"You really think that will work?" Hogan asked.

"Oh yeah. Chicks dig that kind of stuff," Annie assured with a smile.

"I'll have to think it over. Thank you." Hogan then took his post at the wall opposite Lucas.

Annie, Dos, and Adrian looked at Lucas and then each other.

"Where's Vita?" Annie asked first.

Lucas wasn't sure if he should be the one to explain it. He simply said, "She's home, sick."

"Sick?" Dos echoed skeptically. "We do not get sick. Our elements protect us from disease."

"Is she okay?" Adrian asked.

"She will be," Lucas answered firmly.

When he saw her this morning, she had lain in bed, refusing to speak with him. June had reported that it was impossible to get Vita to eat. It was partially why Lucas had been late this morning. He'd refused to leave until Vita had eaten a few bites of food. For a girl with such a large appetite, he was hoping for more but accepted this as progress.

Dr. Wilson entered the room with Dr. Guyer in tow. For the first time in Lucas's life, he watched Dr. Guyer walk without a cane. He strode into the room with a renewed vibrance in his step and a brilliant smile.

Anger twinged in Lucas's gut. How dare Dr. Guyer smile while Vita lay heartbroken. How dare he force Vita into such a horrible position. How could anyone feel joy about diminishing such a bright spirit? Surely, he must have known what would happen to her.

Dos and Annie took one look at Dr. Guyer before they widened their eyes at Lucas. He wished there were an emotion that said, *I should have listened to you.* Perhaps, regret.

Dos looked down with that unreadable mask. He'd received the message.

"Good morning, all!" Dr. Guyer chirped, clapping his hands together.

"Good morning, Dr. Guyer," the guardians greeted.

"I know you must have noticed we are missing our dear Vita," Dr. Guyer started with an empathetic frown. "She insisted on selflessly healing me, as she was terribly worried about my health. Although I am not yet cured, she managed to take most of my illness away at a great cost to herself. Due to the strain that she endured, her abilities have been temporarily subdued. She is at home recuperating until they return."

The elementals collectively sucked in a breath, horror masking their features.

"She can't use her abilities?" Adrian asked.

"Unfortunately, no."

"But . . . could the plants not heal her?" Dos wondered.

"They could not. That is a feature of her abilities, and therefore unavailable to her once she healed me."

"So, she can't talk to her friends?" Annie sighed and shook her head. "God, she must be devastated."

"Well, a good person to ask would be her guardian. Guardian Sawyer, you saw her this morning, correct? How was she?" Dr. Guyer asked.

Discomfort built in Lucas's back as all eyes turned expectantly to him.

Lucas cleared his throat. "Well, she seems all right physically, though she's a bit weak."

"But how is she?" Annie pressed. "Honestly."

"Honestly?" Lucas repeated in a sigh. "Devastated just about covers it. She has trouble sleeping and eating. She won't leave her bedroom. It's like she gave up on herself."

"That is because our abilities are who we are," Dos said, his eyes glowing. "It is not merely a fun attribute to us. It is the very essence of our souls. The angel gave us our abilities, yes, but his blood only enhanced what was already inside us. Imagine if everything you love had been stolen from you. Then multiply that pain by a hundredfold. Vita is an Earth elemental and feels every emotion with severe intensity. It is a despair that humans cannot fathom."

Lucas met Dos's eyes. "Can you feel it from her? Even from here?"

"I feel an emptiness. Much like a deep cavern."

"Can you reduce it at all?"

"I wish I could. But unfortunately, her emotions are too strong right now. Powerful emotions such as depression or rage are more difficult to manipulate, and with Vita's heightened emotional range . . . it is nearly impossible for me. If she were to calm down some, I could, but she is at the peak of her despair. There is not much I can do. I really am sorry, Guardian Sawyer."

The elementals all collectively looked miserable for her. Even Hogan seemed disappointed. Vita had worked hard to befriend him, bringing him fruit and flowers for his home, and had made him more comfortable with the elementals.

"This is an unfortunate event," Dr. Guyer said. "But we all know Vita to be a strong young lady, so I have high hopes for her. Of course, we are doing everything we can to ensure her recovery. I feel terribly guilty. If only we could go back in time and reverse the damage done to her. I'd give anything."

Sure, you would.

"Is there anything we can do?" Hogan asked.

"Why don't we take a half day today?" Dr. Guyer suggested. "You can pay her a visit when we're done. Dr. Wilson, we can take this day to discuss the upcoming festival with everyone."

"What's there to discuss?" Annie asked. "We're doing some kind of stupid talent show and leaving, right?"

"That's at the end of the night, during the dance," Dr. Wilson answered. "The festival is a full-day event. There's the tournament, games, and there's a strong chance you might be approached by potential suitors to carry on the elemental line."

"You want me to get with the people here?" Annie pointedly looked at Guardian Boyd and faked a gag.

Boyd scowled at her and said nothing.

"There are just a few details to go over," Dr. Wilson continued. "First, Adrian, what is your talent?"

"Um ... football?" Adrian offered.

"No, no. An *artistic* talent. You *do* have one, correct?"

"Um, yeah, but ..." He scratched the back of his head. "It's kind of lame. I don't play an instrument or anything like that."

"What is it you do?"

Adrian sighed and shyly muttered, "Origami."

Annie snorted. "No way. Mr. All-American folds paper into cute little shapes?"

"It's relaxing," Adrian defended. "Let me show you. Anyone got a dollar I can use?"

Lucas raised an eyebrow but pulled out his wallet and handed Adrian a one-dollar bill.

"Thanks, bud. Here, y'all watch this, it'll blow your mind." Adrian proceeded to fold the dollar in several ways until he held it up in the shape of a heart. "Ha! I learned how to do this when I asked my girl to prom. I folded a bunch of money to pay for her nail appointment. Cool, huh?"

Lucas was impressed, but it seemed no one else thought it was enough.

Adrian sensed that as well. "I can do elephants too. Here, give me another dollar."

Lucas gave him another and watched in amusement as Adrian folded it until he produced a tiny elephant. "Look at that! What do you think?"

Dr. Wilson pinched the bridge of his nose and slowly exhaled. "I suppose that will do on such short notice. Let's move on to attire and behavior."

CHAPTER 36

WATER

The elementals were given half an hour in the training room to start planning their artistic displays for the festival. Annie set up an easel and took over an entire table with paint supplies, Dos looked through sheet music for him and Vita, and Adrian had been given a stack of colorful paper and an origami book that the guardians had probably dug out of the children's library.

Dr. Guyer sat at his desk, reading through an old journal while Dr. Wilson argued with Annie over what would or would not be an appropriate painting. From the sound of it, Annie was losing this debate.

Adrian always liked origami. It was easy to let his mind rest while he went through the motions, and he could practice it anywhere so long as he had paper. He'd been caught plenty of times folding paper on the sidelines of a football game until it was his time to play. His coaches always had a stack of scrap paper on hand for him because they realized he always thought better while he was folding away.

"Can you do otters?" Hogan asked Adrian.

"I thought your house animal was a rabbit?"

"It is, but there's someone I'd like to attract that's from House of the Otter."

"Ah. Well, I'm a sucker for love, so let's see." Adrian thumbed through the little book until he found an otter. "Um, I can try? Fair warning, it might look more like a boat than a . . ."

He drifted off as thoughts started trickling in his mind. Dr. Guyer's thoughts.

The hidden prophecy . . . no one can know . . .

"Adrian?" Hogan said, observing his glowing blue eyes. "You're not reading my thoughts right now, are you?"

"No. Pretend you're talking to me."

"I am talking to you." Hogan shrugged and started chattering about random things that Adrian wasn't really listening to. On the outside, Guyer was reading through some charts at his desk, but on the inside he was panicking.

I cannot allow anyone to find it . . . It is hidden in my desk in the archives room. Burn the documents to be safe. It will have to wait until after the tournament practice . . .

Adrian tuned back to Hogan's conversation.

"Once that couple decides to start courting, she'll wear a charm with the man's house animal to represent her loyalty to him. My mother has rabbit earrings and—"

"What are you talking about?" Adrian cut in, eyes fading back to their mossy green.

"Oh," Hogan blinked. "Well, you said to pretend like I'm talking to you, so I started talking about our courting rituals. It's been on my mind a lot. Were you able to do what you needed to do?"

"Yeah. I'll be back." Adrian left his table and hurried over to Dos, who was sitting in a corner with a neat pile of sheet music beside him. "Hey, tell me about that prophecy thing again. What did that old alchemist say about us?"

Dos rattled it off like second nature. "Beware the children of this day for they shall change humanity forever. They will mirror Generation 6 and wield powers of the mind."

Adrian lowered his voice so only Dos could hear. "I was just in Guyer's mind. He confirmed a hidden prophecy exists."

Dos finally looked up. "So, it really is true then. One can never be sure when it comes to these rumors. Many alchemical legends are myths, created by alchemists to distract enemies from the truth. John Dee himself created entire codes to keep his work secret. Signed his documents with *007* to let his apprentices know that the document held truth."

Adrian blinked. "I'm sorry, did you just reference James Bond?"

"Who?"

"James Bond. Super suave British spy. The notorious double-O seven?"

"I have no idea what you are referring to. John Dee created the code 007 during his work as a spy for Queen Elizabeth. The zeros were meant to be watchful eyes, and the seven was to bring good fortune, as it was considered a lucky number. Anyway, many of his documents were damaged or plundered. Historians are still trying to sort out the truth of whatever was left. His prophecies were damaged, so there was a rumor that we do not have the completed works. As a matter of fact, our generation, twenty-three, was the last written prophecy he'd made before he died. Guardian Sawyer and I discovered that Dr. Guyer suspected a hidden prophecy, but we did not confirm whether he found it."

"Guyer said, or thought, that he couldn't allow anyone to find it," Adrian said. "He's gonna clean out his desk after some tournament practice."

"Angels, that's this weekend. All the competitors for the tournament are gathering for sparring practice. It will be so busy that nobody will notice if Dr. Guyer is missing."

Boyd walked over to them with his hands clasped behind his back. "What are you two talking about?"

"This poor selection of sheet music." Dos answered. "It is all trivial, children play this. If you expect myself and Vita to deliver a noteworthy performance, I will need something better. I have yet to see a single Vivaldi piece in this mix."

Boyd had a hint of a sneer. "Is this true, Adrian?"

Adrian nodded. "Yeah, man. I bet even I could play this stuff."

"Guardian Boyd," Dos said. "I believe there is another box of sheet music in the library. It would be very helpful if you could get it for me."

"I am not a delivery boy," Boyd snapped.

"Guardian Boyd," Dr. Guyer sighed from his desk. "On your way back from the library, you can bring me John Dee's book of the Enochian language. Thank you."

Boyd pressed his lips thin and shot a glare at Dos before leaving the room.

"I thought you took some oath of honesty?" Adrian asked Dos.

"Dr. Guyer took the same oath when he became the leader of Elondoh, and yet, here we are. We will go to the archives room tonight," Dos whispered to Adrian. "Tell the others via thoughts. Perhaps leave Vita out of this. She will need more time to recover."

"Right." Adrian left Dos and sat back down at his table that was littered with colorful origami paper. He tuned in to Annie's mind to tell her about the plans, but instead found that she was thinking about Dos.

Interesting. He'd just come back to her later. For now, he dove into Sawyer's mind and found that he was thinking about Vita.

Well, what the hell? Adrian thought. *Am I supposed to play Cupid or something?*

Lucas physically jolted in his spot and glared at Adrian. *Will you at least warn me before you go into my head like that?*

Oops. Sorry, I thought I was already out. Party at the archives room tonight.

Lucas spared a glimpse at Guyer before nodding once in response. Adrian delivered the same message to Annie, then checked in on Vita.

Hey. Heard the news. You feeling okay?

She didn't respond. Adrian dipped fully into her mind until he could see through her eyes. She was sitting in bed, staring at a small succulent in a little blue teacup. There was a forgotten plate of food at her bedside table, a glass of water that hadn't been touched, and a book that she hadn't felt like opening. She really was just giving up on herself.

Adrian conjured a recent memory to send over to her. The elementals and their guardians had all sat outside for lunch, and Vita was telling them a funny story from her childhood. The story itself didn't matter; it was the joy she had at making everyone around her laugh. He played that memory in her head and felt her lighten just a bit.

Hang in there, Adrian said. *We're rooting for you.*

Vita didn't say it, but he could feel her desire to say thank you. He slipped out of her mind and went back to folding his paper.

CHAPTER 37

AIR

Annie stepped off her balcony and floated down, using her air abilities to offer just enough wind resistance that she wouldn't simply plummet. Dos waited for her in the shadows of the night with only his glowing red eyes to give him away. Once Annie landed, she walked up to him and smirked.

"Hey, hothead. Ready?"

He nodded and motioned down their path. "You are always happier when you fly. Do you prefer it to walking?"

"There's a certain freedom that comes with flying. When I'm in the air, there's nothing to hold me down. Nothing to hurt me. I'm a cloud or a bird or even a gust of wind. I come and go wherever I want. I'm *really* free. Can't get that from being trapped on the ground. Doesn't using your element ever feel that way for you?"

"I cannot use my element for recreational use. It might hurt someone. But there are moments when I use it for good, and it makes me more appreciative of it. This morning before training, I took a walk through the park, and I saw a little girl fall and start to cry. She was not really hurt; she was just scared. I sent her some happiness, and she got back up and continued playing with her friends."

"Did that make you feel free?"

"It made me realize that I may not be as naturally cruel as I once believed I should be. So, yes. I suppose I did feel a bit freer than usual."

Annie smiled and nudged him. "Cool. Is Adrian going to meet us there?"

"Yes. He and Guardian Sawyer are ahead of us."

Once at the lab, they met up with Adrian and Sawyer, and hurried down to the archives room. It was going to take a few more visits before this place didn't give Annie the creeps. Were there spiders down here? She hoped not. It was damn near impossible to keep up a bravado when one of those eight-legged hairy monsters crawled near her.

Now, Annie emptied a desk drawer and sorted through its documents. Most of them looked like recipes for different elixirs. There were two other drawers on the desk that Adrian and Dos were going through while Sawyer sorted through the piles on top of Dr. Guyer's desk.

"I'm not finding anything," Annie said with an irritated sigh, putting her papers back. "Adrian, are you sure you heard Dr. Guyer say it was on his desk?"

Adrian huffed, probably because this was the third time she'd asked him tonight. "His exact words were that it was hidden in his desk. He didn't exactly give me a location."

"Well, can't you dig into his mind and find out?"

"I can't, he's sleeping. I'll only find whatever he's dreaming about."

"This is pointless. We're not finding anything. I bet you heard him wrong, meathead."

"I'm sorry, Airhead Annie, maybe next time *you* should dig into the dude's mind and find all the answers yourself!"

"Enough, you two," Sawyer cut in.

"Look who's talking." Annie shoved the drawer back into the tracks of the desk. Something must have gotten stuck because the drawer wouldn't slide all the way in.

"Yeah, you're the one who's always fighting with Vita," Adrian said to Sawyer. "And now you're getting on our case for arguing?"

Annie slid the drawer out and tried again, shoving it in harder but once again coming up short. She grunted in frustration and tried it again with a little more force.

"We don't fight anymore," Sawyer argued. Then he rolled his eyes at Annie. "Will you stop that? You'll break the whole desk."

"The stupid thing is stuck!" Annie pulled out the drawer, haphazardly dropping it on the stone floor, and felt inside the empty space for whatever was sticking out. She found purchase on a small circular item, about half the width of her palm. She pulled it out and frowned. It was a wooden coin with some weird symbol carved into it. It looked like a squished version of the horseshoe-shaped omega symbol.

"The hell is this thing?"

Dos looked up from his papers and creased his eyebrows. He took the coin from her and ran his thumb over the carving. "This is an Enochian symbol for *Mals*. In our language, it translates to the letter *P*. John Dee and Edward Kelley created the Enochian language and claimed it was the language of the angels. That's how we got the name for Elondoh."

"*Elo* meaning 'first' and *Londoh* meaning 'kingdom,' " Sawyer added.

"No one speaks it anymore. Where did you find this?" Dos asked.

Annie waved to the desk. "It was stuck in there."

Dos's eyes suddenly lit up with discovery. "Dr. Guyer did not say the prophecy was *on* his desk . . . he said it was *in* it."

He crawled under the desk and lay flat on his back. "Aha!"

Annie exchanged a bizarre look with Sawyer and Adrian before lying next to Dos and cursing under her breath. The underside of the desk was carved with weird symbols, leaving one empty space in the middle of what might be a sentence.

Dos ran his finger across the symbols and muttered to himself.

"You can read this? What does it say?" Annie asked.

"No one taught me how to read Enochian, as I am not meant to know. But I have spent enough time reading these books that I've managed to pick up a few phrases. This is the name of an elixir famed for granting Dr. John Dee the supposed ability to speak to the angels. This should go right here . . ."

Dos slid the coin into the circular spot and pressed it in. A series of clicks sounded right before the underside of the desk dropped by an inch and released a cloud of sawdust. Dos and Annie squeezed their eyes shut, turning their faces inward to avoid catching any debris in their eyes.

Annie blinked away dust, smiling when she saw half of Dos's face covered in sawdust. They were already squished together under the desk, but now their faces were inches apart.

"Careful," she teased, gently brushing the dust off his face. "You might start a fire down here."

Dos could somehow master never revealing his emotions, but he couldn't seem to help the brilliant blush that crawled up his cheeks when she touched him. Had he ever been touched by a girl before? With lips like those, how could anyone resist him?

"Angels above!" Sawyer shouted. "It's here. We found the prophecy!"

Annie rolled her eyes, and she and Dos started to scoot out. "You're welcome."

They all marveled at the new compartment that had popped out of the top of the desk. Sawyer pulled out a small scrap of parchment and unrolled it. Annie stood on the other side of Sawyer and read the writing out loud.

"'The fourteenth son shall mend the divide between man and the heavens. His power has never been seen before, and his might is unmatched. He will vanquish the gatekeeper. For immortality to be attained, the breath of life must be paid.'"

CHAPTER 38

GUARDIAN

"It can never be simple, can it?" Lucas groaned rubbing his forehead. "There *must* be one mystery after another. It's as if the angels are playing a terrible trick on us. Are we sure this is the right prophecy?"

"Do you see any other prophecies lying around?" Dos sighed, rereading the paper. "It is in John Dee's own handwriting, and it would explain why the rest of the prophecy was torn on the bottom. Look." Dos pointed to a small scribbling of the numbers 007.

"It's the James Bond thing!" Adrian exclaimed.

"It is the John Dee thing," Dos corrected. "It means that it is authentically his work. Someone must have ripped it free."

"Obviously Dr. Guyer," Annie said.

"Yeah, but why?" Adrian asked. "Who's the fourteenth son, and what's he got to do with us?"

Dos rubbed his chin in thought. "We have a few things to figure out. Who is the fourteenth son, what power does he wield, and who is the gatekeeper? Obviously, the last line refers to the philosopher's stone. I believe the fourteenth son is a reference to a potential fifth elemental. That would explain Dr. Guyer and Novak discussing *V.* The Roman numeral for five."

"A fifth elemental? But that isn't . . ." Lucas was going to say it wasn't possible, but based on his most recent discoveries, maybe he didn't know what was impossible anymore. He shook his head.

"Let's make a written list. I think better when it is all written down."

Dos pulled out a pen and notebook from his book bag, then flipped to an empty page, where he wrote out a list and the entire prophecy.

Beware the children of this day, for they shall change humanity forever. They will mirror Generation 6 and wield powers of the mind. The fourteenth son shall mend the divide between man and the heavens. His power has never been seen before and his might is unmatched. He will vanquish the gatekeeper. For immortality to be attained, the breath of life must be paid.

Then he circled the last sentence and read it out loud again.

"'For immortality to be attained, the breath of life must be paid.'" He looked at Lucas. "That sounds like it should mean something to me, but I cannot recall why."

Lucas shrugged. "It sounds like a complicated way of saying that the stone brings eternal life."

Dos tapped his chin with his pen as he looked over the prophecy. He murmured to himself as if getting closer to the solution. "Breath of life . . . breath of life . . ."

"You don't think that means we'll have to sacrifice ourselves for the stone, right?" Annie asked with a shiver. "No offense to humanity, but I don't care enough about it to kick the bucket."

"Life must be paid . . ." Dos's brow furrowed deeper.

Adrian sat back against the desk and crossed his arms. "I don't get it. Can't modern medicine be enough to cure diseases? Do we *need* the stone?"

"The stone is the entire purpose of the Elondoh community," Lucas argued. "We would be pointless without the creation of it."

"Breath of . . . oh." Dos closed his eyes for a moment. "Angels above, tell me I am wrong."

"What?" Annie asked.

He looked at Lucas nearly apologetically. "Which element has always represented life in the lore of the elementals?"

Dread immediately knitted in Lucas's gut. "Earth. I know where you're going, but there are a multitude of alternatives. Those are just stories."

"Vita's full name, BellaVita, means 'beautiful *life*.' "

"Stop it, Dos."

"For immortality to be attained, the breath of life must be paid. You see the prophecy. You have seen what Dr. Guyer has already done."

"No!" Lucas barked. His heart raced. "I've heard enough. A man from the sixteenth century couldn't have possibly predicted this to the finest detail. He couldn't have known so much about Vita. You are jumping to conclusions."

"John Dee was able to predict that Generation 6 would lose control," Dos argued, but his tone was nearly pleading. "He predicted we would have the connection abilities. Sawyer, he knew everything. Why else would Dr. Guyer be so sure that this generation would create the stone? You have to face the facts. It is written in the prophecies."

Lucas shook his head, lungs shriveling in his ribcage. "No, it can't be. There must be another interpretation, another meaning. We must keep searching. She *can't* be written in that prophecy. Because if she is, then . . . then I won't be able to save her. We will lose her."

Dos, though mostly stoic, slumped with the weight of sympathy. "I am sorry, Sawyer. In twenty-three generations, there has never been a prophecy that was not completed. I do not wish to lose her either; she is my friend. But I do not know how to prevent what was written."

"You're telling me that there's not a damn solution in this entire library?" Annie asked, eyebrow cocked. "Have you checked every book, scroll, and forgotten slip of paper?"

Dos shook his head. "There are thousands of works here. Of course I have not read them all."

"Okay, so we start there. We look for whatever we can find that might save Vita. There were other people who supposedly created the stone, right? Maybe we can find their methods and make it work. We also need to figure out that other list of questions this prophecy involves. If we can turn copper into gold, we can save our friend."

Dos looked to Lucas again as if asking for confirmation.

Lucas nodded. "That is a good plan, Annie. We'll meet here every night, same time, until we can piece together some answers."

"We should not tell Vita of this discovery," Dos said. "Imagine the dread it might bring to know you are meant to be sacrificed at any moment."

"I agree, and knowing her, she will jump at the opportunity to cure humanity of disease," said Lucas. "Do we all agree to keep this from Vita?"

"Hold on, now," Adrian said. "I don't think that's fair. Doesn't she have a right to know what's waiting for her?"

"You wish to burden her with this?" Dos asked incredulously. "After all she is going through right now? Adrian, I feel her emotions. I really do not believe she can handle any more negative news at the moment."

"Obviously, we have to consider timing, but this is her life we're talking about. She should know."

Lucas shook his head. "If we tell her about this, she will sign up to be sacrificed, and we won't even have a chance to save her."

Adrian sighed and relented. "I still think she should know, but I'll drop it for now. But Sawyer..." He glared at him. "You better do something about all those damn feelings you've got locked up for her. It's screaming in my head every time I get near you. It's like a bad R&B song on repeat. If you're going through all this trouble to save her, you might as well tell her the truth."

Lucas glared back. "For the angel's sake, please stop reading my mind without permission."

Annie rolled her eyes. "Even Hogan knows you've got a thing for Vita, and the dude has the social IQ of a monkey."

"We've gotten off topic." Lucas pointed out. "Let's focus on the task at hand, shall we?"

It's not that obvious, is it? Lucas asked himself, shuffling the papers together.

Adrian gave him a knowing look, his eyes glowing blue.

"Damn it, Adrian!" Lucas shouted.

"All right, sorry." Adrian held up his hands and left him alone.

CHAPTER 39

EARTH

Vita lay in bed with hair still damp from the shower she'd forced herself to take. A week had passed since she'd lost her abilities. Otis and Lula watched over her, though she couldn't hear them.

She so *desperately* wanted to hear them.

Her ability to embrace the earth had been Vita's one remaining tie to her father. Now it was gone. She had never felt so empty. Like she were a glass of water and someone tipped her over, spilling every last drop on the floor.

Even worse, she could still feel the hum of her gift coursing through her like a gentle whisper in her veins, but it ignored her as if it found her offensive. *I'm sorry,* she thought. *I'm sorry I took you for granted. Please come back.*

But, of course, they didn't.

She couldn't cry anymore. She'd cried so much that her swollen eyes couldn't produce any more tears. Her skin was dry, but she didn't care enough to use moisturizer. She only left her bed to shower because her mother had practically dragged her out, claiming she was starting to smell like Otis.

Her mother tried to convince her to eat, but Vita had no appetite. She couldn't convince her body to sleep. She would close her eyes and lie there, hour after hour, counting backward from a hundred at least ten times, but she still could not sleep. Now, she sat up in bed and watched through her balcony doors as the pastel colors of morning painted the clouds.

"Vita?" her mother said. "Lucas is here."

Vita didn't say anything. Despite the terrible loneliness, she wanted to be alone. She didn't want anyone to see her right now. She felt ugly, like everything about her was wrong. The last person she wanted to see her like this was Lucas. But he stopped by twice a day, every day, for the past week. Despite her silence, her failure to look at him, and her refusal to interact, he always came back like clockwork. Every day was a new attempt at getting her to speak. Usually after a failed attempt, he'd just sit next to her. Sometimes he would talk, and other times he would let the silence settle in.

He knocked on her doorframe and stepped in with a paper bag in his hand.

"Good morning," Lucas said, getting comfortable on the chair by her bed. "I brought muffins from the bakery. Would you like a strawberry or lemon poppy seed?"

Vita stayed quiet. She didn't have the energy to eat or to bother with conversation.

Lucas pulled out the muffins. "Lemon it is, then. It comes with a gift."

Lucas stuck a folded piece of paper on top of her muffin and held it out to her. She blinked at it, and the words just popped out before she could consider them.

"Is that an elephant?" she asked, voice hoarse from disuse. It was the first time she'd spoken in a few days.

Lucas lit up. "It is. Adrian made it. He's all yours if you eat."

"I'm not hungry."

"It's just a few bites, Vita."

"I don't want to."

"Well, you can't just waste away. You have to try." At her silence,

Lucas sighed and tentatively rested his hand on hers. "Please. I just need you to try."

"Why are you here, Lucas?" Vita muttered tiredly. "Why do you keep coming back every day? Why do you keep trying when you know it's useless?"

"Because I am your guardian. That means I protect you, even when you think there is nothing left to save."

Her chin trembled. Damn those tears for never listening to her. It felt like a cruel joke that her Earth abilities wouldn't respond to her anymore, yet she still had to deal with these heightened emotions.

She glared at him through the glossiness in her eyes. "Can't you see how empty I am?"

Lucas shook his head, swiping her rogue tears away with his thumb. "I see how full of life you are."

"Dos once said that the elementals in Generation 6 lost their abilities because the angels didn't think they were worthy anymore. I made the angels mad, Lucas. I must've done something awful. The . . . the Earth doesn't love me anymore . . ."

She couldn't get through it. She wanted to scream and throw things and sob until there was nothing left. She wanted Lucas to stop looking at her as if he still recognized the empty shell that had once held her soul. That was gone now, couldn't he see that? Couldn't he see she was rejected by not just the earth but also by the angels? She wasn't worthy of anyone's care.

"No," Lucas firmly demanded, brushing away the hair that stuck to her wet cheeks. "Stop it. Yes, that generation lost their abilities, but you are not like them. They slaughtered people. You help people. Your abilities will come back, but until then, you *need* to rebuild your strength. You have to show the angels that you care enough about your abilities to take care of the vessel that holds them. Show them how strong you can be."

Vita leaned her head closer to his hand. The slightest bit of warmth flushed through her. It was fleeting, but for a moment she felt . . . alive. He'd never lied to her before, so she had to believe he was telling the truth now. That she *would* get better, that there was hope for her. Even if she didn't feel it right now.

"Okay, I'll try to eat," Vita relented. "But I think that's all I can do right now."

He offered her a small smile. "That's more than enough. Thank you."

Vita picked up the muffin and forced herself to take the first bite. She'd always had a sweet tooth, but right now the muffin didn't taste as good as it should have—like anticipating a spoonful of ice cream and instead getting a mouthful of sand. She ate anyway and listened to Lucas's plans for the day. Apparently, there was some practice session he needed to go to for the tournament.

"Will you come back when you're done?" she asked.

He checked his watch. "Um . . . I might be able to fit in a quick visit."

"Oh, if you're busy, don't worry about it. It's Saturday, isn't it? I'm sure you already have plans."

"I'm sorry. I have dinner with Dr. Guyer, and I can't miss it. But I'll stop by tomorrow morning as usual."

"Have fun."

He did look sorry about leaving her. He stood, cleared his throat, and scratched the back of his neck. "Vita? Um, it's really good to hear you speak again. I missed your funny accent."

She forced herself to give him a tired smile. "I'll see you later."

Vita watched him walk out, and when he left, the warmth left with him.

CHAPTER 40

GUARDIAN

Lucas breathed in the early afternoon air and stretched while Dos rattled off his list of potential fifth elementals. The field past the orchards housed an open arena big enough to fit the few hundred spectators that might attend the tournament. Many Elondohnians attended so they could decide where to place bets for the actual tournament, even though gambling was strictly illegal here. The authorities usually turned a blind eye on this day and even tossed in some money themselves.

Dos and Lucas stood far enough away from the forming crowd so no one would overhear them. Dos had collected his list by studying the original families of Elondoh.

"The families we have yet to consider are the Dawsons, the Joneses, and . . . oh." Dos sighed. "The Boyds."

Lucas scoffed and adjusted his leather armor. "You can go ahead and scratch the Boyds off the list. The fifth elemental will still have the beauty of angels and the worthiness of knights. Jason Boyd lacks both of those."

"It would be reckless for us to disregard him," Dos said.

"Very well, if you think you must. Have Adrian read through his mind and see what he can dig up. My family is having dinner with Dr. Guyer, so that should buy you about an hour in the archives room."

Dos nodded and slid his notebook in his bag. "How was Vita this morning?"

Lucas leaned against a nearby light post and smiled to himself. "She's talking again, and she ate an entire muffin. I think we're making progress. I'm hoping I can get her to go on a walk with me tomorrow. Maybe to the bakery."

"The bakery?" Dos repeated. "Would this be a date?"

"Angels, no. Don't be silly. She likes sweets, so I'm hoping I can bribe her with some ice cream. The fresh air will be good for her."

"Right. Well, I hope she agrees to your non-romantic ice cream."

A call went out over the speaker for the participating guardians to gather on the field for practice to begin. Lucas parted ways with Dos and jogged into the center of the field. Many of the older guardians were leading the sparring practice with Chief at the head. The tournament wasn't required, and anyone could sign up for it, but many of the younger guardians viewed it as a chance to attract introductions, so the court of the arena was filled with male guardians. Women could have signed up, and some had won past tournaments, but this year there weren't any volunteers.

They ran drills and tested agility, strength, and swords-manship. They did a few rounds of practice fights and learned new techniques.

None of this was too difficult for Lucas, who dedicated all his off hours to training. He always had somewhat of a knack for predicting patterns in his opponent's moves, which gave him a great advantage. He could almost *feel* their movements half a second before they made them. He had a lifetime of his father's training to thank for that.

Chief smiled proudly at him and frequently used him as an example. Of course, that led to jealous glares from the others, but Lucas brushed them off. The only one who was friendly about it was Hogan, but the man didn't have a mean bone in his body.

The crowd cheered them on when something impressive

happened. Girls cheered extra loud when some of the guardians removed their shirts. Lucas thought that was the most impractical thing the guardians could do. Their shirts were designed to soak up sweat and keep them cool. Not to mention, weren't they the least bit concerned about sunburn?

Thankfully, the sparring went by quickly, and a few hours later, Lucas was removing his gear and wiping sweat from his brow.

Ethan stood next to Lucas and nudged him. "That was a good run, wasn't it? Did you see the way I won over Guardian Stevenson?"

"Yes, you did well," Lucas answered distractedly. He checked his watch. If he hurried, he could shower and still have half an hour to see Vita before dinner, but he needed to leave now.

"I've been meaning to ask you," Ethan said. "I tried calling Vita's home this morning to check in on her, and her mother mentioned she was busy with another visitor. I'm assuming that was you?"

Lucas sighed. He did not have time for this. "Yes, as her guardian, I visit her to ensure she is doing well."

"That is more than guardian's work, Sawyer. I've noticed your behavior lately. You're interested in her, aren't you?"

This was getting ridiculous. Lucas didn't answer. He couldn't lie, but he certainly did not want to divulge the truth now.

"You know," Ethan continued with an empathetic frown. "I don't blame you, of course. I mean, just look at her. I've thought about Annie, too, but she spews venom anytime she speaks, so I thought it best to avoid her. But Vita? She's truly sweet, isn't she?"

Lucas kept his expression bored as he dared himself to meet Ethan's eyes. "What is your point?"

"My point is, I'd understand if you were a little confused. But as your friend, I must remind you of the position you're in. My mother and her friends still talk about your mother moving in here from the outside world and stealing the chief. It's a role meant to be filled by someone who grew up here. As wonderful as Vita is, she doesn't fit that mold, does she? You would only be bringing further strife upon yourself, and we both know how much image matters to you. Or at least it should matter. I just caution you to perhaps back down from someone so . . . controversial."

"How kind of you, but I can make decisions for myself."

"Sawyer, come off it." Ethan now huffed. "You get everything else in Elondoh. Can't you leave one thing alone?"

"What's Vita's favorite color?"

Ethan blinked. "Excuse me?"

"Her favorite color, do you know it?" Lucas asked again. "How about her favorite food? Favorite candy? What is one thing you must never say around her, lest she lose her mind with rage?"

Ethan stammered wordlessly for an answer.

Lucas nodded and felt a surge of pride course through him as he continued. "Yellow because it is a happy color. Grilled cheese with tomato. Caramels, specifically with cream in the middle. Never call her animals 'pets' because the term implies ownership when they are as free as she is. The difference between you and me is that you only want her because, to you, she is a prize to be won. A pretty trophy to brag about. Me? I know she is better than that, and she deserves someone who is going to bring her a life of happiness. When you can show me that you do that for her, *then* I will back down. Until then, I suggest you keep yourself more focused on your duty than my personal life. Maybe then you'd start earning more favor. And don't ever call Vita a thing again."

Lucas picked up his gear and walked away, feeling taller and stronger than he ever had before. But as he started his walk, he caught Chief's wide eyes centered on him from only a few feet away. Chief had heard the whole damn thing, and now he knew.

Horrified, Lucas pushed past Chief and hurried home.

Lucas's hands shook as he tried his tie again. He kept making it too short, too fat, or somehow crooked. It wasn't perfect, and each failed attempt irritated him even more. Chief knocked on his doorframe, watching him through the mirror's reflection. Lucas briefly looked up before focusing on his tie again.

"It's not what you think," Lucas grunted. "It's a silly crush, that's all."

"Lucas," Chief started.

Lucas interrupted. "I'm remaining professional. I am more than these feelings. I won't act on them."

"Why?"

Lucas yanked off his now crinkled tie and threw it on his bed before facing his father. "Because I will be a good chief! I understand my duty, I know what I am expected to do, and I am happy to serve my community. Vita Eastwood is the opposite of who I am meant to be with, and I know that. If I pursue her instead of an Elondohnian woman, my community will never take me seriously. I know the other guardians are waiting for me to fail and allow room for another to step up and take over as chief, but I will not allow it. I will not be the reason that the Sawyer family loses our honor. It does not end with me. I will make our family proud."

Chief sighed and called over his shoulder. "Natalie? Lucas and I are going to the Guardian Club early. We'll meet you there."

Mom poked her head out of their bedroom holding a tube of lipstick. She looked at Lucas then at Chief and raised an eyebrow. "Is everything all right?"

"Yes. We're going to get a drink," Chief said.

Now Lucas raised his eyebrows. In the outside world, people couldn't drink until they reached a certain age, but there was no set drinking age in Elondoh. No one could consume alcohol until their fathers granted them their first drink. It was a rite of passage. Many fathers saved it for their son's or daughter's wedding as a way of saying, "You are my equal."

What had Lucas done to earn this now?

Chief motioned for Lucas to follow him. "Come on. We both need a drink."

CHAPTER 41

GUARDIAN

"Remy." Chief patted the bar as he and Lucas sat down. "Two of my usuals."

Remy, the bartender, nodded and got right to work. Lucas kept his eyes away from Chief, knowing how the conversation was going to go. There would be a lecture and probably a list of Elondohnian girls who would better suit Lucas. It would be embarrassing and unnecessary, but Lucas would sit through it anyway.

Chief didn't speak until the drinks were set in front of them. "It's just whiskey on the rocks. You'll like it, but drink it slowly."

"Um, thanks?" Lucas sniffed and winced at the sharp smell. He set down his glass and waited.

"So, you have feelings for Vita?"

"No. I mean . . ." He couldn't lie, especially not to Chief. "Yes. But I will not act on it. Elondoh needs me to remain focused and choose someone who best represents the community. Vita doesn't even like it here."

"Does she like you?"

"It doesn't matter."

"Why doesn't it matter?"

"Because . . ." Lucas sighed, his shoulders slumping. "Because nobody thinks I can be a chief as it is. I hear what they say about me. They think I'm too soft. If I drag Vita into it, I wouldn't be proving that I can choose Elondoh over myself. I would be selfish."

Chief took a sip of his drink before speaking again. "You know, I have always felt this community asks too much of you. Even when you were a baby, there were expectations set upon you that you didn't ask for."

"I am willing and able to meet those expectations. I will uphold my duty with a sense of gratitude. Just as you and every Sawyer before you did. I will not disappoint you."

"You know, my father used to say the Sawyers are loved by all except by their own fathers. It's the price we pay." Chief traced the rim of his glass with a finger, his eyes staring at the amber liquid without really seeing. "We sell our souls for our purpose and ignore anything else. You would think that in a long line of men, one of them would stand up and change that, but no. When I found out your mother and I were expecting, I swore I would be the one to break that pattern. You would know I was proud and that I loved you, and that would be enough for you."

"And you've done well. It's *my* problems that are an issue, but it won't stop me."

Chief shook his head. "No, because you see, I forgot to teach you one thing I wish I was taught."

"What is that?"

"If you must make a decision between a duty you did not choose or your own happiness, always choose your happiness. You've sacrificed so much of your childhood, and there is more yet to come that you will have to face. So, for the angels' sake, allow yourself to choose at least one thing. One day when your world is falling apart, you will look next to you and find one person who is your safe haven. Who is that person?"

Lucas knew without even thinking. "Vita."

"Then choose her if she will have you. I will back your decision against this entire community if I must, but I will *not* allow you to give until you have nothing left. Being a good chief does not mean selling your soul for a community that will so easily toss you aside."

It was like Chief had lifted heavy chains off Lucas's shoulders. For the first time since he'd met Vita in the plant nursery, he could breathe again. Because now he was given permission to choose. He was given backup if he did end up facing criticism. He was given a peace of mind.

Lucas released a breath and shyly muttered, "I don't know the first thing about talking to women."

Chief chuckled and shrugged. "Nobody really does. For some reason, they still seem to like us. Really makes you question their sanity, doesn't it?"

Lucas laughed. Chief lifted his glass, and Lucas clinked his against it.

The psycho got rid of his entire desk! Adrian shouted in Lucas's mind.

Lucas flinched and accidentally bit too hard onto his fork. Luckily, no one seemed to notice at his table. He was sitting at a circular table with his mother, Chief, and Dr. Guyer. Their entrées had just been served, and Lucas had just taken his first bite of steak when Adrian reported in.

Lower your voice, Lucas thought back. *The entire desk is gone? What about the papers in them?*

We're looking now.

Tell Dos to refer to that list I had him make. We took an inventory of everything in the desk even if we didn't fully read it yet.

"What do you think, Guardian Sawyer?" Dr. Guyer asked,

jarring Lucas out of his thoughts. "Any inclinations as to who the tournament champion will be?"

Lucas smiled. "Well, sir, I do not mean to sound cocky, but as you know, I took an oath of honesty. I believe I have a fair chance."

Dr. Guyer and the Sawyer parents laughed, continuing their conversation.

Smooth, Adrian said. *Dos said the only thing we haven't gone through yet are a few family trees. We're looking for them now.*

"Guardian Sawyer," Dr. Guyer cut in again. "Do you think you've felt any different with the elementals around? I know you get quite sick when they are transmutating materials."

"He does?" Lucas's mom asked, her smile dropping. "How long has this been going on?"

"Oh, he hasn't told you? Every time they've combined their elements, he gets terribly nauseous and often must excuse himself from the room. It started about a month ago."

"Why haven't you told us?" his mom demanded.

"I assumed it was just an allergy to the sulfur." Lucas said, blinking at his mother's sudden worry. "I didn't think it was serious."

"Of course it's serious."

"Natalie," Chief spoke up gruffly, giving her a knowing look. "I'm sure it's fine."

She pursed her lips and picked up her wine glass. Dr. Guyer smiled and checked his watch. "My, look at the time. I must get going. There's work at my office."

"No!" Lucas blurted. He felt a wash of panic as the three sets of eyes settled on him.

Adrian, he mentally said.

Yeah, I heard. We're dealing with problems of our own at the moment. Stall.

"I . . ." Lucas stammered, then said the first thing that came to mind. "Dr. Guyer, I heard a rumor that there was a hidden part of the prophecy."

His mother jerked so suddenly that she spilled her wine all over the table.

That's your way of stalling? Adrian hissed. *That's so stupid! Let me handle this, you focus on getting out of there.*

"Angels," his mother breathed, while a waiter rushed over to mop up the mess. "I'm so sorry. I'm usually so careful."

Dr. Guyer didn't seem to notice her rambling and smiled at Lucas. "You were saying?"

"I know it is only a myth, as nobody has ever actually seen it before, but I thought if anyone would know about the prophecy, it would be you."

"Why has this particular topic come to mind?"

"Vita. I'm concerned about finding a solution to help her. Perhaps some hidden prophecy might contain something that might help."

"I already explained to you that Vita's abilities will come back naturally over time," his mother hissed. "We must not meddle in myths and legends."

"But surely John Dee must have predicted something about her," Lucas argued. "The fact that she lost her abilities in a Stone Generation is notable, isn't it?"

"Indeed, it is," Dr. Guyer mused, an intrigued light sparking in his eyes. "You believe the hidden prophecy might contain something about Vita?"

"Yes."

"This is not the proper conversation for dinner," his mother said. "We should go. Dr. Guyer has work to do, and my dress is ruined."

"Oh, I can put off my work for some time to hear the theories of a young man, but you are welcome to leave, Natalie," Guyer said dismissively.

"How dare—"

"Natalie," Chief cut in again. He shook his head at her.

"I only want to know whether or not the rumors are true," Lucas said. He never intended to cause so much strain on his mother. But why was she so upset?

Dr. Guyer rubbed his chin and gave Lucas a knowing smile. "All rumors are based on a grain of truth. Perhaps there is a hidden prophecy, perhaps not. Whatever is not in our possession is either locked away in a museum somewhere or severely damaged."

We're out, Adrian reported. *Dos grabbed a few things, but he thinks we need to steer clear of the archives room for a while.*

Excellent work.

"I'm sorry," Lucas said to his mother. "I don't wish to hold us up any longer for such silly things. Goodnight, Dr. Guyer."

"If you ever have more questions or theories, you know where my office is."

The moment they returned home, Lucas's mother turned on him and shouted, "Don't *ever* go digging into such things again! Meddling around in rumors and prophecies, it will drive you crazy. Esoteric fools disillusion themselves all the time; don't be stupid like them. I suggest you put such myths out of your mind for good and leave it alone."

She stormed upstairs to her room before Lucas even had a chance to defend himself. Not that he had much of a defense, mostly questions. He spared one for Chief, who was laying down his wallet on the kitchen counter.

"Why did that upset her so much? It was only a question."

Chief sighed and rubbed his forehead. "Just leave it alone, Lucas. It's best not to pry."

"Best for who?"

Chief glared at him and made his way upstairs without answering.

CHAPTER 42

WATER

D own in the archives room, Adrian had just stuffed another scroll into Dos's bookbag when he felt the brush of another mind joining the vicinity.

That was the cool thing about his abilities: he could keep a sort of mental radar to sense whose mental frequencies were around him. It sounded more complicated than it was, but it was nothing more than a sort of sensation. Like having multiple radios on at the same time, then choosing which to ignore and which to listen to. He could tell Dos was thinking like crazy behind him, Annie was mentally cursing out these dead alchemists at a bookshelf to the left, and another mental frequency cut in upstairs at the end of the hallway.

It was Boyd's. His thoughts were cold and calculating. He was sent to Dr. Guyer's office to complete a task. *Damn it.* Dr. Guyer was coming soon.

"Hey, y'all?" Adrian said quietly. "We got a problem."

After Adrian's explanation, the three elementals peered through the crack in the door of the archives room. Boyd was flipping through one of Dr. Guyer's notebooks and muttering to himself before he opened a drawer in Dr. Guyer's desk and pulled out a phone.

"An iPhone, seriously?" Adrian muttered. "It's not fair. I can't call my girl, but Boyd can text people?"

"Focus," Dos hissed. "What is he thinking?"

Adrian slipped further into Boyd's mind and kept himself as quiet as possible. He didn't want Boyd to know they were here.

Dinner with the Sawyers . . . so pathetic. They think they're so perfect, so esteemed. My time will come, and soon it will be Lucas Sawyer who is sent to run errands while I dine with Dr. Guyer. Sawyer has no clue what is coming for him.

He put the phone to his ear. "Yes, I am calling on behalf of Dr. Joseph Guyer. He would like to approve the most recent project he discussed with you . . ."

"I think I can send him away," Adrian whispered. "I've always wanted to try this."

Adrian dug around into Boyd's mind and plucked a few words. *My. Guyer. Help. Needs. Now.*

Then he arranged the words in a sentence and pressed at it over and over again so that Boyd heard it as his own thoughts.

Guyer needs my help now.

Boyd suddenly straightened up, and his face contorted in confusion. Adrian played the sentence louder. Boyd cursed to himself.

I must trust my intuition. Guyer needs my help now. I must go.

He dropped the phone on the table and ran out of the office. Adrian waited until he felt Boyd's mind completely leave the building and then motioned for the other two elementals to follow him out.

"Who was that call to?" Dos asked, picking up the phone. His brows furrowed at it. "How do you operate this?"

"Give it here." Annie snatched it and quickly scrolled through the call log. "Number's not saved, but it's been dialed three times in the past week."

"Call it," Dos suggested, then looked to Adrian. "Can you read the thoughts of those on the other line?"

Adrian shook his head. "No can do. I tried the other night in hopes that I could reach Naomi and couldn't get to her mind—it was too far."

"That's a gross invasion of privacy, you perv." Annie dialed the number and put it on speaker.

The line rang three times before a gravelly voice answered. "Patterson's Logging Company."

Annie hung up and immediately deleted that call from the log. "Any guesses on why Dr. Guyer would need a logging company?"

"Maybe he's extending Elondoh's community?" Adrian suggested.

"For what?" Dos wondered. "We have all that we need, and there is still an abundance of living units for growing families."

"Dunno. We should go though. Dr. Guyer will be here soon. Sawyer bought us some time, but they just wrapped up dinner."

"I think we should refrain from coming back here for a few days," Dos said. "We are coming too close to Dr. Guyer detecting us. I will study the family trees and report my findings."

"Great. I'm happy not to come back here anytime soon," Annie said.

Adrian followed them out and kept an eye—or a *mind*—out to ensure they wouldn't run into anyone. While walking home, he checked on Vita one more time.

She was sleeping, so all he could get was her dreams. Right now, she was dreaming about a memory with her father. They were in their backyard, back home in Georgia. Vita looked around fourteen. Her dad laughed and threw a ball across the yard, watching a puppy version of Otis trample after it.

That was the hard part about Adrian's abilities. When he looked into someone's mind, he couldn't just hear their thoughts or see through their eyes. He could see their memories and every thought that came with it. Some were good, like this one, and some were bad, like Dos's memories of his childhood. It was hard not being able to offer any help for the bad ones, and he wasn't going to walk up to people and admit that he saw their deepest darkest secrets.

There was really no other way to help than to be a supportive friend, but he wished there was more he could do.

Sometimes it really sucked to be a mind reader.

CHAPTER 43

GUARDIAN

Lucas watched the elementals practice their waltz for the festival in the training room. Annie and Dos danced together, and since Vita wasn't there and Adrian refused to dance with any girl who wasn't his current girlfriend, Hogan volunteered to fill the spot and took the role of follower with Adrian.

Having grown up in Elondoh culture, Dos already knew all the dances and traditions, so he had no problem teaching something as simple as the waltz.

"I feel stupid," Annie said for the fifth time.

"You are looking the wrong way," Dos answered in a soft voice as he tilted her chin toward him. "Look at me, just like that."

Something about Annie shifted. Her back straightened, and the softest gleam sparked in her eyes as they met Dos's.

"Yeah, that's a lot better," Annie breathed.

It was probably a good thing that Dos gave her a little extra confidence. Adrian, on the other hand, couldn't stop giggling.

"I don't understand what is so funny," Hogan said, though he was grinning as well. "I am a lovely young lady who has asked you for a dance. Ouch, if you keep stepping on my feet like that, then *nobody* will want to dance with you!"

"That's kind of the point, my guy."

"You mean 'my lady.'"

It was clear that Adrian wouldn't entertain the idea of dancing with any potential suitors, which Lucas had to respect. Dancing could be intimate with the right partner.

Lucas immediately thought about Vita. She'd eaten an entire plate of breakfast this morning and managed to tell him about a book she was reading, but she'd tired quickly after that. Would she have liked to dance? She loved music and often spoke of the artists that she missed the most from the outside world. Motion also seemed part of her personality. She was always tapping, humming, or spinning around in a field of flowers.

An idea popped into his head. But he wasn't sure if it would be improper . . .

"Do it!" Adrian said, eyes glowing blue. "She'll love it."

"Adrian!" Lucas barked. "We talked about this."

Adrian grinned and turned with Hogan, focusing on his dance. Ethan gave Lucas an evaluating glare, and that sealed it for Lucas. He was going to try his idea. To start, he needed to convince Chief to allow something that was technically against the rules.

"Good evening, Mrs. Eastwood," Lucas greeted June. It was after training, and Lucas was stopping by as he usually did. This time, he'd brought a box of cookies from the bakery.

"Hey, honey, come on in," June smiled, letting Lucas inside. "What have you got?"

"Chocolate chip. They're for you. I was wondering if you'd be all right with me escorting Vita through the garden tonight."

"If you can convince her to leave her room, please be my guest."

He left the cookies with her, offered quick pets to Otis and Lula, and hurried upstairs.

Vita was sitting on her balcony with a blanket wrapped around her shoulders as she watched the setting sun. As always, Bo rested in her hands. She looked over her shoulder and offered a glimpse of a smile. A real one, not a forced one. This was *major* progress, and it sent hope right through Lucas's heart.

He knelt beside her and smiled. "Hey. It's a lovely evening for a walk, don't you think?"

Vita grimaced. "I don't want to."

"It'll be a half hour, Vita. I've got a surprise for you. You'll like it."

"I'm tired."

Lucas sighed dramatically and plucked the blue teacup from her hands. "I didn't want to do this, but you've forced my hand."

"What are you doing? Give him back."

"I am going to plant him back in the garden."

"No, you're not! You don't know the first thing about plant care. You'll hurt his roots!"

"Suppose you'll have to stop me then." He stood up and walked out of her room.

Vita scrambled up and ran after him. "Lucas Sawyer, you give him back right now!"

"Make me." Lucas grinned and hurried downstairs. In guardian training, the students were taught several methods to capture an enemy. One of those methods was using a distraction to lure out the target and then sending in a small team to capture the target. This wasn't the exact way it was taught, but it would work regardless.

He ran past a startled June, nearly tripped on a snoozing Lula, and had to skirt around an excited Otis. Finally, he made it outside a moment before Vita collided into him. Lucas held the teacup in the air and smiled.

"Oh, look at that, you're already outside!" Lucas said. "One loop around the garden and I'll give him back."

Vita glared at him. "You must think you're so clever."

"I do, actually." He held out his arm. "You haven't even seen my surprise yet."

She rolled her eyes and aggressively took his arm, allowing him to steer her to the gardens. Vita was tense at first, glaring at the ground and remaining silent, but as they walked past the rose bushes, something about her softened.

The cool breeze danced through the flowers, carrying scents of oncoming rain. Rustling sounded from scurrying rabbits. She lightened her grip on Lucas's arm as they got closer to the playground area. Vita stopped and looked around, as if seeing everything for the first time. A ladybug fluttered toward her, and she held up a finger for it to land on.

"What will you wish for?" Lucas asked.

She pursed her lips in thought and finally blew at the ladybug. It fluttered away toward the flowers. "So, what was your big surprise?"

"Ah, right." Lucas dug into his pocket and pulled out Vita's phone from the outside world. She lit up and looked to him for an explanation. The elementals had any modern form of communication revoked when they entered Elondoh. Vita had once complained that she had hundreds of songs, photos, and virtual books saved on her phone that she missed.

"I talked to Chief and made an agreement," Lucas said. "You can have this only when I am with you, and you cannot use it to communicate with the outside world. At the end of the night, I have to turn it back in, but you can have your music back."

"Lucas! Thank you." She took the phone and scrolled through it, her eyes shifting quickly over the screen.

"I figured maybe you could pick a song and I could show you how to waltz?" His stomach tightened nervously. "The other elementals are learning it for the festival, and someone might ask you to dance, so you should know how. Unless you don't want to. I would understand."

Vita smiled and angels above, it was a beautiful sight. "Okay. Teach me to dance. I've got the perfect song."

She selected a piano arrangement in the perfect time signature and slipped the phone into Lucas's front pocket. He briefly explained the waltz, making sure to mention that in Elondoh, they started with a curtsy, had a few turns, and ended with a lift. Then he settled the teacup down on a park bench and held out his hand to Vita.

It took exactly one full rotation for Lucas to realize that Vita already knew what she was doing. She followed his lead and danced like a dream, not once questioning her step.

"You already know how to waltz!" Lucas accused.

"My daddy taught me when I was a kid. I used to watch him and my momma dance around the kitchen together."

"Why didn't you tell me?"

She gave him a sly smile. "You seemed so excited about it, I just thought I'd let you have your fun."

"So, you were lying."

"I never said I *didn't* know how to waltz. You just never asked."

"Clever. Here comes the first turn." Lucas held her hand and slowly twirled her around in a circle, pulling her back into his arms to continue their dance. "Beautiful."

The music swelled, as if the orchestra was playing just for them, with the silver shine of the moon providing a spotlight. Vita pressed herself closer to him, watching him with a smile as soft as silk.

"Ready to try the lift?" Lucas asked.

"Promise you won't let me fall?"

"I promise." It was a quick lift, only a couple of seconds long. They finished the dance with a bow, then Vita threw herself into his arms in a full embrace.

It wasn't as shocking as it had been the first time she hugged him. It felt so natural to embrace her, as if they were made to hold each other.

"Thank you," she whispered against his ear, sending goose-bumps down his spine. "You made my ladybug wish come true."

"What was your wish?"

"I wished I didn't feel so alone anymore."

"You were never alone. It's you and me, remember?"

She pulled back enough to smile at him. "How could I ever forget about you and me?"

Angels, she's breathtaking.

"What?" she asked. "You've got a weird look. Is something wrong?"

Oh. Damn it, Sawyer. Get it together.

He tried to play it off by checking his watch. "I was just thinking we should probably head back soon. I promised your mother it would be a quick walk."

"What a shame," she muttered.

Vita scooped up Bo's teacup and smiled at it, as if expecting to hear something. When her eyes didn't glow, her smile wavered. She looked at Lucas and studied him for just a second before nodding firmly to herself. Lucas knew then that she'd be all right. She was resilient enough to pull herself out of her sorrows. He'd simply be there to remind her of that.

Lucas held out an arm, and together, they walked home.

CHAPTER 44

GUARDIAN

The next morning, Lucas walked up to Vita's doorstep and was surprised to see her already dressed and waiting for him. She held Bo, and Otis was by her side.

"Good morning," he greeted. "What are you doing out here?"

She stood and nervously pushed a curl behind her ear. "I was thinking . . . I'm ready to go back to training now."

"Really?" His eyebrows shot up. "There's no rush. I understand you've been feeling . . . lethargic. You can take as long as you need."

"I know, but I'm not gonna get any better locked up in my room. After you dropped me off last night, those four walls felt so suffocating. I had a thought. Maybe being around the others will encourage my abilities to come back. But I'm a little afraid to be honest with you."

"Why are you afraid?"

She looked down at Bo and traced the handle of his teacup with her thumb. "Because I'm feeling good again. Not totally back to normal, but I have more energy, and I think I'm ready to be happy again."

"Why does that scare you? That sounds like a good thing."

"Because . . . I want to keep getting better, but I'm worried that seeing the other elements in use without being able to use mine might send me back to that dark place. I felt awful that whole time, and I don't think I'm totally out of it yet. What if I start to spiral again and it gets worse?"

Worse? Lucas didn't want to think about what that would look like, but he'd do anything to avoid it. "We don't have to go to training today. I'll let Hogan know that I won't be in attendance, and we can just stay here, if you'd like."

Vita shook her head, raising her chin up. "No. I want to try. But if I start to feel that way again, could you just . . . I don't know. Maybe just remind me of something good. Like you and me."

"I will." He wondered if she could see how proud he was of her. It must have been difficult to come to this decision, but she'd done it anyway. She was as powerful as she was gentle.

"And Lucas? Could you do me one more thing?" she asked.

"Yes, anything you need."

"You gotta stop looking at me like I'm frail. You have a habit of doing that, and it won't help me. If I'm being honest, it's probably one of the reasons I kept getting mad at you when we first met."

He winced. "I didn't realize. I'm sorry. I only wanted to—"

"Take care of me," she finished with a smile. "I know. But save it for when I need it. Should we go?"

He returned her smile and nodded. "Yes. After you."

Lucas rested a hand on the door handle of the training room, then stopped to ask Vita one more time, "Are you sure you're ready?"

She clutched Bo's teacup and nodded firmly. "Let's do this."

He opened the door and followed her in. Vita hesitantly walked farther into the room and was immediately greeted by the other elementals.

"Hey!" Annie exclaimed. "Back from the dead, I see."

"Welcome back, champ." Adrian held up a hand for a high five.

Dos nodded politely to Vita. "Good morning, Vita."

She smiled, her tense shoulders relaxing. "Hey, y'all. What'd I miss?"

They all dove into conversation about the upcoming festival while Lucas took his usual post by the front door. Hogan offered a smile to Lucas from across the room and mouthed, "Good job."

Ethan watched Vita with a dissipating smile. She hadn't once looked at him, which Lucas was sure made him feel downright heartbroken. But she didn't come here to impress anyone; she wanted to be around the others again.

Dr. Guyer's entourage walked into the room, starting with Dr. Wilson, then Boyd, and finally Dr. Guyer, who straightened up at the sight of Vita. "Vita dear, you're back! Are your abilities . . .?"

"No, sir," Lucas said, stepping in. "We thought maybe—"

"I can speak for myself," Vita interrupted, shooting Lucas an annoyed look. *Right.* She wasn't frail. He gave her an apologetic look and stepped back while she talked. "Maybe being around the others might encourage my abilities to wake up."

"An excellent idea," Dr. Guyer said. "We were going to run over some ground rules for the festival today. Afterward, you'll all go your separate ways to work on your presentations. Unfortunately, we can't work much on the philosopher's stone until your abilities come back, so we're filling the time with other necessary activities. Take a seat, everyone."

Vita sat next to Annie at a table and placed Bo's cup on the corner where he'd get the most sunlight. Otis settled himself next to Vita, eyeing Boyd from across the room. Lucas wondered if dogs had a good sense of people and if Otis could detect that Boyd carried disdain over the elementals. Dr. Guyer whispered something to Boyd, who glanced at Lucas and then nodded.

Dr. Wilson discussed the expectations for the festival, most of which Lucas drowned out, as he already knew them all. He took the time to think about Dos's latest report from their last adventure in the archives room.

Boyd had made a call to a logging company, but why? They

still couldn't think of a good enough reason why Dr. Guyer would need such a service. Perhaps he needed the wood for some kind of construction? Was Dr. Guyer thinking about expanding Elondoh? Either way, it didn't seem like a good idea to carry dead trees into a community where an Earth elemental lived. There had to be a way to ask about it without Guyer getting suspicious.

Boyd walked over to Lucas and stood by his side, speaking in a whisper. "How did you manage to convince her to come out of the shadows?"

"Why do you care?" Lucas asked, already annoyed.

"Only curious. I heard Guardian James had called her, sent flowers, and even offered to take her out to dinner, but nothing worked. She wouldn't even see him. But you somehow managed it? I want to know your secret."

"She volunteered to attend today. I didn't convince her."

"No? That's not what I heard. I heard she was seen walking to the gardens with a certain guardian last night. Alone and late at night. Rather risqué, don't you think? But then, she *is* a girl from the outside world. I'm sure you know how they are."

Boyd had a way of saying the right things to provoke a certain reaction out of anyone. He could make a nun curse if he really wanted to. He'd always been that way in school and was no different now. Lucas swallowed his irritation and kept his eyes forward.

"Guardian Boyd," Lucas said quietly. "I suggest you refrain from speaking poorly about the elementals."

"Or what? You'll file a report? It's what you do best. But it won't matter because Dr. Guyer will toss it away."

"My reports don't go to Dr. Guyer. They go straight to Chief Sawyer. If you don't mind, I'd like to focus on my task, which does not include chatting with you."

Boyd scoffed and left Lucas's side to return to his post next to Dr. Guyer. On the way over, he passed by Vita's table. Lucas's stomach tightened just half a second before Boyd swiped his hand across the table and knocked Bo's cup over, starting a whirlwind of commotion.

The teacup shattered, sending the tiny succulent and all its dirt across the floor. Vita gasped sharply and jumped to her feet. Annie started cursing at Boyd. Otis began to bark and pushed himself between Boyd and Vita, which blocked Vita from getting to Bo. Boyd smiled cruelly at Vita and lifted his boot over Bo. Vita screamed when his boot came down and squished the little plant.

Lucas surged forward to Boyd but skirted to a stop when Adrian crossed the room and tackled Boyd to the floor.

"Angels!" Ethan shouted as he pulled out his impulse bracelet. Hogan hurried forward as well, casting a quick glance at Annie to ensure she wasn't going to react. Dr. Wilson shrieked and cowered next to Dr. Guyer, who kept his eyes on Lucas.

Adrian was back on his feet before any of the guardians could get to him. He stood tall and strong, like the wall of a tsunami building up and threatening to take down a city, but he made no moves just yet.

Lucas held up a hand to the other two guardians, causing them to halt in their steps. Adrian was the element of peace; he was naturally wired to avoid violence until it was necessary. Lucas wanted to trust that Adrian would make the right decision now.

"You think it's funny hurting someone like that?" Adrian growled. "Well, come on then. Stand up and face your consequences like a man."

Boyd sneered up at him. "You're forbidden from using your element against anyone."

"I don't need the water to kick your ass."

"Aren't you going to do anything?" Boyd said to Lucas.

"I might file a report. It's what I'm best at," Lucas tossed back. Still, he stood next to Adrian and placed a hand on his shoulder.

"I'll handle it from here. Guardian James, take Adrian to cool off. Hogan, get us a broom. Dr. Guyer, I suggest Guardian Boyd's dismissal for the remainder of the day."

Dr. Guyer waved a dismissive hand. Ethan nudged Adrian out, Hogan hurried to get a broom, and Boyd stormed away with a glare that could melt snow.

Lucas could now focus on Vita, who sat on the floor, crying. She cradled Bo in one hand and several of his leaves in the other. Her hands had small bloody cuts from scooping up the remains of the shattered teacup.

"Angels, you're bleeding. Are you all right?" he asked.

Vita could barely form a complete sentence. Dark streaks of her makeup stained her cheeks. "His . . . his roots are all torn up. He must be hurting something fierce, and I can't heal him. He's just a baby."

"It'll be okay. We have to clean your cuts. There's dirt in them." Lucas tried to reach for the disfigured plant, but she yanked it toward her chest.

"Don't touch him! You're all careless monsters!"

"Vita," Lucas said, crestfallen.

Annie patted Vita's back, looking a little out of place doing it. "Let's get you cleaned up. You can take him with you."

Dos's eyes glowed red as they centered on Vita. He strained his face as though he were pushing against a brick wall. Vita's tears slowed enough for her to stop hyperventilating and allow Lucas to help her up. Annie and Otis walked Vita out of the room while Hogan walked in with his broom.

"How did she feel, Dos?" Dr. Guyer asked.

"Is it not obvious?" Dos uncharacteristically snapped.

"I meant her exact emotions," Guyer snarled.

"She was scared. Heartbroken. And there was distinct rage to her anger, something I have never encountered before."

"Violent?"

Dos hesitated. "She was just extremely angry."

"That has potential," Dr. Guyer muttered to himself, rubbing his freshly trimmed beard.

Potential? Lucas thought. *For violence? Not Vita, of all people.*

Hogan had swept up most of the mess and lifted up the dustpan. "Can we mend this cup? I'm sure we could borrow some glue from the school."

"There's so many tiny pieces," Lucas said. "I don't think we can glue it all back together."

"You could melt it," Dr. Wilson suggested. Then he blushed and pushed up his glasses. You might be able to use the crucible."

For all the coldness that Dr. Wilson carried, it obviously wasn't enough to deflect Vita's warmth. Her persistent kindness to him was paying off.

"That is a good idea," Dos said, taking the dustpan. "We can use the gold we made from transmutation to mend it. It is a Japanese practice I read about. Guardian Sawyer, could you help me clean the pieces?"

Lucas followed Dos out to the bathroom, where he suspected that Dos would want to talk privately. Dos turned on every faucet and checked every stall before whispering to Lucas.

"Dr. Guyer set that whole ordeal up."

"How do you know that?"

"His emotions. Everyone else was either frightened, angry, or in Vita's case, sad. He was excited. There was a sense of giddiness about him."

"That doesn't make any sense. Why in the angel's name would he be excited about what just happened?"

"I think he is trying to get a reaction out of Vita. Perhaps he is trying to get her abilities back so that the prophecy can come to fruition. Which means when her abilities *do* come back, he cannot know. You must keep her as far away from him as possible. Actually, keep her from Boyd. Dr. Guyer keeps his hands clean, which is why he has chosen a lackey to complete his dirty work for him."

"I'll talk to Chief and see about Boyd. There's no way he'll allow a rogue guardian to hurt an elemental like that."

"Just remember, Sawyer," Dos gave him a knowing look. "We do not have allies in the senior staff. Chief Sawyer might want to help, but that does not mean he can. At the end of the day, Dr. Guyer gets whatever he wants. We might be on our own in this."

CHAPTER 45

FIRE

Dos had just finished piecing together the fragments of the teacup using the melted gold to shape it back together. One of the positives of being a Fire elemental was that Dos could not be burned, regardless of the heat's intensity. This made it possible for him to touch the melted gold with his fingers to accurately place the pieces together.

Now, Dos was in one of the music rooms in the upper-level school setting up his cello. This was where the general education took place for every Elondohnian until they took up a career path. The music room was small and limited, as most students spent their time outside for athletic activities. Music was not a serious enough contribution for it to be considered a career in Elondoh.

But if it were up to Dos, he'd always play his cello.

Guardian Sawyer and Vita walked into the music room. Vita was holding a newly potted, yet crumpled, plant. The clouds of her despair had significantly lightened from earlier, but there was still such a vast emptiness within her. At least her emotions were now light enough that Dos could maneuver them into more positive ones.

"It's beautiful, Dos." She sat on the piano bench and placed the cup on the top of the piano. "Thank you."

"Will your plant be all right?"

"We'll have to wait and see."

Dos's eyes glowed as he nudged some peace her way. A

lilac-colored fog seeped into her despair, the scent of lavender overcoming that of thunderstorms.

Vita's shoulders relaxed, and she gave Dos a knowing smile. "Thanks."

He nodded and handed her a stack of sheet music. "I am afraid that most of our selection is rather dull."

"Oh, let's do this one." Vita plucked a selection from the stack and held it up. "'Bring Him Home.' This song is full of love and hope. There won't be a dry eye in the room."

"You purposely want to make people cry?"

"In a good way. Haven't you ever heard something so beautiful it just makes you want to cry your eyeballs out?"

"No. I was thinking perhaps we could write our own music to perform. Something challenging and beautiful."

Vita lit up, a tiny burst of happiness flurrying about her like a butterfly. "That's a great idea! We could tell a story about—" She stopped and looked at Sawyer, who was standing against the closest door. "You gotta go."

Sawyer blinked in surprise. "Why?"

"You can't hear it before everyone else does. Scoot."

He rolled his eyes and begrudgingly stepped out of the room, closing the door behind him. Vita turned back to Dos and smiled. "I have an idea. We could tell a story about the joy of discovering others who are similar to you, and the rush of forming wonderful bonds. Maybe even with a twist of romance in there. Like falling in love with someone you didn't expect."

"I like it. Do you plan on telling Guardian Sawyer that it is for him?"

She went through a mixture of expressions in a matter of seconds. The neon orange of shock, the ginger scent of embarrassment, and ending with a sigh of realization. "How long have you known?"

He tilted his head as he thought about when he saw their first shared sense of attraction. "I believe it has been a month. It was mild at first, but now when you two are together, the sight of the emotion is nearly blinding. I always wonder why neither of you have acted upon it yet."

"Are you saying he feels the same way?"

"Is it not obvious?"

"Well, I can't see emotions like you can. I had a hunch, but I wasn't sure. I know the kind of girl he's meant to be with, and it ain't me."

"Sawyer has been carrying a stronger sense of defiance recently. Particularly when it comes to you."

"You know about defiance now?"

"Yes, I have learned it from Annie. It seems to be her favorite emotion."

Vita smirked. "You must've learned a lot from Annie. Possibly attraction?"

Dos stilled, panic stabbing through his heart. "How did you . . . ?"

"The only time I've ever seen you blush is when she smiles. You've got it bad, honey. Are you gonna ask her out?"

"It is forbidden. Elementals are not to mix, thanks to Generation 6."

Vita creased her eyebrows. "What do you mean?"

"I have not told you? Angels, it must have slipped my mind. We are distant cousins, you and I. Our ancestors fell in love and had children together. Some of the head alchemists believed that the mixing of their bloodlines was what caused an angelic reaction. Because of that, we are no longer allowed to mix."

"But you really like her, don't you? The way I feel for Lucas, that's how you feel for Annie." At his shy nod, Vita gently nudged him. "Then forget those stupid rules. You could just keep it a secret."

"I am afraid of the punishment she would have to face because of my selfish desires," Dos admitted, his left thumb brushing over the fading scars on his right wrist. Dr. Guyer wouldn't simply punish Annie; he was much more calculating than that. He'd find her most personal fear and force her to drown in it. He would tear her confidence to shreds until there wasn't any personality left in her. Dos could never live with himself if that happened to her.

"I would face a thousand days of cruelty to feel her love, but I would never condemn her to such a fate just for me."

"What if she thought you were worth it?" Vita asked. "And before you say 'I'm not,' just remember that you're not allowed to lie."

Dos released a mix of a breath and a laugh. It was amazing that Vita could endure such heartbreak and still find the room to uplift others. She was a life-giving elemental, so it came naturally to her. But it weighed on Dos's heart because he knew the fate that awaited her. The truth that Sawyer failed to accept, but there was no alternative.

Not a single prophecy predicted by John Dee had ever been wrong before. From the most mundane to the most extravagant, they had all come true. The odds of this one failing didn't exist. Vita was meant to die, and Dos knew that. He knew it would be soon, and there was nothing he could do to prevent it.

Of all the lives to be cut short, hers deserved it the least. She deserved a long life of joy and laughter. There was a difference between the affection he had for Annie and what he felt for Vita. With Annie, it had an exciting physical aspect. A desire. But with Vita, there was a kinship and warmth. He'd never felt gratitude before, but he'd read about it and was sure this was it.

"Vita?" Dos said, feeling a lump form in his throat. "Thank you for being so kind to me. I hope your every wish comes true and that you are fulfilled in life. You make me feel . . . gratitude."

Vita smiled. "What's the color for gratitude?"

He studied her and watched a blurry gray halo form over her head. The emotion still didn't have a scent or color. "I am unsure. This is the first I have felt it. Something warm, though, and inviting."

"How about orange? Like the sunset."

The halo shimmered to a deep golden orange, with the warm scent of freshly baked cookies to pair with it. He nodded. "Yes, orange is the right color for it. Good choice."

"We should name the piece 'Gratitude.' I think it fits."

"I agree."

Vita held up a hand, and Dos carefully returned the high five.

CHAPTER 46

Guardian

"Oh, this is my favorite song!" Vita exclaimed as she held her phone in the air. She demanded that they go outside for lunch, and because Lucas was with her, she could go through her phone again. The sky was filling with rain clouds, the air carrying a cool breeze. It would definitely rain soon, but it wasn't going to start for another few hours. While they walked to the picnic benches in the garden, Vita played her music and told him all about the things she loved most about the outside world.

Dos said he'd given Vita a high dosage of happiness at the end of their session so she would be in a much lighter mood. Lucas was glad for it, and it would seem Vita was too.

They sat at the benches and enjoyed the afternoon sun. Vita pulled up the photos on her phone. "This is my friend Christy and me at a Hunter Hayes concert. Look, we were so close I got a picture of the singer. He is fine as all get out, I tell you what."

Lucas creased his brows. "Is that someone you dated?"

"Goodness, honey, I wish. He doesn't even know I exist. In the outside world, there are things called celebrity crushes. They don't mean anything, but they're fun to have."

"So, these are people you would not pursue but are fond of?"

She nodded. "I don't suppose you have any?"

"Well, the closest thing to celebrities that we have here are the elementals."

Vita fluttered her lashes and pressed her hand over her heart. "Lucas Sawyer, are you telling me it's possible you might have a celebrity crush on me?"

Lucas froze and could barely speak around his sudden stutter. "Well, I mean . . ."

Vita giggled and nudged him. "I'm just teasing, calm down. Anyway, I took a ton of pictures at that concert. Thought the lighting would do me justice, but it all came out blurry."

He leaned closer to her and observed the different photos she flipped through. She was wrong about them. Every photo of herself was wonderful, even the blurry ones.

Vita smiled. "This is the perfect lighting. Let's take a picture together."

"Right now?"

"Yeah." She held up the phone at arm's length.

Lucas cringed at the sight of himself. "I can't do pictures."

"What's there to do? You look at yourself and smile."

He sighed and stared at his reflection. He'd never cared much about his appearance, but he hated pictures. His mother was notorious for filling scrapbooks with family pictures, and they were all awful.

Vita leaned against him and said, "How do we know the ocean is friendly?"

Lucas blinked. This was another one of those outside-world jokes. Vita had once called them "dad jokes," but that didn't make any sense because none of the fathers in Elondoh were very funny.

"How?" he asked, already biting back a grin.

"It waves." Then she snapped the picture as soon as Lucas started laughing.

A storm had rolled in shortly after lunch, so training was dismissed for the remainder of the day. Lucas had just gotten home and was shrugging off his raincoat when he heard Chief's deep voice from the dining room. He must have gotten home early too.

Good. Lucas still needed to make that report about Boyd.

Chief was sitting at the table, cursing under his breath at the reports in front of him. He briefly glanced up at Lucas. "Oh good, you're home. What's this I see about you allowing an elemental to attack Guardian Boyd?"

Lucas groaned and rolled his eyes. "He attacked Vita first. Adrian got to Boyd before I could."

"He claims you encouraged the incident."

"I did no such thing. Boyd stomped on Vita's plant just to provoke her. Adrian knocked him down, but he didn't use his element, nor did he strike Boyd at all."

"Did you attempt to stop Adrian?"

Lucas huffed. "No. I knew he wouldn't take it too far."

"Lucas, you are their lead guardian. You cannot just let a serious event like this happen. What do you think would have happened to Adrian if he *did* take it too far? You think Dr. Guyer would have let it go unpunished?"

"I take full responsibility, but sir, Boyd attacked Vita first. Unprovoked, might I add. I would like to request for his immediate removal under guardian code three dash—"

"Denied."

Lucas's jaw dropped. "Sir, he *attacked* her. Looked her in the eyes and destroyed—"

"Did he touch her?"

"You know as well as I do how much Earth elementals value plant life."

"Did he *touch* her?"

"He could've caused an angelic reaction and—"

"Guardian Sawyer!" Chief barked, banging his fist on the table. "Did. He. Touch her."

Lucas's entire back tightened as he forced himself to not shout back. "No, sir."

"Then there is nothing we can do. He is protected under Dr. Guyer's rule. For all intents and purposes, Boyd is untouchable. I don't like it either but that's how it is. What he did was wrong, but you cannot change it. You are meant to keep the elementals under control, and today you did not prove you could do that. You must show more restraint with your emotions, or else everything under your watch will fall apart. Do you understand?"

Lucas stared in aghast at his father, the man he looked up to the most. The man who was dismissing an obvious problem. For what though? Politics?

"I know there is a secret you are trying to hide. I know there is something nefarious that Dr. Guyer is working on," Lucas admitted in a strained voice. "He plans on harming the elementals, and you know about it, don't you?"

Chief stood until their heights were matched. His face turned red, his mouth pressing into a furious line. He said nothing. Probably because he couldn't lie, but he couldn't tell the truth either.

"You promised you had my back against the entire community. Now is your chance to prove it. Is Dr. Guyer going to hurt Vita?"

A muscle twitched in Chief's jaw. "What makes you think that? Did somebody tell you that?"

"Does it matter?"

"I asked you a question."

"So did I, and you are avoiding it. Can't you look me in the eyes and tell me the truth? Am I not worthy of that?"

"You do not understand the decisions we've had to make and the events that are to pass. We must save lives or else Elondoh's efforts will be all for naught. Thousands of years of effort will mean nothing if we do not make certain sacrifices."

"If you said that to Mason Eastwood, how do you think he'd respond? Would he still call you a friend afterward?"

Chief's expression darkened with a mixture of rage and shame. "Don't think for one moment that I haven't prayed for his forgiveness."

The door opened, allowing in the thundering sound of rain, and Mom walked in. She closed her umbrella and stared at them with wide eyes. Then she huffed a sigh and looked heavenward. "I swear to the angels above, this day has been far too long. What happened?"

"Nothing, ma'am," Lucas answered, stepping back. "Excuse me, I have a report to write."

He coolly stormed upstairs, where he locked his bedroom door and slumped down on his bed. Dos was right about this. They would have no help and would be completely on their own in this silent war.

One guardian and four elementals against Elondoh's most powerful man.

CHAPTER 47

EARTH

V ita settled Bo's patched-together teacup on her desk and opened her balcony doors. It was raining sideways outside. Despite it being early afternoon, the gloomy, dark rain clouds made it feel like evening. Vita breathed in the scent of the rain and listened. Plants sang when they were watered, and they had the most beautiful voices, like a choir of a thousand angels. They didn't sing in words, rather with *ooh*'s and *ah*'s.

But she didn't hear the singing today. Her abilities were still numb.

It's okay. They'll come back soon. I'm not alone.

She'd chanted that to herself at least a hundred times today. It was the only thought that kept her from feeling totally empty. Lucas helped as a distraction when her mind was running too fast for her to keep up. He somehow seemed to know when she was sinking because he'd look at her with those gentle brown eyes and offer a firm nod. A silent "you can do this."

Earlier, Lucas had rested a hand on her shoulder, gave her that stern but warm gaze, and simply said, "You and me, okay?"

It was a simple reminder that she wasn't alone and that she'd be okay. It helped ease the sting enough for her to get through the day. And Dos also helped her when he'd sent her that burst of happiness. She was glad he understood it enough to be able to share it now.

Her hands still bore tiny cuts from picking up the ceramic

shards. They didn't hurt, and they didn't even bleed a lot, but it was a cold reminder that she couldn't heal herself. She couldn't heal Bo, and she couldn't ask him if he was okay. She couldn't do anything.

Vita sucked in a sharp breath and squeezed her eyes shut, trying to stop the spiral of cruel thoughts. She was okay. Her abilities would come back. She was not alone.

Picking up the watering can, she went about watering the indoor plants in her room, finishing with Bo. Per usual, she spoke positive affirmations over them. Like any living thing, her plants grew better with some encouragement.

"Look at how green you've gotten! You just can't stop growing, can you?" Vita tilted the watering can over Bo and smiled. "Bo, I'm really proud of how resilient you are . . ."

As soon as the water hit Bo's soil, Vita heard music.

A soft, childlike voice singing a simple *oh*. Then came the other voices, like parts of a choir joining the song to form one full and harmonious performance. Vita froze and listened, just to be sure.

Her hand shook as she rested a finger on Bo's crumpled form. He sang even louder as his squished leaves reformed and his tattered stem was fully healed. Still, she was unsure whether it was real or just a dream.

Vita ran over to the mirror and gasped at the sight of her glowing green eyes. Then she stepped out onto the balcony, ignoring the cold drops of rain bouncing off her skin.

The earth was singing to her.

The watering can slipped from her fingers and bounced against the floor as Vita whipped around and sprinted out of her room.

"Vita!" Her mom shouted, startled by Vita's sudden franticness.

Vita didn't answer, nor did she stop to grab a coat or even put on rainboots. She just ran outside to get to the garden as quickly as possible. Her feet splashed against the mud, cold rain drenched through her clothes, and her lungs burned, but she kept following the voices, terrified she'd lose them again.

Then she was in the middle of the garden surrounded by the earth. The oak trees and evergreens chanted in their deep, rumbling voices. The hydrangeas and roses harmonized, their tones dancing around each other like lovers in a ballroom. And lavender—beautiful, delicate lavender—floated above all those notes in an airy melody, like birds fluttering in the wind.

Their voices collided and rose in one powerful, breathtaking crescendo until it felt like their song had taken root within her bones. Hot tears slipped out of Vita's eyes and joined the cool rain on her cheeks. Little pink flowers sprouted by her feet, and vines reached toward her as if asking for a hug. Vita gasped out a sob and sank to her knees, overwhelmed by the surge of gratitude and relief.

The earth had welcomed her back. She could feel its energy again, feel the heartbeat of every root beneath her feet. She was enveloped and uplifted by the love that the earth had for her. She was protected and adored.

Vita dug her fingers into the muddy grass and felt a rush of golden euphoria. The cuts on her hands had healed as if they'd never even existed.

"I missed you," she cried to the earth. "I missed you so much, and I love you. Please don't ever leave me again."

Even though there were no words, she somehow understood what the flowers were trying to tell her in their song. They had never left her and they never would. They were always right there, patiently waiting for her to sing with them.

She was loved. She was home.

———————————————

The next morning, Vita sat on the front steps of her townhome while she waited for Lucas. The sun peeked out from the leftover clouds, and a cool breeze brought in the crisp scents of an upcoming fall. Vita shared a handful of freshly picked blueberries with Otis while Lula stretched in a patch of sunlight next to them.

"Vita," Lula said, rolling on her back. "Now that you can hear us again, I need more catnip. Drool-face over there ate my last batch."

Vita giggled and fed Otis a blueberry. "So, that's why you were so sleepy yesterday. Sure thing, Lula. I'll grow some more when we get home from training. Today's the last day of training for the week. With the festival this Saturday, Dr. Guyer wanted to give the guardians time to prepare for the tournament. I guess it's a pretty big deal here."

"Think you'll invite Lucas over?" Otis asked excitedly.

"Can't. He's training for the tournament too. I don't want to throw off his focus."

"I like Lucas," Lula said. "He slipped me a piece of his lunch once. I like a guy who feeds me."

"Same here," Vita agreed as she offered both animals a scratch behind their ears. She always said she wouldn't date anyone if the animals didn't like them. They had great instincts, sometimes even better than Vita's own judgment.

Speaking of which, Ethan was the first to walk up to the row of townhomes, and he smiled brightly at Vita. She'd been avoiding him ever since their last brunch together.

"Good morning," Ethan said. "I'm so glad I caught you. How do you feel?"

"Hey, Ethan," Vita greeted. "I'm good, thanks. Better than ever, actually."

"Oh good. So, I was thinking we could go to the festival together. It's been a while since our last date."

Lula scrutinized Ethan with her bright-yellow eyes and then turned to Vita. "No."

Otis sniffed Ethan's hand, but Ethan flinched back and grimaced as he wiped dog drool from his hand. Otis stiffened up and snorted. That was a hard no from Otis.

Just as well. Vita had been putting off this conversation for long enough as it was. Ethan appreciated himself a bit too much. On their dates, he discussed all the things that made him a good match and even mentioned how other girls would be envious of Vita. For some reason, he thought that was a plus, but Vita wasn't interested in being enemies with any Elondohnian girls. Not to mention, he never argued with her. Whatever she said, weird or not, he simply agreed with. It made conversation with him boring. Good looks only went so far, and that little stunt he pulled with Lucas at brunch had just about sealed it for Vita.

"Ethan, um . . ." Vita sighed, then just said it outright. "I think we should just stay friends."

Ethan's perfect smile dropped. "Is there someone else you're interested in?"

"Red flag," Lula said. "Break his heart and send him away."

Vita ignored her. "I don't really want to talk about it."

"It's Sawyer, isn't it?" Ethan asked, chuckling without any humor. "He always gets everything he wants, doesn't he? Don't you see that, to him, you are simply a conquest? Sawyer gets the best of the best without even trying for it, and now he gets you too?"

"That's strike two," Lula warned, pupils dilating at his shoelaces. "Say the word, Vita, and I'll take him down."

"You're supposed to go for the neck, not the ankles," Otis said, standing tall.

Vita stood so she could face Ethan instead of looking up at him. "There's a little thing in the outside world called minding your own beeswax. I think you should practice it now. If I want someone, I'll have him, and I don't need to explain it to you."

"He's meant to marry an Elondohnian girl. He won't seriously pursue you; he cares too much about his image. This is just a rebellious phase he is going through, surely you see that. He will eventually break your heart."

"I think you're forgetting one major thing, honey. My parents are Elondohnian. Maybe I grew up an outsider, but my blood came from here. Now, I think you and I are better as friends, but you keep talking and we won't even be that."

At that moment, Lucas walked up, eyeing Ethan. "Good morning, Guardian James."

Ethan scoffed and shook his head. "Sawyer." He breezed past Lucas and headed back to Adrian's doorstep with a sour look on his face.

"Everything all right?" Lucas asked.

Vita waved a dismissive hand. "Yeah, he'll be fine. I've got something to show you. Ready?"

"Okay?"

Her eyes glowed green as the briar rose bushes by her steps flourished and fully bloomed, releasing the sweet scent of apples. Lucas gasped, as he watched each delicate pink petal unravel from its bud.

"Glory to the angels . . ." he said in awe.

Vita plucked a rose from the bush, after using her abilities to sink the thorns into the stem so it was safe to hold. Then she held it out to him and grinned. "Surprise."

CHAPTER 48

GUARDIAN

W*hen her abilities do come back, he cannot know.* Dos's warning played in Lucas's mind as he watched the flowers bloom around Vita.

"I can't wait to show everyone." Vita smiled at the flower in her hand. "Let's stop by the gardens! I want to bring the best bouquet to training today."

Lucas winced and mentally scrambled for a viable excuse. "Actually, would you mind keeping your abilities a secret?"

Vita blinked, and her smile faded. "Why? Dr. Guyer's been asking about my abilities. He seems really concerned."

"Yes, I know but . . ." Angels forgive him, he would have to lie. He feigned a bashful smile, as if he were embarrassed to admit this. "Dr. Guyer is giving us the rest of the week off for the tournament, but if he hears that your abilities are back, he'll want to schedule more trainings and . . . well, I'm nervous about the tournament and would like the extra time to train some more."

Vita laughed and playfully nudged him. "You little rebel. Fine, I suppose a little secrecy won't be so bad."

"Thank you. We should get to the laboratory before we're late." Lucas led her and Otis away, mentally panicking. The excuse would buy them a few more days, but it certainly wouldn't last forever, and they were no closer to finding a solution for Vita.

Angels help us, he prayed. *Give us something to work with.*

During lunch, Lucas stood next to Hogan in the buffet line in the dining hall when some of the gardening staff came in carrying heavy bushels of dirty potatoes. One of the workers, a woman with big, curly blonde hair, struggled with her basket. Hogan froze when he saw her.

"What?" Lucas whispered. "What's wrong with her?"

"Wrong? Nothing, she's perfect," Hogan muttered shyly.

"Oh," Lucas observed her again. "She's pretty. Has she introduced herself to you yet?"

"No. Annie suggested I give her something called a smolder."

"She suggested you burn the girl?"

"Apparently in the outside world, it is a way they look at each other to attract romance. She taught me how to do it. What do you think?" Hogan contorted his face so that his eyes were squinting, one eyebrow was raised in a questioning manner, and he chewed on his lower lip. "Do you feel attracted yet?"

"Uh, not quite," Lucas admitted, trying not to grimace too hard. "Maybe try squinting a little more."

The woman fumbled with her basket and dropped it, sending a tiny herd of potatoes bouncing across the floor. "Oh, not again!"

Lucas and Hogan hurried to help her, joining her on the floor and gathering the potatoes in one pile.

"Angels bless you," she said, brushing back her hair. "One of these days, I'll stop dropping the harvest. Oh, I'm sorry, did you get dirt in your eyes?"

Hogan had attempted his awkward smoldering, looking like he was trying very hard to see far away. He dropped the face and his eyes widened like saucers. "Oh, no, I was . . . you're . . . you're beautiful."

Lucas thought he would die of embarrassment right there and

looked around for a viable exit from this horrible situation, but then his jaw dropped when the girl smiled and held out her dirt-covered hand.

"My name isn't Beautiful, but you can call me Violet Harper. House of the Otter."

Hogan smiled and took her hand. "Timothy Hogan, House of the Rabbit. May I help you carry this basket?"

"Thank you."

Did Hogan just fumble his way into an introduction? Sure, he was decent-looking, but he was also supremely awkward. Most women laughed at Hogan but this one must've seen something no one else did. Lucas handed over the last fallen potato and watched them walk away.

Dumbfounded, he picked up his lunch tray and wandered back to the elementals' table. They had another hour of training, and then they'd be released for the weekend.

Vita nudged him and smiled. "That was nice of you to help that girl."

"Oh, thank you." He glanced at Hogan and Violet, who were deep in conversation. "She gave Hogan her introduction."

Annie followed Lucas's eyes to the couple. "Yes! I *told* him the smolder would work."

Lucas chuckled to himself and shook his head. "The smolder had nothing to do with it. He was just . . . himself. Somehow that worked."

The night before the tournament, hours after training had ended, Lucas was wielding a wooden sword against a training dummy, making sure to perfect his lunges and footwork. The dull thump of wood against dense foam echoed against the walls of the guardians' training hall. Lucas had waited until the other competitors left the gym for the night so he could practice alone.

Practically speaking, the guardians were trained in modern methods of combat: firearms, hand-to-hand, and various knife-wielding techniques. But they still maintained the art of sword fighting, just as their original knights had. For the guardians who attended outside-world missions, it wouldn't be as helpful as knowing how to reload a gun and fire accurately, but traditions mattered in Elondoh. Lucas Sawyer, future chief, needed to be the best in that arena or he might as well turn in his rank now.

Sweat rolled down his temple and dripped off his jaw as he made one last lunge against the dummy's chest. He stepped back and wiped his forehead while he caught his breath. A single set of applause broke out at the doorway, and Lucas whirled to find Vita smiling and clapping for him.

"What are you doing here?" he asked, still breathless. He checked his watch. "It's nearly curfew for you."

She shrugged the shoulder that was carrying the strap of her bag. "Yeah, one of the security guys mentioned that. I told him Guardian Sawyer would escort me home, and he left me alone. I brought something for you. Might bring you some good luck."

Vita dug into her bag and pulled out a roll of purple fabric. Lucas raised an eyebrow and unraveled the fabric, revealing a gold-embroidered lion. It was his house flag, about the size of a piece of paper.

"Dos told me that y'all have to wear flags for the tournament, but he said it was just plain fabric. I thought the future chief deserved something better, so I made it," Vita explained. "Just a thank-you gift for helping me after my abilities left."

Lucas smiled, a blush coating his sweaty face. "Angels, Vita, this is beautiful. Thank you. I'd hug you, but . . ."

"Yeah, keep all that sweat over there. Think you can walk me home though?"

He nodded and put his practice tools away before leading her out. After yesterday's rainfall, the night air was cool and welcome against his hot skin.

"You know," Vita started, "I never got to thank you for helping me when my abilities were gone. You stood by my side even when I pushed you away. Now whenever I heal, I feel like I'm giving back rather than making up for my past failure of not being able to heal my dad. I just want to heal everything I can."

For immortality to be attained, the breath of life must be paid.

Lucas hadn't told her about the prophecy yet. He wasn't sure how. He thought about the conversation he'd had with the others and felt his stomach tighten.

"Can I ask you something?" Lucas said. "If you knew you could rid the world of every disease but it would require your life, would you still do it?"

"Yes," Vita answered without hesitation.

"You would sacrifice your life to heal random people you don't know? Some of them could be horrible people. They will never know your name or the price you paid, yet you would still die for them?"

"They aren't just random people to me, Lucas. They're little girls waiting by their daddy's bedside, watching their hero wither away because of a disease. They're parents praying that their baby's gonna make it to the next morning. They're Christmas dinners with one less person at the table. They're people who would bring good into the world if they only had a little more time. Sure, there's some bad folks out there, but I believe the good outweighs them, and if I can give them at least one more day, then why wouldn't I?"

"But what about your mother? Or your friends, or ..."

Or me?

Vita hugged her elbows, and the weight of grief clouded her usually bright eyes as she spoke in a soft voice. "When my daddy died, I thought my whole world was ending. I felt so small and lost. It was suffocating how painful his loss was, but at least it was quick. I remember him strong and full of joy. I can't imagine how scary it would've been to see him suffer day after day in a hospital bed. To lose someone is hard, but to watch them fade away into nothing? That's haunting. I would give everything if it meant helping those people. If the price is as small as me, then I see it as a bargain."

Lucas shook his head. "That's too high a price. You're too valuable to be given away like that."

Vita raised an amused eyebrow at him as they reached her front porch. She stopped and leaned against the railing to face him. "Now, don't tell me you'd actually miss me and all my—what did you call it? Unbearable wildness?"

"Maybe I would. I'd miss your wildness, your funny accent, and how you always insult me in phrases I don't understand. I'd miss you and me."

She reached out and gave his hand a quick but reassuring squeeze. "It's all hypothetical anyway. You're stuck with me for a while, Lucas Sawyer."

"At least until the stone is created."

She shrugged. "Or I find a reason to stay."

"A reason like Guardian James?"

"No. Actually, this morning I told him I wasn't interested in a relationship. We're just friends."

"Really?" Lucas asked a little too excitedly. He tried fixing his expression into a casual interest, but his heart leaped a thousand times. "Why?"

"He just wasn't my type. I think I need someone who's not such a peacock, if you know what I mean."

He didn't know what that meant, and he didn't ask. "Oh. I assumed you two would be going to the festival together."

"Nope. I'm flying solo, I guess. Unless someone happens to ask me between now and tomorrow morning." She stared at him, as if expecting a specific response.

Lucas's body grew hot. He was still covered in dry sweat, wearing his workout gear, and frustratingly unprepared to ask her on a date. Was he supposed to wait for an introduction from her? Did it technically matter anymore?

Angels, this was complicated.

"Have a good night," Lucas blurted, already making his way down her porch steps without letting Vita say goodnight.

"Okay?" she muttered with a sigh.

Son of the angels, Guardian Sawyer! If Hogan can stumble into an introduction, you can ask Vita on a date.

"Wait!" He turned and faced her. "Let's go together. To the festival, I mean. As a date or . . . whatever. No, not whatever. It would be a date. I am asking you on a date."

Vita raised an eyebrow. Again, an amused smile played on her lips as she waved a hand for him to continue. "Well, go on. Give me your proposition. I want pros and cons."

He smiled and straightened his posture. "If you attend the festival with me, I will bring you to the best vendors that Elondoh has to offer. I'll be sure to get you an authentic medieval meal— vegetarian, of course—and I'll win you a prize at ring toss. In exchange, you must promise me a dance at the end of the night."

Vita hummed in thought and tapped her chin. "Cons?"

"You'll have to share any dessert with me. Especially if it has chocolate."

She grinned and held out her hand. "It's a date then. You and me."

He took her hand and surprised himself by planting a kiss on the back of it. The amount of boldness her smile gave him was dangerously exhilarating. "I'll see you tomorrow then, Miss Eastwood."

Vita somehow blushed in the most graceful way as she watched Lucas walk off. Meanwhile, Lucas hurried away until he was sure he was alone, then pumped his fist in the air. Yes, there were a few important things that required his attention. Namely, the prophecy, Dr. Guyer's selfish intentions, and the well-being of the elementals.

But for at least one day, he could allow himself to just be a man and have fun.

CHAPTER 49

GUARDIAN

The next morning, Lucas stood in a large tent outside of the arena, adjusting his leather armor. The other competing guardians lounged around the tent, stretching, chatting, and practicing movements. They wore traditional black tunics and linen pants with a vest baring their house color and animal. Around the waist was a leather belt that held their house flag.

Lucas absentmindedly toyed with the flag Vita had made for him on his belt and listened as the game master explained the rules to the audience.

The rules were simple: it was an ordinary sword fight, but the winner had to be the last standing with their flag still on their belt. If a guardian was struck in a kill zone—such as their head, chest, or back—the losing guardian had to remove their flag and toss it at the winning guardian's feet as a show of conquest.

Lucas poked his head out of the curtain and scanned the crowd of spectators. Dr. Guyer sat on the highest raised platform. Chief and Dr. Sawyer sat at his right-hand side. The elementals had the honor of sitting on the left-hand side as his guests. Vita was missing from the group. Perhaps she hadn't arrived yet.

Chief's uniform was like Lucas's, except that he wore a golden sash around his tunic with his rank printed on top. His mother wore a flowing purple dress, and delicate gold lion combs pinned back her hair. They glinted in the sunlight as she turned her head to talk to Chief.

It was tradition that when a couple began courting, the man presented the woman with jewelry bearing the man's house animal as a way of showing loyalty to each other. His mother had had those combs since she and Chief had started courting, and she only broke them out on festival days, as most women did. After the wedding, they usually wore simple gold wedding bands and kept the charm for special occasions.

Lucas distantly wondered what kind of jewelry Vita would like. She hardly wore any, but he thought a necklace would look nice on her. Something gold.

Don't get ahead of yourself, Sawyer. Get through the date first.

The chatter of the tent halted and was replaced with the soft murmur of whispers as if someone important had walked in. But all the high-ranking people were still in the stands. Lucas looked over his shoulder and stilled when he saw Vita peeking into the tent and offering polite waves to the competitors.

Ethan walked up to her with a bright smile. "Vita, it's so wonderful to see you before the competition. Your beauty is sure to give us good luck."

"Thanks. Have you seen Lucas?" She looked around him and smiled when she spotted Lucas. "Hey! Could I steal you for a second?"

All eyes turned to Lucas, most of them surprised. Hogan flashed him an excited grin and a thumbs-up. Ethan's smile curled down into a grim line of annoyance. Lucas flushed from all the attention and walked up to her.

"What are you doing here?"

She glanced around at the mass of curious eyes and tried not to laugh. He could tell because she always pursed her lips when she withheld it. "Come with me."

Murmurs broke out, and Lucas could piece together what most of them were saying. They all definitely thought there was something between Lucas and Vita now. Lucas ignored them and followed her a short distance out of the tent until they were beneath the shade of a tree.

"I just wanted to wish you good luck before the tournament. I was searching all morning for one of these and finally found one. Came across a bunch of ladybugs, too, so I made a ton of wishes for your victory." Vita tucked a four-leafed clover into the top notch of his chest plate. "I know you're not really a superstition kind of guy."

"Thank you," Lucas said. "Anything helps. I'm glad I got to see you before we begin. The costume suits you."

For the Clarice Day Festival, Elondohnians wore medieval-inspired clothing. Women wore long linen dresses and some kind of covering on their heads, while the men wore doublets adorned in gold or silver. Vita wore a green dress with a crown of tiny white flowers on top of her head.

She was stunning, but he didn't know how far to go with compliments. He now believed that she liked him, but he wasn't sure how deep those feelings went yet, and he didn't want to scare off his chance at earning her favor.

The speaker overhead coughed out static before announcing that all competitors must meet in the arena in two minutes.

"I have to go," Lucas said, both excited to compete but disappointed to leave her.

Vita hopped up on the tips of her toes and kissed his cheek. Lucas's breath caught, his face burning hot.

Vita looked as surprised as he was, a hand flying to her mouth as her eyes flashed green. Little pink flowers sprouted from the ground near her feet.

"Good luck, Guardian Sawyer. I'll be cheering for you." She bobbed him a curtsy before running off to the stands.

For a moment, Lucas stood there with his hand on his cheek

and a dreamy smile on his face. The kiss had lasted only a moment, but he could still feel the heat from her lips and smell the vanilla from her perfume. The small flowers remained in the spot where she previously stood, as if a monument to her.

Something small fluttered past his ear as a ladybug flew by. Lucas smiled and held out a finger for it to land on.

"Vita says you make wishes come true," he whispered. "I wish to find out if she feels the same way about me."

Lucas lightly blew the ladybug and it fluttered away. Today was going to be a wonderful day.

"Lucas!" Chief barked behind him, pushing the curtain aside.

Lucas jumped and whirled around to face him. "Yes, sir?"

"Didn't you hear the call? You're due in the arena. Let's go!"

"Yes, right." Lucas blinked himself back into reality and scurried into the tent.

"Hold on," Chief grabbed Lucas's elbow and scrutinized his cheek. "What's that stuff on your face? Is that ... *lipstick*?"

Lucas's eyes widened as he rubbed his cheek with the back of his hand, and sure enough, there was a pink smudge from Vita's lips. "Um, I was ... eating berries and it, uh ... smeared."

"Berries. The best excuse you could come up with was *berries*?" Chief rolled his eyes and pushed Lucas forward. "Son, I know we discourage lying, but angels above, if you're going to do it, at least come up with something sensible. Now get your game face on or that'll be the last kiss you get."

"Right. Yes, sir."

"Wait." Chief held Lucas back and lowered his voice. "Vita?"

Lucas couldn't hide the shy grin as he nodded. Their relationship had been tense recently, but their bond of father and son was strong and ran deep. If anyone would understand, it was Chief.

"My boy." Chief smirked proudly and shoved Lucas into the arena.

Lucas unsheathed his sword, the straps of his shield snug on his left forearm.

House of the Lion. I can do this.

Twenty competing guardians stood in a circle in the pit of the stadium watching each other with gritted intensity as they waited for the gong to sound off.

The families of the competitors waved their banners, cheering loudly for their sons. The families who were not competing simply waved Elondoh's banners and cheered on the violence.

The guardian to his left kept eyeing Lucas, leaning ever so slightly toward him. He was probably going to make Lucas his first target, or at least he'd attempt it. Lucas pretended not to notice and focused his attention on the center of the field, just as Chief had taught him. Tournaments were his favorite part of Elondoh's culture, even when he had been too young to participate and could only watch. This being his first year as a competitor, Lucas was more than excited to start.

The gong went off and Lucas whipped to his left, bringing up his shield just in time to block a hit from a guardian's sword. With a quick swipe, Lucas brought his sword across the guardian's abdomen. If it were a real sword, that boy would have been sliced in half.

Instead, he cursed and tossed his red flag at Lucas's feet.

On to the next, Lucas whirled and kicked another guardian at center mass. The guardian stumbled back into two other fighters, who only took their attention off each other to give him a quick stab. A pink flag flew into the air from the center of the fray.

One by one, he allowed the others to come at him for a fight. Blurs of colorful flags hit his feet as he danced around the other guardians, staying on the offense. He took a few blows to his arms and legs, but as they weren't considered kill zones, he was allowed to continue fighting.

And fight he did.

A shield collided with his face, his nose throbbed as he quickly recovered and punched the opposing guardian's face with the hilt of his sword. As his opponent stumbled back, Lucas sliced upward against his chest. A green flag fluttered to his feet, signifying his victory.

A dark shadow crept up behind Lucas. He dove down just in time to avoid a sword. Lucas swept his leg back, knocking his opponent over. Before the guardian could hit the ground, Lucas drove his sword hard against his chest plate. A white flag and a not-so-friendly curse fell at Lucas's feet.

It was down to four guardians now, Lucas included. Boyd had just knocked out Hogan with a blow to the head and leaped over to Lucas.

Finally, an excuse to punch him, Lucas thought as he adjusted his grip and raced up to Boyd.

He crossed Boyd's sword with his own, pushing back. Boyd stumbled, giving Ethan the room to jump in and go for a strike. But it was too predictable.

Boyd managed to knock away Ethan's sword and swipe down at his wrist, forcing Ethan to release his shield.

Lucas dove in, keeping his feet light as he moved around Boyd, their swords clanking together as they fought each other. Boyd was definitely fighting with his emotions. His sword struck Lucas's shield with enough force to cause Lucas to stumble.

With a quick kick to the stomach, Lucas was able to force Boyd backward. He saw an opening and swiped his sword down on Boyd's hand.

With a curse, Boyd dropped his sword and stumbled backward into Ethan's arms. Ethan held Boyd back and nodded once at Lucas.

A swipe at his chest and Boyd was out of the game. Ethan tossed him to the ground with a laugh.

Boyd cursed viciously and threw his yellow flag in before storming off the field.

Lucas and Ethan laughed with each other, sharing victorious smiles until they realized they were the final competitors.

Ethan sighed and adjusted the grip on his sword. "Sorry, old friend."

"I'm not," Lucas half joked, fixing his posture and striking first.

There was a reason why Ethan had always been a close second to Lucas in training. Both were incredibly light on their feet and were not afraid to make daring moves. But Lucas had that uncanny knack for predicting moves a few moments before they happened.

Ethan made a quick swipe at Lucas's head. Lucas raised his shield just in time to block it. Then he pushed with all his might against his shield, knocking Ethan back a few steps.

Lucas kicked hard at the dirt, sending a cloud of dry dust in Ethan's face.

"Agh!" Ethan instinctively covered his eyes.

Lucas dropped low to the ground and swiped his feet behind Ethan's legs. Ethan slammed to the ground with a resounding thud, knocking the air from his lungs.

Ethan coughed and quickly raised his sword in defense. Lucas knocked Ethan's sword with his own before stepping over Ethan's wrist.

Before Ethan could make another move, Lucas pressed the

tip of his sword to his throat. Both guardians were out of breath, dirty, and covered in sweat, waiting for the other to make the next move.

Ethan might have been able to fight back, but the likelihood of his success was pitifully low. At this point in the game, Lucas could now do one of two things.

He could make a move in the kill zone, take Ethan's flag, and wave it proudly in the air for his victory. Lucas would be crowned the winner, and the community would applaud him. He'd be known all over Elondoh as this year's tournament winner.

Or he could choose chivalry and show mercy. Lucas could tell Ethan to keep his flag and display unity between the houses of the Black Bear and the Lion. There would be no crowned winner.

Plus, there was a slim chance that Ethan could choose to continue fighting Lucas, though that would be highly unchivalrous. If there was anything Lucas knew about Ethan, it was that the man valued class.

Just as Ethan reached for the flag at his belt, Lucas sheathed his sword and held out his hand.

"The House of the Lion will not fight the House of the Black Bear tonight," Lucas announced.

A collective gasp swept through the stadium as the community waited for Ethan's next move. He could still deny the offer of mercy and attack Lucas in pursuit of the victory.

Ethan grinned at him and accepted his helping hand, pulling him into a rough bear hug when he stood.

Both guardians held up their flags as a show of unity, and the crowd erupted with cheers. Much to Lucas's surprise, the community seemed to love watching the two houses align, and even threw roses at their feet like they would have for the victor. This wasn't exactly how Lucas had imagined his first tournament would end, but he could appreciate it nonetheless.

Ethan roughly patted Lucas's back and rested an arm around his shoulders. "Look at those girls. They're all radiantly in love with you now! You could have anyone you want."

Lucas glanced at the crowd, but his eyes landed on the girl who smiled brilliantly and somehow found a way to cheer louder than the others.

"Yes, I could. But all I want is her," Lucas breathlessly said, mostly to himself, as Vita tossed a pink rose at his feet.

CHAPTER 50

FIRE

Dos held his breath, wanting to shake some sense into Vita. The rose had simply grown out of the ground and into her hand. Dos watched in silent horror as Dr. Guyer caught a glimpse of Vita's glowing eyes just moments before she tossed the rose.

"Vita, dear girl, have your abilities returned?" Dr. Guyer asked.

Vita hesitated. "Um . . ."

Dos stepped in. "Vita, I did not realize. Congratulations!"

Now that Dr. Guyer knew her abilities had returned, Dos would make sure he didn't find out that Vita had withheld that information from him. She wouldn't be able to handle the punishment that lying would bring upon her. Sawyer mentioned that her abilities had returned, but he'd convinced her not to tell Dr. Guyer. She must have forgotten.

"How wonderful!" Dr. Guyer cheered. "All the excitement of the tournament must have triggered it. We should run some tests to ensure their strength."

Dos winced. He knew the type of tests Dr. Guyer preferred.

"Today?" Vita asked. "We're supposed to have the day off for the festival."

"I wouldn't want to waste a minute. They might flicker away again if we do not nurture their strength."

"I don't think so. To be honest, it's been a couple—"

"Dr. Guyer, if I may make a suggestion?" Dos interrupted

before Vita could unknowingly condemn herself. Annie and Adrian stiffened in their seats. "Perhaps it should be done on Monday? Vita has had a bit to drink today, and that may lead to inaccurate results."

Vita hadn't had a drop of alcohol, but it wouldn't be unusual for an occasion like this, and they needed a cover. Thank the angels that she went along with his lie.

"Oh..." Dr. Guyer frowned. "Very well. We start Monday then."

"Excellent idea, sir." Dos said. Dr. Guyer nodded, then walked down the steps of the stadium.

"So, you gonna tell me what that was about?" Vita asked Dos once Dr. Guyer was gone. "I get that we weren't telling him before so we could have the rest of the week off from training, but what does it matter now?"

Dos exchanged a quick look at Annie and Adrian before choosing to lie to her as well. "We should not let Dr. Guyer know that you lied. He takes the philosopher's stone very seriously, and he would be most disappointed if he found out we had delayed any progress for a silly festival. That is all."

"Oh, okay. I get that. Well, it's out of our hands now."

Dos withheld his frustration and nodded. She was right, but she didn't know the repercussions of what she just did or what was to come. He wanted her to enjoy today. It would likely be her first—and only—Clarice Day Festival.

"You are meeting with Guardian Sawyer today, correct?" he asked, hoping to lighten the mood.

She nodded with a bright smile. "Yeah, we're gonna meet later by the flower booth. What are y'all gonna do?"

"I told my folks I'd hang around them until the dance," Adrian said. "I'm starving though, and I smell food, so I'm gonna hunt that down. What about you two?"

Annie shrugged, already appearing bored. "I don't really want to spend my Saturday playing stupid games, and this godforsaken corset makes me want to scream. I'm probably gonna go home until we have to show up again for the dance. Dos, what are your plans?"

"I usually go home after the tournament as well. I am not one for games."

Vita shot Dos a meaningful look. "Dos, you could escort Annie home so she doesn't have to go alone, ya know?"

Dos looked at Annie and held out his arm. "If you are ready, I am too."

She shrugged again and accepted. They walked out of the arena together and started their short journey home. The field was full of Elondohnian families rushing around to enjoy the festivities. They barely seemed to notice the two elementals walking in the opposite direction.

"What are you going to do until your music performance?" Annie asked.

"Perhaps read or practice the piece a few more times."

"Sounds boring," Annie said. "You might as well come over to my place. My dad's going around with the other parents, so it'll just be us."

She wanted to spend time with him? What did he have to offer her?

It would be terribly inappropriate, even if they weren't elementals. For a man to be alone in a woman's house, with no supervision and no courtship? Rumors would spread like a disease if anyone caught them.

But then, everyone was at the festival. Except for Dr. Novak, but she was working at the lab, so she wouldn't spot them anyway.

"All right," Dos finally said as they approached her townhome. "Thank you."

Annie followed Dos in and shut the door behind them. He

immediately felt out of place in her house, noting the outside-world decor and furniture. Instead of everything being the standard issue white of his own residence, Annie's house had color to it. Blue couches, paintings on the walls, pictures of Annie and David on the mantel. It was obvious that a family lived here.

Annie motioned for Dos to follow, and he did. She led him upstairs to her room, then yanked the flower crown off her head and tossed it on her desk. Dos stayed in the doorway, maintaining an arguably respectful distance. Her room smelled like her jasmine perfume. Her walls were littered with pictures, dark clothing hung in her closet, and paint supplies were scattered across her desk.

"What kind of music do you like? We're lucky I went through a vintage phase or else we'd be screwed." Annie flipped through a stack of CDs on her desk. She finally looked up and noticed him standing in the doorway. She snorted. "You can come in. I don't bite."

Again, Dos ignored the warning bells in his head that told him this was wrong and took a step in. "I did not want to give the wrong impression."

"I've already got an impression of you, and believe me, it'd be hard to change my mind." Her eyes flicked from his shoes up to his eyes, and she smirked.

"What does that mean?"

"Can't you tell? I mean seriously, you read everyone's emotions all the time, and I hear you asking Adrian and Vita about the ones you don't understand, but you never say anything about mine."

"Emotions are intimate features of our souls. I do not wish to offend you by reading your emotions without permission."

"Read me now." She tilted her chin up at him.

His eyes glowed as he watched that familiar ash-colored ribbon flourish around her chest. Heat formed within his core with the lightest shine of ice-blue attraction.

"What are you feeling?" Dos asked. "You've worn it around me before, but I can never find the name for it."

"What does it feel like?"

"It feels ... rebellious. Addicting. Reckless. Once I felt it for the first time, it was all I could think about despite trying not to. Tell me its name."

Dos couldn't handle it anymore. This emotion haunted him. As much as he scoured his books, he couldn't find anything like it. His body reacted in ways he couldn't understand, and damn it all, he *would* find the name for it.

Annie's smile grew slowly, one side quirking higher than the other. That emotion grew hotter, more intense, prickling through his skin as she walked toward him. "Do you feel it around me too?"

He nodded, then felt his heart raging when Annie rested a hand on his chest. She looked down at his lips then up to his eyes. "It's called lust. We're not supposed to feel it for each other, but here we are."

That ash-toned ribbon now took on a rich, warm color, as if reflecting the glow from a carnelian stone. The musky scent of extinguished fire enveloped him, like hands dragging him further into the depths of Annie's spell.

"We should separate before these emotions get out of hand," Dos muttered, quickly becoming breathless.

"Is that what you want?" Annie lifted her hand away.

Without even thinking, he stopped her, gently taking her wrist and flattening her palm against his chest again. He couldn't bear to be away from her touch for a moment longer. What did another person's hands feel like when they weren't striking him?

"No," he said. "But just being alone with you is enough for a hoard of guardians to separate us and lock us away. Dr. Guyer will say this is wrong."

"Who cares what that tyrant has to say? I don't see anyone in here but us. We both know we've been avoiding this for a while. We might as well just see what happens."

"I cannot allow my feelings to endanger you. You are all I think about, and that is a deadly thing."

Annie shrugged and pulled her hand away. "I'm not scared. Either way, I already said this corset is killing me, so I'm taking it off. You're welcome to stay or leave. Just as long as you choose what you actually want and not what other people say you should do. You're a Fire elemental. You once told me that even kings bowed to us. I'd like to see a bit of that now."

Dos was the son of angels and knights. But under the shadow of Dr. Guyer and Dr. Novak, he was nothing. He was always considered a liability. A waste. His thoughts, his soul, his independence were never accounted for. Their threats and abuse were always the one leverage they had, but now he was stronger and better. He was the only living Fire elemental, for angel's sake.

What could they do to him that he could not simply fight against? At the core of it all, they could never truly take his power away. If there was something worth fighting for, wasn't it the right to choose his own life?

Annie pulled at the thread of her corset, giving him an expectant look. With a few clever tugs, her dress fell to her ankles, and Dos finally saw that design inked on her hip. It was of a woman in flight. It was Annie at her freest.

Dos turned from her and walked toward the bedroom door, resting his hand on the knob. "There is another emotion that I need you to explain, for you are an expert at it."

"Yeah? What is it?"

"Freedom." He smiled to himself and locked the door, shutting

Elondoh away and leaving the two of them alone.

CHAPTER 51

WATER

Adrian finished his meat pie and went in for another. He was having lunch with his parents in one of the food tents. Elondohnian food was so plain and lacked seasoning, but the festival food was decent. Maybe they saved up their seasonings for such an event. He was hungry anyway, so he dug in. Once the stone was created and he was free to go, the first thing he'd do was eat good food again. Elondoh had nothing on South Carolina cooking.

"Excuse me?" A woman with long red hair came up to his table and smiled at Adrian. *Oh no, not another one.* "I am Elizabeth Ashley, House of the Falcon."

Adrian's parents collectively sighed and picked up their drinks. Adrian swallowed his last bite and offered an empathetic smile. "Sorry, I'm already taken."

"Oh," Elizabeth said, just as disappointed as the other four girls who had introduced themselves to him today. Guess they weren't so scared of the elementals now.

Adrian's eyes glowed blue as he quickly scanned the room. Sitting in the corner among a group of guardians was a blond man who watched Elizabeth with a furrowed brow.

How am I to compete with an elemental? She will never introduce herself to me now.

"That guy over there," Adrian said, nodding in the guardian's direction. "He likes you. You should go talk to him."

Elizabeth looked in that direction and lit up. "Really? I thought he was interested in someone else. He's rather cute, isn't he?"

"Uh, sure."

"Thank you. Enjoy the festival." She confidently made her way over to the guardian.

"I swear, one of these people better name their kid after me or something," Adrian said, getting back to his food. "If football doesn't work out, I could always be a matchmaker."

His mother rolled her eyes. "Dream big, honey. In the meantime, we've got to stick a sign on your forehead that tells girls you're not interested."

"He's such a stud, isn't he, Tabby?" Adrian's dad joked. "Like his old man."

His mom smiled and quirked an eyebrow at her husband. "Robert Jackson, did you just call yourself old? You still look as young and handsome as you did when we first met."

Adrian rolled his eyes and continued eating, scanning the room again for any entertaining thoughts. He ended up stumbling on one mind that made his mouth run dry.

Dr. Guyer sat at a table with Boyd and was speaking to him in a low voice. Adrian slipped into Dr. Guyer's mind and looked through his eyes.

"Call the logging company and have them start tomorrow," Dr. Guyer said.

"Tomorrow is a Sunday, sir," Boyd argued. "And it is short notice. Will they be able to pull it off?"

"Tell them price is not a problem. They've already started, we just need them to continue their work for another hour or so. You'll convince them if you want the rank of chief."

"Yes, sir. Will Guardian James be in attendance as well?"

Dr. Guyer scoffed. "No. He is too weak and will not be able to complete the task at hand. You will go in his place. I will handle him. Your team will be sent to help stop a wildfire that broke out near Elondoh. See to it that the windows of the bus are open, that is vital. Do not let anyone stop you from—"

Dr. Guyer suddenly looked up and spotted Adrian's glowing blue eyes and shocked expression.

"Damn it," Adrian muttered, looking away, but it was too late.

Dr. Guyer was already walking over with that fake pleasant smile. He was at the table before Adrian's parents could even ask why Adrian was fidgeting so much.

"Hello!" Dr. Guyer greeted happily. "I'm sorry, I know I am interrupting your delicious meal, but could I borrow Adrian for just a moment? I need his assistance with something right away."

Adrian's parents both shared the same disdainful look, but Adrian stood anyway. "It'll just be a second."

He followed Dr. Guyer outside and kept quiet. If he didn't admit to anything, Dr. Guyer had nothing to accuse him of.

Dr. Guyer stopped just outside of the tent and continued smiling at Adrian. "How was your Naomi before you left? Was she doing well?"

Adrian blinked. That definitely wasn't what he thought Dr. Guyer would say. "Uh, yeah, she was good."

"And her elder brother? He is in the Navy, is he not? Works on submarines?"

"Yes?"

"An exciting job but very dangerous. Something could happen to him and no one would know for quite some time."

Ah, Adrian realized with dread. *I know where this is going.*

"I'm sure the Navy can handle most threats," Adrian said.

"Oh, I know they can!" Dr. Guyer chuckled, but there was a coldness in his eyes. "I know many things about them because I often work with them, and I have so many connections. They're wonderfully accommodating as well. If I say I need help, they help me. No questions asked, so long as I keep providing them with our guardians. Isn't that so kind of them?"

Horror seeped in and tightened every muscle in Adrian's body. He swallowed and said nothing.

"They are impressively good at keeping secrets as well," Dr. Guyer continued, as if not noticing that Adrian's fists were balled by his side. "That's something that keeps them alive. If men shared the first thing they learned, we'd never survive and neither would our loved ones."

Adrian nodded once to show he understood.

Dr. Guyer clapped his shoulder. "Always good to see someone who understands. Well, thank you for our chat, son. Enjoy the festival."

Adrian drifted back into the tent and numbly sat down with his parents.

"What did he want?" his dad asked.

Adrian shrugged and picked up his half-eaten meat pie. "Just asking about my relationship with Naomi."

"Always so intrusive," his mom grumbled. "He was like that when your father and I were children too. Heaven forbid we ever knew something that he didn't."

His dad scoffed. "You'd think with all the influence Elondohnians freely give him, he'd be satisfied, but it was never enough. The man just *had* to have control over the elementals. Make sure he doesn't get control over you."

Adrian nodded wordlessly, took a bite of his meat pie, and watched Boyd walk out after Dr. Guyer. The food all tasted like sand now, and he was done with it. He was done with all of this.

An old, evil alchemist had just threatened Adrian's girlfriend and her family over some secrets he was not supposed to know. He didn't even know what he'd just found out, but it was obviously something bad. What was he supposed to do about it?

Naomi's family was like his own, and if something happened to them because of Adrian's loose lips, he'd never forgive himself.

He would have to keep quiet. *No one can know.*

CHAPTER 52

GUARDIAN

After the tournament, Lucas raced home to shower and change, then ran back to the festival grounds to meet Vita. She stood like a vision in the golden sunlight next to the florist's stand, no doubt chatting with all the flowers there. A crowd of excited Elondohnians were playing carnival games like ring toss, bottle knockdown, and darts. There were easier games for the smaller children, and this year, it looked like a basketball hoop from the outside world had been set up. Lucas didn't know much about that particular game, so he'd stay away from it for now.

Lucas took a deep breath and approached her, holding out his arm. "I believe I owe you a prize, Miss Eastwood."

Vita smiled and took his arm. "Assuming I don't beat you at the game myself."

"No offense, but I'm well trained in accuracy."

"Sorry, honey, but you're about to be humbled. I'm the ring toss champion where I come from. Don't worry, though. When I win, I'll let you keep the prize."

Lucas grinned. "We'll see about that."

She did win the first few rounds. Admittedly, Lucas had let her win, but she was quite good. He wasn't simply joking when he'd said he was good at games like this. If he focused on the target, he could throw the dart, ball, or bean bag and always land it where he wanted it to go. But Vita liked competing, and she lit up beautifully when she hit her target, so Lucas simply tweaked his aim to miss a few times.

Of course, there were a few rounds he had to win. He still had to impress her, after all.

They continued their day through the festival, playing games, eating, and always laughing. Lucas fell more and more for her every time he heard her laugh. Conversation wasn't difficult with her, even in the few moments that they didn't speak. He didn't have to think too hard about every word he was going to say or wonder how a chief would react to any given moment. Vita was his comfort, his breath of freedom. He could just be Lucas around her, not Guardian Sawyer or future Chief Sawyer.

If this were a glimpse into his future with her, by all the angels above, he couldn't wait for the future to begin. It was nice to not dread the pressures ahead, for once.

Finally, when the sun started to set and the dance was about to begin, Vita and Lucas made their way to the large white tent. Flowers and candles were set up on every table, and a small quartet got situated on a newly built wooden stage. In the center of the tent was a dance floor where children ran around despite not having any music to dance to yet. Older patrons stood around the bar or picked at a small buffet of hors d'oeuvres.

Dos, Annie, and Adrian were talking to each other by the buffet table. Vita hurried over to them, leading Lucas by the hand.

"Hey, y'all!" Vita greeted happily. "How did you like the festival? What did y'all do?"

"I ate and carried my mom's bags," Adrian said, picking at finger sandwiches. "I swear, even in a hidden community in the middle of nowhere, the woman finds a way to shop. It's a gift."

"Nice. What about y'all two?" Vita asked Dos and Annie.

Annie shrugged. "Nothing exciting. Hung out and listened to some music."

Dos motioned to the stage. "Vita, are you ready perform?"

"Yes, I'm so excited!" Vita rested a hand on Lucas's arm and offered him another one of her shy smiles. "Think of you and me when you listen to it."

Angels, it was so easy for her to make him smile. He nodded and gently squeezed her hand before releasing it. She and Dos headed toward the stage and chatted happily among themselves. Dos had a new confidence in his walk and stood a little taller than he had before. He tilted his head just enough for Lucas to spot a small bruise peeking out from his collar.

"Angels," Lucas said to Adrian. "Was Dos bit by something? There looks to be a terrible bruise on his neck."

Annie froze for just a second and turned bright red, despite wearing her typical bored expression. "I don't see anything. You're delusional."

"No, I could have sworn—"

Adrian draped an arm around Lucas's shoulders and guided him to one of the tables. "Don't ask questions you don't want answers to, my guy."

They sat at one of the round tables as the tent quickly filled up with Elondohnians. Some of them gathered at a stand where Adrian's origami animals were displayed. Annie's watercolor painting of the apple trees in the orchard stood on an easel.

Dr. Guyer walked in with two of the most prominent families in Elondoh: the Sawyers and the Boyds.

Lucas's mother wore her fake smile as Mrs. Boyd spoke to her. Chief didn't bother paying attention to whatever Senior Guardian Boyd was saying. Jason Boyd stuck close to Dr. Guyer's side and offered Lucas a nod that wasn't returned.

Everyone got seated and the room fell silent. All eyes settled on the musicians.

Vita nodded at Dos, then released a deep sigh and started on the piano.

A light melody, more of a voice rather than an instrument, sang to Lucas. Soft and gentle, welcoming him into the song the way a friend welcomed someone into their home.

Dos started his section, deep and low in response to her notes. Like a conversation, they carried forward throughout the song, music dancing around each other hesitantly yet intimately. The way someone learned to trust for the first time.

Think of you and me, she'd told him. In each note, he remembered every apology, every silly joke, and every smile they'd exchanged. He remembered the moments they argued and the moments they depended on each other.

And he swore he heard the angels themselves sighing in awe of the music.

Dos and Vita finished their song in a delicate flourish, then glanced up from their instruments seemingly remembering there was a world outside of their music. Applause broke out, accompanied by a standing ovation, which Lucas proudly joined.

Dos and Vita offered a graceful bow before relinquishing the stage to the quartet. Of course, June rushed to Vita and pulled her into a tight hug before giving Dos a hug as well. Dos seemed much more comfortable returning this hug than he had the first time he was hugged and he seemed a little surprised when June told him, "I'm proud of you." Lucas joined in time to hear Dos mutter his thanks.

When June's eyes got misty, Lucas produced a tissue from his pocket. Good guardians were prepared even on holidays.

June gave Vita a knowing smile. "Oh, don't let me hold you two up. Dance the night away. I'll be at the bar drinking all the wine with Natalie like the good old days."

Lucas and Vita exchanged amused looks before walking together to the dance floor. June said to dance the night away, and so they did. Song after song, even as the night hours passed and other dancers dwindled off to go home.

So long as the quartet played, Lucas held Vita and danced with her like it was the last thing they'd ever do together.

CHAPTER 53

Generation 23

GUARDIAN

I t was around five o'clock the next morning when Lucas awoke to Chief shaking him harshly. "Son, you need to wake up," Chief commanded.

Lucas blearily blinked open his tired eyes and grunted. "What? What's wrong?"

"There was a fire that broke out in a valley not too far from here. It's spreading fast, and Dr. Guyer wants to send the elementals to stop it before it can reach Elondoh. You must get ready to go now."

Lucas clumsily rolled out of bed, racing to get ready. Fires spread so quickly in the mountains, and if it reached Elondoh, the whole community could be destroyed. If it was too much for a local fire department to handle, and therefore necessary for Dr. Guyer to risk sending the elementals, then the fire must have been close.

Lucas's mother and Chief stood in the kitchen, watching Lucas with worried eyes.

"Darling, be safe." His mom wrung her hands together.

"Yes, of course," Lucas said, shoving on his coat.

"Son," Chief said in an uncharacteristically soft voice. "We love you."

"Love you both. I'm sure I'll be back by lunch." Lucas waved them off and hurried out the door.

A bus was waiting at the front gate, already loaded with the elementals and an additional squad of guardians. Unfortunately, that included Boyd, but for an event like this, every hand was needed.

Though, it was strange to note that Ethan was nowhere in sight.

Lucas nodded at the driver to go and then addressed the group. He briefly read over a report given by the surveillance corps and quickly formulated a plan.

"All right, we've got a wildfire about thirty miles from Elondoh. According to this, it just began, so we might be able to stop it before it spreads too far. Dos, you'll keep the flames centralized in one location. Annie, take away as much oxygen as you can from the flames to try and kill it. Adrian, according to the maps, there's a lake not too far from the fire. We'll take you there to gather water to extinguish the flames. Vita, you'll be damage control. We've got your vitamin shots to help you, but be warned, you may not be able to heal all the trees if the damage is too large. Do not strain yourself. Guardians, we will serve as protection and additional assistance where needed. There is protective gear in the back. Boyd, you'll maintain communication with Elondoh command. Hogan, you'll serve as my second-in-command. The rest of you, be prepared for anything. Understood?"

A chorus of "yes, sir" broke out from all except Boyd, who merely watched Lucas with an amused smile.

"Did you understand me, Boyd?" Lucas asked.

"Of course, Guardian Sawyer," Boyd drawled, leaning back in his seat.

Lucas dismissed the attitude and walked toward the back

where the elementals sat with each other. Lucas sat in the seat across from Vita and offered her a warm smile.

"Good morning. Did you sleep well?"

She yawned and nodded. "Not as long as I wanted to, but it was all right."

They had been one of the last couples to leave the dance last night, and it was nearly midnight when Lucas had walked her home. Vita had given him another kiss on the cheek before he left her, and for the better part of an hour, he had lain in bed thinking about her. He didn't get a lot of sleep, but she was worth it.

"I suppose our brunch plans are ruined now," Lucas said.

"You'll make it up to me another time." Vita leaned her head against the seat. Her eyebrows twitched inward as if something bothered her, but she rubbed her eyes and brushed it off.

EARTH

They drove for another long fifteen minutes before the screams started.

It was faint at first, drowned out by the rushing wind of the open windows. Vita thought she was just exhausted, but they kept growing louder and more desperate.

Help us . . . please . . . help us . . .

Vita sucked in a sharp breath and looked around to see if anyone else had heard it, but nobody seemed to react. Who was screaming? What was hurting them?

Please . . . end this . . .

Then a hot, blinding pain seared through Vita's chest as if a thousand nails clawed through her heart. She grunted and placed her hand over her racing heart. It was getting difficult to breathe.

The screams grew louder from hundreds of unseen sources. They surrounded her from every angle, pleading for her help. Their deep voices rumbled from within her, and then she knew who it was.

"The trees," Vita cried out. She pressed her hands over her throbbing ears. "They're hurting. I . . . I hear their screams."

"Vita?" Lucas reached for her, but she recoiled from him.

The sight of him, the smell . . . it made her physically sick. The selfishness that naturally lived within him, the greed and acceptance of murder . . . it disgusted her.

"Sawyer, should I call someone?" Hogan asked from a few seats away. Had he always been so useless? Wasting the precious air that the trees worked so hard to produce?

"Yes, call Dr. Sawyer. Perhaps she can recognize the symptoms. Vita, what's wrong?"

The bus sputtered, releasing a loud grinding noise before acrid gray smoke puffed up from the hood. The driver cursed and pulled the bus to the side of the road.

"Something's wrong," the driver announced. "We'll need to call Elondoh command and ask for repairs."

"What? We have an injured elemental. You can't just drive it back to the compound?" Lucas demanded.

"Can't drive what won't start, sir. I'll see what I can do." The driver opened the doors and hopped out, letting in more screams from outside.

More pollution. More waste. More blatant disregard for the other souls that inhabited this planet. They were all so . . . *evil*.

Vita forced her watery eyes open to see where they were. She froze. Construction workers in bright-yellow hard hats operated various heavy machinery to cut down layers of trees and then shove the logs into wood grinders.

Hatred boiled within her, protective rage building until it

cinched her throat. The trees begged for mercy, released blood-curdling screams, bargained for their loved ones, but nobody heard them and nobody cared.

Nobody cares about them. I am the only one.

The humans were cutting down the trees and mercilessly shredding them in front of their families. They were murdering the innocent souls for their own selfish gain, and Vita *hated* them for it.

She wanted them to hurt, to bleed, to suffer. She wanted to cleanse the earth of the parasites that skittered among its pure soil. All they ever did was take; there was no give. No empathy. She needed to protect the innocent, to save them from this terror.

Vita needed to kill the humans.

Her vision blinked in and out, her breath ragged, sweat glistening on her skin. These thoughts weren't hers, but they were loud and overpowering. God, she just needed to *breathe*.

Lucas knelt in front of Vita, calling her name, and tried to get her to look at him.

She wanted to cry to him, beg him to make the screaming stop, warn him of the terrifying hatred that overtook her thoughts. But she couldn't. They were too strong.

I must protect them.

She surrendered to the thoughts and, in a blink, everything faded away.

The screams stopped.

FIRE

Dos had felt her rage before he put together what was happening.

He'd never felt such a level of pure hatred before, not even from the cruel scientists who abused him. Vita's hatred appeared like dark blood dripping from the top of her head, the scent of blood so powerful that it nearly made Dos gag.

It was so terrifyingly unlike her.

He heard the logging machinery, felt the rumbling of their operation through his body, and he knew with a terrible dread what was happening. Vita was having every elemental's worst nightmare.

She was having an angelic reaction.

Each of the elementals had a quality they were to defend. It was not their choice, nor could they prevent the repercussions of it. Innocence was always Earth's quality, and Vita said the trees were the most innocent. Dos knew she could hear their terror and feel their pain. He could feel her own pain amplified through her. If they needed defending, her angelic genetics would simply react. She'd have no way of stopping it; her body was no longer in her control.

And it all aligned far too well.

The logging company, the supposed fire, the setup from Dr. Guyer. This was the prophecy being fulfilled in real time. The guardians were trained that if an angelic reaction were to happen, they must disable the elemental. If that wasn't possible, they were to kill the threat.

Vita was meant to die today.

"No," Dos said out loud, suddenly shaking with righteous anger. "No. I will not let this pass."

"Dos, not you too," Sawyer said, still trying to get Vita to look at him.

"Guardian Sawyer, this is the prophecy." Dos's eyes glowed red. "Vita is about to have an angelic reaction. I will try to stifle her emotions, but we *must* get her away from these trees."

Guardian Sawyer cursed, looking out the windows, and cursed again at the construction site.

Vita suddenly exhaled as if in relief, but her emotions read differently. She opened her eyes and revealed glowing green eyes, whites and all.

"Angels above . . ." Guardian Sawyer breathed, reaching for his impulse bracelet. "Vita? Can you hear me?"

A vine surged through the open window from the nearby trees and ripped Sawyer away from her. He crashed into the seat and grunted in pain, tied together by the vines. Dos stood at the same time Vita did and sent her as much peace as he could muster.

"Please do not do this," Dos said in a soft whisper. "We are your friends."

His emotions didn't sink into her the way they normally did. Rather, they bounced off like a ray of light reflecting from a mirror.

Vita raised her hand and shot another vine toward Dos.

WATER

Adrian cursed when Dos dove out of the way and nearly landed on his lap, the vine cracking like a whip. The guardians all scrambled to get to Vita, but more vines lashed in and pulled them away before they could reach her. Adrian tried to hijack her thoughts, but it was like a steel wall had formed around her mind. No matter how hard he prodded, he couldn't get in.

"This is the prophecy!" Dos had to shout over the machinery and the panicked commands of the guardians. "We must stop her before the guardians do!"

Another guardian was thrown against the wall of the bus before slumping down, unconscious. Vita glided off the bus, her movements too fluid and calculating for her usual demeanor. Annie tried to reach out to her but had to duck away from another one of Vita's vines.

Sawyer finally cut himself loose from the vines using a knife from his belt and called out to Dos. "Stop the guardians from reaching her!"

"Sawyer, she could kill you!" Dos argued.

Sawyer knew that, but he didn't seem to care. He ran after her anyway.

Most of the construction workers scrambled away at the sight of the growing vines curling around the machinery and hurling them into the air. One of the workers stayed while his friends ran away. He threw some kind of tool at Vita and hit her in the head. She summoned another vine and strung him up by the throat, lifting him so high that his boots lifted off the ground as he kicked and gasped for air.

This was what Dr. Guyer had planned yesterday at the festival, and Adrian had said nothing. His friends could all die, and he had done nothing to prevent it. How selfish could he be?

Adrian, Annie, and Dos all scrambled off the bus before the guardians could recover.

"Form a barrier," Dos commanded. "Do not let them pass. We must buy Sawyer some—"

The ground shook in a terrible earthquake. Vita opened craters in the earth to sink the machinery and crush it. She had somehow dashed several yards away in a matter of seconds and was now causing the ground to shake.

The guardians fell on top of each other and tried to recover from the shaking ground. Adrian and the other elementals struggled to remain standing through this earthquake, but now they were supposed to fight too?

Guess it was a good thing they did a refresher course on using their abilities for combat.

"Can you take the water from the air?" Dos asked.

"Uh, I can try." Adrian had only done it a couple of times in training, and he couldn't get much then, but he needed to push harder this time. Their lives were at stake.

Boyd was the first to rise and get his footing, soon accompanied by another three guardians. Boyd glared at the elementals and reached for his belt of weapons.

"Move," he demanded.

Dos swiped his hands out in front of him, igniting a wall of fire to act as a barrier between the elementals and the guardians.

Adrian reached out and pulled with everything he had. Water droplets formed from thin air and surged toward him, forming a growing ball of water.

A guardian pointed his tranquilizer gun at Dos and fired. Dos jerked out of the way, but his focus was lost, and the fire barrier broke.

One of the guardians tried to go through a gap in the flames, but Adrian was quicker than that. He sent the ball of water toward the guardian's feet and froze him to the ground. Another guardian tried to shoot his tranquilizer gun, but Adrian dodged out of the way just in time.

But that was a bluff too. Because as soon as Adrian straightened up, a tranquilizer dart pierced his thigh and sent a numbness throughout his body.

Adrian was the first to fall out of the fight.

AIR

Annie swiped her hands upward, sending a gust of wind through the heart of the flames, igniting the wall of fire until it towered over them.

Adrian grunted next to her and collapsed in a heap. The ice that had frozen around the first guardian's feet instantly melted, allowing him to start running.

Annie sent him flying back with a powerful burst of wind. Unfortunately, that took away her focus from the flames, which lowered their height. Dos skirted and dodged the tranquilizer darts that were flying through the air. Of course, the guardians were focused on bringing Dos down first. He was the biggest threat of the two standing elementals. The ground trembled and roared, causing gaps to break in the barrier of flames. Another guardian slipped through an opening, forcing Annie to take her attention off the fire and focus on stopping the guardians. Dos would have to keep up the flames himself.

She locked eyes with Hogan, who had stayed near the bus, watching in horror. She didn't want to hurt the guy, but if he tried coming after Vita, she'd have no choice.

Instead, Hogan dropped his tranquilizer gun and held up his hands. He didn't want to fight them either.

Annie nodded in thanks and kept working on the other five guardians who were coming after her. She had just thrown one back when Boyd catapulted a small metal ball—no bigger than a strawberry—toward her. It flashed with a beeping red light and sparks of electricity.

"No!" Dos shouted, panic clear in his eyes. He lunged toward the metal ball and threw his body over it just seconds before it exploded into a burst of electricity. He writhed in pain, his body locking up as he coughed out a scream. He was being electrocuted, and it was only because he didn't want Annie to feel that pain. He'd taken it for *her*. But his flames died out with nothing but a wisp of smoke in their place.

"Dos!" Annie cried out, reaching for him.

He sucked in a ragged breath, his skin pale and covered in sweat. "Run!" he gasped.

Another grenade flew through the air toward Annie. She swiped her hand just in time to deflect it, but while she was distracted, a sharp pain pierced her side. She lost feeling in her limbs and felt herself sinking to the ground.

The last thing she saw was Hogan helping Dos to his feet and telling him to help Sawyer.

At least there was one guardian who would help, because it seemed like there was no other option. Vita was going to die and maybe the other elementals too. Annie didn't want that. She desperately didn't want that. Whether it was from the terror of this situation or the drug in that dart, Annie for once couldn't hide the tears that rolled down her cheeks.

CHAPTER 54

GUARDIAN

Lucas was only twenty feet away, still calling Vita's name. His throat burned and his legs ached from clambering around the trembling earth. Still, he ran for her with an impulse bracelet clutched in his hand. He just had to reach her.

Boyd raced unsteadily toward them. Lucas knew the hatred he had for elementals. He knew the man wouldn't just try to disarm Vita. He'd kill her.

Vita finally released the construction worker who had thrown something at her. His body crumpled in a lifeless heap, his neck bearing a dark round bruise. He was dead, and Vita was his killer.

She raised her hands above her head, and the acres of trees that had been chopped down were now rising, regrowing in defiance against their killer's weapons. Blood poured from Vita's nose as she screamed and pushed her element harder. The ground split apart as the trees grew taller and stronger than they had before.

Lucas knew that he'd never forget the echoes of her unholy screams, and for the first time in his life, he felt incredible trepidation toward the angels. But even more so for the humans who had pushed the angels this far. This was Dr. Guyer's doing—his cruel desperation, and now people would suffer because of it.

Boyd got into position, raised his gun, and aimed.

Lucas leaped toward Vita. "Get down!"

The shot fired just as Lucas's boots left the ground, his arms wrapping around her waist and bringing her down. He latched the impulse bracelet onto her wrist and twisted in midair so that she'd land on top, already knowing that the bullet should have found home in his back.

He gritted his teeth as they hit the ground and prepared himself for the pain. The earth finally stopped shaking, which meant the bracelet was working.

Please let me live long enough to protect her.

He felt the stickiness of warm blood on his hands. He sucked in a breath and waited, but the pain never came. Nonetheless, he blurted to Vita, "It's going to be okay. I'll be fine—"

His words drifted when he heard her whimper and watched her shakily push herself up. Her brown eyes squinted in pain, and she clutched her stomach.

Her hand was covered in blood.

"No . . ." was all Lucas could say in his horror. He'd been too late. Too slow. Vita had been shot, and it was his fault. All those years of training and he couldn't save her.

She took quick, ragged breaths as she brought up her eyes to his. "L-Lucas?"

"No, no, no!" He scrambled up, barely catching her in time as she fell over. "It's going to be okay. We . . . we'll take you to a tree!"

"No!" She coughed, blood trickling from the corner of her lips. "Don't take . . . from the trees . . ."

Lucas dug frantically in his pocket for the bracelet key. "I'm sorry, but I can't leave you like this. *Where's the key?*"

He searched but couldn't find it. It must have fallen out when he was stumbling to her.

"Someone give me your key!" he shouted desperately. None of the guardians made a move. "What are you doing? I need your key now! She must heal herself."

The guardians glared him down and did not move. He pressed his hand over Vita's wound to stanch the bleeding.

"I'm s-sorry, I'm so sorry," Vita huffed, tears slipping out of her dazed eyes.

"You'll be all right. Just hold on, you'll be okay," Lucas promised, his voice shaking.

Vita raised a bloody hand to his cheek, weakly turning his face so that she could look in his eyes. "I . . . I love you, Lucas Sawyer . . . I love you . . ."

Lucas thought of the ladybug and the wish he'd made. How he'd wished for Vita to return his feelings. Wishes did come true. If only it hadn't come to this for him to realize that.

"I love you too, Vita. I was too afraid to say it before, but I won't be anymore. I promise, I'll tell you every day that I love you. I'll tell the whole world and I won't be afraid. All you have to do is stay."

"It's . . . okay, Lucas. You'll be okay without me . . . I know you will."

"Don't talk like that. Don't give up." Lucas looked around and saw a glint of silver in the grass just past the wall of guardians. His key. "I'm going to get the key, okay? Just hold on."

Vita whimpered in pain with his slightest movement. Just as Lucas started to move, the guardians raised their guns in a threatening manner. Lucas froze on his knees, calculating his next move.

"Lower your weapons," Lucas warned. "She is an elemental. We need to save her!"

Boyd shook his head. "Move and I'll shoot her again."

But Lucas needed to get that key.

"It's okay. I'll get it, it'll be fine," he promised Vita, preparing himself for a fight.

"Don't leave," Vita requested softly, coughing again. She clutched his shirt with feeble fingers, her skin getting colder.

"But Vita . . ." Lucas stopped short, horrified at the blood trickling from her lips. He didn't notice until now that her blood stained the grass beneath them, pooling at his knees. Every blade of grass was now a haunting dark red.

She shivered violently. "It's so cold, Lucas . . . I'm so cold. Just . . . hold me until—"

"Shh, don't." Lucas pulled her body closer, her head resting against his chest. Vita hated the cold. "Please don't leave me . . . don't go. You *must* stay, Vita. You must. For you and me, remember?"

She gave him the best smile she could muster, and despite the blood on her teeth, she still managed to maintain the grace in her eyes. "It's . . . it's always you and me."

Hogan and Dos were finally making their way toward Lucas. A spark of hope reignited in his chest as Lucas called to Hogan, "Your key! I need your key, Hogan, hurry!"

"Stop right there!" Boyd demanded, pointing his gun at Dos.

Dos skirted to a stop, holding up his hands. The other guardians backed up Boyd, pointing their guns at Dos as well. One guardian latched an impulse bracelet onto Dos's wrist and forced him to his knees. Hogan tried to proceed forward, but Boyd wouldn't allow it.

"Not another step!" Boyd ordered.

"Boyd, please!" Lucas begged. "*Please* let them help!"

"What are you doing?" Hogan snapped at Boyd. "We'll lose the entire Earth line if we don't help her!"

"I said don't move."

"You would shoot me, Jason?" Hogan asked, hurt clear in his eyes.

"I have orders that I *will* follow," Boyd snapped.

Dos and Lucas locked eyes, sharing in their desperation.

"Vita, just hold on," Lucas gasped, feeling the air grow thin around him. "I'll get you out of here, I promise."

Her hand slipped from his chest, falling limply at her side. Despite his begging, her eyes fluttered closed, head lolling back.

"No, *no!*" he cried, shaking her shoulders. "Vita, wake up. *Wake up. Vita!*"

If only he could heal her like she did to him. The blood sucking back in and the skin stitching closed. But he couldn't help her. She was going to die in his arms if he couldn't convince her just to stay.

"Don't go. Don't go. Please don't go . . ." He tearfully begged. He pressed his lips to her forehead. "Stay for you and me. Just stay."

"Bring her to a tree!" Dos cried out. He didn't know that Vita wouldn't be able to heal herself even if Lucas did bring her to a tree. "Sawyer, hurry!"

Boyd hit Dos with the butt of his gun and hissed at him to shut up. Dos fell to his side, covering his split lip and glaring up at Boyd. His eyes flashed red once before the bracelet shocked him into submission.

Vita's skin grew pale. Under Lucas's fingers, he felt her weakened pulse.

Thump . . . thump . . . thump . . .

Then no more. Her heart stopped beating, right under his touch.

"No," Lucas gasped, looking up at Dos as tears spilled out of his eyes. "I . . . I failed. She's gone."

A pained scream left his lips, dully piercing his eardrums.

Complete chaos ensued around Lucas, and yet the world felt so terribly numb and still. Everything was already so tragically empty without her. Lucas watched through tears as Hogan tried to get to them, only to be stopped by the guardians. One of them finally hit him with a Taser and forced him into handcuffs next to Dos, who sat frozen in shock.

Lucas shivered violently though he could feel nothing, not even the slightest breeze. He couldn't even tell if he was breathing anymore. Nothing felt right, nothing made sense.

He glanced at Vita. This beautiful, vibrant, witty girl who exemplified life itself, and yet she lay lifeless in his arms. Her dark blood painted his hand as if to remind him, *You couldn't save her.*

His vision blurred before his eyes, and the scene before him shifted into a dark abyss that he couldn't tell was real or a figment of his numbed imagination.

Lucas felt weightless, as if he didn't really exist in this dark nightmare. He heard his own voice pounding around him in a cacophony of insulting questions that he had no answers to.

Is this what life is meant to be like?

How was he ever to listen to the rain without her next to him? This couldn't be right; this couldn't be the end.

Lucas felt one thing only: the unrelenting desire to lie next to her and never get up again. He couldn't dare to face the world and all of its looming trials without her belief in him. Without hearing her voice say his name once more.

I love you, Lucas Sawyer . . . I love you . . .

As if turning on a switch, a bright purple light glowed painfully in his eyes and vacuumed him back to Earth.

Back to Vita.

Back to her killer.

Lucas's body shook with white-hot rage and adrenaline as he locked eyes with Boyd. Men like Boyd shouldn't have been allowed to live. Men who liked to hurt others, who gained power through cruelty. Vita had once warned Lucas that men like Boyd existed, and he didn't think much of it. How could anyone be so vile?

Humans like claiming power over things that can't fight back. It's their way of feeling strong.

If that was what Boyd wanted, that was what he would get. Lucas would show him what it meant to be afraid, what it meant to be unable to fight back.

"His eyes!" someone shouted. "They're glowing!"

"Sawyer . . ." Dos said. "It is him . . . he is the fifth elemental. The fourteenth son."

Lucas's irises glowed a vibrant royal purple, nearly as fierce as his bloodlust. A hot, burning sensation spread along his right wrist. Bright-red lines etched into his skin. Two consecutive triangles, one inverted, with two parallel horizontal lines crossing through them.

His elemental symbol.

Which meant only one thing to Lucas. It meant he could make things right. He could give Boyd his due justice.

If Vita is taken away from me, then I will take him away too.

Lucas lifted his left hand toward Boyd. Gravity seemed to pull toward Lucas, tingling his fingertips in a bristle of electricity. A rush of unyielding power surged through his veins, causing the hair along his arms to stand on end. He had never felt so indestructible.

An omnipresent buzzing screamed in Lucas's ears like a thousand firecrackers.

The air around Boyd shifted. What started as a spark now grew into a basketball-sized hole, shifting and blacker than night. Boyd's arm was lifted against his own will, inching closer to the hole as if sucked in by a vacuum.

Boyd cursed and dropped his gun. He pulled and fought, but

the hole now consumed his forearm. Boyd screamed as his arm dissipated into the hole. Lucas felt unrivaled joy at hearing Vita's killer shout in pain. He gritted his teeth and willed the black hole to pull closer.

The wind rippled around Boyd, and fallen leaves and branches were sucked into the black hole like a vacuum.

Lucas didn't know how he did it, but the black hole grew bigger until it had Boyd's elbow. The guardians rushed to Boyd and tried to free him from the gravity of the black hole but to no avail. Lucas could feel the smallest tug at his arm when the guardians tried to pull Boyd out. He pulled back even harder and watched with a cruel, righteous satisfaction as the guardians abandoned Boyd and scrambled away to save themselves from being sucked in.

You will not get away from me. You will pay for what you've done.

All the wonderful memories of Vita rushed through Lucas's mind. Her laughter. The smell of her perfume. The joy in her smile. The golden rush that her healing carried. He could almost feel it now, that precious euphoria tingling through his skin, almost as if flowing out of him.

He was so focused that he didn't expect Dos to slam the butt of a rifle into his temple. As Lucas's body careened sideways, he heard the black hole slap closed on Boyd's screams before all went dark.

As Lucas's body hit the ground, his bloodied right hand opened—the one that had been firmly pressed over Vita's wound. When his fingers slackened, a bullet tip slipped from his palm and rolled into the lush green grass.

CHAPTER 55

GUARDIAN

The stifled cries were the first to greet Lucas from the depths of unconsciousness.

"He is my son!" a woman cried. "Not your little experiment."

"This was always going to happen, Natalie. You knew that when you signed the contract eighteen years ago," a male voice purred.

"Please . . . he's just a boy," begged another male voice.

"Oh, he's more than that. He is my magnum opus."

The woman sobbed as Lucas drifted back to sleep.

It was easier to wake up the second time. Lucas opened his eyes and was nearly blinded by the fluorescent lights.

He took a deep breath and smelled a familiar scent, but not like the disinfectant of the hospital. The bed wasn't soft either, but rather thin like a cot.

Lucas sat up and saw the ballistic glass wall in front of him. His mother, and Chief sat on the other side. His mother's face was bright red and puffy as she spoke quietly to Chief. Neither of them knew Lucas was awake yet.

But he knew right away where he was. Lucas was in a cell in the observation hall where the elementals were to be brought if they reacted dangerously in Elondoh. He noticed he was wearing scrubs and white canvas shoes. A dull ache greeted him when he touched his head. His wrist stung, a fresh burn shining brightly on his skin. At the sight of the symbol, his memory jarred back.

I am the fifth elemental.

He thought about the family tree he'd found in the archives room. He'd never bothered to count how many men there were in his lineage, but as he thought about it, there were thirteen before Lucas. When the elementals had discovered the fourteenth son's prophecy, they immediately dismissed Lucas as an option because he had no special ability. They hadn't even considered reading his tree.

He stood, catching the attention of his parents.

"Lucas!" his mother cried, pressing her hands on the glass. "Oh, my sweet boy. Are you okay?"

Chief watched him with wary eyes. "Son, can you hear us?"

Lucas approached the glass and pressed his hands where his mother's hands were. He looked her in the eyes and saw no fear, no anger, no shock. She knew. They both knew.

"What did you do to me?" he asked in a hoarse voice.

His mother sniffled and wiped her tears with a damp tissue. "Lucas, we never meant for it to happen this way. You have to know that this isn't what we wanted for you."

"Tell me what you did!" he demanded, heart thundering.

"I had just gotten pregnant with you when Dr. Guyer found a hidden prophecy from John Dee describing a fourteenth son. We'd just found out we were having a boy, and my pregnancy was . . . complicated. I nearly lost you because the human genetics I gave you weren't strong enough to withstand your forming abilities. Dr. Guyer said he created a serum to help your genetics accept your abilities. He said that you were destined to create the philosopher's stone. At the time, we just wanted to serve him.

Clarice was dying, and you were fated to save us all from disease. I wanted my baby boy to live. So, we agreed to let him inject you with the serum. If the prophecy was true, then you'd become an elemental. If it wasn't, then you'd just be a normal man. After the injection, the pregnancy was smooth. You were healthy again. You were the prophesied fourteenth son. Nobody could know, so we kept it a secret."

"'His power has never been seen before and his might is unmatched,'" Lucas recited, understanding all the signs now.

Mom and Chief stiffened.

"How do you know it?" his mother demanded. "Dr. Guyer told you, didn't he? He promised he wouldn't say anything."

"He didn't." Lucas sighed and rubbed his aching forehead. "We discovered it. But now that I am thinking about it, I remember thinking it was all too easy. The simple cipher, the clues, the thoughts that Adrian heard . . . Dr. Guyer had planted it all. He knew we'd go searching for it. I *knew* there was something off about all that. It was too obvious."

Chief sighed heavily, the weight of his lies aging him. "He never physically said anything to you. He led you right to the answers, hoping you'd discover it. Son, you were destined to create the philosopher's stone. That's why you kept getting sick when the elementals practiced their transmutation. Dr. Guyer claimed your abilities were trying to activate, but the process wasn't stimulating enough."

"Why didn't either of you say anything? Why didn't you prepare me for this?"

"We wanted to make sure you could grow up like a normal boy. The serum was created to help you, but there was no guarantee that your abilities would even develop. Everything about you is so unknown. John Dee left us with nothing to prepare you. Dr.

Guyer promised us that we could raise you how we saw fit until your element activated. We agreed not to tell you about it so you could live free of the burden."

"Why am I just getting my abilities now?"

"Supposedly, your abilities wouldn't activate until you felt that the other elementals needed you. Your 'element' is a response to theirs. So, when we brought you to them and the element didn't activate, I assumed it had failed. I thought you would get to live a normal life."

"And what *is* my element?"

"Molecular control," Mom answered tiredly. "In theory, if you can imagine it, you can create it. It activated when you saw Vita get hurt."

"Vita . . ." Lucas's heart raced as he remembered. His eyes burned with tears as he gripped his hair and sank to his knees. "Angels above, Vita . . . no, no, no."

"Darling . . ."

A sob shook his shoulders. Every time he closed his eyes, he could see the blood staining his hands. "Boyd, he—he shot her. He killed her. Dr. Guyer gave him the order. The prophecy stated that her breath of life must be paid, and Guyer had her killed. Oh angels, we have to tell June . . ."

"Lucas—" his mother tried.

"*Did you know?*" Lucas snapped. "Did you know that Dr. Guyer would kill her?"

"No, of course, not. We would have *never* allowed it."

"How can I trust anything you say? You've lied to me my entire life. She's *dead* because of all of you!" Lucas cradled his head, sobs tightening his throat. "She's dead . . ."

"Lucas, she's alive," Chief interrupted.

The air left his lungs as he met Chief's eyes. "What?"

"Vita is alive," Chief repeated carefully, pain evident in his eyes. "As we said, you are able to mimic what you see. You've seen Vita heal, and you were able to imitate it."

"But . . . her heart stopped."

"I'm still not really sure how," his mother admitted, "but you stopped and reversed the damage of the wound. We've never seen anything like that before. Even Vita can't restart hearts. Dr. Guyer thought perhaps you'd produced enough electricity to resuscitate her. Lucas, darling, you brought her back from the dead. She's alive, resting at home. And June knows you saved her daughter."

New tears burned Lucas's eyes. "She's . . . she's alive . . . I want to see her."

"You will soon," Chief promised. "Things are tense right now. The elementals have been under house arrest since returning. When that's lifted, she can see you."

"How long have I been here?"

"Three days," his mother answered.

"Things will be different for you, son," Chief warned, lowering to one knee to look him in the eyes. "You have to do as Dr. Guyer says. You're not like the others. People don't quite understand what you are or what you'll do."

"Am I to live as Dr. Guyer's prisoner from now on?" Lucas asked bitterly.

"No. You'll receive training on your ability, and you'll live life as you have before. But you must promise to behave. Things are tense for you because of everything with Jason Boyd. He . . . didn't make it."

Lucas shook his head. It felt like trying to interpret spoken language under water. He could barely speak his next question, afraid to hear the answer. "What will become of me?"

"I don't know," Chief admitted. "There will be a trial for you soon to determine the consequences. As your father, I am not allowed to contribute to the discussion, but as Chief, I will present evi-dence to the judge. Boyd was aware of the operation; it's why he and those select guardians went with you. They were assigned to kill Vita if she reacted. This entire time, Boyd was trying to get a reaction out of you by provoking Vita. This time, Dr. Guyer instructed them to only allow you to help her, but he didn't tell them why. Even I didn't know of this. I'm sorry, son. I never wanted this for my best friend's daughter."

"And yet, you did nothing to prevent it. So much for your protection from this angel-forsaken community," Lucas snapped. "When can I go home?"

Chief's broad shoulders sank. "We can take you home now."

———————————

Lucas sat in his room and stared at the now-necessary impulse bracelet on his wrist. There were already burns on his skin from the shocks. Chief had promised that Lucas would only have to wear it until he gained control over his abilities. But Lucas didn't want to use his abilities. He didn't want any of this.

It was well past midnight now. Lucas hadn't been able to sleep, and he didn't think he'd ever get to now. The walls seemed to slowly cave in and the air seemed to thin. His head was heavy with fear and grief. He was a killer, a failure of a guardian, and he'd nearly lost Vita.

I love you, Lucas Sawyer . . . I love you . . .

Lucas jolted to his feet, adrenaline coursing through his veins as panic settled in. He couldn't stay here any longer. He didn't care if he'd get in trouble; he needed to see her. To see that she really was alive.

Lucas quietly slipped out the front door and jogged his way

to her townhome. Realistically, house arrest only meant that the elementals weren't allowed to leave. No one had said anything about them being unable to accept visitors.

He tossed pebbles at her balcony window and whispered her name.

"Vita . . . Vita!"

Finally, a vine from a nearby tree gently wrapped around his waist and lifted him up. He swung his legs over the balcony railing and stepped into her room.

Vita ran into his arms. "Oh, Lucas. Oh my gosh, they told me what happened. Are you okay?"

Lucas held her, tears burning his eyes once more. His fingers felt for her pulse on her neck. With every thump, his own heart shook in relief. "You're okay . . . thank the angels, you're okay."

She ran her fingers through his hair, her other hand gripping the back of his shirt. "I'm so sorry, Lucas. I don't remember a thing, but they said I reacted to something bad and forced all this to happen. I'm so sorry."

"You don't remember anything?" he asked, pulling away.

She shook her head. "Everything is blank. They said you're an elemental, like us. That I got hurt and you healed me. How is that possible?"

Lucas pulled her into another hug, clinging to her as if she were the only thing holding him up right now.

"You scared me so much. I thought I'd lost you. I wouldn't know what to do if . . . if you . . ." He couldn't finish the thought without his voice breaking.

"You saved me," she whispered, gently rubbing his back. "I'm standing here *because* of you."

"I want to pretend that none of this exists. That I walked into the plant nursery that day and we became friends and had berry cobbler together. I want to pretend that you showed me around a no-name town in the middle of nowhere. I just want to be safe with you and pretend that everything is still okay."

Vita pulled away and slid her thumb across his cheek, wiping away tears he didn't know he had. Her voice was a gentle hum and uplifting like a ray of light. "Now, who says it's only pretend? It feels real enough to me."

"I'm afraid," he admitted in a small voice. "Everything's going to be so different. I don't truly know who I am now or what I am capable of. What do we do now?"

Vita gave him a warm smile and rested a hand on his cheek. "We start a new adventure."

Acknowledgments

First, thanks for reading this book and even daring to read this little section! I hope you're enjoying this adventure as much as I am.

I want to thank my husband and best friend. Jacob, you're the very definition of an honorable man. You've dried every tear, squished every doubt, and listened to every rant. When I didn't believe in myself, you believed in me and encouraged me to persevere. You were my first reader and soundboard when no one else would listen. You're my favorite person.

Hailey and Richard, you both amaze me with how supportive and excited you got when I told you about my crazy story idea. You leaped at the opportunity to beta read for me and gave me hope that maybe I could actually write exciting books. Thank you. Brandon, you're pretty cool too, I guess.

I'd also like to thank my dad. I know he's up in the heavens right now, but I like to imagine that he's watching over me and nudging past literary legends while saying, "That's my kid! That's my storyteller." Dad, thanks for believing in me and for introducing me to the crazy world of reading.

Also, I wanted to extend a quick thanks to the people in my life who told me I wasn't smart enough to be an author. I thought about your words every time I wrote, and as I write this section, I can't help but laugh. Thank you for giving me something to prove wrong.

Andrea, I can't believe how patient you've been with me! Thank you for guiding this story in the right direction and dealing with my limited literary knowledge. I feel smarter just from reading your edits! Grammar flaws have got nothing on you. Of all the editors I could have been paired with, I'm immensely grateful that I got to work with you.

Last, thank you to Terri Leidich and the incredible team at Boutique of Quality Books. You took a chance on a dreamer, and I couldn't be more thankful. Your expertise and enthusiasm are both refreshing and heartwarming. Thank you all for being so supportive and welcoming.

About the Author

Cassie Corbin is a Panamanian-American writer who has claimed the coast of South Carolina as her home. She has a background working for a non-profit, where she has the opportunity to meet all kinds of people within the medical field.

When she's not spending time with her husband and her Yorkie, Cassie can be found at the beach, imagining what it would be like to share a cup of coffee with her favorite authors.